Heart-warming, uplifting romance

Etti Summers

Copyright © 2021 Etti Summers
Published by Lilac Tree Books

This book is licensed for your personal enjoyment only. This book may not be re-sold or given away to other people. If you would like to share this book with another person, please purchase an additional copy for each recipient. If you're reading this book and did not purchase it, or it was not purchased for your use only, then please purchase your own copy. Thank you for respecting the hard work of this author.

This story is a work of fiction. All names, characters, places and incidents are invented by the author or have been used fictitiously and are not to be construed as real. Any similarity to actual persons or events is purely coincidental

The author asserts the moral rights under the Copyright, Design and Patents Act 1988 to be identified as the author of this work.

All rights reserved. No part of this publication may be reproduced, stored in a retrieval system or transmitted, in any form or by any means without the prior consent of the author, nor be otherwise circulated in any form of binding or cover other than that which it is published and without a similar condition being imposed on the subsequent purchaser.

For my Dad…
for taking me riding all those times, when he would have preferred to be doing something – *anything* – else x

SPRING

CHAPTER ONE

Early morning was the best time of day, as far as Petra Kelly was concerned. And by early morning, she really did mean early, because when you had animals to see to you couldn't spend half the day lazing around in bed, no matter how comfy and warm you felt. By six a.m. she'd already freed an excited cluck of chickens from their overnight prison (in other words, the coop), had fed them, and had collected the warm brown eggs from the straw. She left the chickens to squabble and squawk over the grain she'd spread on the ground, and went off to check on Princess.

She always saw to the chickens and the goat first because they were the creatures which caused her the greatest headache if she left them until later. The chickens would make a racket and refuse to lay, and the goat kicked the walls of her stall and bleated incessantly.

Princess was on her hind legs with her front ones on the half-open door of her stall as usual Petra noticed, as she entered the barn. Petra had built a goat-proof stall for her on one side of the building, so the animal could see out but couldn't get out. Which was a good thing, because if she was left to her own devices, she'd eat everything she could get her sharp little hooves on.

The goat bleated loudly as Petra opened the barn door, Queenie hot on her heels. The dog accompanied her everywhere, both around the stables and away from them. And if her dog wasn't welcome, then Petra simply didn't go there; like the fancy restaurant that had opened on the edge of the village, for instance. Not that she had any intention of eating there anyway, because she didn't. But if she'd had a mind to spend lots of money on tiny portions of food with ingredients she'd never heard of, the restaurant's dog-unfriendly ways would soon put her off.

Petra clipped a rope onto the goat's halter (god help it if a goat wasn't tethered, because the blighters were better escape artists than Houdini) and walked her across to a field. Hammering in a new stake, she tied Princess to it and let her loose on the brambles which were springing up in response to the increased levels of sunlight and the warmer weather.

As well as early mornings, Petra also loved the spring. All those fresh green shoots and sweet grass, the bluebells carpeting the woodlands, the primroses poking their heads out of the hedgerows – it was a lovely time of year. And she couldn't forget the tiny lambs, the busily nesting birds with demanding chicks to feed, and the calves on the farm next door. A pair of barn owls were nesting in the barn (funnily enough), she'd noticed, and the swallows were back; she'd spotted them swooping and diving yesterday evening as she was bringing the horses and ponies in from the field for possibly the last time this winter. It was time to let them stay outside overnight, now that the risk of bad weather had passed.

All except for Hercules, her pride and joy. He was too precious to leave outside overnight and risk him damaging himself. Not that he probably would, but he could be a bit feisty sometimes and lash out with his back legs if one of the others got too close. An ex-racehorse, he was high-spirited and high-maintenance, and she loved him all the more for it.

She heard a vehicle trundling along the lane long before she saw it (sound travelled further at this time of day) and she waited in the yard for the girls to show up. Faith and Charity were twins, and Petra guessed that if they had been part of a set of triplets, the third sister would have been called Hope.

They were as alike as two peas in a pod, and it had taken her a while to tell one from the other; but now that she could, the differences were obvious. Faith had a couple more freckles scattered across her nose than Charity had, and Charity sported a tiny scar on her cheek, courtesy of an encounter with some barbed wire. There were subtler differences, too, which Petra couldn't for the life of her describe but which she was aware of nevertheless, and altogether they added up to make the two girls distinct and separate.

But as far as personalities went, the sisters couldn't be more different; Faith was outgoing and the life and soul of the party, while Charity was shy and introverted. They did have one thing in common, though – their love of horses.

They'd been coming to the stable for years, ever since they were little and long before Petra had taken over from her great uncle, Amos. Amos was still around, but nowhere near as involved as he used to be – a heart problem had seen to that. These days he was content to let Petra get on with things (as long as she did them the way he used to, that is) and he spent his days pottering around doing the things he liked and was still able to manage.

Faith and Charity kept their own horses at the stables for free in exchange for their labour, and Petra didn't know what she'd do without them. She could only afford to pay one person and that was Nathan, whom she could hear whistling as he headed for the tractor. Today he was planning to fix the fence in the bottom field and the tractor's trailer was loaded up with posts and coiled lengths of wire.

'Morning,' she said, as the girls got out of Faith's bright yellow Beetle.

They were dressed, as was Petra, in green wellies, olive waxed cotton jackets and dark-coloured jodhpurs, every item old and worn, and utterly suitable for mucking out a succession of stables.

Methodically the two of them started at one end of the stables and worked their way along the stalls, whilst Petra jumped onto a pony and rode the mare bare-back, using only her legs and her body weight to steer her, as she took another couple of ponies to the field furthest from the house. To be fair to the ponies, they knew exactly where they were going, and they had a spring in their step as they half walked, half trotted, the scent of lush grass in their nostrils.

Petra slid off Beauty's back and opened the gate, the ponies almost pushing her aside in their eagerness to reach the new grazing, and she paused for a moment to watch them trot into the field, kicking up their legs and prancing. She waited until they settled down with their noses buried in the grass before walking back to fetch the next lot.

The sun was bright and there were only a few clouds in the sky, and it promised to be a nice day.

Her breath misted in front of her as she strolled along the path, as it was still chilly at this time in the morning so early in the year, and she could see dew on the spiders' webs which were draped over the bushes on either side. A slight breeze ruffled her hair and she stopped to take in the view.

How she loved this place! She honestly couldn't imagine living anywhere else or doing anything else. She'd been horse mad since she was a child and had spent every waking moment she was allowed (and many when she wasn't) at these very stables. It had been the happiest day of her life when Amos had told her he wanted her to work for him.

That had been when she was nineteen, adrift with no real job to speak of, and no idea what she wanted to do with her life. Twelve years later, she was running the stables and was totally and utterly happy with her lot.

The animals were her life and she dedicated every waking minute to them. If she wasn't actively doing something with them or for them, then she was thinking about it, or planning it. And one had to be organised when one was responsible for running a stable, and she spent quite a lot of time planning weeks or months ahead. It wouldn't do to get to November and realise that she was out of silage or hay, would it? By then it might be too late to buy any in, or the price might be sky-high, or the weather might be so bad that the delivery lorry wouldn't be able to get through. Planning ahead, being organised and having a routine was what she was all about. And right now her mind was on the annual gymkhana in the summer, as well as making sure the mucking out this morning was done to her satisfaction.

She'd just returned from another field, having dropped the remainder of the horses into it, and had come back for Hercules. He was a bit of a prima donna, and considerably more challenging than the rest of the equines in her stables. Unlike the three small ponies that she'd taken to share Princess's field, he didn't fare well on rough grass. They were content to nibble on the rough stuff. Hercules liked good-quality grass and she had to supplement his feed with oats and other grains, as well as hay.

'There's my lovely boy,' she called, seeing his rich chestnut head hanging over the lower door of his box. His ears pricked forward at the sound of her voice and he blew softly through his nose at her in greeting.

As she approached, he shuffled from foot to foot in anticipation, and when she finally got to him he thrust his head at her, butting her gently. She reached around his neck and put her arms around him, breathing in his familiar comforting horsey smell. He rested his chin on her shoulder and nibbled at her cheek, his soft hairy lips making her giggle.

'Get away with you,' she said, scratching between his ears.

They stayed in that position for a few minutes, until it became clear Hercules wanted his breakfast.

Petra went to fetch a full hay net and heaved it up onto the hook in the horse's stable. Then, while he was busy munching, tugging at the dried strands with his whiskery mobile lips, she checked him over, running her hands down his neck, over his shoulder and down his leg, picking up the hoof and checking it. She stroked his back, feeling the massive muscles of his hindquarters quiver at her touch, then her questing hands slid down his near-side hind leg and she did the same with that hoof. Then she moved around to his off-side and repeated the process.

Damn. He'd thrown a shoe on one of his front legs. It would probably be in the deep hay somewhere, but to be honest it wasn't worth hunting for. He was due a new set of shoes soon anyway, so she might as well have all four feet done at once.

With a resigned sigh, she gave the horse a final pat and went in search of her own breakfast.

'All set?' Ted asked, as Harry Milton opened the van door and sank into its saggy warmth. The van had seen better days and the springs on the passenger seat weren't as firm as they could be, but that was the least of Harry's worries.

He nodded at Ted, not feeling "all set" in the slightest. This was a big step for him. Not the farrier part (he'd been shoeing horses for a good many years), but the buying a new business part and moving halfway across the country.

'We are going to Petra Kelly's stables first. Her stallion's thrown a shoe, but he'll probably need all four renewing. She's a tough bird. No nonsense. Don't expect any chit chat.'

Ted, Harry had discovered, was a man of few words himself, so Harry was grateful he was taking the time to share details of his clients with him. Soon though, they wouldn't be Ted's clients any longer; they'd be his. Of course, he'd have to earn them. They didn't come with the business, but Harry would take over Ted's round and hopefully Ted's clients would be happy with his work and would keep him on.

'Looking forward to retiring?' Harry asked, trying to make conversation.

'Nope. Gonna miss this.' Ted waved an arm at the scenery on the other side of the windscreen.

Harry had to admit that the patchwork of fields with the moorland above and the wooded valleys with streams running through them was a landscape a person could become very attached to. He was already falling in love with it, and he'd only been here two weeks. He'd moved to the area as soon as the sale of Ted's business had been agreed, and he couldn't wait to get started. There was one fly in the ointment though…

Harry tried to shy away from thoughts of Timothy; he needed to concentrate on work right now, not on his brother's problems, but it was hard not to focus on the worry that had consumed him ever since he'd fallen into the role of guardian when their parents had died so suddenly and so tragically. For the past fourteen years, he'd been both mother and father to Timothy. He still was and he didn't begrudge Timothy a single day of the love and care he'd lavished on him.

But for once, he was doing something for himself, and Timothy was old enough to decide what he wanted to do with his life. He'd decided to stay in the house they'd inherited from their parents. It was a sensible choice; his friends were there, his job was there, and so was his girlfriend. It was time Timothy stood on his own two feet, without Harry stifling him. He needed the space to grow into the adult he'd become, and Harry was aware that by living in the same house, the pair of them playing the same roles, he was holding his brother back. All Harry hoped, was that Timothy would be happy. Happiness was all he'd ever wanted for his little brother. His own was inconsequential.

Until, that is, he'd been flicking through a nag rag (one of the horsey newspapers) while attending a meet at Cheltenham Racecourse, and had spotted an advert for a farrier business for sale in the cutely named village of Picklewick. It was high time he branched out on his own, so he'd contacted Ted, and here he was, two months later, about to take over from Ted and begin a new chapter in his life.

'It is beautiful,' Harry agreed, especially with the landscape having a definite feel of spring in the air.

'Not that. I can see a field whenever I like. I'm gonna miss the freedom.' Ted spoke the last word with deep feeling. 'The missus has already got stuff planned.' His face fell into woebegone folds, and Harry suppressed a smile. He could empathise. He longed for freedom, too.

'This is it,' Ted announced, hauling the van's steering wheel to the right and heading up a rough track towards a cluster of buildings. Horses and ponies grazed the fields either side of the pitted track, and he wondered which one of them they were here to shoe.

Nerves knotted his stomach – this was his very first job, with his very first client. Ted might be with him (he'd kindly offered to accompany him for a couple of weeks to introduce him and to vouch for him), but Harry was under no illusion that he had to step up to the mark, or risk losing everything.

Ted brought the van to a halt in a very clean-looking yard, and hopped out. He might be getting on in years, but you'd never know it, Harry thought, extricating himself from the seat with far less agility.

'Don't say nothing,' Ted said out of the corner of his mouth, even though there didn't appear to be anyone around. 'Leave the talking to me. She'll come round. Petra is a tough nut, but she loves her horses.'

Great. His first client sounded a right old battle-axe, and his stomach clenched tighter.

Please let me get this right, he thought.

Then he gave himself a mental shake.

He could do this. He *had* been doing it; for years and years. He'd dealt with all manner of horses, from hideously expensive racehorses to the smallest of Pony Club mounts. He'd dealt with all manner of owners, too, and they had often proved to be more difficult than their animals.

He'd be fine. Wouldn't he?

CHAPTER TWO

Petra leant back in the saddle, one hand resting on her thigh, the other holding the reins loosely in order to allow the horse to pick her way over the rough track. Mabel was an elderly lady with a calming influence on the other ponies, who were all old hands themselves. They knew what they were doing, and what was expected of them, which allowed Petra to enjoy the hack rather than having to worry about her young charges. Easter was always a busy time for the stables, and especially this one what with the school holidays being late and the weather being so much better than earlier on in the year. Parents were happier letting their kids sit on the back of a pony for a couple of hours when they knew they wouldn't be blue with cold by the time they got back.

Petra, though, couldn't be choosy about when she rode, because the animals in her care needed exercising regardless of the weather conditions. But today was gorgeous, the early morning promise having been kept as dawn turned into mid-morning and the sun grew warm on her face as she turned it up to the sky.

Her body swaying gently to the rhythm of the mare's stride, Petra closed her eyes for a moment as she breathed in the scent of growing things, horse, and leather. It was better than any perfume, she thought, no matter how expensive. The clip and plod of the horses' hooves, along with the occasional snort and the creak of leather, provided an accompaniment to the orchestra of bird song and the rustle of little feathered bodies darting amongst the branches.

How could anyone prefer to work indoors on a day like today, she mused, shuddering at the thought of being confined to a desk in an air-conditioned office, unable to feel the breeze in her hair or listen to the sounds of nature. It was unnatural, that's what it was.

'Queenie, come here girl,' she called to the spaniel, who'd gone tearing off into the undergrowth, probably catching the scent of a rabbit or another small creature.

The dog returned to the horse's side, her tongue lolling and her tail wagging furiously.

Petra glanced behind her to check all was well, knowing it was from the steady plod of four sets of hooves and the occasional snort or shake of the head, but wanting to make sure anyway.

The ponies were in single file, practically nose to tail, appearing to be almost asleep, yet she knew they would respond in an instant if asked to do so. As soon as they came down off the hill and the terrain levelled out, she'd urge them into a canter. The final race for home was what her clients enjoyed the most, as the ponies made a controlled dash to the stable, anticipating a quick rub down after their tack was removed and then being released into the field.

Petra would bring them in again later for the early evening rides which were booked, but for the moment they'd be free to enjoy a long afternoon in the spring sunshine.

As soon as she thought it safe, she held Mabel back to allow the other ponies to walk ahead of her. Mabel, for all her advancing years, knew the score and as each pony trotted past, their ears pricked and their heads held high, she pranced and cavorted, as anxious as the rest of them. All the riders took off across the field, hanging onto the reins as they tried to control their mounts' speed, and Petra brought up the rear, prepared to intervene if anyone got into difficulties, only slowing when a gate hindered their progress.

Once through, there was a fast trot up the lane, then a clatter of hooves as all five animals skittered over the cobbles and across the yard.

Petra noticed that Ted's van was already there, and she nodded in satisfaction. Hercules would get his new set of shoes shortly and all would be well in his world.

All wasn't as it should be in hers however, as she spotted a stranger standing next to the farrier. He was possibly in his early to mid-thirties, tall, not bad looking if you liked clean-shaven, well-groomed men, and on her property when he had no right to be there. She wasn't expecting anyone and, come to think of it, how had he got here, because the only vehicles in the parking area were ones which were supposed to be there.

He could have walked, she conceded, but he didn't look the type to go for an aimless stroll around the countryside. His Wellington boots were too clean for a start. Despite the burgeoning spring weather, it was still muddy and slippery underfoot so if he had walked he'd stuck to the roads, and how boring was that!

She dismounted and handed her reins to Faith

who came dashing out of the barn when she heard the clatter of hooves on cobbles, and walked over to the two men to find out what was going on.

'Morning,' Ted said. 'I'll fetch Hercules.' He nodded to her and stomped off in the direction of the horse's stall. A man of few words, Ted was better at dealing with equines than people. His age was indeterminable, although Petra suspected he was in his late sixties; his strength was undeniable (she'd seen him control a rearing horse which a lesser man would have had to have backed away from); and his patience was insurmountable – with horses and other animals, that is. With people, not so much.

Petra didn't mind. In fact, she liked it because she knew where she stood with him. He was down-to-earth and straight to the point. Much like herself.

She waited for Ted to move out of earshot, before turning to the stranger and saying, 'Who are you and why are you here? If you're trying to sell me feed or wormers, I'm not interested.'

'I'm Harry Milton,' he replied, 'And I'm taking over from Ted.'

Petra blinked at him, hoping she hadn't heard correctly. 'You're doing what?'

'Ted is retiring and I'm taking over from him.'

That might explain what he was doing in her yard and how he'd got here, but she wasn't happy about it. She hadn't any inkling that Ted was about to retire, and she didn't like the idea one little bit. She was used to Ted and he was used to her. He'd been shoeing her animals for years and he knew all their little foibles. What if this new bloke wasn't any good?

She wasn't sure she wanted to take the chance, but what choice did she have, other than to look around for another farrier. But if she did that, then she still wouldn't know if that one would be any good, either.

Darn it – she didn't like change. It didn't sit well with her.

But for the moment, she would have to put up with it, because Hercules needed shoes today, not in three months' time when she'd found someone suitable.

Petra glared at this new guy. 'He didn't tell me he was hanging up his horseshoes.'

'That's why I've accompanied him today, so I could meet his clients and introduce myself.'

Petra huffed. 'Are you any good?'

'I'll let you be the judge of that,' he said, as Ted emerged from a horsebox with Hercules on the end of a lead rope.

'I'd prefer Ted to shoe him,' Petra said as Harry stepped forward.

The man stopped and looked at her, his expression inscrutable. 'As you wish.'

'Right, young fella,' Ted said to the new man, as he tethered the horse to a nearby post. 'Take a look at him.'

'I'd prefer it if he didn't,' Petra said.

Ted raised his eyebrows. 'That's up to you, but if this 'un don't shoe him, the horse won't get done today.'

'Why ever not?'

'I've got a problem with my back.'

'Since when?' Petra was surprised; Ted had always seemed so fit and robust.

'For a while.'

'Is that why you're retiring?'

'Partly.'

'I see.'

'And then there's the missus,' he added.

'Oh?' She didn't know he was married; then again, why should she? The only things they ever talked about were horses, and the weather – and the latter was only discussed if it was unduly unusual.

'Harry will see you right,' Ted said.

'He will?' She still wasn't convinced.

'Aye.'

It appeared that was all Ted was prepared to say on the matter, as he closed his mouth and stared at her.

She'd have to take his word for it; at least Ted was here to supervise. He might not give a hoot about people, but he would never let anything happen to a horse.

Harry was conscious of Petra's eyes on him the whole time, from the second he approached the horse – murmuring softly to the animal and letting the horse sniff him before running his hands down each leg and lifting it to check the condition of the hooves – to shoeing the last foot, replacing it gently on the ground and giving the horse a pat on his solid rump.

'All done, fella,' he said. 'You were a good boy, weren't you?'

Hercules turned to look at him out of one eye and blew down his nose. His tail swished across Harry's face and he laughed. He could have sworn the horse was laughing too.

Petra wasn't. She looked as po-faced as when he'd first set eyes on her.

Ted had been watching closely as he worked, nodding now and again in what Harry hoped was approval. He knew he was good at his job; he'd worked with one of the best farriers in the country. So why did he feel as though he had just sat some kind of exam, which he wasn't entirely sure he'd passed.

He intercepted a look between Ted and Petra and almost jumped out of his skin when the woman said, 'You might as well meet the rest of my animals, while you're here. I don't want any work done on them today,' she added in a warning tone. 'They don't need it.'

'Go take a look, lad. I'll wait here.' Ted leant against the side of the van and folded his arms, so Harry obediently followed Petra, who was already halfway across the yard, a black spaniel trotting at her heels.

He hurried to catch up.

'I've got seventeen ponies, three horses, a donkey and a goat. The goat is the only one of those who doesn't need your services.'

'I can take a look at it while I'm here?' he offered.

Petra shot him a sharp glance. 'I can trim her feet myself, thank you.'

'I'm sure you can—'

'Can I just say that I'm not happy Ted's retiring,' she broke in. 'I get on well with Ted. He doesn't bother me and I don't bother him. He just gets on with his job.'

He'd gathered that she wasn't ecstatic he was here. He also gathered that she wasn't the friendliest of clients. He vowed to cause her as little bother as possible. He might need her custom and she might need his services, but that didn't mean they had to become bosom buddies.

The rest of his visit took place in silence, interspersed with the occasional stilted comment or brief question and answer, so Harry was glad when the tour was finally over and he could return to the far more garrulous and friendly Ted (and that was saying something!).

'I didn't realise you had a problem with your back,' Harry said, once they were on the road to the next job.

'I don't.'

'But you said—'

'I know what I said.' Ted chuckled. 'Worked, didn't it? And she'll accept you next time. Petra is a bit like a flighty filly being introduced to a stallion — she needs a firm hand.'

Harry's eyebrows rose. Never in a million years would he have compared Petra to a filly. Neither would he have called himself a stallion. He was more like a weary old carthorse and she was a stubborn mare.

He had to admit that she was rather attractive in a girl-next-door kind of way, with her make-up free face and honey-coloured hair gathered into a messy knot at the nape of her neck. She had arresting eyes, too — they were almond-shaped and green-blue in colour, and she'd used them to scrutinise him.

He wondered what she'd seen when she'd stared at him.

He wondered what she'd thought of him.

Then he shoved his wondering to one side. It didn't matter a jot as long as she thought he was professional, could do a good job and would use him on her animals again.

CHAPTER THREE

Petra stowed the pitchfork back in the tool shed and sighed deeply. It had been another tiring day. The days were all tiring lately, and she wondered if she was getting old. Thirty-one was hardly considered old, but she found she wasn't able to work for quite as long or quite as hard as she'd done when she had been in her twenties. It was as though a dial had been turned down a notch on her thirtieth birthday and it had yet to be turned back up.

'I've bedded the terrible twosome down,' Charity said, appearing from behind the stable block. 'Is there anything else before I go?'

The terrible twosome was a pair of Shetland ponies who refused to go anywhere without each other. If only one was needed for a ride, the other had to go too, albeit riderless. Petra knew she should try to loosen their dependency on each other, but what harm was it doing? She didn't mind, and if it made the little creatures happy then who was she to separate them.

'No, you get off, thanks,' she said. 'How are you fixed for taking a trek out on Saturday for a couple of hours? I wouldn't normally ask but I've got that kiddies' party booked in, and this is for seven people, so...'

She knew Charity would pick up on the subtext – a booking for seven people for a two-hour trek was a substantial amount of money when every penny counted. Running a riding stables wasn't cheap, which was why Petra was branching out into other activities, such as pony parties, where children could enjoy all the fun of a birthday party combined with horsey games.

'I'm working, but I'll ask Faith. I think she's got this weekend off.'

'Thanks, love.'

Petra watched the girl head for her car and sighed. Faith and Charity were hardly girls anymore, although they had been when they'd first started stabling their horses with her. She'd watched them grow from awkward teenagers into the charming young women they were today. Not only did it make her feel old, it also worried her – she depended on their help so much that she didn't know what she'd do if marriage and babies eclipsed their love of horses. And it was bound to happen – husbands and children took up so much time and attention, it was inevitable that once the twins settled down they wouldn't be able to be at the stables as much. They might even decide to sell their horses.

The thought horrified her. It was bad enough when an animal died (she recalled how heartbroken she'd been when Prince dropped dead last year – it was from old age and he'd had a long and wonderful life, but the knowledge didn't ease the hurt), but to actively move a horse to a new home went totally against the grain as far as Petra was concerned. She simply couldn't imagine doing such a thing.

Although to be fair, she couldn't imagine having a husband or children either. And neither did she want to. She had everything she needed right here. Besides, she didn't have the time for love. Human love, that is. She had all the love in the world for her animals.

As if sensing her thoughts, Fred stalked up to her and pecked her boot.

'Yes, I know, it's time you and your ladies were tucked up in bed,' she told the cockerel, who was strutting around her feet making soft little noises of contentment.

Fred had a great deal to be contented about, Petra thought, as she rounded up the hens and shepherded them into the coop for the night. They were allowed to wander at will during the day, and with plenty of food, all that grubbing around and fresh air, they had perfect lives for chickens. That perfection filtered through to the wonderfully tasting eggs they laid.

'You reap what you sow,' she murmured to herself as she ensured the lock was securely fastened, and she smiled as she heard the pre-bed squabbling taking place inside. Each bird might roost in the same place every night, but it didn't stop them having a tiff about it. Chickens tended to enjoy a good squabble.

After a final check around with Queenie at her heels, Petra finally headed to the house, her supper and Amos.

'Finished for the day?' her uncle called from the kitchen when he heard her enter the boot room.

Petra smiled. He always asked the same thing. 'Yep, everyone is in bed,' she shouted back, easing her wellies off and wriggling her toes. Queenie shook herself and clambered into her basket, snuggling up to Tiddles, who was already there.

The grey cat gave Queenie a narrow-eyed stare, but allowed the dog to join her in the basket. It might belong to Queenie but as far as the cat was concerned she had squatters' rights and it was first come, first served.

'Anything I can do?' Amos asked this question every evening, too. One day she'd surprise him and suggest something. He'd probably like that, she thought, but he had enough on his plate these days with keeping the house going and staying on top of the accounts. His days of hauling bales of hay around were long gone.

'What's for supper?' she asked, sniffing appreciatively. She'd never been much of a cook, but that didn't mean she didn't enjoy food, especially when someone else prepared it for her.

'Lamb chops, with roast potatoes and the last of the carrots.' Amos had a small veggie plot at the back of the house and he took great pride in providing fresh food for the table whenever he could. The carrots had been overwintered in the root cellar, a leftover from when the stables had been a working farm many moons ago.

The pair of them ate their meal whilst discussing the events of the day.

'Ted retiring!' Amos exclaimed when she told him the news. 'Well, I never. He kept that quiet. He brought a new guy with him, you say?'

'Yes, a young chap. He seemed to know what he was doing though.' Petra still wasn't sure about Harry, but time would tell, and the fact that Ted was vouching for him gave her some confidence

'How young?'

'Early thirties.'

Amos spluttered. 'When you said "young" I thought you meant a teenager.'

'He might as well be one – it'll be a long time before he's got Ted's experience. He shoed Hercules okay, though,' she added grudgingly.

'What's his name?'

'Harry Milton.'

'What's he like?'

'I told you – younger than I'd like him to be.'

'Does it matter how old he is, as long as he knows what he's doing?'

Petra shrugged. 'I suppose not.'

'What's he like?' Amos repeated.

'Not bad looking, tall, broad-shouldered…' She trailed off. 'What?'

'I meant, what's he like with the horses.' Her uncle gave her a quizzical look and Petra blushed, the heat creeping up her neck and into her cheeks.

'Oh, I see, um, good. He was good. Hercules liked him.' What on earth had got into her? Of course Amos wouldn't have wanted to know what Harry looked like. His looks, good or otherwise, were irrelevant.

Amos was still staring at her oddly. 'What?' she demanded irritably.

'You like him, don't you?'

'I do not!'

'Hmm.'

'Don't "hmm" me. I told you, I don't like him.'

'You think he's good-looking – you just said so.'

Petra stuck her nose in the air and refused to answer.

'I miss your Aunt Mags,' he said out of the blue, and Petra immediately softened.

'I know you do,' she said, reaching across the table to lay her hand on top of his. She was well aware he missed her. How could he not, when her aunt and uncle had been together for so long. Her death had been a blow to everyone. And no matter that it had happened years ago, Petra could vividly recall how upset she had been, so she couldn't even imagine what her uncle must have gone through. Was still going through.

'Don't leave it too late,' he said.

Confused, Petra asked, 'Leave what too late?'

'Finding love. It's the only thing that truly matters. If you spend your life alone, you'll miss out on so much.' His eyes were glossy with unshed tears, and Petra felt close to crying herself. Not because she didn't have a man in her life (she neither wanted one, nor needed one) but because her uncle was still in so much pain at the loss of his wife. If there was something – anything – she could do to alleviate even a fraction of the hurt he was feeling, she'd do it in a heartbeat.

'I'm fine as I am, Amos.' She *was*. She didn't need a man to complete her; she was already complete. Running the stables and being with horses all day was all she'd ever wanted, and she considered herself truly blessed. She had enough people to love – well, horses, although she obviously loved Amos, and she cared deeply for Nathen, Faith and Charity. Anyone else would only be a distraction and a hindrance.

'You're past thirty,' Amos pointed out. 'Don't leave it too late.'

'Thirty isn't old,' Petra scoffed. 'And I'm only just gone thirty.'

Amos pounced. 'Ha! So you *are* open to love.'

'No! Didn't I just say so?' He was trying to trip her up with this convoluted way of thinking, but she wasn't having any of it.

Her uncle smiled sadly. 'Petra, my sweet, I'm serious. Everyone needs a special someone in their life. It's high time you found yours.'

Petra rolled her eyes, and instead of responding to his ridiculousness she got to her feet and began clearing the table.

Why, oh why, though, did the image of the new farrier pop into her mind?

Harry relaxed into his sofa with a deep sigh, a bottle of ice-cold beer in his hand, and he thought about the day he'd just had.

All in all, he thought it had gone quite well. Aside from making necessary visits to those clients who Ted had been scheduled to see, they'd also made the odd detour or two to pop in on a few other locals so that Ted could introduce him and explain he was taking over the business.

Most people, especially those whose animals he had tended to, were sad to see Ted go, but seemed happy enough that Harry was taking over.

There was only one person who still appeared to have reservations about him after he'd done his job (under Ted's watchful eye, of course) and that was Petra.

What was her problem? He'd shown he was more than capable, so what more did she want from him? Ted had told him that she didn't like change, but that was tough – change happened all the time. And him replacing Ted was hardly a major one. He'd only see her a few times a year, even with him living in the nearest village to the stables. Muddypuddle Lane was over a mile long, and the stables were at the far end of it. He might bump into her occasionally in Picklewick, but on the other hand she might prefer to do her shopping further afield. Either way, his arrival could hardly be described as a life-changing event for her.

So, he asked himself again, what was her problem?

Maybe it was him, personally. She might have taken an instant dislike to him, for some reason. He didn't think he was a particularly unlikeable bloke, but he supposed it was possible. You heard of love at first sight – so maybe Petra had experienced hate at first sight the second she clapped eyes on him, though perhaps "hate" was too strong a word.

Oh well, he thought, you can't please all the people all the time, and if the only client who was displeased with him was Petra, he could live with that. It would be a shame if she took her custom elsewhere, though; she was by far one of the biggest clients in his patch. Maybe he could reduce his rates for her, a kind of bulk buy thing. Or maybe not – margins were tight as they were, without making them worse.

He'd have a think, see how things went. It could be that they would agree not to like each other and he could still retain her as a client.

He paused as a thought struck him; he didn't dislike her in return, and he wasn't referring to the fact that he found her attractive either (although she undoubtedly was). And that was quite odd – to like someone when they didn't like you.

Harry took another swig of his beer, his head

beginning to ache with all the second-guessing he was doing, and he deliberately dragged his thoughts away from Petra and her stables, and directed them to his cottage. He had taken out a six-month lease on it with the idea that he'd settle into the area first before he thought about buying. Although, if he was honest, this little cottage with its three outbuildings was perfect. He didn't need any more than two bedrooms (one for him and one for Timothy when he came for a visit) and the larger the place, the more there was to clean. He preferred outdoor spaces, and this cottage had an enchanting garden backing onto a field in which a pair of horses grazed.

He ran his eye over them, automatically noting their configuration and their general state of health. Their coats shone in the last rays of the setting sun as they cropped the grass, and the scene was one of peace and contentment.

Harry had considered sitting outside this evening but it was still rather early in the year, and once the sun dropped lower in the sky, winter's chill returned as if reluctant to let go and admit defeat.

Movement caught his eye and he watched as a woman strode across the field, a bucket in one hand and a couple of lead ropes in the other. Her voice calling to the horses carried faintly through the window, and Harry wondered if Petra had brought her animals in for the night yet.

Then he frowned because he didn't want to think about her right now, so why had she popped into his thoughts again?

The horses had gone to the woman willingly enough, their heads pushing at her as both of them tried to stick their noses in the bucket she held, and

Harry smiled. He hadn't ridden in a long time. Too long. Maybe that was why he kept thinking about Petra and her stables – he should book a hack with her. It would be good to ride again, and hacking in the hills around the village would help him explore the area.

And you never know, he said to himself as he finished his beer, she might even begin to like him a little bit. Although why that should matter to him, he hadn't the slightest idea.

CHAPTER FOUR

Petra was rather touched to be invited to Ted's retirement party. She hadn't thought they were all that close, but when she climbed the stairs to the function room on the first floor of the Black Horse and saw how many people had turned up to wish him well, she didn't feel quite so special. Still, it was nice to see that the residents of Picklewick and the surrounding area thought so highly of the old farrier. All she hoped was that the new one would be as good at his job.

She had no reason to believe that Harry wouldn't be, and he'd done a competent enough job on Hercules – she'd checked the horse's hooves after Ted and Harry left. It was just that she was used to Ted, and he was used to her. She'd get used to this new one eventually, of course she would.

As though thinking about the new farrier had conjured him into being, she spotted him at the bar and she quickly turned away before he realised she'd noticed him. There were far too many people at this party who'd expect her to chat with them as it was, without throwing his name into the hat. People like the glamorous and opinionated Cher, whose daughter Thaila (pronounced Taylor – Petra had been told the first time she'd met the child, who was as precocious as her mother) used to have riding lessons every week until Petra told her where to stick her suggestions.

Cher had always wanted to chat – and although "chat" was the word Cher used, Petra thought "harangue" was a far more accurate description of what actually passed between them. She pitied Thaila's teachers, but she pitied the owner of the riding school Thaila now attended, even more.

Oh dear, Cher had spotted her and was heading in her direction.

Petra hastily swallowed what was left of her wine and using the need for a top-up as an excuse, waved her empty glass at the woman bearing down on her and dashed to the bar, only to find herself next to another person she wasn't too keen on engaging in conversation with this evening. She was beginning to wish she hadn't come.

'Harry,' she said. It sounded more like an accusation than a greeting, and she tried to temper it with a friendly nod.

He appeared to be amused. A small smile played about his lips and his eyes crinkled a little at the corners. He scrubbed up well, she noticed. The old jeans and hoodie had been replaced with charcoal chinos and a white button-down shirt with the sleeves rolled up, showing his muscular forearms. Petra looked away.

'Nice to see you again,' he said politely. 'How is Hercules?'

'He's very well, thank you.' She'd ridden him several times since he'd been shod and she hadn't been aware of any issues. 'I rode him today, in fact,' she added, as though Harry had been privy to her thoughts.

'I've been meaning to ask you…I'd like to go out on a hack sometime.'

Petra blinked. 'Um, okay,' she stuttered, then she pulled herself together and rallied. 'I'll have to assess your riding ability first,' she told him sharply. 'I can't have any old Tom, Dick or Harry—' She halted and bit her lip.

Harry, she saw, was trying not to laugh.

'What's so funny?' Cher's voice inserted itself into the conversation, quickly followed by the rest of her as she pushed her way between them.

Petra took a step back.

'So, you're the new farrier, are you? Ted has told me *aaalll* about you,' Cher drawled, and Petra watched her scan Harry from the tip of his loafers to the top of his dark hair. Petra could tell that the other woman clearly liked what she was seeing.

She took another step back, hoping to slip away unnoticed.

No such luck.

'Petra, aren't you going to introduce us?' Cher demanded. She did a lot of demanding, did Cher. And she was perfectly capable of introducing herself. Did the woman think she was living in the nineteenth century?

Sullenly Petra replied, 'Harry, meet Cher. Cher meet Harry. Now, if you'll excuse me, I have people to see.'

'No problem, run along,' Cher said, waving her hand dismissively, her attention on Harry. Petra could almost see the drool coming out of those too-red lips.

Petra "ran", but not before she caught a glimpse of the pleading look on Harry's face as she left.

Ha! She thought, serves him right.

Although, what it served him right for, she didn't have the faintest idea. She felt a twinge of guilt at abandoning him to deal with Cher on his own, but she pushed the feeling away by telling herself that all was fair in love and war, and when it came to Cher Reynolds, it most definitely *was* war.

'Sorry,' she mouthed at him before turning away and disappearing into the crowd, and in a way she *was* sorry. Not because she was leaving him in the tender care of a woman like Cher (she had no doubt Harry could take care of himself) but that he might find the woman attractive.

Cher was a single mother, and she made it clear she wasn't averse to changing that status.

Petra fervently hoped Cher didn't get to change her single status by netting Harry Milton. And by that, she only meant that she couldn't abide the idea of her new farrier being married to a woman she actively disliked and who, she suspected, had bad-mouthed her stables on more than one occasion.

No wonder she preferred horses to people, Petra thought as she smiled a greeting to the parents of a little lad by the name of Simon who loved horses as much as she did. You knew where you were with horses. People were far trickier.

But every now and then, throughout the evening, she couldn't help her gaze seeking out Harry to check that he wasn't as interested in Cher as Cher clearly hoped he would be.

Harry was not amused. He'd spent most of the party trying to avoid that Cher-woman who Petra had introduced him to. He could have sworn Petra had been laughing at him as she slipped away, using the flimsy excuse that she had other people to speak to.

Not that he particularly wanted Petra to stay and talk to him (he didn't), he simply hadn't wanted to be left alone with Cher. The woman scared him – she'd kept putting her hand on his arm and leaning too close so her perfume made his eyes water.

When he'd eventually escaped, saying he needed the loo, her eyes had been on his back (he could feel them boring into him) as he weaved his way to the door. He'd washed his hands, spent a few minutes giving himself a mental talking to, then had sidled back into the party hoping his entrance would go unnoticed.

His tactics hadn't worked. Cher had positioned herself near the door, and she spotted him as soon as he reappeared; it was only Ted wanting him to meet someone that saved him from an evening of being hounded.

As soon as he was free of Cher's clutches, he looked for Petra, hoping to tease her about her abandonment of him, but he couldn't see her.

He didn't see her for the rest of the party, and when he put his weary self to bed later that night his thoughts had filled with all the new people he'd met, but the only image to stay with him as he drifted off to sleep was that of Petra mouthing "sorry" at him, and the twinkle in her eye as she abandoned him to his fate..

CHAPTER FIVE

Not even her beloved Hercules could lift Petra's mood. She'd been as grumpy as a badger with a snout full of bee stings ever since Ted's retirement party on Friday night, and she had no idea why.

She could try to blame it on having a Sunday filled with back-to-back lessons, followed by a trek with a group of giggling teenage girls who had spent as much time looking at their phones as they had in paying attention to their mounts until she was sick of yelling at them to pull their ponies' heads out of the verges.

She couldn't blame the ponies for taking the opportunity to snatch at the grass – after all, equines were eating machines, spending up to sixteen hours a day grazing if left to their own devices. However, she didn't leave them to their own devices; she expected them to work for their hay and grain, and too much rich grass could lead to all kinds of problems, especially when it came to a greedy creature like Tango, a cob who was prone to laminitis if she didn't watch him.

She made a mental note to pop a grazing muzzle on him before she turned him out into the field. It didn't prevent him from grazing, but it limited his intake of grass and made him work harder for it. He hated wearing it, but Petra knew it was better than trying to treat any resulting laminitis. As well as the pain the horse would be in, laminitis meant numerous visits by both the vet and the farrier as they tried to treat the swelling of the hoof and the bone. The vet was expensive, and she was already seeing far more of the farrier than she wanted to.

By the time she'd arrived back at the stables and the girls had left, she was in a foul mood. Wrestling with Tango didn't help, as he kept tossing his head in annoyance and his nose had dealt her a glancing blow on the chin, making her yelp in pain.

'Tango!' she shouted at him, and he glared at her balefully, eyeing the muzzle with dislike. 'It's for your own good.'

Eventually she managed to slip it over his nose and buckle the strap behind his ears. Then she smiled gently at the sad expression on his face.

Bless him. He looked awfully sorry for himself.

His expression mirrored her own she noticed, as she caught sight of her reflection in one of the old farmhouse windows a short while later, and she couldn't believe how glum she looked.

Snap out of it, she told herself. She had nothing to be miserable about; the stables were doing well (she'd never be rich, but the income was steady), she had a job she loved, and she was happy (wasn't she? – of course she was).

What more could she possibly want?

When Harry's face popped into her mind, she angrily shoved it away. He had no right to invade her thoughts and she had a good mind to tell him so. And she would too, apart from the fact that she didn't want to admit that he seemed to have taken up residence in her head.

Okay, she admitted reluctantly, he was damned attractive, but handsome is as handsome does as the old saying goes, and no good would come of it. Look at the problems he had with Cher. That woman was a man-eater if ever there was one. She made no secret that she was hunting for a husband, and at one point she had set her sights on a locum doctor. Now she appeared to be targeting the new farrier.

Petra's one consolation was her memory of the wide-eyed helpless stare he'd sent her as she'd left him to Cher's tender mercies. Harry's discomfort had cheered her up no end.

'Have you got the number for the new farrier?' Faith asked Petra a couple of days later. 'Midnight has thrown another shoe. I honestly don't know how he does it.' She grimaced. 'I'm beginning to think he's doing it on purpose; like he's in his stable every night, working out how to prise them off.'

Petra laughed. How long horses kept shoes on their hooves depended on a variety of factors such as how fast the hoof grew, what terrain the horse walked on, or overreaching by the hind feet.

Midnight was notorious for losing his.

'Yes, it's on the wall in the office, above the phone. Have you found the shoe?' Sometimes the horseshoe could be found in a field or a stable, but more often than not it simply disappeared. And even if it was found, it couldn't always be reused.

'Not yet.' Faith heaved a sigh. 'He's costing me a fortune.'

Petra sympathised. Owning a horse was expensive and riding wasn't a cheap hobby. Which was why the arrangement she had with Faith and her twin to house their horses at the stables for free in exchange for help around the place, suited all three of them. Including the horses, who were sometimes used for lessons and hacks if either of the twins didn't have time to exercise their animals.

Apart from throwing his shoes on a regular basis, Midnight was a sweet fella, and Petra had a soft spot for him. 'I'll see if I can find it after I've sorted the others out,' she said, knowing that the girl had to go to work. 'It can't have gone far.'

Which were famous last words, she thought sometime later as she was rooting through the straw on the stable floor. It wasn't quite like looking for a needle in a haystack because a cast shoe was a fairly substantial item, but it certainly felt like it.

'Is he in one of the fields?' a man's voice called, making her jump.

She straightened up and whirled around to see Harry leaning against the door, watching her.

Great. He'd had a perfect view of her backside as she'd been scrabbling around on the floor.

'In the bottom one,' she muttered, then instantly regretting using the word "bottom". In a rare display of embarrassment, she felt heat flood into her cheeks. This was the second time this man had made her blush. Cross with herself, she added briskly, 'Can you find it on your own, or do you need some help?'

'I dare say I can manage. Which horse is it?'

'Midnight.' She was about to describe the horse when Harry spoke.

'Ah, dark brown, sixteen hands, gelding,' he said.

Petra raised her eyebrows.

'I paid attention when you showed me around.'

She was impressed. Although she tended to remember horses better than people, she was aware most folks weren't like that.

'Besides,' he added with a grin. 'If I couldn't work out which animal in the field had lost a shoe, I wouldn't be much of a farrier, would I? So you can carry on doing what you're doing – I'll fetch him myself.'

His smile was infectious, and she found her lips curving upwards in response. Hastily, she dropped the smile; she didn't want him to think she was interested in him. She didn't want to come across like Cher did, all giggles and dimpled cheeks. The blushing was bad enough, but at least she could put that down to straightening up suddenly. Not that he'd mentioned it; but if he did…

'Right then,' he said. 'I'll get on. Is he wearing a halter?'

Guilt pricked at her – it wasn't a farrier's job to go chasing around a field after a horse. The animal should be ready and waiting. 'I'll get him,' she said, and he stood aside to let her pass.

'I may as well come with you,' he suggested, and she couldn't think of a reason not to let him. Actually, she could, but she wasn't prepared to share with him the information that he made her uncomfortable.

Not uncomfortable, exactly. More…out of sorts. She couldn't describe it to herself, so trying to explain it to the man striding down the track next to her would be difficult. She was far too aware of his nearness for her liking. She could see his profile out of the corner of her eye, she could smell the subtle scent of him – citrus and fresh – and she could almost feel the warmth of his arm as it swung by his side, matching her pace for pace.

Suddenly aware that she was practically running along the path leading to the field, she slowed a little, feeling slightly breathless. Which was odd because she was extremely fit. A bit of walking shouldn't make her heart beat faster, or her pulse throb in her ears, and neither should she feel as though she couldn't catch her breath.

Maybe she was coming down with something? If so, it would be a damned inconvenience that she could do without. Surreptitiously she felt her forehead, hoping she didn't have the beginnings of a temperature. But although she was feeling all hot and bothered, her brow was cool enough.

Thank goodness for that. She was far too busy to be ill, and she knew she was a horrid patient. But her lack of a temperature didn't explain why she was feeling so odd.

Petra left Harry at the gate whilst she went into the field to catch Midnight, which was easier said than done as the horse had only been turned out a couple of hours ago and didn't fancy being brought back in because it usually meant he had to do some work.

She caught him eventually and led him to Harry who, she saw, was gazing intently at them. Yet another blush threatened to flood her cheeks at his scrutiny, and she willed her body to behave. This was becoming quite ridiculous. She was regressing into a teenager with a first crush.

Her eyes widened and she came to a stop.

That's what was wrong with her! She was behaving like a filly faced with a handsome stallion (not that fillies gave a hoot for a stallion's looks), and she gave herself a mental shake. How absurd, her having a crush on the new farrier. She wasn't behaving any better than Cher, but at least Cher was being honest with herself and with the man she fancied. Harry knew where he stood with Cher.

'Everything okay?' he called, and she jumped, her sudden movement making Midnight toss his head in annoyance.

'Fine. Sorry, miles away for a minute.' She carried on walking as he opened the gate and led the horse through it.

'I was watching him as you brought him up the field and apart from the cast shoe, he looks a little lame in his nearside back leg, to me,' Harry said, and Petra suppressed a groan. He hadn't been studying her at all – he had been examining the horse. Of course he had – that *was* why he was there.

Feeling incredibility foolish, she carried on walking without saying anything until they reached the usual place where she hitched any horses who were about to be shod.

She tied Midnight up then headed back to the house, calling over her shoulder, 'Let Faith know what you find. You can leave him there when you've finished – I'll see to him later.'

Ignoring the eyes she could feel on her back, she marched across the yard, darted into the house and as soon as she was safely out of sight, collapsed into a chair and rubbed a slightly shaking hand across her face.

Dear god, she didn't need this. She didn't need him, or any other man for that matter. She was happy as she was; but even as she told herself that, she could sense the doubt in the back of her mind asking if she truly was happy, or whether she'd said it so often she had come to believe it.

When she heard the sound of Harry's van pulling out of the yard sometime later, she finally looked up to see Amos staring. She hadn't heard him come in and he was sitting in one of the other chairs. How long he'd been there she had no idea, and she wondered what he was making of her strange behaviour this morning.

Then he said, 'Don't leave it too late,' and she knew precisely what he was thinking.

And she also knew precisely what she was going to do with his advice.

Ignore it. Because she was happy just the way she was.

CHAPTER SIX

Mondays, Ted had informed Harry before he'd handed over the reins of the business to him for good, tended to be busy. Horses and ponies were ridden more at the weekends and owners tended to notice thrown shoes more, and they all wanted their animals seen to as soon as possible. For Harry, weekends had always been business as usual as he'd often attended races as the on-site farrier. It was a welcome change to have weekends off, although he was still on call in an emergency. So far, no one had needed him and everything had been routine.

Today he was attending a stable some thirteen miles from Picklewick. Several animals were due to be re-shoed (every six weeks for working horses was quite common) and he'd set aside a chunk of time to do just that. He'd just finished and was stowing his equipment in the back of Ted's (now his) van, when he saw a familiar figure trotting towards him.

It was Cher, and his heart sank.

'Harry? I thought it was you.' She tottered over to him in heels far too high to be worn in a stable yard. 'What are you doing here?' she asked, then she put a hand to her mouth and gave a tinkling giggle. 'Silly me. You're working.'

'Yes, I am,' he agreed.

She stared at him and he realised he was supposed to ask her what she was doing here in return. He didn't. Instead, he told her, 'I've got to get on; another job to go to.'

'I was hoping to bump into you,' she said, laying a hand on his arm. 'I wanted to ask you something.'

'Oh?' His mind whirled with possibilities and he dreaded what she was about to ask. She'd come on to him fairly heavily the other night and he knew she'd been flirting outrageously with him.

'I need your advice and your help,' she said.

'What with?' His reply was cautious.

'Can we have a chat about it some other time? I've got to pick Thaila up from school and you've said you've got a job to go to.'

'Um, okay.'

'How about we meet for coffee? I can do tomorrow.'

His curiosity piqued, Harry said, 'Lunchtime?' He had a couple of things on in the morning, but he had set the afternoon aside to work on his accounts, starting as he meant to go on, although he wasn't entirely convinced he'd keep his good intentions up. A quick coffee would split the day up.

'Lunch it is!' Cher twinkled at him.

He'd never seen anyone twinkle before, but he'd definitely been twinkled at. And he was sure he hadn't agreed to lunch, not in the way Cher was implying.

'We can go to the Black Horse, if you like?' This time she simpered, and he bit his lip. Her frivolous behaviour might appeal to another man but he was a more down-to-earth guy, and he found her a bit over the top. Petra was more his type.

His eyes widened as the thought took him by surprise.

'Or maybe not,' Cher said, seeing his expression. 'Let's avoid temptation, shall we?'

'Temptation?' he repeated blankly, his attention on the silly notion he'd just had. Petra wasn't his type at all – she was too grumpy for a start.

'Ooh, you naughty thing!' Cher tapped him on the arm in mock admonishment. 'I was referring to drinking at lunchtime.'

Harry hadn't been referring to anything at all, and now he was slightly bewildered and very much regretting agreeing to meet her.

'Let's go to Blake's Café in Picklewick,' she continued. 'They do some fantastic open sandwiches, or homemade soup if you prefer. Or maybe both – in your line of work you need to keep your strength up.' She eyed him up and down and he resisted the urge to squirm like a small boy needing the loo.

'Indeed,' he said, not knowing how else to respond.

'Shall we say twelve-thirty?'

'Fine. See you there,' he said, lifting his rolled-up bag of tools into the van and closing the door.

'I'll look forward to it,' Cher said, her smile revealing dimples in both of her cheeks.

Harry smiled back and gave her a wave of acknowledgment as he climbed into the van. He had to admit that she was an attractive woman, and she obviously took care of herself and had pride in her appearance. She wore the kind of make-up that made it appear she had hardly any on (he'd learnt that from one of Timothy's many girlfriends), her hair was glossy and bounced on her shoulders whenever she moved her head, and she had a good figure.

But when he compared her to the girl-next-door freshness and lithe frame of the owner of the stables on Muddypuddle Lane, he knew which woman he preferred.

It was just a pity Petra Kelly wasn't as interested in him as Cher Reynolds was.

He froze, his hand on the gear stick.

Why was Petra's lack of interest in him such a pity? What—?

Cher tapped on the glass and waved to him, pulling him out of his thoughts. He waggled his fingers at her, started the engine and hurriedly made his escape.

As he made his way to his next appointment, his mind was churning.

By the time he pulled into a field where a fellow with a massive Shire horse was waiting for him, hooves larger than serving platters, he'd arrived at the conclusion that he wanted to see more of Petra Kelly and it wasn't because of her equine charges, either.

She, however, hadn't shown the slightest inclination that she wanted to see any more of him. Quite the opposite, as her behaviour last week had shown.

The realisation was rather disappointing.

○

The following day Harry spotted Cher as he neared the café. She was sitting by the window and was watching out for him because the second she saw him she waved and beckoned for him to hurry up. He frowned a little – he wasn't late, he was early, because he'd been hoping to arrive before her so he could get his bearings.

Cher unsettled him. Not in a good way like Petra (stop thinking about her, he told himself) but in a "please-get-me-out-of-here" way, and he was anxious to hear what she had to say so he could leave. His plan was to have a half-drunk cup of coffee already in front of him, so as soon as she'd discussed what she wanted to discuss, he could make his excuses and dash off. However, she'd scuppered his plan, and now he was forced to sit through the ordering process, the wait for their orders to arrive and the imbibing of them, and all the while he simply knew she'd flirt.

She looked so pleased to see him when he sidled past the other tables to get to the one she was sitting at, that he immediately felt guilty. It wasn't her fault that she wasn't his type he thought, as Petra's pretty but scowling face appeared in his mind – Petra was the only woman he'd met who had piqued his interest since he'd moved to Picklewick.

Okay, more than pique, he admitted as he smiled politely at Cher and took a seat.

'You're early!' she exclaimed with pleasure, and he felt himself deflate even further.

Dear god, please don't let her think it was because he couldn't wait to see her. He didn't want her to get the wrong end of the stick, and he wasn't the type to lead her on.

'Sorry,' he said.

'Don't be.' She glanced quickly around, her gaze coming back to rest on his face. 'This is nice, isn't it? The two of us having lunch together.'

'Just a cup of coffee for me, I think,' he said,

calling the waitress over, and he felt a right heel when Cher's face fell. He should never have agreed to meet with her today. Or any other day, for that matter. 'What advice do you need?' He decided to cut to the chase and get this over with before he upset her further.

'Oh yes, right. Um, Thaila wants a pony. She's been riding since she was three and she's been nagging for a horse for simply ages. I had said no, but her father – we're no longer together – has said he'll buy it for her. But he doesn't know the first thing about horses, so I told him that I'd have to choose it for her.' She put a hand on her chest, the varnish on her long nails shimmering. 'I'm no expert when it comes to horseflesh, although I do know more than my ex-husband, so I was hoping you could help?'

Harry pulled a face. 'I know about hooves and legs,' he said, 'but I'm not as hot on the rest of the animal.'

'Don't be so modest,' she giggled. 'I bet you know a pretty filly when you see one.' She fluttered her eyelashes.

Repressing a grimace, Harry said, 'I really wouldn't like to influence any decision you might make.'

'I won't hold it against you – not unless you ask me to,' she added with another suggestive giggle.

Crumbs, she was laying it on thick, making sure he knew she fancied him. 'I don't think I can help you,' he said, meaning he was certain he couldn't.

'Come with me then, for moral support.'

'I've got a better idea,' he said, suddenly struck with inspiration. 'Why don't you ask Petra?'

Cher's expression hardened. 'I don't think so. If she were the only person in the world who could tell one end of a horse from another, I still wouldn't ask her.'

'Oh.'

'Thaila had to move riding stables because of her.'

'Oh,' he repeated, not wanting to hear any more, and hoping Cher would take the hint.

'Petra Kelly is the rudest person on the planet. All I did was make a couple of suggestions which, I might add, would have made the whole riding lesson experience better for the grown-ups and she shot me down in flames. So rude.'

'I see.'

'Good. So then, will you come with me?'

'What were your suggestions?'

'Oh, um, some central heating in the indoor arena for the mums – it's mostly mums who have to sit through the lessons – a comfy sofa or two. Just little things to make the wait more bearable. It's so cold in the winter and those plastic chairs are awful. It's like being back in school.'

Harry barked out a laugh. Central heating, indeed? Sofas? Did the woman not realise that the arena was a converted barn and any heat would immediately leak out? And as for a sofa, plastic chairs were ideal because they could be washed down easily and they wouldn't rot.

'I know, right?' she carried on, mistaking his laugh for agreement. 'You still haven't answered my question. Please say you'll come.'

'Sorry, no. I don't think it's a good idea. Let me get these,' he added as their waitress approached with a tray. He took a note out of his wallet and handed it to the woman after she placed their drinks on the table. Then he rose. 'I've got to run. Sorry I can't help.'

And with that he hastened out of the café as fast as he could and drove home as though the hounds of hell were after him.

Petra hoisted her bag onto her shoulder yet again. It kept slipping down her arm and was starting to annoy her and she wished she hadn't bothered to bring it. She usually stuffed her bank card, money and phone in a pocket, but today she felt as though she needed a bag.

She'd also redone her ponytail before she'd left the house, and had changed out of her wellies and into a pair of trainers. She'd even swapped her jodhpurs for a pair of jeans.

Petra had drawn the line at applying a coat of lipstick though, despite picking it up and staring at it. She'd had the silly idea that a bit of colour on her lips might brighten her face, then she'd decided against it. She'd only do what she always did and lick it off before she'd got to where she was going.

Today she was going into the village. They were out of some essentials such as bread and potatoes, and she also wanted to pop into the deli for some of their artisan rose jam and organic cheese. She wanted to take a book to the nursing home, too. There was a little library there, just a couple of shelves, and although Petra didn't have a great deal of time in which to read, she enjoyed a good book, and when she finished with it she took it to the nursing home for others to enjoy.

Picklewick wasn't very large and most people knew everyone else, so as she made her way down the main street she constantly nodded and said hello, and had a couple of quick conversations along the lines of "how are you", "how is Amos" and so on; it was all rather pleasant and a change from the peace of the stables – if you ignored the various horsey noises, the chickens, Princess's frequent bleating, farm machinery…

It had been a while since she'd done anything more than dash into a shop, grab what she wanted and dash back out again, so she took her time in the deli, choosing with care, picking out things she knew Amos would enjoy such as the caramelised onion and walnut chutney to go with the slice of game pie she also bought for him.

'Morning, Petra. We don't see you in the village very often,' a man's voice said from behind and Petra turned to see William Reid, who managed the care home, standing at her elbow waiting to be served.

'Hello, William, how are you? Oh, I've got a book for you.' She drew the paperback out of her bag, wishing she had more than the one to donate.

He took it from her and read the back. 'Thanks, this will be very welcome. There are several residents who get through a book every couple of days and it's hard to keep up with demand.'

'I must pop in for a visit,' she said, feeling guilty. Some of the elderly people in the home had very few relatives who visited them. 'How about if I bring Queenie? Would that be okay?' She knew many of them loved animals, dogs and cats especially, but no longer got a chance to pet any.

'What a lovely idea,' William said, and they made arrangements for her to drop in next week.

Feeling more contented with life than she'd done in a while, she paid for her goodies and strolled further along the street, glancing into shop windows as she went. Faith and Charity's birthday was coming up and she needed to buy something nice for them. Maybe something girly and personal, rather than the horse-related presents she normally gave them. The problem was, she didn't do girly and had little idea what they might like.

Hoping inspiration would strike, she continued along the street. Easter displays were in evidence in shop windows, and dotted along the pavements were large wooden flower beds bursting with spring blooms. Petra loved this time of year, when winter was finally over and the horses and ponies could gorge themselves on the new spring grass (all except poor Tango), and she smiled happily.

Abruptly, her smile disappeared when she saw who was sitting in the window of the café she was walking past, as if they were on display themselves – Harry and Cher, all cosied up and having an intimate discussion by the looks of things.

Petra bit her lip and glanced away. That was that; Harry was more into Cher than Petra had hoped. She'd been right to keep him at arm's length, and she vowed she'd try to keep him out of her thoughts too.

Unfortunately, she had the feeling such a vow might be easier made than kept.

'Timothy?' Harry had arrived home and had just spread out all the paperwork, invoices and receipts he needed to wade through in order to bring his accounts up to date, when his brother phoned. 'Is everything all right?'

'Why shouldn't it be?'

Why, indeed? Harry was so used to being the adult in their little family of two, that he was finding it hard to let go. Timothy was a grown man; he could cope on his own. Part of Harry's reason for moving to Picklewick was to allow him to do just that.

'I can ring my big brother for a chat, can't I?' Timothy added.

'Of course you can, but are you sure you're okay?'

'I'm sure. I'm more concerned about you. I haven't heard from you for a few days.'

Harry blanched. Crikey, Tim was right. The first week he'd arrived in the village he had phoned his brother every day (sometimes twice a day) anxious to ensure he was managing without him. Then Harry had deliberately eased off to every other day.

But it came as a shock to realise he hadn't spoken to Timothy in four days.

'I've, erm, been a little distracted,' he said.

'About time!' his brother exclaimed.

'Eh?'

'What's her name?'

'Whose name?'

'The woman you've been distracted by.'

'I've not been distracted by any woman.'

'Oh, sorry, bro, I just thought…' Harry heard Timothy's sigh. 'What's the distraction, if it's not a girlfriend?'

'Work.'

Timothy snorted. 'You know what they say about all work and no play.'

'Ha ha, very funny.'

'I'm serious, Hal. New job, new home, new woman. Actually, any woman, because I can't remember the last time I saw you with a girl.'

'I've been somewhat busy, if you hadn't noticed.'

'Yeah, sorry about that.'

Harry spluttered, 'You've got nothing to be sorry about.'

'If it weren't for me, you'd—'

'Stop it! I love you, you're my brother. No regrets. Anyway,' Harry took a deep breath and threw the next sentence out there, hoping to alleviate some of the guilt Timothy felt at Harry having to give up his place at university and come home to look after his little brother. It had been a dark time. Harry wasn't entirely sure they'd emerged into the light yet. 'There is someone I'm interested in, if you must know,' he said.

'I knew it!' Timothy crowed. 'What's her name, how did you meet her, is she fit?'

'Slow down. Her name is Petra Kelly and she owns the stables on Muddypuddle Lane. She's got over twenty animals and—'

'Trust you! I want to know about *her*, not her horses.'

Harry heard Tim's exasperated laugh. 'She's um, early thirties I think, slim, fairly tall, blond hair, green eyes. No, they're blue. No, green – they're green. And she's got a couple of freckles on her nose.'

'She sounds cute.'

'She is.'

'Harry?'

'Yes?'

'You really need to get close enough to check out her eye colour, man.'

'Green-blue,' he said, decisively.

'Are you sure you're not making her up, like an imaginary friend?'

'I'm not making her up. I'm not sure if she's a friend, though. I don't think she likes me much.'

'How can she not like you? You're the best guy I know.'

'You're biased.'

'And you need to turn on the charm and try harder.'

'Thanks for the advice,' Harry replied in a dry voice.

But maybe his baby brother was right. Harry had taken his cue from Petra, but perhaps he should be a bit more forthright. She might not realise he was interested in her.

On the other hand, she might not *want* him to be interested in her and any advances on his part might be unwelcome. And if that were the case, she might decide his services as a farrier were unwelcome too, and he'd be in danger of losing an important client, a client who hadn't been all that convinced of him in the first place.

His instinct was right; it was best if he carried on behaving the same way towards her, and hope he'd recognise the signs if she did want anything more than a professional relationship.

As far as Harry was concerned, the ball was very firmly in Petra's court.

CHAPTER SEVEN

Petra had just shoved a large forkful of pasta in her mouth when the landline rang. With a garbled curse and frantically chewing, she went to answer it. Clients rang at all times of the day and night, and although she wished they'd stick to reasonable hours – to be fair, it was only seven p.m. so this call wasn't totally unreasonable and some evenings she'd still be in the arena at this time teaching a lesson – she didn't want to miss a potential booking. Or a cancellation.

Hoping it wasn't the latter, she swallowed her mouthful and picked up the phone.

Her heart did a funny little skipped beat when she heard the voice on the other end.

'Hi Petra, it's Harry.'

'What do you want?' She knew she was being rude, but she couldn't help it. Besides, it was usually her who called the farrier, not the other way around.

There was a slight hesitation then he said, 'I was checking that we're still on for tomorrow.'

Eh? Still on for what? As she was racking her brains, he spoke again.

'I've got Ted's diary in front of me and he has put the stables down for a possible re-shoe of nine animals.'

'Ah, yes, I see.'

'Do you still want me to come?'

'I suppose. Ted never used to ring – he just turned up.'

'I like to double-check. There's no point in a wasted journey.'

Petra did a rapid run-through of the condition of her charges' hooves. Although she checked each horse and pony thoroughly every day, she couldn't for the life of her remember who needed re-shoeing. She always left that to Ted, trusting implicitly that he wouldn't re-shoe an animal when it didn't need it.

'You'd better come. What time have you got me down for?'

'Early. Eight o'clock.'

'I'll see you then,' she said and hung up before he could say anything further.

As she returned to the table, she noticed Amos was frowning at her. 'What?' she asked, sliding back into her seat and picking up her cutlery.

'I take it that was the new farrier on the phone?'

Petra nodded, her attention on her meal. For some reason, her appetite had deserted her.

'Why were you so abrupt with him?' Amos asked.

She moved her pasta around in the bowl and didn't answer.

'What has he done to upset you?' her uncle persisted, and she could feel his eyes on her. 'I know you can be a bit grumpy—'

'I am not grumpy,' she interrupted grumpily.

'Cranky, then?'

'No! And cranky means the same thing as grumpy. I prefer the word "succinct".'

'I prefer the word "cross" and "rude",' Amos retorted.

'That's two words.'

'They both fit.'

'They do not!'

'You know they do, but you're not usually this bad.'

Petra placed her knife and fork neatly together in the bowl. 'If you must know, I'm not too keen on the company he keeps.'

'Oh? Pray tell.'

'Cher Reynolds. They're an item, and I'm surprised, that's all.'

'What do you mean? I thought he was single.'

'I saw them together. They looked very cosy in the café in the village.'

Amos frowned again, his already craggy brow creasing even further. 'I'm sure there's nothing going on between them.'

'It certainly looked as if there was, to me.' Petra knew what she saw – a lunchtime date. Cher hadn't been able to keep her hands off him.

'I heard on the grapevine that Cher is thinking of buying Thaila her own pony. Or rather, her ex-husband is,' Amos said.

Petra's eyes widened. 'I hope she doesn't think she's going to stable it here.'

He chuckled. 'I doubt it. There's no love lost between you two, is there? Anyway, I don't think she's going to bother after all. I heard that she was all for the idea and had asked Harry to accompany her, but she seems to have gone off the boil when he said no.'

'Hmph, they looked friendly enough to me when I saw them.'

'Looks can be deceiving. I heard he didn't even stay to finish his drink.'

'You hear an awful lot,' she accused, wondering where he was getting his information from.

'That's because I go out and talk to people. Which reminds me, you couldn't drive me to the Black Horse later, could you? It's darts and a chippie supper tonight.'

'You've just had your evening meal,' she protested.

'Aye, but I'm not going to turn down a pint and a plate of chips in the pub.'

As Petra cleared away the dishes (Amos had emptied his bowl – she'd hardly touched hers), she thought about what her uncle had told her. She could have sworn Harry and Cher were a couple, or at least on the brink of becoming one, but maybe she'd got it wrong. Admittedly, she wasn't as good at reading people as she was at reading horses. Her animals mightn't be able to speak, but she was able to tell what they were feeling much better than she was able to tell what was in people's minds.

Hell, she was having trouble knowing what was in her own, because for some reason the news that Harry was single and wasn't interested in Cher had lifted her spirits immensely.

And she knew she was in trouble when she found herself humming along to the radio after she'd dropped Amos off at the pub.

She knew she was in *serious* trouble when she took the long way home – past the cottage Harry was renting.

Lights were on behind drawn curtains, and her treacherous mind couldn't help wondering whether he was thinking about her as much as she was thinking about him.

Harry wasn't pleased. His perfectly polite and reasonable phone call to Petra had left him feeling cross and deflated, and he failed to understand what was wrong with the woman. He'd been nothing but friendly to her, his conduct utterly professional, but she'd been rude and rather dismissive in return. He was beginning to think that Cher had a point.

A low-level feeling of dread crept over him; he wasn't looking forward to visiting the stables on Muddypuddle Lane tomorrow, and he debated whether or not to cancel the appointment. But that would mean calling Petra back, and he seriously didn't fancy speaking to her again this evening. She'd spoilt his mood enough already. Then there were the horses to consider; they could last another week or two without being seen by a farrier, and although Harry wasn't under the illusion that he was the only one for miles around (he wasn't – farriers were quite common, especially in rural areas), they did tend to be booked up.

Taking a deep breath, he resolved to attend the stables tomorrow, and whilst he was there he'd have it out with her. He didn't want to lose her custom, but neither could he work for someone who clearly disliked him so much. Ted had given him the impression that she was offish with most people, but the way she was with him took being offish to the extreme. He was used to surly trainers, brusque farmers, and the like, but she took the biscuit.

Harry paused. Or, did she? When he thought about it, she had behaved no differently to that of a number of other horsey people he'd encountered, so why did her attitude towards him bother him so much?

It was because he fancied her, he decided, and he'd taken it as a personal affront. If she'd been a bloke would he have reacted the same way? Probably not. Therefore the problem lay with him and not her. Petra was, as far as he could tell, simply being Petra. He needed to grow a thicker skin and get over himself.

Vowing not to take it personally and deciding he wouldn't take her to task about it after all, he nevertheless spent the rest of the evening trying to keep thoughts of Petra out of his head.

Hope for the best and plan for the worst; Harry couldn't remember where he'd heard such sage advice, but the following morning he drove the old van up the bumpy track to Petra's stables, filled with optimism that she would be pleasant (or should he say, pleasant*er*) but fully expecting his visit to be as disagreeable as the last time he'd met her.

Several curious faces peered out of the horseboxes, ears pricked, following his progress across the yard to his usual parking spot.

Horses were intelligent creatures and he had no doubt that they recognised Ted's van and knew what it signified.

He cut the engine and clambered out, stretching his back and rotating his shoulders. Blacksmithing was a physical job and he hadn't rested too well last night (Petra had featured quite heavily in his dreams, but he couldn't for the life of him remember any of them this morning) and he was feeling rather tired and in no mood for her unfriendly attitude, despite his vow yesterday evening to not take it personally.

'Morning.' Petra appeared from around a corner and smiled at him.

Harry nearly lost his balance. 'Morning,' he replied cautiously, wondering why she was smiling.

'Nice day.'

It certainly was, bright, sunny, and fresh, yet with a hint of warmth from the spring sun. 'Yes, it's lovely,' he agreed. 'Are they all here?' He gestured towards the animals in their stalls.

'Yep, all there. Most of them are okay with being shod, except for Gerald. He doesn't have shoes, but he will need to have his hooves trimmed.'

'Remind me, which one is Gerald?'

Petra pointed to an empty stall.

Harry squinted then he laughed. He could just about see a pair of incredibly long equine ears waggling over the top of the half-door and realised they belonged to the donkey.

'He came to us in a dreadful state,' Petra was saying. 'I was only supposed to have him for a couple of weeks while he got his strength back, but I ended up keeping him.'

'That was good of you.'

She shrugged. 'He earns his keep at Christmas,' she said. 'Nativity plays and so on.'

Harry wasn't fooled. He understood that, as far as Petra was concerned, Gerald earning his keep didn't matter one iota to her, and despite the barriers she put up to keep people at bay, she had a heart of gold when it came to animals. He suspected she might also have one when it came to people who needed help too, but he couldn't prove it.

She didn't wait for a response from him, but went to the nearest stall and led out a small creamy-coloured cob. 'This is Parsnip. Named for the colour of his coat and for the way he digs his heels into the ground when he doesn't want to do something.'

Harry smiled at the metaphor – parsnips had long taproots and were sometimes difficult to dig up. The pony was a beautiful colour though, especially with the early morning sun shining on him. It gave his coat a soft gold sheen. He was about to say so, when he glanced from the pony to the woman who was holding him, and the sight stopped his breath.

The same sun shone on Petra's hair, and he was reminded of those religious paintings where the subject had a halo around their heads. Some of her hair had escaped from its customary bun and her face was framed in shades of gold and bronze. Her face was also illuminated by the rays and her skin appeared luminous, her eyes bluer than he remembered; he could have sworn they had more green in them—

'Is everything all right?' she asked, bringing him back to himself with a start.

'Oh, yes, fine. Great. Never better.' He was stammering and stuttering like an idiot, but he didn't seem able to get his brain to work, and what was coming out of his mouth was nonsensical drivel.

'Good.' She shot him a curious look, but he turned his attention back to Parsnip.

'Right, I'll get started on these. Is there anything else I should know about?' he asked.

'Nothing, except Blaze – he's the chestnut without a blaze – doesn't like his hind feet being played with, so if you can get away with not shoeing him today, it would be good.'

'Blaze *without* a blaze?'

Petra smiled at him again and his heart somersaulted. God, she was incredibly pretty when she smiled. She was pretty anyway, but her face lit up like a Madonna when she did that. A beautiful Madonna—

'Are you sure you're okay?' she asked. 'You look a bit strange.'

'Do you fancy going out for a drink sometime? Or a meal?' He stopped abruptly, appalled at what he'd just asked her.

She sent him another odd look. It seemed like odd looks and smiles were the order of the day. 'You don't look as though you want me to go anywhere with you,' she pointed out and he hurriedly rearranged his expression.

'Oh, I do, believe me, I really do,' he insisted.

'In that case, yes. Just the once, mind you; don't think I'm going to be making a habit of it.'

He didn't care that she was only planning on going out with him once. It was a far cry from not going out with him at all. And you never know, he said to himself, once might very well lead to twice.

'Brilliant!' He beamed back at her. 'Tonight?' He held the grin in place, but at the same time he was berating himself for sounding so keen. Or desperate, which was possibly more accurate.

'I can do eight. I've got lessons booked until seven-thirty.'

'Is eight going to give you enough time to get ready?' From past experiences (not that there had been a great many of them) he was under the impression that women could take hours to get ready to go out.

Petra gave him an incredulous look. 'I don't need long,' she replied frostily, 'unless you think it's going to take hours to get this,' she swept a hand from her head to her knees, 'to look presentable.'

'I…no…that's not what I meant,' he stammered. 'You can come as you are, I don't mind.'

This time she looked more amused than affronted. 'Covered in horse hair and smelling of manure?'

'I didn't mean that either. What I mean is, you're beautiful anyway and a posh dress or lipstick won't make you any more beautiful than you already are.'

Petra studied him for a long while, then she said in a small voice, 'That's the nicest thing anyone has ever said to me.' And with that she shoved Parsnip's lead rein into his hands and was off, almost running across the yard.

Harry watched her go, so many emotions tumbling through his chest that he didn't know where to start in sorting them out.

But when she stopped as she reached the corner of the stable block and turned to him, he saw the delight on her face, and then his overriding emotion was pleasure. He'd made her happy, and as a consequence, it made him happy too.

In fact, he was happier today than he could ever remember being, and all that had happened was that he'd asked her out and she'd said yes.

Lord help him, he was smitten. And it felt good.

That was unexpected, Petra thought for the umpteenth time that day, as she hurried to get ready for her date with Harry. The twins were happy to see to the three ponies which had been used for the lesson that had just finished, although they did keep shooting her curious glances and whispering between themselves.

They thought she hadn't noticed, but she had, and their odd behaviour set her teeth on edge. So what if she was having a quick drink with a man this evening? It wasn't the first time – although, she was forced to acknowledge, it was probably such a rare event everyone had forgotten about it. In fact, she was struggling to remember when the last time was and who it had been with.

Despite telling Harry that she didn't spend hours getting ready, Petra had spent hours mentally going through her wardrobe and wondering what she should wear. At least her hair had been freshly washed that morning, so all she needed to do was to release it from its band and give it a quick brush after the fastest shower in the history of mankind; she was well aware that l'eau de horse wasn't to everyone's taste, and even though Harry might work with horses himself, he probably didn't want his date smelling of one.

That *was* what this was, wasn't it – a date?

She'd assumed so, but what if she was wrong? Had she read too much into what might have been a casual suggestion, and this was nothing more than a swift half down the pub?

Now look what she'd gone and done; she was second-guessing and overanalysing. Just turn up and see what happens, she told herself. As long as she didn't make a fool of herself and she let him make the first move (if, indeed, any first moves were going to be made), then all would be well.

But as she drove into the village, which was thankfully only five minutes away by car, she was seriously wondering why she'd agreed to have a drink with him at all. She didn't normally go out at night. For one thing she was often too tired, for another she couldn't be bothered because there was nowhere to go in Picklewick except for the Black Horse, and for a third, no one asked her.

Petra was sorely tempted to turn her SUV around and send Harry a text to say something had come up.

But she was here now, she argued to herself, as she drew to a stop in the pub's car park. Just one drink wouldn't hurt and perhaps a quick bite to eat because she hadn't had any supper yet and she was starving.

She glanced down, checking that she looked decent enough in her jeans, smart leather pumps and flowery top (the effect was somewhat spoilt by the old and worn waxed-cotton jacket she'd slung over the top because it was decidedly chilly this evening) and came to the conclusion that she'd do. This was as close to dressing up as she got. He'd have to take her or leave her.

From the look in his eyes when he caught sight of her from his table near the bar, she guessed he must like what he saw. He did a sort of double-take, swiftly scanned her from head to foot, then his gaze came to rest on her face, and she was certain there was admiration in it. There was a hint of something else too, but she wasn't sure what.

He got to his feet as she approached and held out both hands to her.

Cautiously, she took hold of them and he pulled her gently towards him, kissing the air near to one side of her face then the other.

With a sharp intake of breath, she pulled her hand free and stepped back.

For a second there, she'd thought he was about to go in for a proper kiss, and while she would have pushed him away, a little part of her was disappointed that it was only a peck on the cheek.

Mystified, she sat down. Harry remained standing.

'What can I get you?' he asked.

'Erm, soda and lime, please.' Petra watched him walk to the bar, taking in his long legs encased in dark denim, his broad shoulders beneath a plain white tee shirt, the set of his back, the shape of his behind.

Oh my, this wouldn't do at all.

Not only had his extremely friendly greeting disconcerted her, now she was ogling his backside. Having never been much of a hugger (not when it came to people), she wasn't used to such familiarity, and although she was fully aware that many people greeted each other like that, it wasn't her way, and now her heart was thudding and she had butterflies in her tummy. Surely a simple 'hello' and a nod would have sufficed?

Or maybe this was a proper date, and that's how datees usually greeted each other these days?

Harry returned with their drinks and a couple of menus. 'I don't know about you,' he said, 'but I'm starving. I didn't have a chance to grab anything to eat before I came out; I got stuck over Willow Hill way, working with a vet to treat a lame gelding.

'Oh?' Petra was interested – anything horsey was of interest to her and at least she was in her comfort zone when she was talking about equines. She might learn something too, so as they chose their meals and waited for their food to arrive, Harry explained that the horse in question had severe laminitis.

Petra shuddered. Laminitis, she knew, could be very serious and she thought about Tango and how he made her feel terribly guilty about putting his grazing muzzle on him. 'One of mine is prone to laminitis,' she said.

'The bright chestnut one?'

Petra smiled. 'Tango – yes, he is rather bright, isn't he? It makes him easy to spot. He's a sweetie but he hates having his muzzle on.'

'I bet he does,' Harry said, leaning to one side as a plate of steak and chips was placed in front of him. 'Imagine being given a meal like this and being told you had to eat it through a straw, which is what I imagine trying to graze on all that new grass whilst wearing his muzzle must feel like to him.'

Petra laughed. 'That would be awful.' She eyed her food with appreciation. 'Mmm, this looks good.'

'Do you often miss your evening meal?' he asked, spearing a chip.

'Only when I'm asked to go to the pub.'

His expression was neutral. 'Does that happen much?'

'Never.' She may as well be honest with him. 'I haven't been on a date in years.' As soon as the words passed her lips she immediately wanted to take them back. If this wasn't a date, then she'd just made a right fool of herself.

'Neither have I,' Harry said, and Petra blinked in surprise.

'A good-looking man like you? I'm shocked.' She really needed to give her mouth a stern talking to, because it was saying things her brain hadn't given it permission to say. What was wrong with her this evening? She was behaving like a gauche schoolgirl. Although, saying that, the schoolgirls who frequented her stables were far from gauche – they were self-assured, precocious and confident. The total opposite of Petra, and she was double their age.

A smile spread across his face. 'You think I'm good-looking?'

She gulped and examined her plate, wishing the ground would open up and swallow her. Now, please.

'I think you're beautiful,' he said.

She risked a quick glance at him. He didn't look as though he was joking.

'I mean it,' he added. 'You're lovely.'

'Thank you,' she whispered. Unused to compliments, she was unsure how to deal with this.

'Thank *you*, for agreeing to come out with me this evening,' he countered. 'I didn't think you would. I didn't think you liked me.'

Her gaze shot to his face once more. 'I didn't.'

'But you do now?' He looked like a hopeful puppy begging for food.

She nodded.

'Good, because I like you, too. Now we've got that out of the way, shall we continue with our meal?'

Thankful for the distraction of her supper, Petra tucked in, and while they ate they chatted once more about horses until she felt at ease again.

'Have you always worked with horses?' she asked him.

'Yes, my mother loved to ride, and I learnt to ride before I could walk, so I grew up around them.'

'Does she still ride?' Riding, unlike many other sports, could be carried on until well into middle-age and beyond.

'My parents died when I was twenty. Car crash.'

Petra's heart ached for him. 'I'm so very sorry,' she said, wanting to reach out but not knowing where to start.

'It was a long time ago,' he said, but she could hear the anguish behind his words and see the sadness in his face.

'Did you ever want to be a professional rider or trainer?' She knew she was changing the subject but his sorrow made her want to weep for him.

'I thought about it but my brother took up most of my time.'

'You've got a brother? I wish I had a sibling or two. What's his name? How old is he? Where does he live?'

'He's called Timothy, he's twenty-four, nearly twenty-five and he's still living in the family home near Cheltenham.'

Petra did the maths. 'That meant he was quite young when…?' She trailed off, dismay and pity flooding through her. 'That must have been tough.'

His smile was small. 'It was. I was at uni when I got the call. I jacked in the course to look after him.'

'You must have been devastated.'

He shrugged. 'We were, but we had no choice other than to get on with it. I didn't want Tim to go to my aunt and uncle, although they did want him to.

He insisted on staying in the house he'd always known as home. I stayed to look after him, and fell in with a local farrier who offered to train me. He knew my mum and what had happened to our parents, and was kind enough to let me work for him and fit my hours around Tim's school holidays. He sometimes used to let me bring Tim with me, and Tim loved it. Not the farrier side of things, but the horses. He'd learnt to ride when he was tiny, too.'

'What does he do now?'

'He's a vet,' Harry said proudly. 'He's working for a practice which specialises in equine health back in Cheltenham. It's only a locum position, but at least he's earning a wage and it's good experience for him.'

'What were you studying at university?' she asked, but she had a sinking feeling she knew the answer.

'Veterinary Science.'

He'd confirmed her suspicion. 'Now that your brother is fledged, so to speak, do you think you'll go back to it?' she asked.

Harry laughed. 'Not a chance! I've seen how hard Timothy works and I don't fancy the unsociable hours, either. I'm happy doing what I'm doing, thanks.'

'That's good.' She meant it. It would be awful if he was regretting not being a vet, and he did have a point about the unsociable hours. As a farrier, he might get the odd call-out on the weekend, but they would be few and far between. She worked worse hours than he did, because her busiest times tended to be weekends and evenings. Vets, though, were often on-call throughout the night and on weekends.

'What about you?' he asked her. 'Amos is your uncle, isn't he?'

Petra nodded. 'I've been horse-mad ever since I can remember. My parents live in Norwich but we used to come and visit Uncle Amos and Aunty Mags a couple of times every year, and I used to howl fit to burst when they took me home. I wanted to stay so badly that they eventually gave in when I was about eighteen and let me move in with Amos. Aunt Mags had passed on by then, so I think they thought I might be company for him. Little did they know that I'd be here and still loving it twelve years later.'

There was a small pause in the conversation, then Harry said, 'I take it there's no significant other in your life right now?'

She gave him a level look. 'I wouldn't have agreed to have a drink with you if there was.'

'Fair enough, I had to check.'

'How about you?'

Harry grinned and said, 'I wouldn't have asked you to have a drink with me if there was.'

Petra raised her almost empty glass and tipped it towards him. 'Fair enough,' she echoed back at him.

'Do you fancy a proper drink?' he asked.

'I'd love one, but I'm driving.'

'I can walk you home, if you like. It's not that far and the exercise will do me good,' he offered.

'Just the one, then.'

He bought her a pint of ale and one for himself, and they drank and chatted until it started to get late.

Petra was amazed at how quickly the evening passed, and to her surprise she found she didn't want it to end. She was enjoying herself immensely.

After the initial horsey-talk, the conversation moved on from families and onto things that had nothing at all to do with equines or stables, blacksmithing or businesses. They discussed the cinema and books, the news, favourite places, favourite food.

'What's your favourite time of the year?' he asked.

'Spring.'

'Mine, too. I think it's the promise of summer.'

'What's your favourite time of the day?' she asked. It was a silly, frivolous game, but Harry seemed to be enjoying it as much as she.

'Early morning,' he replied.

'And mine! Everything is so fresh and new.'

'I used to like early mornings because Timothy was asleep and not playing loud music, or stomping around the house,' Harry explained. 'Of course, it's different now I'm living on my own. If loud music is playing, I only have myself to blame.' He looked at his watch.

Petra checked the time on her phone.

They arrived at the same conclusion at the same time – it was getting late and both of them had to get up early.

Not caring if she looked a mess in it, Petra slipped her old jacket on and did the zip up. Harry was wearing the sort of jacket hikers favoured, so both of them should have been warm enough as they walked along Muddypuddle Lane. But for some reason Petra shivered and no sooner had she done so, than his arm came around her shoulders and he pulled her into him.

'Is that better?' he asked and she nodded, her cheek rubbing against his shoulder.

He smelt divine, citrus with a hit of wood, and she breathed deeply, drawing the scent of him into her and savouring it. It was also nice being held by him, his chest warm against her side, his solid arm curled around her.

She didn't want him to release her but of course he had to, giving her another one of those double-kisses as he did so.

'I enjoyed myself this evening,' he said.

'So did I.'

'Does that mean you'll come out with me again?'

'Yes.'

'When?'

'I'll have to check my diary,' she said, then hastily added, 'I really will have to check it – I can't remember what's booked in.'

'Okay. You've got my number.' He hesitated, and she wondered if he was about to kiss her.

When he didn't, disappointment flowed through her.

She was still disappointed when she fell asleep a short while later. But at least he'd said he wanted to see her again, so she had to be content with that for the time being.

CHAPTER EIGHT

Harry lifted the horse's hind leg so that the animal's hoof rested in the foot stand, and unrolled his bag of tools. He had to remove the old shoe, then trim the hoof in preparation for the new one. The horse he was working on was familiar with the process and stood patiently munching on a hay net and totally ignoring the human messing with his feet.

Harry wished he was as calm as the horse.

His head was full of Petra and nothing he did and no matter how busy he was, could drive her image from his mind. That she'd agreed to see him again made his stomach knot with anticipation and his heart thud.

The impulse that had made him ask her out had been a good one, despite how he'd felt about it at the time. He'd enjoyed himself last night, and he was delighted with the way the date had gone, although he had been worried that she hadn't considered it a date. But she had, and he was so pleased with himself, he was like a dog with two tails.

Petra, he'd discovered, was good company and they had more in common than he would ever have guessed — aside from the equine connection, of course. Once you got to know her she wasn't in the least bit grumpy, but he realised that she didn't suffer fools gladly and tended to prefer animals to people.

He could relate to that. He'd had to be gregarious because of Timothy and also because of his job, to a certain extent. He might deal with surly owners on a regular basis, but owners, surly or otherwise, didn't appreciate a surly farrier. Ted had been an exception; he'd built up a good reputation and people had become used to him. Harry was in a new area with new clients – he couldn't afford to cheese any of them off. That didn't mean that when it came to certain people (he was thinking of Cher Reynolds) then a pony was definitely preferable. Being his own boss suited him and for the most part he was usually left alone to get on with the job of shoeing.

If he had a choice he tended to gravitate away from people, so he and Petra were more alike than he'd thought. He simply hid it better. Although one person he would like to gravitate towards was Petra herself.

Harry shook his head in annoyance. He needed to concentrate on what he was doing. The horse he was shoeing was unconcerned but no matter how gentle the animal, horses were flighty and unpredictable. Letting your guard down and day dreaming wasn't advisable. But no matter how hard he tried to concentrate, Petra's sweet face or something she'd said popped into his head, and he found he couldn't wait to see her again.

As soon as he'd loaded his tools and assorted equipment into the van, Harry was unable to resist the urge any longer – he had to phone her. He might not be able to see her right now, but he could hear her voice and if he knew when their next date was he might be able to relax.

His stomach clenched when she answered, and he wondered where she was and what she was doing right now. He wanted to ask, but was worried he might come across as a bit stalkerish, so instead he said, 'How are you fixed for later? Have you got any lessons?' She was almost certain to be busy, but he had to ask.

'Gosh, you're keen.'

Yes, he was. He couldn't deny it, and he hesitated, wondering how to respond.

'I was planning on taking Hercules out for a ride,' she continued, ignoring his embarrassed silence. 'He's not been ridden for ages and he gets bored easily. I caught him nibbling the lower part of his door this morning. If he's not careful he's going to be pooping wood.'

'I could come with you?' he suggested, suddenly.

The phone went silent and Harry hoped he hadn't overstepped the mark or misconstrued their connection last night.

Eventually, she said quietly, 'I'd like that,' then she added, 'Be at the stables at four-thirty.'

Harry couldn't wait!

The clang as an iron shoe struck a stone provided a backdrop to the rhythmic percussion thud of hooves on earth, and Petra relaxed in the saddle as the familiar music soothed her. Riding out on the open moors above the valley was her happy place. For her, nothing could beat being on horseback on a surprisingly warm spring afternoon, surrounded by nature, and with no sign of people apart from the steady drone of a tractor in the distance and a line of fencing disappearing over the brow of a hill.

Oh, and the man at her side.

She was extremely aware of him, all right, especially the way his body gently swayed with the horse's gait, the curl of hair poking out from underneath his helmet, his strong forearms with their rolled-up sleeves, one of them resting loosely on his thighs. Those thighs didn't escape her notice, either. Clad in black jodhpurs, they were muscular and she was more aware of them than she could ever remember being of anyone else's legs.

His thighs weren't the only part of him she was aware of. Every so often his citrussy scent laced with woody undertones and another delicious smell she could only assume was his own unique scent, would waft across her nose. Together with the aroma of horse, leather tack and the great outdoors, she thought she might be becoming slightly intoxicated. She felt a little lightheaded and it wasn't an unpleasant feeling at all.

Then there was his profile, and she also caught glimpses of the rest of his face as he gazed at the countryside unfolding around them. Now and again their eyes would meet, and Petra would swiftly look away, but not before she saw the smile he gave her.

Petra was used to having other people with her when she rode because she was frequently supervising a group of riders who liked to hack, and this didn't bother her because riding was riding no matter who accompanied her – and riding was better than anything else in the world.

But her absolute favourite thing to do was to ride solo. She loved her alone time with her horse and her dog, who was busily sniffing every blade of grass and every rock; Queenie's tail was wagging so hard it was little more than a blur. Being alone gave her the opportunity to recharge her batteries, and she guarded it jealously.

But when Harry suggested he came with her on her ride, she was intrigued. She wanted to see how well he rode for a start – and she also wanted to see what it would be like to have him by her side.

It wasn't a date, more of a trial run for being in a relationship, because she'd never felt like this about any man. She had never given anyone else the opportunity to get close to her, and she was scared by her feelings and worried at how he'd fit into her life – if, in fact, things got that far. She reasoned that it was better to know now rather than to wait until she was even more invested in their growing relationship to find out.

Then there was also the issue of what if she fell in love (although she feared she might be half-way there already) – what was she supposed to do about it? Was there any room in her busy life for love?

Pushing the unsettling thoughts away, Petra tried to concentrate on the new buds on the branches of the trees and shrubs dotting the path. Some of the leaves had already unfurled and the array of green made her spirits soar, as did the complicated song of a blackbird perched on the very highest top of a nearby tree. His bright yellow beak contrasted sharply with his black plumage and she wished him all the luck in the world in his quest for a mate.

The bird's sweet song followed them as they rode higher, soon leaving the neatly fenced fields behind as they negotiated a gate which led onto the hillside above.

Petra breathed deeply, the fresh air invigorating her and making her feel more alive than she had in a long time. Although she forced herself to acknowledge that it may well be partly due to Harry's aftershave, and she longed to get close enough to him to bury her nose in his neck.

Unable to bear her jumbled thoughts any longer, Petra urged Hercules into a canter, then before she knew it the pair of them were galloping wildly along the dirt track, the horse's mane snapping, the wind buffeting her face, her heart pounding with the sheer unbridled joy of a horse and rider at one with nature.

She whooped in exhilaration, letting Hercules have his head, trusting him to take care on the path, and allowing him to run at his own pace. She was dimly aware of Queenie racing alongside, bounding through the tufts of grass, a black shadow with a pink lolling tongue and flapping ears.

She was also aware of Harry keeping pace with her, Midnight's nose almost touching Hercules's flank. When she risked a quick look over her shoulder she saw that he was up in his stirrups and crouching over the horse's neck, trying to keep wind drag to a minimum, and she laughed. He'd need all the help he could get if he wanted to keep up with her; Midnight was no match for Hercules.

Desperate to leave him eating her dust, she urged her mount on with a shout and a slap of the reins on his neck. Hercules, though, had other ideas, and he gradually slowed.

Harry pulled on Midnight's reins and his horse slowed in tandem, ensuring he stayed a few paces behind her.

Was Midnight as blown as Hercules, or was Harry being a gentleman and allowing her to "win", even though they hadn't officially been racing and there was no finishing post as such, although she had been heading for a stand of trees which she knew signified the start of a small valley with a tumbling brook running through it.

As her horse came to a walk, his sides heaving and blowing hard, another idea came to her – maybe Harry had been staying slightly behind her just in case she fell off (she wanted to scoff at that, but she had been known to come a cropper now and again), and the thought warmed her immeasurably. Most other riders would have done their best to win, especially with Hercules flagging – bless him, he was getting on a bit and he wasn't as fit as he had once been. Still, she could tell he'd enjoyed himself, because he kept tossing his head with his neck arched and he even managed a little prance for a step or two.

Petra watched Harry out of the corner of her eye as he drew level, Midnight just as winded as Hercules, and once again she saw his easy grace in the saddle and his confidence in his ability to work with his horse – because it was partnership, not dominance, that made her own relationship with Hercules so special.

Calling Queenie to heel (or as near to the back end of a horse as the dog felt comfortable getting) Petra guided Hercules into the trees, the ground dropping away and forcing her to lean back in the saddle to counterbalance her weight with the gradient. She allowed the horse to pick his way down the path, confident that he knew where he was going.

And as she rode, Amos's advice about not leaving it too late rang in her ears.

So when they reached the little clearing, the brook widening into a small pool, she brought her horse to a halt.

It was now or never, she said to herself, sliding from the saddle, her heart in her mouth and ponies cavorting in her tummy.

Harry had still been panting a little when Petra had turned Hercules towards a clump of trees and began to head down the hillside, following the woodland which was lining the sides of a narrow valley.

The gallop had been fun – he hadn't ridden like that in ages, and he'd forgotten how exciting it could be. It was also hard work on the body, and he knew he'd feel the effect tomorrow, despite being relatively fit, especially his thighs, shoulders and behind.

The little valley was barely more than a crease in the landscape, yet it was a different world to that of the relatively bare hillside above. Sounds were more intimate with the mottled and gnarled trunks muffling noise, yet the birdsong was clearer, sharper and far more numerous. The little creatures flitted and darted, chattering and chirping as they went, and the spaniel was in her element as she tried unsuccessfully to chase them. Once or twice she came across a squirrel digging amongst the dead leaves, searching for the last of the winter's stored nuts, but they were always too quick for her, bounding for the nearest trunk and leaping up it, leaving Queenie to snuffle and sniff in frantic circles as she tried to work out where it had disappeared to, and Harry chuckling at the dog's antics.

He was so engrossed in Queenie's confusion, that he almost failed to notice that Petra had brought Hercules to a halt. Wondering what she was doing, he watched her lift her leg elegantly over the saddle and slide off the horse's back to land lightly on her feet amongst the fallen leaves.

The stream they'd been following had flowed into a small clearing and had formed a little pool, which was a perfect place to water the horses, so he dismounted too and led Midnight to it.

Both horses slurped noisily, sucking the cool liquid into their mouths with mobile lips. When they'd had their fill, Hercules entertained himself by pawing at the water, sending spray into the air to fall back in sparkling droplets. Midnight had his fun by blowing bubbles and snorting, the fuzzy hairs on his nose and chin soaking wet.

When he attempted to rub his face in Harry's coat, Harry gathered up the reins and prepared to mount up. He was just about to put his foot in the stirrup when he noticed Petra throw Hercules's reins over the nearest bush, and the horse immediately dropped his head and started cropping the tufts of grass which grew along the banks of the stream.

Intrigued, Harry waited for a moment but when it became clear that Petra didn't intend to leave the pretty clearing yet, he took care to tie his horse up after briefly debating whether to do the same as her and hope Midnight didn't realise he wasn't secured to anything. Not wanting to take the chance and certainly not wanting to chase after the gelding as it headed back to the stables, he double-checked the knot before turning around to see what Petra was doing.

She was standing close, her face lifted to the canopy, a dreamy expression in her eyes.

Harry stilled; he'd never seen her look dreamy before and he wondered what she was thinking. She looked gorgeous with the sun shining through the new leaves and dappling her skin and hair with light and shadow. It reminded him of a woodland nymph he'd once seen in a painting – she looked as though she was cloaked in magic and touched by fairy dust as little motes danced around her head.

My god, she was so beautiful it took his breath away.

'I love it here,' she said. 'Not many people come down this way because the path runs out further along.'

'It's beautiful,' he agreed but he was referring to her and not the clearing.

Harry waited for her to say something else but she continued to stand motionless, so he did too, allowing the peace of the place seep into him, hearing nothing but the soft stamp of a hoof, the jingle of tack, and the sounds of nature.

It was so peaceful, he thought he could hear her heart beating. He could most definitely hear his own.

'I come here to refill my soul with all that is good,' she said, breaking the silence.

Harry knew what she meant. 'I've missed this. I've been so busy, so wrapped up in Tim, work and life in general, I think I'd forgotten how to live.'

He stared at her.

Her eyes were luminous, her lips slightly parted, and he knew that if he lived to be a hundred, he'd never forget the sight of her.

Petra's gaze locked onto his and she took a step closer to him.

Then another.

He couldn't tear himself away – her eyes were greener than the gurgling pool, unfathomable depths where a man could easily lose himself and drown.

He might be drowning right now; his chest was tight, the air heavy in his lungs, his thoughts languid. She was bewitching him, bespelling him to fall in love with her like the mystical naiads of ancient Greece, who lived in pools and lakes and were irresistible to men.

Harry didn't want to resist her. He didn't think he could…

Another step brought her close enough for him to gather her into his arms if he wanted.

And he did want, very much. But he instinctively knew that he had to take his cue from her. If he was too eager or made any sudden move, he was terrified she might slip into those mysterious waters and be lost to him forever.

She tilted her chin and her lips parted a little more.

Harry resisted the urge to lick his own in nerves.

The sounds of the brook, the chirping of the birds, the rustle of the leaves overhead as the wind sighed through them, had all faded. The only noise was the pulse in his ears and his heart hammering a staccato beat.

'Then I shall have to remind you how to live,' she murmured, and she stretched up on tiptoe, her arms snaking around his neck as she drew his head down to hers.

And in that wonderful moment when their lips met, Harry forgot everything – except for one thing. He remembered what it was like to be truly alive.

CHAPTER NINE

'Hey, bro, how's it going?' Timothy sounded upbeat and cheerful on the other end of the phone.

'Great. How about you?' Harry was more than great, actually... The kisses he'd shared with Petra floated through his mind, making him smile.

'Eh, you know. Work, eat, sleep, work, Xbox, work...' his brother said. 'What have you been getting up to?'

'I went riding yesterday.'

'With your imaginary friend?'

'How can you possibly know that?'

'Because I know you. You sound different. Happy.'

Harry *was* happy, but he didn't think he'd been unhappy before. 'Gee, thanks.'

'You *do*,' Timothy insisted. 'And I'm happy for you. I take it she's decided she likes you after all?'

'I haven't said I went riding with Petra, or anyone else for that matter.'

'Harry...' Timothy growled.

'Okay, I went riding with Petra.'

'And? Crikey, man, I know guys don't talk about stuff like lurve and relationships, but this is me you're talking to.'

Harry chuckled, imagining his younger brother running a hand through his perpetually messy hair in exasperation. It was odd having the tables turned – in the past it had been Harry who had been trying to drag girlfriend details out of Timothy. His questioning had been more in the vein of "where the hell were you last night, and why didn't you tell me you wouldn't be home?"

'And…we kissed,' he admitted, a huge grin on his face.

'Yes!' Timothy shouted.

Harry jumped and held the phone away from his ear and Timothy's yell. 'Calm down, Tim, it was only a kiss.'

'For you, a kiss is a momentous occasion. When's the wedding? I feel an urge to buy one of those hats with the netting over your face and a feather in it.'

'You are *not* wearing a hat to my wedding.'

'Ah ha! So you *are* hoping it'll get serious?' Timothy teased.

'I'm hoping no such thing. I plan on taking it slowly and one step at a time and see where it goes.'

'Don't take it too slow,' his brother warned. 'She might lose interest and go find someone livelier.'

'Are you saying I'm boring?'

Timothy's voice sobered as he said, 'You are the least boring person I know.' Then the cockiness was back with a vengeance as he added, 'Except for me, of course. Seriously, if you like her, don't hang about. Life's too short and too damn unpredictable.'

Timothy was right. It was. And he should know.

'You've got a face like a slapped arse,' Amos pointed out when Petra popped in for a spot of lunch. 'What's wrong. Has lover-boy upset you? I saw you go out for a ride with him yesterday.'

'Don't call him that! And I haven't spoken to him today.'

Amos smirked knowingly. 'I see.'

'See what?'

'The reason for the glum face is because he hasn't phoned you.'

'I don't care if he hasn't phoned me,' she protested. But she was lying, she did care, even though she didn't expect him to be in touch so soon. But that wasn't the reason for her discontent. In fact, she wasn't sure why she was restless and disgruntled. She just *was*.

Yesterday had been wonderful (the kissing part especially) and her insides glowed with the memory of how he had hesitated at first, his lips tentative against hers, but then he'd crushed her to him and kissed her so deeply and thoroughly she'd thought she might faint. And when they'd broken apart, she'd found herself wobbly-legged and breathless, and longing for more.

He'd helped her mount Hercules, although she was perfectly capable of launching herself onto the horse's back by herself, and they'd ridden back in delighted silence.

She hadn't known what to say, and it seemed he hadn't either, but they shared several lingering looks and the occasional smouldering glance, and she had to be content with that. There had been too many people around when they'd clattered into the yard for him to kiss her again, although she'd desperately wanted him to. So they'd hidden their feelings and she'd said goodbye as though he was another customer that she'd taken out for a hack.

But that wasn't the reason for her mood today.

Something was wrong, she could sense it; she just didn't know what it was.

Heidi and May slid from their ponies' saddles with a little help from their respective parents. Petra listened to their excited chatter as Heidi told her mum, Rose Walker, all about her lesson. May was a little more subdued, and Petra put that down to her dad missing the thrilling sight of his young daughter attempting the first stage in her jumping career, which consisted of walking the pony over a pole lying on the ground. The pony in question was a rather good jumper, but he was also well-versed in having novice riders on his back, and he knew what was expected of him.

For six-year-old May, though, this was a brand-new and dangerous experience, and she'd expected her father to have witnessed it.

'Sorry I'm late, pumpkin, I got stuck in traffic,' he said, giving Petra a sheepish smile.

Petra smiled as May pushed home her unexpected advantage over her father. May was always brought to her lessons by her mum, who then had to shoot off, and her dad picked her up. Petra knew he tried not to miss a single minute of it, but sometimes he was late. Whenever he was, May insisted on being allowed to stroke the "big horses", instead of being taken straight home.

With an exaggerated sigh her father agreed, and Petra watched the little girl dart off in the direction of the stables, her dad following more sedately behind.

'See you next week,' he called over his shoulder and Petra nodded.

It was great to see the little ones come to her stables, many of them not having sat on the back of a horse before, and leaving at the end of their lessons full of wonder and delight at being able to control an animal so very much bigger than they were. Of course, it didn't happen all at once, but after a year of lessons May, in particular, was doing brilliantly.

Petra frowned as she checked the time. Harry still hadn't called. Maybe it was unreasonable to expect him to. She didn't have a great deal of experience when it came to dating, so she might be expecting too much from him. But there had been a definite connection between them – she didn't doubt that was true.

Having shortened the ponies' stirrups so they were resting on the saddle and not slapping against the animals' sides as she led them into their stalls for the night, Petra was surprised to see Charity hurrying towards her, a look of concern on her face.

'Charity? What's wrong?'

'I think you should come and see this. May Halligan dragged her dad off to pet the bigger horses, and when she came back I heard her ask her dad why Hercules was trying to kick himself in the tummy, and did he have an itch. I went to check on him and...' Charity paused and Petra felt her blood turn to ice. 'I think he might have colic.'

'Here, see to these,' she said, thrusting the reins into Charity's hands, and shouting 'Please,' as she shot to the door.

Not colic, please not colic, she prayed as she scurried out of the arena and down the row of stables. It was still quite light out, but she flicked the master switch on as she ran past, illuminating the yard and the individual stalls. She wanted to have a thorough look at the horse in good light, before she called the vet.

Petra heard Hercules before she saw him. He was pawing the concrete floor of his stable, which wasn't an unusual thing for a horse to do as they churned up the deep straw bedding under their feet, but she also heard a loud bang, signifying a steel-shod hoof had connected with the wooden partition of his stall.

When the bang was followed by a squeal, dread swept over her.

Those were the sounds of an animal in distress, and she was abruptly aware that this was what must have been bothering her all day. Animals were far, far better at hiding pain and discomfort than people were, and she must have subconsciously noticed that Hercules wasn't quite himself earlier. It was a damned pity that her conscious mind hadn't also noticed, because colic was the number one reason for horses having to be euthanised. The sooner it was treated the greater was the chance of his survival.

Steeling herself, she looked inside his stall.

The horse stood with his head hanging down, a sheen of sweat darkening the hair on his neck. His ears were laid back and his nostrils were flared.

When he uttered another squeal and brought one of his hind legs up to kick at his flank, Petra flinched.

It was colic, all right. The signs were unmistakable.

With a desperate look at the stricken animal, Petra ran to the house. 'Amos! Amos! Call the vet – Hercules has colic. Then can you phone Nathan to help me move him into the barn?'

Amos appeared from the kitchen, wiping his hands on the apron he liked to wear whilst he was cooking. He gave her a brief nod, his expression grave, and she heard his steps on the parquet floor of the hall as he hurried off to make the phone calls.

Petra hurried outside again, this time heading for the barn. There were a couple of chickens scratching about and Tiddles glared down at her from the top of several bales of hay where the cat had probably been waiting for mice to appear as dusk fell, but she couldn't see anything to hurt Hercules.

By the time she'd returned to the animal's stall, Amos was marching across the yard.

'The vet will be as quick as he can,' her uncle said. 'Have you been inside Hercules's stable yet?'

She shook her head. 'I wanted to wait for Nathan.' Hercules could be unpredictable sometimes; he was temperamental and highly-strung when he was upset, and although he wouldn't deliberately hurt her, she didn't want to take the risk of him lashing out because of the pain.

But neither could she leave him in his stall. Horses with colic had a tendency to roll onto their backs in an effort to relieve their painful stomachs, and if he rolled within the confines of his stable he might injure his legs on the walls of the stall as he thrashed around or, worse, he might not have enough room to get back up again. It was imperative she took him into the barn where she could also keep him moving. Walking a horse with colic could help to relieve the symptoms and the movement encouraged the gut to keep working, which in turn sometimes helped to relieve the pain.

Hercules lashed out with a hind leg, his hoof connecting with the wooden wall and a loud crash reverberated throughout the small space, making her wince.

'How long did Nathan say he'd be?' she asked – the sooner they got the horse out of his stable the better.

'I couldn't get hold of him. You'll have to make do with me.'

Petra bit her lip. 'Are you sure you'll be okay?' Amos never spoke of his angina, but that didn't stop her worrying about it and she knew he'd been advised not to overexert himself.

'I'll be fine,' he insisted, and all she could do was take her uncle's word for it.

She held out her hand, her arm inside the stall, and clicked her tongue. 'Come here, lad,' she crooned. 'Let me take a look at you, boy.'

The horse tossed his head, the whites of his eyes showing, but he stepped forward until he was close enough to the door for Petra to reach for his halter. Expertly she clipped a lead rope onto the metal ring underneath his chin.

Then she looked at her uncle, nodded, and opened the door.

Hercules lunged out, immediately crabbing sideways, but she hung on to the rope and the horse settled enough for Amos to get a second lead rope clipped onto his halter. With two of them controlling the animal, they should be able to get him into the barn.

'Are you okay?' she asked Amos again, her attention on the horse. She had to remain alert – a horse in pain might try to rear or bolt, kick or bite, but Hercules was relatively calm considering the circumstances.

'For the moment,' her uncle replied, and she knew it wouldn't be long before he started to struggle, and fresh worry gnawed at her.

He was already starting to look a little blue about the lips, but she didn't know whether that was from the chill of the spring evening air, or because he was feeling unwell.

Without wasting any more time, Petra led the horse towards the barn, Amos hanging onto the other lead rope, and between them they managed to get Hercules inside without incident.

As soon as the barn door was closed, Petra unclipped one of the lead ropes. 'I can take it from here,' she said to her uncle.

'I think I should stay.' He leant against one of the bales of hay and she could hear him wheezing. He didn't look at all well.

'How about if you go into the yard and wait for the vet?' she suggested. 'And take one of your heart pills before you do,' she added sternly. She knew what he could be like – he tended to deny he had a problem and sometimes she had to badger him not to do too much or nag him to take his medication.

Amos gave her a long look before nodding, and she sighed with relief. Her uncle had had enough excitement for one evening.

'You could bring me a sandwich later?' she suggested as she began walking Hercules around in a wide circle. She knew from experience that it was going to be a long night, and she also knew Amos liked to be useful. If all he could do was keep her fed and watered, then that would be enough.

All she could do was to keep the horse moving and try not to worry.

The first was easy – it was the latter she was having trouble with.

Harry was dozing in front of the tv and thinking he should take himself off to bed when his phone rang. He considered ignoring it – he'd had a long day and it was late – but it might be a customer. It wasn't unheard of for someone who wanted an animal to be shod to call him at an ungodly hour. Or it might be his brother, he thought suddenly, and a frisson of fear made the hairs on his arms stand on end.

Hoping nothing was wrong, he scrabbled around for his mobile.

'Petra?' He recognised the number immediately.

'It's Amos here, Petra's uncle.'

'Oh, hi.' Please don't tell me something has happened to her, Harry prayed, his mouth suddenly dry and his heart pounding. 'Is anything wrong?'

'It's Petra. She needs some help. I can't get hold of Nathan, and I'd do it myself but…'

'Do what? What help does she need?' Harry could hear the older man's harsh and fast breathing down the phone.

'One of the horses has colic.' Amos coughed and Harry waited for him to catch his breath. 'The vet came out a couple of hours ago. He thinks it's gas and maybe an impacted gut from Hercules chewing his stable door.'

Harry closed his eyes briefly. Hercules must have been feeling a little off-colour yesterday which would explain how Midnight had been able to keep up with him.

Amos carried on, 'He's been given a laxative to get things moving again, and a tranquiliser to help with the pain, and now Petra is walking him. She's going to be at it all night.'

As Amos was speaking, Harry was already changing out of his slouchy jogging bottoms and back into his work clothes. 'I'll be there in five minutes,' he said, grabbing his car keys.

Petra's uncle was waiting at the top of the lane for him, as Harry drove up. 'She's in the barn,' he said. 'I'll bring you a flask of coffee in a while.' He hesitated and seemed to be choosing his next words carefully. 'Thanks for coming. She might not show it, but she'll be pleased to see you.'

'It's what you do, when you care for someone,' Harry replied.

'I'm glad you feel that way, because I believe she cares for you, too.'

Embarrassed and delighted in equal measure, Harry said, 'I'll go on in, shall I?' He gestured towards the barn and the light leaking around the door.

Petra, Harry discovered, wasn't at all thrilled to see him. 'What are you doing here?' she demanded.

'I've come to help.'

'I don't need any.'

'I beg to differ.' It wasn't yet midnight and she was already looking exhausted. Hercules didn't look much better, and between them they'd worn a path through the compacted dirt which comprised the floor of the barn.

'You can beg all you like,' she retorted sharply. 'I'm fine doing this by myself.'

'Amos doesn't seem to think so.'

'Amos had no right to call you. I told him not to.'

'I'm glad he did.'

'I'm not,' she grumbled.

Harry might have felt deflated by her attitude if Amos hadn't had warned him. He guessed she was tired and worried, and her original prickliness had reasserted itself as a coping and defence mechanism. She was so used to managing on her own that he thought maybe she'd forgotten how to accept help from anyone, no matter whether she cared about them or not. And no matter whether they cared about her.

As Harry walked over to her and took the lead rope out of her hand, ignoring her protests, he came to the conclusion that he more than cared for her. He was falling in love with her. She might have more thorns than a holly bush, she might be proud, stubborn and independent to the point of causing him despair, but he didn't care. It was what made her, her. And he loved her for it.

He also loved her for her caring nature, for her love of her horses, for the odd moments when she let her guard down and allowed the sun to shine out of her. He loved her for her dedication, for her passion and for her strength. He also loved her for her vulnerability.

And this was where he stepped in.

She no longer had to cope alone. If she'd let him, he'd give her as much support as she needed and probably more than she wanted.

If she'd let him…

'I'm here now, let me take a turn at walking him,' he said, leading the horse on yet another circuit of the barn. He watched her go to the nearest pile of bales and sink down onto one of them, then he turned his attention to Hercules.

The horse didn't look good. But he didn't look as bad as Harry had feared, either. Sweat had dried on his neck and flanks, leaving a white tide of salt on his coat. He was walking willingly and not kicking up a fuss, but the droop of his head and the plod of his hooves told Harry that Hercules had had enough. The poor guy was tired, and although Harry would love nothing better than to let the horse rest, he knew it was better to keep him moving.

And throughout that long night, that was what the two of them did, taking it in turns to walk Hercules around and around the barn, with Amos popping in frequently to check on progress and bringing them fresh coffee and snacks to keep them going. During one of Petra's turns, Harry rearranged a couple of bales of hay to form a makeshift couch, and he found some horse rugs which had been neatly folded away until next winter when the horses and ponies would need them again. He spread two of them across the couch and used another to drape over himself. It grew chilly if you didn't keep moving and even the gentle pace of the circuits they were doing helped to keep the blood flowing, but the one who was sitting out was at risk of frostbite.

Queenie, bless her, did her best to keep the both of them warm, curling up next to whichever one of them was sitting it out but despite the furry hot water bottle, the dipping temperature, the worry and the tiredness gradually began to take its toll.

Petra looked shattered and Harry guessed he probably didn't look much better.

Then, finally, as the witching hour clicked over to four a.m. Hercules farted.

It was an incredibly long and drawn out affair, and after an initial gasp of relief, Petra started to laugh. Harry chuckled too.

The horse broke wind again, louder and longer than the last time, then they were laughing so hard tears streamed down their cheeks and Harry doubled over with the force of it.

The horse's ears pricked and his dark, liquid eyes gazed from one to the other. Even Queenie wondered what was going on, and she whined uncertainly until Harry tickled her under the chin.

'I think we can safely say Hercules is over the worst of it,' Harry said.

It was what they had been waiting for. The horse wasn't out of the woods yet, but the release of so much trapped gas meant movement was afoot. The next milestone would be the appearance of poop.

They didn't have long to wait.

During the following half an hour, Hercules seemed to take great delight in dropping little presents all over the floor of the barn. He looked perkier too, more like his old self.

'Let me,' Petra said, getting to her feet and coming over to him.

'You've got ten minutes before it's your turn. Make the most of it,' Harry joked.

'It's my horse, my rules, and I want a go.'

She was smiling as she said it, the first smile Harry had seen since he'd arrived, so he handed her the lead rope and sat down next to Queenie, who huffed out a deep sigh at being disturbed yet again by these pesky humans. She edged over to him and rested her head on his lap, then shut her eyes tightly, intent on trying to get back to sleep.

Harry poured himself another cup of coffee from the flask. It wasn't as hot as he liked it, so he set it to one side, had a drink of water instead, and watched Petra stroke Hercules. Her nose was close to the horse's and he could hear her murmuring to the animal, soothing and reassuring him.

Harry closed his eyes for a moment.

'Queenie likes you,' Petra said, jerking him awake and he cleared his throat, hoping she hadn't noticed he'd been dozing. 'She doesn't normally bother with anyone other than me and Amos.'

'I like her, too. She's a sweetie.'

She was also warm snuggled against him and soft, and he absent-mindedly stroked her silky ears as he watched the spaniel's mistress resume her trudge around the barn.

Harry knew Petra would keep this up until the vet returned in the morning to check on Hercules, and once again silence descended, the relief of knowing the horse was getting better superseded by exhaustion.

When he took his turn for the umpteenth time that night, Harry was conscious of just how quiet it was. There were no sounds apart from the muffled thud of the horse's hooves, the creak of the barn's beams contracting as the chill of the night deepened, and the rustle as something moved in the straw.

It was surreal, as though they were on another planet, or in another era. Nothing outside the barn existed. The world had shrunk to the two of them, the horse and the dog.

The next time he walked close to the hay-couch, Harry's gaze came to rest on Petra and he smiled softly; she was fast asleep, her eyelids fluttering, her fingers twitching. Queenie was awake, guarding her mistress, but her tail thumped with approval as Harry broke off his horse-walking to drape another rug over Petra and tuck it in around her. Then he took his jacket off, pulled his fleece over his head, folded it into a pillow and eased it under her head.

Petra shifted slightly and made a cute little noise, but she didn't wake, which Harry was pleased about. She needed the rest and he could handle things from here.

As he put his jacket back on and zipped it up, his eyes roamed over her face, thinking how vulnerable she looked in sleep, and how beautiful. It had hurt him to see her so upset, and as he stood there he made a silent vow to himself and to her – he intended to do anything and everything in his power not to let her feel that way again. He had an overwhelming urge to protect her, to look after her, to cherish her. To love her.

If only she would let him…

Petra screwed her eyes shut as tight as they would go. She didn't want to wake up. She was stiff, cold and uncomfortable, but it was too much of an effort to re-join the world of the sentient.

Then the memory of last night flashed into her head and she sat up with a start.

It was early; the sun had only just risen, she guessed from the light creeping around the edge of the barn door. The dawn chorus was in full flow outside, but it was strangely quiet inside.

Harry, she saw, was slumped in a corner of the hay-couch and when his eyes met hers, he smiled, and she knew everything was all right. Hercules was dozing in the way horses do, with his head down and one hind foot cocked, the hoof's tip resting on the ground. A huge pile of poo had built up on the floor behind him, and never had Petra been so pleased to see so much manure. He was going to be fine; he *was* fine.

She got to her feet to check, nevertheless.

As soon as she was satisfied that her initial assessment was correct, her attention came back to Harry. He was fine too; he had dark shadows under his eyes, his shoulders were slumped and stubble coated his chin, but he'd be as right as rain after a nice long sleep.

It hadn't escaped her notice that at some point when she'd been sleeping, he'd slipped his fleece under her head and thrown another rug over her. It gave her a warm glow to think he'd cared enough to do such a thing.

'He's doing okay,' he said, getting awkwardly to his feet.

'So I see. I'm sorry I fell asleep.'
'Don't be. Hercules and I were fine on our own.'
She smiled. 'So I see,' she repeated.

Petra moved closer to him, reached out a hand and slipped it into his, lacing her fingers through his.

Harry gently squeezed her hand.

She leant into him, her head resting on his shoulder. He kissed her hair.

Then he kissed her forehead.

She lifted her face to his. 'Thank you.'

'There's nothing to thank me for.'

'I think there is. Not everyone would stay up all night to help a friend.'

'Is that all I am – a friend?' She heard the dismay in his voice.

'Yes, you are. But you're also more than that.'

'I am?' He sounded a little more hopeful

She nodded, enjoying teasing him if only for a moment; she knew how she felt about him. And she knew Amos was right. She wasn't going to leave it too late – she didn't intend to let this wonderful man slip through her fingers. He was kind, considerate, thoughtful, fun to be with, and he loved horses as much as she did. What more could she ask for?

Actually, there *was* one thing…

'You are…I mean…' She was lost for words. She knew what she wanted to say but she didn't know how to say it. She didn't know if she should. Panic and fear held her back. If he didn't feel the same way about her, she'd be devastated.

Harry came to her rescue yet again. He cupped her face in his hands, his lips inches from hers. 'I love you,' he said.

'Yes, that's it,' she whispered. 'That's exactly what I wanted to say.' And it was also the other thing she asked for; that he loved her.

From the look in his eyes, she realised that he did.

Finally, for Petra, as for everything else on Muddypuddle Lane, spring had brought new love, new hope, and a brand new beginning.

SUMMER

CHAPTER ONE

Rose Walker clapped enthusiastically as her eight-year-old daughter Heidi guided her pony over jumps no higher than about a foot off the ground.

It might not appear to be a great deal to anyone else, but to Rose it was an achievement to be noted. Heidi had progressed from walking Parsnip over poles laid on the ground to actually jumping over said poles, all in the space of three lessons, and Rose watched and clapped as a succession of children popped the ponies they were riding over the same jump. All in all, there were nine children in the group riding lesson today. Heidi wasn't the youngest – little May Halligan was, being only six years old – but she was close to it, and although Rose knew that children younger than her daughter were able to jump far higher, they were usually the ones who were lucky enough to have their own ponies or whose parents could afford more than one lesson per week.

Horse riding wasn't the cheapest of hobbies, but her daughter had been horse-mad ever since Rose could remember. The child seemed to have been born with horses in her heart, and she could clearly recall the first time the not-yet-walking Heidi had seen a horse, and the child's squeals of excitement, followed by bereft sobbing as Rose had to take her home, would be etched in her mind forever.

After that, Rose had bought her a plush pony toy to cuddle and a succession of miniature plastic horses to play with. But it wasn't enough. Heidi was adamant that she wanted to firstly stroke a pony, then, once she'd achieved that goal, she wanted to get on its back. Her daughter's drive to learn to ride had been relentless, and it was Rose's one regret that she couldn't afford to buy the child her own pony.

Rose had resisted Heidi's pleas to have riding lessons for as long as humanly possible. But her daughter had been adamant and implacable. As she grew older, whenever Rose asked her what she wanted for Christmas or her birthday, the answer would be the same – a horse; or, if she couldn't have a horse, riding lessons. Rose had eventually given in, even though the cost made her wince, and from then on she'd had to sit in the viewing area of the indoor arena (which was a converted barn) no matter what the weather. Too hot in summer and absolutely freezing in winter, the experience wasn't a particularly comfortable one, and the hard plastic chairs put out for the parents to sit on didn't help either.

Heidi popped her pony over the tiny jump again and Rose called, 'Well done,' earning herself a disapproving look from Petra Kelly, who ran the stables. Petra was one of those people who preferred animals to humans, and Rose sometimes wondered if the woman actually preferred her horses to her farrier partner, Harry.

Heidi almost always rode Parsnip. Petra did her best to match rider with the horse or pony, and she liked to pair the two of them together for every lesson so they could get used to one another. Rose had begun to wonder which mount Heidi would be allocated when she outgrew Parsnip. Her daughter was almost there already, her legs a little bit too long for the animal, the proportions no longer quite as right as they had once been, and seeing the pair of them together reminded Rose of a child outgrowing a bike and needing a slightly larger frame.

Heidi and Parsnip popped over the jump once again, relatively fluidly, although Petra scolded Heidi for allowing her elbows to stick out.

Heidi took the telling off good naturedly. If Rose had tried to tell her off like that, Heidi wouldn't have been quite so accepting. Sometimes her daughter could be as stubborn as the pony she was riding – he had a tendency to dig his heels in when he didn't want to do something.

'Oh, well done!' Rose cried, when little May Halligan, who was sitting on the back of a sweet Shetland pony, progressed from walking her mount over the poles on the ground to trotting over them. She watched the little girl rise into the trot, her cute face shining as she controlled an animal many times bigger than her.

Rose risked a quick glance at May's father, Jason. She didn't know much about him, apart from his name, and the rumour that he was a single dad. The woman who dropped May off at the stables for every lesson was the little girl's mum. She seemed pleasant enough, giving May a quick hug and a kiss before handing her over to Petra, who promptly handed the child over to one of the girls who helped teach the lessons.

For quite some time Rose had thought that Faith and Charity Jones were one and the same person, until she saw them side by side and realised they were twins. They kept their horses at the stables in exchange for helping out, and when Rose had learnt that, she had a vision of the future as she fully expected Heidi to suggest the same arrangement as long as Petra Kelly was in agreement.

Rose didn't want to think about that just yet; it was enough to bring Heidi to the stables once a week for an hour-long lesson, without having to ferry her daughter here every waking minute that she wasn't in school.

Finally the lesson was over and the children dismounted on their own and handed their ponies over to one of the adults, who shortened the stirrups then led any animals who wouldn't be used for the next lesson out of the arena.

Rose watched Heidi unbuckle her helmet and pull it off her head. Her blond ponytail was all askew, and strands of hair were falling around her face. Rose thought she looked adorable; but then she would, wouldn't she, because she was rather biased. It warmed her heart when Heidi, on noticing May struggling with her own buckle, went over to help the younger child.

Heidi was a good kid. Rose had never had a moment's trouble with her, and she could hardly complain about her obsession with all things equine. Not in the summer, anyway; however, the winter was a different matter.

Rose hated sitting there in the cold, bundled up and wearing practically everything she owned, shivering on the hard plastic seat while darkness descended rapidly outside and her breath steamed in front of her face.

No matter how many hot cups of coffee she drank from the vending machine in the corner, she invariably failed to keep herself warm.

Yet, on an afternoon like this, when it wouldn't get dark until about nine-thirty and the air inside the barn was warm and smelt of hay and horses (to her surprise she'd found she actually quite liked the smell of horse) it was much more pleasant. When she emerged from the indoor arena and she saw there was still a whole long evening of daylight ahead of her, she heaved a contented sigh.

The riding school was situated in rolling hills, with lush fields and hedgerows all around. The actual buildings themselves were constructed of old stone, which gleamed golden in the rays of the late afternoon sun. The drone of a tractor in the distance competed with the buzz of bees as Rose stepped outside to await her excited child. She smiled at the chickens scratching about in the yard, hunting for their supper, and she reminded herself to buy some of the eggs that Petra often had for sale. The yolks were so yellow they didn't look real, and the taste of them was far superior to anything she'd bought in a shop.

When Rose felt a small nudge on the back of her leg, she looked down to see Queenie, the stables' resident dog, staring up at her with large dark eyes.

'Hello sweetie,' she crooned, bending down to fondle her silky ears, and the spaniel wagged her tail. Rose actually enjoyed coming to the stables on evenings like this. Although Picklewick was hardly a metropolis, the village was a hive of activity compared to the peace and tranquillity which surrounded her here.

She'd just knelt down to tickle Queenie's tummy, the dog lying on her back with all four paws in the air and looking up at her hopefully, when the peace was shattered as Heidi dashed around the corner and skidded to a halt.

'Mum, Mum, you must come and see this!' She pulled at Rose's sleeve, and Rose clambered to her feet.

'Sorry, Queenie, maybe next week,' she said to the dog, who reluctantly rolled over onto her front and lay there looking at her reproachfully. 'What is it?' Rose asked her daughter. 'Don't tell me Petra has got another horse?'

Heidi very often demanded that her mum meet any new arrival at the stables, whether it was a new horse (which had only happened once), or some fluffy chicks that one of the hens had brooded.

'It's Tiddles, she's had babies! Come and see.' Heidi tugged at her again, and Rose allowed herself to be reluctantly dragged along. It wasn't that she was averse to seeing kittens – far from it – but she knew exactly where the conversation was going to go.

'Can we have one, Mum, please, can we?' Heidi pleaded.

Rose sighed. At least it was better than asking for a horse, she conceded, or a dog; they'd had that conversation, too. 'We'll see,' she said, which was her go-to comment when she meant "no" but she couldn't be bothered to argue.

Heidi whined, 'That means no.'

'Probably.'

They watched the kittens for a while, the cat giving her and Heidi a gimlet stare but not seeming to be unduly bothered by the attention, then Rose said,

'Come on, sweetie, we must get home. I don't know about you but I'm starving.'

'What are we having?'

Rose was just about to answer her when she heard a child's raised voice. Holding Heidi's hand, she came around the side of the building to head towards her car, and spotted May standing in the middle of the yard, her hands folded across her chest, her chin down, scowling up at her father from underneath her eyebrows.

'I'm sorry darling, but you can't. There isn't anyone to pick you up. I've got a meeting I can't get out of.' Jason caught Rose's eye and swiftly looked away.

'That's not fair!' May stamped her foot.

Rose tried not to look. It was difficult enough when your child had a tantrum, without having an audience to witness it. She unlocked the car and ushered Heidi inside.

'Why can't Mummy pick me up?' May demanded.

'You know Mummy has to work.'

'I hate you and I hate Mummy, too.' Another stamp, this time accompanied by a sob.

Rose opened the car boot, stowed Heidi's helmet in it, then fished out a pair of trainers and walked around to the passenger side to help her daughter off with her riding boots.

Jason Halligan knelt down so he was at eye level with his daughter, and said something to her that Rose didn't catch.

May let out a howl of despair. 'But that's ages away!' she cried.

Her dad said, 'It's two weeks, May, you'll only miss one lesson.'

'I don't want to miss *any* lessons. You promised you'd pick me up. Mummy said you'd always pick me up.'

Rose could see the conflict on the man's face, and she felt sorry for him. She knew what it was like when life got in the way of parenting.

Heidi wriggled out of her boots and slipped her feet into the trainers Rose held out for her. Rose walked around to the back of the car and popped the relatively clean riding boots inside, leaving Heidi to buckle herself into her seat belt.

'We could take her home with us, couldn't we, Mummy?' Heidi said.

Rose was about to get in the car, but her daughter's suggestion made her pause. She shouldn't interfere, but as they were here anyway, it made sense.

'Excuse me,' she called across to Jason Halligan. 'I'm sorry, I couldn't help overhearing; is your daughter going to miss her lesson next week?'

May's father straightened up. The look he gave her was an assessing one, and Rose wasn't sure she liked it.

'That's right,' he said, his tone clearly indicating it was none of her business.

She was about to turn away and leave him to it, when she caught sight of May's little face. It was streaked with dirty tears, and her bottom lip was wobbling. Her heart went out to the child, so she tried again.

'I could bring her home with Heidi, and you can pick her up from my house, if you like. We're going to be here anyway, so it won't be any trouble,' she added just in case he thought it might be.

'Thank you, but no. I'm sorry, May,' he said, turning to his daughter. 'You're just going to have to miss next week.'

'It's not fair,' May cried, shooting her father daggers. 'Why *can't* Heidi's mummy bring me home?'

'Because I won't be finished until late, that's why.' He sent Rose an apologetic look.

Rose smiled back. At least this was better than the annoyed glance he'd given her earlier. She followed her smile up with a nod, saying, 'That's okay, I don't mind having her until you're ready to pick her up.'

'No, sorry, May. I've made my decision.'

'See,' the little girl said defiantly. 'Heidi's mum doesn't mind. It's you who minds. You don't want me to go riding.'

'That's not true,' her father protested, but May cut in with, 'Yes, it is. I heard you tell Mummy.'

'Okay, I do mind, but only because I worry about you.'

Rose thought she'd better beat a hasty retreat before she caused any more trouble. She got in her car, snapped on her seat belt and started the engine, hissing when she put her hands on the steering wheel. She must remember to face the car the other way and not leave it in the full glare of the sun. She'd forgotten how hot the interior could get, so she wound the window down to try to get some air.

She was about to pull off, when she saw Jason Halligan's exasperated expression. May was having a right tantrum and Rose bit her lip. Oh, dear, this was her fault; if Rose hadn't offered, then maybe he would have talked May around by now.

Feeling guilty, she called through the open window. 'It honestly won't be any trouble to pick her up from riding. In fact, I could collect her from school along with Heidi, and bring them both to the stables. And how about I give her tea afterwards? I'm sure she'd like that.' The damage was already done, so Rose might as well try to make amends.

The effect on May was instantaneous. The little girl stopped crying and clapped her hands together. 'Daddy, can I? Please say yes. Please?'

Jason Halligan narrowed his eyes at Rose, but she guessed he didn't want to come across as the bad guy, because he reluctantly agreed. 'If you're sure?' he asked, clearly hoping she wasn't.

'I'm sure,' Rose hastily reassured him. 'I often fetch other people's children from school and feed them, and they do the same for me when I can't pick Heidi up. It's no trouble, honestly.'

'You'd better give me your address and phone number,' Jason said.

Rose switched off the engine, clambered out of the car and they duly swapped phone numbers, Rose adding her address. 'Don't forget to let May's teacher know I'm picking her up,' she reminded him. 'They're very strict about who collects the children, and I wouldn't want May to be stuck in school while someone is trying to get hold of you.'

'Right, okay. I'll see you next week,' he said, before adding a totally reluctant, 'Thank you.'

As Rose drove away she glanced in the rear view mirror to see May hopping up and down excitedly. She was pleased she'd made the little girl's day a bit better, but she felt awfully guilty for interfering. What went on between May and her father wasn't any of her business, and she'd had no right to step in but, as she'd told him, it was second nature to help out other mums, and they helped her out in return.

She couldn't see any harm in it, so why had Jason Halligan seemed dead set against the idea?

Jason Halligan had no intention of taking Heidi's mother up on her offer. Agreeing to it had just seemed to be the easiest thing to do at the time; he didn't think she was going to take no for an answer, and May was having such a tantrum he was starting to get embarrassed. He would have agreed to anything in order to stem his daughter's tears.

He'd give it a day or two, then have a chat with May and explain. With a bit of time and distance, he was sure she'd understand.

In a way, a little part of him was relieved that she wouldn't be going riding next week. He had never liked the idea of Pamela dropping her off at the stables and the child being unsupervised until he arrived after he'd finished work. But unless he picked her up from school himself, which he wasn't able to do, he didn't seem to have any choice in the matter. Pamela and May had sorted the riding lessons out between them, and had only informed him when it was a fait accompli. Usually he managed to arrive not long after the lesson started, so there were only a few minutes when his daughter was left to her own devices, but he still hated it. Petra Kelly and the girls who helped out with the lessons were marvellous, but May wasn't their responsibility. She was his – and Pamela's, although you wouldn't always know it.

Another reason he didn't like May taking riding lessons was the danger. The Shetland pony she rode might be small in horsey terms, but he was still massively bigger than she was. When Pamela had told him May was having riding lessons, he had been horrified. He still was. Many years ago, when he was a child himself, he remembered a boy in his class whose mum had been a keen rider. He also remembered the devastation on the face of the boy when he'd come into school one day after a period of being absent, and learnt that the boy's mother had suffered an accident whilst riding. She'd broken a bone in her neck and had been paralysed from the neck down. Jason wondered what had happened to her – and the boy, because shortly afterwards the kid had been removed from the school and Jason had never seen him again.

Logically, Jason knew that the odds of something so terrible happening to May were slight. But he'd made the mistake of researching riding accidents on the internet, and it had made him even more reluctant to allow May anywhere near a horse.

He wondered if other parents felt the same. Was it normal to feel such worry that your child might be thrown? How did other mums and dads cope? He supposed it might be easier for the parents of those children who had grown up around horses, or even if he'd had some experience of the animals himself. But the closest he'd got to anything resembling a horse, was a donkey ride on the beach at Weston-Super-Mare when he was little. And that had been before the boy's mother had been injured. Since then, he'd made a point of avoiding the large, hairy beasts; until, that is, May and her mother had conspired against him to let her have riding lessons, and now he seemed to be in a perpetual state of mild panic whenever she was at the stables.

Take today for instance; his heart had been in his mouth when May had guided the pony over the poles laid on the ground. Walking hadn't seemed too bad, but trotting the animal over them had appeared reckless. And Heidi's mother, Rose Walker, hadn't seemed in the least bit concerned when her daughter took a proper jump for the first time. Admittedly, the pole was only about a foot high, but it still meant that for a brief moment all four of the horse's hooves were off the ground at the same time. It wouldn't be long before May progressed to that stage, and he didn't think his nerves could stand it.

'Daddy, Daddy, Daddy!' May squealed, as he tried to get her into the bath. He always insisted she had a bath every evening, and never more so than when she'd been riding, because afterwards she always smelt vaguely of horse.

'I can't wait for next week!' she cried, and his heart constricted. She'd talked about nothing else since he'd bundled her into the car at the stables and driven home. 'I like Heidi,' she said, 'even though she's a bigger girl than me.'

That was another problem – how much older was Heidi than May? 'What year is Heidi in?' he asked.

'I'm in year two and she's in year four,' May said proudly. 'She's eight and I'm six, and she's invited me for tea.'

Technically it hadn't been Heidi who had done the inviting, it had been her mother. Jason wasn't sure how he felt about that. As far as he knew, May hadn't had a play-date after school before, although he knew she'd had one or two during the school holidays because Pamela had told him. He left that kind of thing up to her. After a day at work, the last thing he wanted was to entertain someone else's child. He simply wanted to be on his own with May, so the thought of her going to someone else's house for a few hours and impacting on his precious time with her didn't please him.

It was bad enough when work necessitated May having to go to her grandma's, which was what should have happened next Thursday if he hadn't stupidly given in to letting a total stranger pick her up from school and take her to her lesson. Not only that, the total stranger would be taking his daughter home from that lesson too, and May would have to stay there until he fetched her. This was a woman he'd never met before. Okay, he conceded, he *had* met her before, but he'd never actually spoken to her. The only thing he knew about her was that she had a daughter, Heidi, who was older than May and in year four in school. That was it.

It was hardly a substantial basis on which to allow the woman to take care of his child.

'I like Heidi,' May was saying. 'She's kind. Did you see she helped me take my helmet off, Daddy? I couldn't undo the buckle thing.'

That was true; usually one of the twins who helped with the lessons unfastened the helmet for her. It wouldn't be long before she could do it herself, he thought, with a pang. She was growing up so fast – far too fast for his liking. It seemed only last year she was a tiny babe in arms, and now here she was getting all excited about play dates.

'I can't wait to tell Mummy tomorrow,' she continued, piling bubbles on her head and wetting hair that he'd had no intention of washing this evening.

'May!' he scolded, but his admonishment was tinged with laughter. She looked so silly and incredibly cute with her pink face, wet eyelashes and a bubbly head.

She threw a handful of bubbles at him and giggled at his pretend shocked expression.

Hoping that was the end of the going-to-Heidi's-house conversation, he lifted her warm slippery body out of the bath and wrapped her in an oversized fluffy towel.

No such luck.

As he was dressing her, she said, 'I like Heidi's Mummy. She hasn't got a daddy.' May held onto his shoulder to steady herself as she put one foot into her pyjama bottoms, then the other.

'Rose Walker hasn't got a daddy?' Jason asked, confused.

'No, silly. *Heidi* hasn't got a daddy. Not the way I've got a daddy.'

'Not many mummies and daddies share their children, like me and your mummy do.' This wouldn't be the first time he'd explained their arrangement to her.

'Why not?'

'Because it's usually the mummy who takes care of the children most of the time, and the daddies don't see their children as often as I see you.' He pulled her pyjama top over her head.

'They must be so sad. You'd be sad if you didn't see me every day, wouldn't you?' This last came out rather muffled, then her head popped free of the neck of her pyjama top.

'I would be very sad indeed,' he admitted.

'Do you think Heidi's daddy is sad?'

'I don't know, poppet. I don't know anything about him.'

'I think he is. I think Heidi is sad, too.'

Abruptly, Jason wondered if Rose Walker's offer to pick May up from school was more for Heidi's benefit than to enable May to have her riding lesson. Was Rose trying to fill her daughter's time with friends because Heidi's father wasn't on the scene?

It was entirely possible, and he realised how lucky May was, despite the inconvenience that living between two households caused. He might dislike the arrangement, but it was the best thing for May. Of course, the ultimate best thing for her would be to have both her parents living under the same roof, but that simply wasn't going to happen.

He wished he could blame his ex-wife for their relationship failing, but it hadn't been anyone's fault. Falling out of love had crept up on them both without either of them realising it, and by the time they had, it was too late – the love had well and truly disappeared. Yet they might have carried on living together for May's sake, but Pamela had fallen in love with a builder called Craig and that, as they say, was that.

'I'll cheer her up, won't I, Daddy?' May said.

'You, my lovely girl, are enough to cheer anyone up.'

'I wonder what we'll have for tea?' she mused. 'I hope it's fish fingers.'

For a second Jason was confused – they'd already had their tea. Bath was a prelude to bed, so why was she talking about—? Ah, she meant what she was going to have for tea when she went to Heidi's house.

He was about to try to change the subject, in the hope that if he didn't respond she would eventually forget about her visit to Heidi's next week, but when he looked at her eager little face, he knew he had to take the bull by the horns. May wouldn't forget, and she was looking forward to it so much. He hated to be the one to play bad cop, but it was for her own good and—

She was still looking at him, but her expression now held a hint of worry. 'You *are* going to let me go, aren't you, Daddy? You *said* you would.'

Indeed he had, but at the time he'd felt coerced into it by his daughter and by Rose Walker. 'We'll see,' he said, and watched as May's bottom lip began to tremble.

Wonderful. He should have put his foot down from the start and not given in to pressure. Now he was going to upset her right before bedtime and it would be ages before he would manage to settle her down.

Jason spied the bottle of wine sitting all alone in the wine rack and turned away. As much as he fancied drowning his sorrows, he couldn't. One glass might well lead to two, or maybe more, and having to get up in the middle of the night to see to a fractious child when he'd had a bit too much to drink was never a good idea. Besides, he had work in the morning, and he had to drive May to her mum's house first.

Instead of the wine, he flipped the switch on the kettle and made himself a cup of tea, taking it into the living room and sinking down onto the sofa.

May had an incredible knack of making him feel like the worst father in the world. She'd certainly done so tonight, and, he conceded, she might have a point. First he'd said yes, and he'd built her hopes up, and then he'd said no and had dashed them to smithereens.

He knew she didn't mean it when she'd told him she hated him – all kids said that to their parents at some point, although usually it was when they hit their teenage years, and not at the tender age of six. But May had been through a lot in her little life; despite how much he and Pamela had tried to shield their daughter from the breakup of their marriage, it was inevitable she would be affected.

What the hell was he supposed to do about next week? He knew if he asked Pamela for advice, she wouldn't see the harm in allowing Rose Walker to pick May up from school, take her riding and then take their daughter to her house for some tea.

But his issue was that he didn't know anything about Rose Walker, or her home life. All he knew was that he'd seen her at the school gates occasionally, chatting to other mums, and she and Heidi seemed to adore each other. Was that a good enough reason to allow the woman to look after his daughter?

Throughout the whole separation and divorce, his mother had been the voice of reason. No matter that the divorce had been amicable and inevitable, there had still been a great deal of heartache surrounding his and Pamela's separation, and even more hurt when Pamela had moved in with her new partner. Craig seemed a nice enough bloke, but that was another thing Jason didn't like very much, the fact that May spent nearly fifty per cent of her time in another man's home.

He knew he was a bit of a helicopter parent, but he couldn't help it, even though he had a feeling he was being somewhat over-protective. Maybe he should give his mum a call – her advice was always sage.

After he'd explained the problem, Sheila surprised him. 'I don't know why on earth you're fussing,' his mother said. 'Unless you have reason to suspect this woman won't take good care of May?'

He didn't. 'No…'

'Well then, you've got nothing to worry about. You've got to let go of the reins sometime, you know. May is growing up; you can't keep her wrapped in cotton wool forever.'

But that's exactly what he wanted to do. Ever since his divorce, he'd felt very acutely that she was his sole responsibility, even though he shared joint custody with Pamela. When May was in his care he wanted to make sure he did everything he could to keep her safe.

'You've got to let her spread her wings a little,' his mother added. 'That's the problem with parents today – they don't allow their children to learn to stand on their own two feet and develop some resilience.'

'You've been on one of those training sessions again,' Jason said.

'What if I have? It doesn't make what I'm telling you any less true.'

Jason shrugged, despite his mother not being able to see him. She worked as a learning support assistant in what May called "the big school". His daughter was referring to the secondary school she would eventually go to when she was eleven. He didn't want to think that far ahead.

'What are you afraid of?' Sheila asked.

Crikey, where should he start? For himself, he wasn't scared of anything. When it came to May he lived in a permanent state of anxiety, from the worry of whether he was feeding her enough vegetables, to the very real fear of what would become of her if something was to happen to him.

No one told you that being a parent meant you were faced with a lifetime of worry, and he knew it would only get worse as she grew older. He actually dreaded the thought of her learning to drive—

'Are you going to let her go or are you going to stifle her for the rest of her life?' Sheila demanded, breaking into his thoughts.

'Excuse me?' He was flabbergasted at the stance his mother was taking. For some reason, he'd expected her to agree with him. That she'd taken the opposite position, shocked him somewhat.

'You heard,' Sheila said. 'Let Rose Walker look after May for the afternoon; what harm can it do?'

What harm indeed?

CHAPTER TWO

Rose grimaced as her mobile pinged again with yet another text from May's father asking if May was okay. May was as fine as she had been the last time he'd messaged, which had only been fifteen minutes ago. If Rose had known Jason Halligan was going to be this needy, she would never have offered to pick his daughter up from school and take her riding.

However, when she looked at May and Heidi trotting around the arena, both of them rising and falling in their saddles with effortless ease, her expression softened. The girls were having a wonderful time, and that's what mattered.

Rose left it ten minutes before replying and when she did she also sent him a photo of his daughter smiling so widely that it almost brought tears to her eyes. The child was having the time of her life and had been ever since Rose had picked her up from school, popped both girls home so they could change into their riding clothes, before driving them out to the stables on Muddypuddle Lane.

Heidi and May had chattered and giggled the whole time, talking non-stop about their school friends, their teachers, and their love of anything remotely horsey. Rose was proud of the way Heidi was taking May under her wing, and she could see how May was looking up to Heidi and hanging onto her every word. It was quite sweet to see them together; they could almost be sisters, despite their appearances being very different. Heidi followed Rose in that she had fine blond hair and grey eyes. May's hair fell down her back in dark, glossy ringlets, and she had hazel eyes. With her cute button nose and slight frame, she reminded Rose of a porcelain doll, despite the golden tan she'd already acquired this early in the summer.

Rose had re-plaited May's hair for her as it had come free at some point during the day, and had helped her secure her helmet, checking it was tight enough but not too tight, before she sent both girls scampering off into the arena to await the arrival of their ponies.

Taking her usual seat, Rose had proceeded to answer the third text Jason had sent her (the first had been to ask if she'd picked May up from school, the second had been to ask if they were on their way to the stables, and the third had been to ask whether they'd arrived) and then she had settled down to watch the lesson. It had only just started when Jason had sent her a fourth text, which she'd just replied to.

She wondered how long it would be before he sent her the next. Considering he was supposed to be working, Jason seemed to have plenty of time to send her messages.

She looked up from her phone in surprise as someone took the seat next to her.

It was one of the mums Rose knew from school, Jane Crease. She seemed nice enough, and they'd exchanged a few pleasantries now and again, but they weren't that friendly and Rose wondered what she wanted.

'Did I see little May Halligan getting out of your car?' Jane asked.

Ah, so that's what Jane was after, a bit of gossip. 'Yes, you did.'

'Getting friendly with her dad, are you?'

Jane certainly knew how to cut to the chase.

'Not at all,' Rose replied coolly. 'I offered to bring May to her lesson, otherwise she would have missed it.'

'Bit of an odd setup, isn't it?'

'I don't think me offering to bring May to her riding lesson is that odd.' Rose was busy trying to work out what could possibly be wrong with it.

'Not that; him and his ex-wife.'

Despite not wanting to gossip, Rose couldn't help asking, 'What do you mean?'

'May lives with both of them. Co-parenting, it's called. I think it should be called confusing. I bet the poor little mite doesn't know whether she's coming or going most of the time. She spends the week with him, and the weekends with her. The poor thing is being bounced back and forth between the two of them like a ping pong ball.' Jane seemed to take great delight in telling Rose this.

'May seems happy enough to me,' Rose said. 'Whatever they're doing, it appears to work.'

Jane gave her a shrewd look. 'Kids need stability,' she said firmly, as though she was an authority on the subject.

'Kids need love,' Rose countered. 'And it seems to me that May is loved very much.' Rose had the text messages to prove it.

'It's like that, is it?'

'What's like what?'

'He's rather good looking,' Jane said.

'Who? Jason Halligan? I hadn't noticed.' It was a lie, because it was hard *not* to notice. Not many people wouldn't. But just because she thought someone was good looking, didn't mean to say she had the hots for them, which was what Jane was implying.

Jane snorted, clearly not believing her, and when the woman got up to return to her original seat, Rose realised their brief chat had been a fishing expedition. She guessed news of her bringing May to the stables would be all around the school yard by tomorrow. How ridiculous. It looked like you couldn't do anyone a favour these days, without someone taking it the wrong way.

Rose sat through the rest of the lesson wondering if Jane and the other mums were talking about her, and she was pleased when it finally ended.

Making her way outside, she hoped for a quick getaway, but she'd not taken into account a new notice on the board outside the office, as Heidi and May came haring up to her, all legs and excited faces, and dragged her to take a look.

'Petra says we need to sign up by next week,' Heidi cried, jumping up and down with excitement.

'What are you talking about?' Rose couldn't help laughing at the earnest expressions on both girls' faces.

'The gymkhana! Petra told everyone about it at the end of the lesson. Weren't you listening?'

That will teach her to dash off like she did – she'd missed a vital announcement. She peered at the piece of paper pinned to the board.

'Mum…?'

'Shhh, I'm trying to read it.'

'What's a gymkhana, Mrs Walker?' May asked.

'Oh, it's a bit like your sports day, only with horses. There'll be games and competitions.'

'What kind?' May's eyes were as large as the hooves belonging to the pony she'd just ridden.

'I don't know.'

'Do you think there'll be show jumping?'

'Maybe.'

'What about dressage?' Heidi asked.

'You'll have to check with Petra. I've not really got any idea.' She didn't think there had been dressage at last year's' gymkhana, but she couldn't remember.

'Can you put my name down, Mum?'

Rose fished a pen out of her bag and wrote Heidi's name on the sheet of paper. Then she noticed May's hopeful little face. 'Sorry, sweetie, I can't put your name down – your daddy will have to do that.'

'Mum,' Heidi said, 'Please put her name down – it might get full up. Her dad can cross it off next week if she's not allowed.' She waggled her eyebrows to let Rose know she understood that May's dad probably *would* cross his daughter's name off, but she didn't want May to realise, and Rose's heart swelled with love.

She was so lucky to have such a mature and considerate child.

'Okay, I will, but if her dad is cross, I'm blaming you,' Rose warned her with a smile.

Names written, she hastily rounded the two girls up, ushered them into the car and headed for home.

As she drove, the children chattering in the back, her thoughts strayed to May's father. She hadn't given much thought about the little girl's home life, but now Jane had mentioned it, Rose couldn't help considering it. Jane seemed to imply that the child was pushed from pillar to post on a regular basis, but May seemed happy and well adjusted.

The temper tantrum she'd thrown at the stables last week was perfectly normal; Heidi had thrown far worse in her time, and from what other people had said, it was nothing compared to the teenage angst that was to come. Whatever was going on between May's parents didn't seem to have affected the little girl too badly.

Rose's phone pinged with an incoming text and she shook her head wryly, guessing the latest message would be from Jason inquiring how the lesson had gone and whether May had got through it safely.

He'd have to wait; there was no way she was going to even look at her phone let alone answer a message while she was driving. Anyway, he'd texted her enough times already, and she was getting fed up. The man really needed to loosen the apron strings a bit.

One thing occurred to her though, as she made her way through the village, and that was how she was surprised he allowed his daughter to go riding at all. He seemed extremely over-protective, yet he happily allowed May to bounce up and down astride a creature many times larger than she was. It was quite irritating to think Jason Halligan trusted a Shetland pony more than he trusted her.

Oh, well, she said to herself, there was nowt so strange as folk, as the old saying went. She was pretty sure she wouldn't be helping him out again, despite how sweet May was.

Rose simply didn't need the aggro.

Jason checked his phone for possibly the hundredth time, and sighed when he realised Rose Walker hadn't responded to his latest text. What was she *doing*? It was less than fifteen minutes since the riding lesson ended, so she must still be at the stables. Surely she could take a second or two to send him a quick reply, before she drove the children home?

If he'd been regretting allowing Rose to take May to her riding lesson before, he was doubly regretting it now. He'd been on edge since this morning, first worrying about whether Rose would actually remember to pick May up, then fretting about whether she'd make sure May's helmet was firmly on (even though he knew the staff at the stables would double-check anyway) and that was in addition to his normal worry that May might fall off her pony, or one of the unpredictable creatures might kick her, or bite her, or knock her over. He even had a moment where he was concerned that the cockerel, who for some reason was called Fred, might decide to peck her.

And now that the lesson was over with, he had fresh worry regarding the drive home from the stables to Rose Walker's house, followed by whether the two girls would get on, and accompanied by concerns over what the woman would feed his child for tea.

It was now over twenty minutes since the lesson had officially ended and there was still no word from Rose. No wonder he was going grey. Every now and again he scrutinised himself in the bathroom mirror looking for new grey hairs, his heart sinking every time he found another. At the rate he was going, he'd be totally grey by the time he was forty. No wonder people resorted to dyeing their hair. It had crossed his mind more than once. He was only thirty-six, yet he was starting to look ancient, and he very definitely felt it. No one ever told you that kids would age you so much. But even if they had, he wouldn't swap May and his grey hairs for the absence of worry and a dark barnet.

His phone vibrated and he snatched it up. Finally!

When he read Rose's message he was surprised to see they were already at her house. Gosh, it took him at least twenty minutes to wrestle May away from the stables. She absolutely adored it there and loved every animal, from the smallest of chicks to that massive ex-racehorse which Petra rode. She insisted on saying hello to as many of them as she could, but her favourite was Gerald the donkey, although she had a soft spot for the goat as well.

Jason didn't. Why a creature with eyes like the devil was called Princess he had absolutely no idea. It didn't help that the animal had once tried to eat his sleeve.

He replaced his phone on the table, and tried to concentrate on the conference call he was supposed to be involved in. He didn't like working this late, but his company had clients in the US and it was barely midday for them. The Americans were so gung-ho it made his teeth ache.

He loved his job, he really did, but it wasn't the be-all and end-all. May was that, and he resented anyone and anything that took him away from her. It wasn't so bad during the day because she was at school, but as soon as school was out, he wanted to be too. He was more than happy to work from home once she had gone to bed, but right now he was becoming increasingly more resentful as the minutes ticked on, that someone else was spending time with his daughter instead of him.

He wondered what she was doing now. Was she behaving herself? Of course she was – she always did, apart from occasionally when she was with him. He preferred it that way; being polite and respectful at school and with other people, but allowing herself to have the odd meltdown when she was at home.

He hoped Heidi Walker wasn't teaching her anything he would disapprove of. Or that her mother was allowing them to watch something inappropriate. Or that—

Give it a rest, he told himself; Heidi seemed a perfectly lovely child. Rose seemed a perfectly lovely woman. The children were probably watching a Disney movie, or playing dress-up or something. But he still couldn't help worrying.

He sighed, then was brought firmly back to the present when his boss said, 'Is there anything you would like to contribute, Jason?'

Jason tried not to panic. He had absolutely no idea what they'd been talking about for the past few minutes. Or since the meeting had started, if he was honest. He shook his head. 'No, I think you've covered everything,' he said.

His boss nodded, and Jason let out a small sigh of relief. It looked like he'd got away with it this time. He'd better concentrate from now on, though, he thought.

But less than two minutes after the meeting had ended he was in his car and heading to Picklewick. If he was lucky, he might get there before Rose fed the girls, so he could take May home and enjoy eating his evening meal with his daughter.

Rose was just about to dish up three platefuls of risotto with some spicy chicken (mildly spiced, to cater for younger palates) and roasted vegetables, when there was a knock at the door.

With a cross sigh she went to answer it, wondering who it could possibly be. She was getting slightly fed up with all the interruptions to her afternoon. Thankfully, she'd not had a text off Jason for a while so she assumed he was actually doing what he was paid to do, rather than fretting about his daughter.

How she managed to resist the urge to roll her eyes when she opened the door and saw May's father standing on the other side of it, was a miracle. Dear god, she felt sorry for the poor child, having a father like him. If he was like this now, Rose could only imagine what he would be like when May started going out and about on her own; he'd be horrific. He'd be even worse when May had her first boyfriend. Although, the way Jason was going, May might very well be in her thirties before that happened.

'I didn't expect you so soon,' Rose told him, the irritation evident in her voice.

'My meeting finished a bit earlier than I anticipated,' he said, 'So if it's all right with you, I'll just grab May and we'll be off.'

'Actually, I was just dishing up,' she replied mildly, hiding her annoyance. He could at least let them eat before he took May.

'Oh, we won't bother you for much longer,' Jason said, looking past her into the depths of the house.

Rose invited him in, although she wasn't sure whether she wanted to, but she could hardly keep him out when his daughter was inside. 'She's upstairs, playing with Heidi. I'll give her a shout.' She halted at the foot of the stairs. 'May? Can you come down please, your father is here.'

There was an abrupt silence, then two pairs of heavy footsteps stampeded across the landing, and two heads peered around the bannister.

May did not look pleased to see her father. In fact, she looked positively thunderous.

'Daddy, why are you here?' she demanded.

'To take you home.' Jason smiled up at his daughter who, Rose noticed, failed to smile back.

'You're early. I haven't had tea yet,' May said.

'I know; isn't that lovely? We can eat at our house.'

'I don't want to.' There was a thud, and Rose realised May was stamping her foot. She seemed to do that a lot.

'We can't intrude on these lovely people any longer. It's time we went home.'

'No, Daddy, it's not. Heidi's mummy said she would give me tea, and I haven't had my tea yet, so I'm not going home and you can't make me.'

Rose bit her lip, hoping no one would see her smile. May was a right little madam and a bit of a handful, but she knew what she wanted and Rose could only admire that.

'I could do pancakes…?' Jason said.

'No, thank you. Heidi's mummy is making roasted vegetables. I want those.'

Jason shot Rose an incredulous look. 'Vegetables?'

Rose nodded. 'Cooked in the oven, with some oil and garlic.'

'May has agreed to eat it?'

'Yes, why? She's not allergic to garlic or anything, is she?'

'No, I think it's the vegetables she's allergic to.'

'We're having risotto too, and a little bit of spicy chicken.'

Jason raised his eyebrows. 'Risotto *and* spicy chicken?'

'Yes, you're welcome to stay and eat with us, if you like. There's plenty to go round. I always make far too much and end up having to eat it myself, as you can tell.' Rose cringed as his eyes swept up and down her body. Why on earth had she said such a thing?

'We couldn't possibly—' Jason began, but his daughter had other ideas.

'Yes, we can, Daddy. You said I could stay for tea. If you take me home I'm not eating any of your yucky food.'

'But you like my cooking,' he said.

'Not today I don't. Today I want Mrs Walker's cooking. I've never had roasted vegetables, or spicy chicken.'

'That's because you don't like vegetables very much. I have to hide them in your food to get you to eat them.'

May stared at him suspiciously, and Rose simply knew the child was filing this little bit of information away to use against him in the future. She had a suspicion May would be scrutinising every single meal Jason put in front of her from now on, to try to find hidden vegetables.

'If you don't want to stay and eat with us,' Rose said to him, 'you could always come back in an hour. I must get on though, otherwise everything will be ruined.' She walked into the kitchen, leaving him standing at the bottom of the stairs. He was starting to get on her nerves.

'May, please calm down. It's time to go home,' Rose heard him say, and she also heard his daughter's very firm, 'No! You *promised*.'

Rose quickly put a spoonful of risotto on each plate, and as she was doing so she became aware of someone standing behind her.

She turned, spoon poised. 'Are you sure you don't want to stay?'

'I suppose I'm going to have to, if I want my daughter to eat anything this evening.'

Right. Good.' She was having difficulty keeping a lid on her temper. What an ungrateful man. 'You can make yourself useful and lay the table,' she said, jerking her head at the drawer where the cutlery was kept. 'Is there anything you don't like – how about vegetables?'

'I like vegetables just fine,' he said. 'I just wish May did, too.'

'They all seem to go through these funny fads,' Rose said, doing her best to be pleasant. 'Heidi went through a phase of not wanting anything red on her plate. Considering she loved tomatoes, it was a bit of an issue. I remember her sitting at the table once, bawling her eyes out because she wanted blue tomatoes, not red.'

She heard him clattering about in the draw as he chuckled, 'That's funny.'

'Glad you think so. I certainly didn't at the time. She seems to have grown out of that now, although I'm sure there will be another along shortly. You think you've got over one little hurdle, and along comes another. Thankfully, it doesn't matter in the great scheme of things,' she added, 'but it can be annoying at the time.'

She used oven gloves to put the warm plates on the table, then indicated he should sit down. 'Yours is the one with the biggest portion,' she said to him. 'I'll just give the girls a shout.'

Rose took a second to compose herself as she walked out of the kitchen towards the stairs. Since he'd made the decision to stay and eat with them, he'd mellowed slightly, and she found she liked him all the better for it.

'Heidi, May, your food is on the table. Can you wash your hands first, please?'

A flurry of small footsteps followed her call, then Rose heard the tap running. She was about to walk away, when May's voice floated down the stairs. 'Has he gone yet?'

'No, your father is going to have tea with us.'

'Oh.' May didn't sound pleased about it. 'Do you think he'll let me play afterwards?'

'I don't know, sweetie, you'll have to ask him.'

'Tell him if he's good he can have some wine,' May said, appearing at the top of the stairs with a towel in her hand. Rose saw Heidi's arm reach out to take it from her. Then both children hurtled down the steps, coming to a halt at the bottom.

'He likes wine a lot,' May said in a loud whisper. 'Tell him he can have some if he lets me stay. Do you have any?'

'I do, although I don't think I'm going to get a bottle of wine out right now,' Rose told her, stifling a laugh. She wasn't quite sure whether May was telling her that her father was a lush or not, and she didn't want to find out. She also didn't want him to think she made a habit of swigging back glasses of wine when she was looking after other peoples' children. Although technically, now he was here, she wasn't looking after May. May was now her father's responsibility, but she still didn't want Jason to get the wrong idea about her. Rose had a bottle or two of wine in the house, but she didn't drink often; she actually didn't like the taste very much, and neither did she like the effect when she was drinking it, or the hangover the day after.

'I think you should,' May persisted as Rose rounded up the two children and ushered them into the kitchen.

'What do you think she should do, May?' Jason asked.

'Never mind,' Rose said quickly. She'd assumed this conversation was just between her and May, but May proved her wrong.

'I told her she should give you some wine if you say I could stay after we've eaten our tea,' May said. 'Can I stay for a bit? Please? Heidi said she'll show me how to draw horses.'

This time Rose was unable to hold her laughter in when she saw Jason's stricken expression. He looked utterly mortified and totally embarrassed.

'You can't have any secrets when you've got children,' Rose said.

'It's not a secret,' Jason said, then he added hastily, 'Not that I make a habit of telling everyone how much wine I drink. I don't actually drink much. Just the odd glass now and again.' He was clearly flustered, not wanting her to think the worst of him.

'My vice is chocolate,' Rose confessed. 'Although I only tend to eat it when Heidi is in bed.'

'Mum! You eat chocolate when I'm in *bed*? Why don't I get any?'

'Because it rots your teeth and it's not good for you.'

Heidi pointed out, 'You're old but your teeth aren't rotten.' She turned to May and said, 'Did you know that old people have to have all their teeth out and they have to have plastic ones.'

May's eyes grew round. 'Really?'

'That's not true at all,' Rose said. 'Some people have problems with their teeth, and yes some people do have to have all their teeth removed, but not everyone.'

Heidi put a hand up to her mouth and whispered behind it, 'My great-grandma keeps her teeth in a glass in the bathroom. It's yucky.'

'She keeps plastic teeth in her bathroom?' May asked in fascination.

'I've seen them.'

Rose sent Jason an apologetic look. 'It's true, my grandma does keep her false teeth in the bathroom. Thank god dental hygiene is better today, eh?' Then she giggled. 'I can't believe we're having a discussion about false teeth and dental hygiene.'

She was pleased to see Jason tucking into his meal with enthusiasm, and so were the two girls. Whether May did, or didn't, like roasted vegetables seemed to be neither here nor there, because the chatter around the table was distracting the child enough for her to continue putting forkfuls into her mouth until her plate was empty.

Jason didn't say anything but she could see him looking, and when Rose got to her feet to collect the plates he said, 'You've eaten a good meal, May.'

'That's because it was nice,' the child said, and once again Rose burst out laughing.

'Are you trying to say your dad can't cook?' she asked.

'No, my mummy can't. She's not as good at cooking as Daddy is, and Daddy's not as good at cooking as you are.'

Rose took the compliment. These days she didn't get many, so she wasn't picky where they came from. 'Thank you, young lady,' she said. 'You may come again.' As soon as the words left her mouth, Rose wished she could take them back. She gave Jason an apologetic look, but to her surprise, he didn't seem annoyed.

'Can I stay for a little bit, Daddy? Please?'

'Only if it's all right with Rose. And Heidi, of course.'

Heidi nodded. 'Come on.' She grabbed May's hand and they made a dash for the door.

After the girls left, Rose said, 'Ordinarily, I would insist Heidi helps with the clearing up, but not when she's got guests.'

'Does she do many chores?'

'Not many, just one or two. I don't want her to grow up thinking she has an inbuilt maid. I expect her to put her dishes in the dishwasher and to keep her room tidy. I also expect her to take her school bag upstairs, empty it out, and then give me anything I need to wash, or read, or sign. I don't think it's too much to ask.'

'May doesn't do anything,' he said, and she could see him thinking. 'When did you start?'

'House-training Heidi? From when she was quite small. We used to make a game out of picking her toys up and putting them away before she had her tea.'

'I usually do all the clearing up and tidying up after May has gone to bed.'

'Do you mind me asking you something?' Rose thought he was definitely going to mind, so she added, 'You don't have to say anything if you don't want.'

'Go on.' His voice was cautious, and she thought he was going to tell her to mind her own business.

'You and May's mum don't live together, do you?'

'No, we don't.'

'Does she live with you?'

'She lives with us both,' he said, and he went on to confirm what Jane had told her earlier, finishing up with, 'It's not ideal by any stretch of the imagination, but at least it means she gets to see an equal amount of us both, which she wouldn't do if she lived with one or the other of us.'

'I'm not judging', Rose said, anxious in case he thought she was. 'If it works for you, that's all that matters. Families come in all shapes and sizes these days, and at least May gets to see both of you equally.'

'Does Heidi see much of her father?'

'Not a great deal. Holidays and the occasional weekend, and her birthday – that's about it. I'm lucky my dad is so hands-on with her. She adores her grandad, and she gets some male input into her life.'

'Thank you for picking May up from school and everything,' he said when there was a lull in the conversation. 'I'm sorry I texted you so often. It's just…I worry about her.'

'Don't we all!' Rose exclaimed. 'I think that's par for the course when you have kids. You get handed a whole lot of worry from the minute you conceive and according to my mum, it doesn't end when they enter adulthood, either. She still worries about me as though I'm twelve.'

'I know what you mean; my mother worries about me, too.'

He was helping stack the dishwasher, as if working in her kitchen was the most natural thing in the world, and she was surprised he'd gone from being so tense, to being fairly relaxed. He was actually quite easy to talk to, now that he'd got over his constant worry about May. With his daughter safely playing upstairs and a decent meal eaten, he seemed more chilled.

'Would you like a coffee or a tea?' she asked. 'I don't think the girls are quite ready to end the evening yet.'

He checked the clock on the kitchen wall. 'It's still quite early,' he said, 'although I do want her to be in bed by seven-thirty.'

'Heidi goes to bed at eight, nine o'clock on a Friday or Saturday. To be honest,' Rose added, 'some days I'd be quite happy if she went to bed at half-past seven, too.'

'I have evenings like that,' Jason admitted. 'I love my daughter and I enjoy her company, but crikey, I sometimes think I'm too old for this.'

'How old are you?' Rose wanted to know.

'I'm thirty-seven.'

'That's hardly old, is it?'

They continued to chat back and forth for another half an hour or so, until Jason finally decided it was time to leave. Rose called to the children, smiling when disappointed groans wafted down the stairs, although May was willing enough to collect her things together, with a little help from Heidi.

'Thank you for having me, Mrs Walker,' May sing-songed to Rose and Rose ruffled her hair.

'You're welcome, sweetie. We'll see you at the stables next week, yes?'

May nodded vigorously, then she gasped and slapped a hand to her forehead. 'I just remembered! Daddy, Daddy, there's going to be a gymkhana at the stables and Mrs Walker put mine and Heidi's names down for it.'

Jason looked baffled. 'A what?'

'A gymkhana – think school sports day with ponies,' Rose explained for the second time that day.

'When is this?'

'A month away, so there'll be plenty of time for the children to practice.'

'I'm going to do show jumping,' May announced grandly, not noticing the horrified look on her father's face or the hardening of his jaw.

'I don't think so,' he replied sharply.

'But, Daddy—'

'Hurry up, May, we need to go home. I'm sure Rose has other things to do. Thank you for having her. Us.'

'You're welcome,' she said as Jason hurried his daughter out of the door and into his car.

'Bye, Heidi, bye Mrs Walker,' May called and Rose grimaced – the little girl seemed cheerful enough now, but she guessed it wouldn't last long when her father informed her that she wasn't going to be entering the gymkhana.

Rose felt somewhat guilty about putting May's name down and maybe she should have asked Jason first, but she hadn't seriously imagined he wouldn't allow May to enter. It was the highlight of the riding year (apart from the nativity play) and every child wanted to enter it. May would be devastated.

'May's dad is a bit grumpy, isn't he, Mum?' Heidi said.

Downright rude would be a more accurate description. Why on earth she'd thought he was nice earlier, was beyond her. Nice wasn't a word she associated with Jason Halligan.

Attractive was a word that popped into her mind, but no matter how good-looking he was, she preferred friendliness over sexy any day. And Jason didn't appear to have any of that whatsoever.

That was the last time she'd do him a favour, although it was a pity Heidi and May wouldn't see each other again apart from during their riding lessons and at school. The children seemed to get on exceptionally well – but the adults most certainly did not.

CHAPTER THREE

Jason had been in two minds about whether to take May to her riding lesson the following week. His daughter had been fractious and difficult ever since they'd driven home from Rose and Heidi's house and he'd informed May that she wasn't, under any circumstances, going to take part in any competition involving a horse.

He'd tried telling her she wasn't old enough, but she'd insisted she was, and she'd even managed to get her mother on board. The only thing in Jason's favour, he saw, as he walked into the office to pay for May's lesson and spotted the notice, was that the gymkhana was being held on the third Saturday in June, and that was the date on which Pamela and Craig would be away for a long weekend so Jason was looking after May. If he hadn't been, then it would have been inevitable Pamela would take May to the event.

He and his ex-wife needed to have a serious conversation about singing off the same hymn sheet when it came to their daughter, because right now they were poles apart regarding May and her riding.

Jason saw Rose before she saw him, and he was tempted to wait for May out in the car park because he didn't want to speak to the woman. He couldn't believe she'd put May's name down for the competition without his permission. What a cheek! It had caused no end of problems between him and his daughter – and between him and his ex-wife, who couldn't see how potentially dangerous riding could be. It was bad enough having May dashing around an indoor arena once a week – but he knew that as she grew older and became more confident, she wouldn't be content to merely do circuits of a barn. She'd want to ride outside, and the first step on that slippery slope was the gymkhana.

His heart sank when he caught a glimpse of what his daughter was doing, and he decided he had to stay to see what was going on.

Petra had placed five poles several metres apart along the length of the arena, with the riders and their ponies gathered at the one end. May was guiding her pony between the poles as though she was performing a slalom, weaving in and out as fast as she could to the cheers and whoops of the rest of the riders and the parents in the raised spectator area.

May was about to wind her pony around the final pole and Jason found himself urging her on.

'Go, May!' he shouted and beamed with pride as she cleared the last pole, hauled her pony around it and hurtled back towards Petra and the others. The *hurtling* was more of a fast trot rather than a breakneck gallop, but his daughter seemed to be flying, closing the distance with heart-stopping speed.

Petra blew a whistle when May and her pony trotted over a line drawn in the sandy floor, and everyone cheered and clapped, Jason along with the rest. He'd moved closer to the balustrade without realising and was now standing near Rose, who'd leapt to her feet and was clapping enthusiastically.

'Didn't she do well?' Rose exclaimed, turning to him, her face alight.

Jason found himself nodding. Then he calmed down and asked, 'What exactly are they doing?' Because he had no idea what was going on.

'Practising for the gymkhana.'

'But May's not entering the gymkhana,' he protested. 'I thought this was supposed to be a riding lesson.'

'It is. These events all help with a rider's control of their mount, as well as being fun.'

'She's still not going.' He was adamant about that – and he wasn't pleased they were practising for it, either.

'That's your decision, of course,' she said, but Jason was sure he could hear an undertone of disapproval in her tone.

How dare she question his parenting? It was his job to keep May safe, and he believed by preventing her from entering a reckless and pointless competition he was doing precisely that. Thank god he only had to see Rose once a week, because she was starting to get on his nerves. It didn't matter that he'd enjoyed eating a meal with her, but she'd overstepped the mark by signing May up for this darned event and now he was certain she was silently commenting on the way he was bringing his daughter up.

'Yes, it is,' he replied coolly, then stalked outside to await his child. He knew May would be upset that he was missing the remainder of her lesson, but she'd get over it. It was more important that he had as little to do with Rose Walker as possible right now.

He'd reckoned without May, though, because the first thing she said when she emerged through the large doors to the arena was, 'Me and Heidi are having a play date.'

'Really?'

May nodded emphatically. 'Grandma says one good turn deserves another. It means you have to do something nice for someone if they do something nice for you.'

'I know what it means.' He tried to hurry her away, but May was having none of it.

'Can I tell Heidi she can come for tea today?' she persisted.

'No, you can't.'

'Could she come tomorrow?'

'I'm sorry, poppet, but I don't think that's a good idea.'

May pouted. 'You never let me have any friends over. You're mean.'

'I'm not mean. It's just…' How do you explain to a six-year-old that you don't want her bothering with another child because you don't approve of the child's mother; especially since there was nothing intrinsically wrong with the woman. If he was honest, Rose was actually quite nice – pretty, friendly, helpful, pretty (that was twice in the same thought he'd referred to her as pretty). She was also interfering and judgemental, but he couldn't tell May that; she wouldn't understand, and she also might repeat it.

'You don't want me to have any friends.' May was taking her argument to the next level.

'Of course I want you to have friends.'

'But you don't want me to be friends with Heidi.'

Darn it, his daughter was far too perceptive for her own good.

'You can't stop me being friends with her.' May gave him a sly look. 'I'm friends with her in school, so there.'

'That's fine,' he replied absently, taking her hand and trying to hurry her to the car.

She pulled her hand from his. 'If I can be friends with her in school, why can't I be friends with her when I'm not in school?'

She had him there, and he didn't have an answer – at least, not one he was prepared to share with her. He was already the bad guy in her eyes; he didn't want to make things worse.

'Because I said so.' His reply was vague and didn't make a great deal of sense, which pained him, because he always tried to be honest with his daughter.

'That's not a good enough answer,' she told him, and he was shocked at the sudden maturity in her voice.

'It's the only answer you're going to get, young lady,' he said.

'Don't you like Heidi?' May asked, as he opened the car door and lifted her inside.

'Yes, I do.' He eased his daughter's riding boots off and reached into the back seat for her trainers.

'Do you like Heidi's mummy?'

He hesitated, and that was all it took. May pounced on him. 'Why don't you like Mrs Walker? She's nice. She's pretty, too. Not as pretty as Mummy, though.' She sneaked a look at him from under her lashes.

'No one is as pretty as your mummy,' he said to her, kissing her on the top of her head.

'But, do you think Mrs Walker is pretty, too?'

He'd been thinking that very thing not too long ago. 'Yes, she's pretty. Now—'

'Mrs Walker!' May yelled. 'My Daddy thinks you're pretty.'

'May!' He couldn't believe she'd just said that. He turned around and saw Rose getting into the car next to his. She was looking amused and he felt a blush creep up his neck.

'She asked me whether I thought you were,' he said in his defence.

'I think he likes you,' May continued, and Jason slowly closed his eyes. This couldn't be happening.

He opened them again, glared at his daughter and hissed, 'Stop it!'

May stared innocently back at him. 'What?' she asked. 'You said I always had to tell the truth.'

Grr. Just wait until he got her home, he'd— Actually, what *would* he do? He could hardly chastise her for telling the truth, something he always encouraged her to do.

'What day did you have in mind?' Rose asked. 'May didn't say.'

'Excuse me?'

'To come to yours? The play date? Tea?'

Jason didn't know what to do with himself. Out of the corner of his mouth he said to May, 'Did you already tell Heidi she could come to tea, and did you invite Rose, too?'

'Uh huh.' She nodded. Oh, dear.

His shock must have shown on his face because Rose hastily said, 'You didn't know about it, did you?'

What could he say? His daughter had already landed him in enough trouble and caused him enough embarrassment, without this.

There was only one thing he *could* do.

'Of course I did,' he said plastering a smile on his face and hoping it would stay there. 'We were just discussing which day was best, weren't we, May?' He nudged her foot with his knee.

'Daddy said you can come tomorrow, didn't you, Daddy?'

'Yes, that's right, tomorrow. If that's okay with you?' He hoped May didn't see the fingers he'd crossed behind his back – with any luck Rose would have something else on.

'Um…okay. Tomorrow is good. We weren't doing anything.' Rose smiled hesitantly at him.

'Yippee!' May clapped her hands together and kicked her feet, catching him on the shin.

'I'll text you our address,' he said to Rose. 'Will five o'clock do you?'

'Lovely. We'll see you then. Bye, May.'

'Bye, Mrs Walker.'

'I think if your dad and I are going to be friends, you should call me Rose,' she said.

And all the way home Jason had to listen to May say "Rose this" and "Rose that", until he was sick of hearing the woman's name.

But when he'd put his exhausted daughter to bed he discovered he was still hearing Rose's name in his mind long after May had stopped saying it.

Rose kept herself together until she was in the car, then she couldn't help bursting out laughing.

'What's so funny, Mum?' Heidi asked.

'May's dad,' Rose replied. 'I swear to god he had no idea May had asked us to pop over for tea one evening. Did you see his face?'

'He looked like a bulldog chewing a wasp,' Heidi said with a giggle.

'Where on earth did you get that expression?'

'Nana.'

Rose shook her head. The things her daughter came out with.

'May's dad still isn't happy with us, is he?'

'No, I don't think he is. Did May say anything to you about being allowed to enter the gymkhana?'

Heidi shrugged. 'A bit. She said he's being mean and that her mum said she could enter.'

'I wonder why her mum isn't taking her to it?' Rose mused. 'I thought she lived with Jason during the week and with her mum on the weekend.'

Heidi reached for one of the wipes that was kept in the glove compartment, and cleaned her hands. She then stuffed the used wipe into the side pocket of the car door.

'Heidi, I hope you remember to bring that out with you. I don't need my car filling up with rubbish.' Out of the corner of her eye she saw Heidi pull a face. It wouldn't be long before her daughter was in full teenager mode, and Rose was dreading it.

'May's dad is looking after her when the gymkhana is on,' Heidi told her. 'May said her mum and her stepdad had to go somewhere.'

'That's unfortunate. I got the impression that although he didn't like her riding, her mum didn't mind.'

'That's what May said. You don't mind *me* riding do you mum?'

Rose didn't, because she'd ridden herself when she was a girl, but it was only since she'd become a parent that she realised how much her mum used to worry about her being on the back of a horse. It wasn't so bad riding in the arena, but Rose used to go out for hacks over the hills with her friends. The stables they frequented were quite happy to let the youngsters loose on their own.

It would be unheard of today, and Petra would never dream of letting anyone take her ponies out without supervision, but things had been different when Rose was young. Rose could see where Jason was coming from, even though she thought he was too over-protective.

'I don't *mind*,' Rose said, 'but I do worry.'

'You always worry about everything.'

'It comes with the territory. It's my job to worry.'

Another roll of the eyes from Heidi was followed by a huff.

Rose thought it wise not to say anything further regarding Jason and May. Bringing up May was Jason's business, not hers, and it must be hard for him only having his little girl half of the time. She knew how much she worried whenever Heidi's dad looked after her. It wasn't that she didn't trust Ben – she knew he loved Heidi as much as she did – but she couldn't help it. So she felt a certain degree of empathy for Jason.

She also felt a certain degree of something else, too, and that was attraction. It went against the grain a bit, because he was a grumpy so-and-so and she could do without grumpy people in her life. But on the other hand, she'd seen another side of Jason Halligan when he had eaten an evening meal with them last week. It had been a friendlier, more relaxed Jason; a Jason she found she quite liked.

The problem was he'd reverted to the Jason she had originally met the second May had told him about the gymkhana.

One part of him was Rhett Butler and the other part was more Ashley Wilkes, and she didn't know which one she preferred. The one was moody and enigmatic, and the other was friendly and far more open. The problem was she quite liked them both, and to put them into one package, aka Jason Halligan, was quite a dangerous combination.

Thank goodness she was no Scarlett O'Hara.

CHAPTER FOUR

Rose wondered whether she should take something to Jason's house. She'd spotted May's mum at the school gates picking her daughter up this afternoon, and she wondered if she should say anything. Or whether May would. She gave the little girl a quick wave, then turned away hastily, feeling awkward.

If she took something, would it seem more like a date? Because it quite clearly wasn't – the only date was the play date between the two children, and the fact that May had invited Rose along too, even though her father knew nothing about it. He'd rallied well though, she conceded.

Maybe she should take a bottle of wine? On the other hand, maybe not. Taking wine was more like the sort of thing you would do if you were going to a dinner party. Besides, she wasn't sure it would go very well with chicken nuggets. Although, she may be doing him a disservice by assuming that was the sort of thing their meal would consist of; she had no idea how good a cook he was, and she might be in for a surprise.

Perhaps she could take dessert? But then again, would he think she was being patronising? Or that he'd think she didn't believe him capable of providing dessert? Oh, dear, this wasn't easy. If any of Heidi's other friends' mums had invited her, she knew exactly what she'd do – she'd take cake. That seemed to be the done thing. Not that she'd been invited to anyone's house for tea very often; it was normally a mid-morning or mid-afternoon thing, when cake was entirely appropriate.

Perhaps it was best if she took nothing at all, just herself and her daughter?

Decision made, she supervised Heidi getting changed out of her school uniform and into something more appropriate, before she went off to check her own appearance. Jeans, tee shirt with a cardi slung over the top, and a pair of ballet flats. It was her usual attire, but for some reason she felt she should make more of an effort. But if she made more of an effort, wouldn't that look a bit odd? She was only going to his house for a bite to eat while the two children played: it was hardly an evening out on the tiles.

She had a sudden image of being in a bar sipping cocktails with Jason Halligan, and her eyes widened. Where on earth had that come from? Although she wasn't closed to offers of evenings out from the opposite sex – she'd done her fair share of dating since she'd split from Heidi's father – she wasn't exactly in desperate need of a man. She and Heidi were a unit, and they were quite content together.

For the moment.

Rose was under no illusion that as Heidi got older, she'd want to spend less and less time with her mother. Which would leave said mother at a bit of a loose end. Rose didn't want to rush out and fill the void which Heidi's growing independence would inevitably leave, but neither did she want to become a lonely old maid.

Therefore, she wasn't averse to dating.

But what she was averse to, was imagining she was going on a date with Jason.

Things were too complicated there, even if she *was* interested in him. Which she wasn't. Not really. And he wasn't interested in her, either. She ignored the memory of May telling her that Jason found her attractive. *Pretty* was the word the little girl had used. Jason hadn't been delighted either, but then again, he'd been so embarrassed he probably couldn't even remember what his name was. The poor man – that's what kids did to you. When they were younger they caused you inordinate amounts of embarrassment. Rose was looking forward to doing exactly the same to Heidi when Heidi was old enough. There had to be some compensations, and that was one of them.

Rose checked her appearance in the mirror, deciding she'd have to do. She would have liked to put a swipe of gloss on her lips, but she didn't want Jason to think she'd been making an effort, especially since lip gloss wasn't the sort of thing she normally wore.

'Ready?' she called, and Heidi came bounding down the stairs. Her daughter appeared to be ready for anything. She too was dressed in jeans, but that was where any sign of normality ended. She was wearing wellies on her feet, despite it being summer and there hadn't been a drop of rain for ages, and she had pink glittery angel wings on her back and a swimming cap on her head. Not only that, she'd draped a woollen scarf around her neck.

'That's an interesting outfit,' Rose said mildly.

'I'm not sure what we're going to be doing, so I thought I'd dress for any eventuality.'

Rose shook her head in bemusement. It was a constant source of wonder hearing what came out of her daughter's mouth. She had no idea where the *any eventuality* phrase had come from (although she strongly suspected Heidi's granddad was the culprit), but she couldn't fault the child's logic. Even though she guessed that neither the wellies, the scarf, nor the swimming cap would actually be needed today.

'Could you find my car keys for me, please?' Rose asked. 'I just need to nip to the loo.'

It was a diversionary tactic; she knew exactly where her car keys were and she didn't need the loo. What she needed to do was to stuff a pair of Heidi's trainers and a fleece into her bag, just in case the children played out in the garden and the wellies hindered Heidi from running around.

She was glad she had, because on arriving at Jason and May's house May immediately dragged Heidi outside. 'I've got a trampoline,' she declared and Rose heard the little girl ask, 'Heidi, why are you wearing Wellington boots?'

'I was wondering the same thing,' Jason said as he showed Rose into the kitchen.

'I've no idea. Her fashion choices are a mystery to me. I'm sure there must be some logical explanation, but I have no idea what it is.'

'Is that a...?' He tapped his head.

'A swimming cap? Yes, it is. I've no idea about that, either. Or the scarf.'

'I do like the fairy wings, though,' Jason said, and they both burst out laughing.

This might be easier than she'd anticipated, Rose thought, as he switched the kettle on. She perched on the stool at the breakfast bar and watched him getting some mugs out of the cupboard and pop a tea bag in each. He was quite a bit taller than her, broad shouldered and slim hipped. Not too brawny but not too skinny either. Just how she liked a man. Not that she liked this one – well, she did, but only in the sense that she could admire a decent looking guy without wanting to jump into bed with him.

A blush whooshed up her face. Dear god, did she just think that? She had a sudden image of crisp white sheets and a dark-haired head on her pillow.

Mortified, she pushed it away. This wasn't the time or the place to be having fantasies.

There was an awkward silence and she wondered what to say to fill it. The most logical thing to talk about would be the stables. It was one of the things she and Jason had in common, but it would be fraught with pitfalls if his reaction to May entering the gymkhana was any indication.

'What do you do?' she asked, her brain gratefully latching onto the subject of work. 'For a living, I mean.'

He poured boiling water into the mugs, added some milk and gave them a quick stir before handing one of them to her. 'I work in renewable energies,' he said. 'Behind a desk mostly. What about you?'

'I'm an administrator, so I work behind a desk, too. I'm part-time though, so I only work during school hours.'

'Do you like your job?'

'I do, actually. I work in the care home out on Albany Road. Do you enjoy yours?'

'Yes, I do. I feel as though I'm doing my bit for the planet.' He got a pot out of a cupboard. 'I'm making chilli with rice, if that's okay with you?'

'With hidden vegetables?'

He laughed. 'How did you guess? Shredded carrots are my speciality. May will eat them if they're covered in chilli sauce. She picks out the red kidney beans, though. It's a very mild chilli,' he warned. 'May isn't too keen on spicy.'

Rose wondered if that was strictly true. May seemed to have had no trouble eating the spicy chicken that she prepared last week. The little girl's tastes might very well be changing and Jason might be slow to catch on. It had happened with her and Heidi. In fact, that was the only thing Rose could be sure of with Heidi, that things were in a constant state of change. What might be her daughter's favourite one day, would be looked upon with scorn and derision the next. Rose had learnt to play things by ear and go with the flow.

They drank their tea, then Jason began preparing their meal.

'Is there anything I can do?' she offered.

'Thank you, but no. I've got it all sorted.'

She glanced around the kitchen, wondering whether his ex-wife had had any hand in its decoration. It looked quite functional, but then again it was a kitchen. She hadn't seen the living room and she wondered if there were any throws and cushions. What was it with men and their general dislike of cushions?

Why on earth was she thinking about soft furnishings when she had Jason Halligan standing in front of her, his hips moving slightly as he stirred some mince in a pan.

Those hips were quite delectable. As were his shoulders and his broad back. He was wearing a tee shirt, and she could see the muscles flex in his upper arm and a smattering of hairs on his forearms. He had nice hands, too. Wait, *what?* What on earth was she doing? Anyone would think she fancied him.

Okay, to be honest she did, a bit. But she must stop this. He was the father of her daughter's friend and that's all there was to it. She really needed to go out on another date; it might stop her fantasising about Jason. Although, if her last couple of dates were anything to go by, she might be fantasising about him even more after she'd been on another disastrous one.

Hunting around for a safe topic to talk about, Rose found she was struggling. He didn't want to talk about the stables, and they'd already touched on both their home lives. When he came round to hers last week they had talked about school and teachers. They didn't have much more in common, as far as she could tell.

'When you aren't working or looking after May, what do you do with your time?' she asked, eventually.

'The usual – I read, I do housework, I catch up on my sleep.'

'Your life sounds about as much fun as mine,' Rose joked, then bit her lip. 'Sorry, I didn't mean it to come out like that.'

'No, you're right; what with working all week and looking after May, by the time the weekend comes I'm bushed.' Then it was his turn to bite his lip as he turned to her. 'Sorry, that was a bit insensitive of me considering I do get the weekends to myself and you probably don't.'

'Not much,' she agreed. 'Ben lives too far away to see Heidi very often, but that's okay, I cope. My mother is as good as gold, and she will look after Heidi if I ask.'

There was a clatter at the door, and two small heads peered into the kitchen.

'When's tea ready, Daddy?' May asked.

'About fifteen minutes. Why don't you wash your hands, and you can show Heidi your bedroom. I'll give you a shout as soon as the food is on the table.'

Rose watched them go, May holding Heidi's hand and tugging her through the kitchen. 'She's a credit to you,' she said. 'She's absolutely adorable.'

'She's an absolute madam,' Jason said. 'Look what she did to me last—' He stopped abruptly, and his eyes skittered away from hers.

Rose laughed. 'Don't worry, I know what you were going to say, and that's fine. I'd already guessed that May had railroaded you into inviting us around for a meal.'

'I'm sorry, it wasn't like that.'

'What *was* it like?' Rose wasn't being awkward, she genuinely wanted to know. 'Was it because of the gymkhana?'

'Yes, partly.'

'What was the other part?' Rose felt was holding something back, and she hoped he wasn't going to say he had a girlfriend.

He wiped his hands on a cloth and turned to face her, leaning against the worktop. 'I didn't want it to come across as anything it wasn't,' he said. 'Please don't take that the wrong way.'

'How am I supposed to take it?' Rose was bemused. It wasn't as though they'd been flirting or she'd been coming on to him, so where he'd got this notion from she had no idea.

'It's just I've got to be careful around May,' he said.

'Are you talking about dating? Because if you are, I don't think this is a date.'

Jason frowned and looked at his feet. 'I'm sorry, I'm not expressing myself very well, am I?'

'No, you're not, but I know what you mean. Since Heidi's father and I split, I haven't dated much, and I wouldn't want to introduce another man into Heidi's life until I was absolutely sure it was serious. So far, that hasn't happened yet. There's no need to worry on that score; I'll treat you the same as I treat any other parent of Heidi's friends. Just because you're a man and I'm a woman, doesn't mean our children can't enjoy each other's company.'

There, it was out in the open. It looked like he'd been having similar thoughts as she, but now neither of them needed to worry. All that mattered was that the children were happily playing together, and she and Jason could have a friendly conversation, without either of them worrying that the other thought it meant more than it did.

Strangely, though, it wasn't relief coursing through her, but disappointment. Oh well, it was better this way. The last thing she wanted was to date the father of Heidi's new best friend, and then for her and Jason to fall out for some reason. It would just make things very awkward and very difficult.

This was for the best, wasn't it?

Jason wasn't sure he'd handled the conversation very well. In fact, he wasn't quite sure exactly what he'd said. And neither could he read Rose's reaction. He had the feeling he'd just told her he wasn't interested in her. He wasn't interested in any woman, but something inside him said he was fibbing to himself. He *was* interested in Rose. She was pretty and fun, quite sparky, but in a nice way, not in the way Pamela had been towards the end of their marriage when they seriously hadn't liked one another at all.

But whether he was interested in Rose or not, made absolutely no difference. He wasn't in the market for a girlfriend and he was pretty sure she didn't like him in that way. Which made him feel a bit of a prat, considering what he'd just said to her. She'd made it clear that all she wanted from him was friendship because of their daughters, and for no other reason. On the odd occasion when he picked May up from the school gates (that was normally Pamela's job, then she'd drop May off at his house as she was on the way to work) he'd noticed Rose was always surrounded by other mums, quite happily laughing and chatting in a group. He wasn't kidding himself that she was only interested in being mates because she didn't have anyone else. She appeared to have loads of friends.

May also had plenty of friends in school, and he was well aware Pamela occasionally had those friends around to play, and May sometimes went to theirs. But during the week, when he had May in the evening and overnight, he never encouraged her to go anywhere or to have anyone back to his house. Heidi Walker was the first child, apart from May, to walk through his front door, and Rose Walker was the first woman who wasn't related to him.

He knew he was being selfish in wanting to keep May all to himself, but it wasn't doing her any good. He was aware enough to wonder if some of his antipathy to his daughter having riding lessons was because it impinged on his precious time with her, and not solely because of the hazards. He was also aware enough to know that this precious time would soon be gone. Before he knew it, his daughter would be a teenager and he'd be lucky if he got a grunted hello out of her.

Of course, not all teenagers were like that, and he didn't have any experience of them, but from what his brother, who had two teenage boys, had told him, he was fully expecting it.

He turned his attention to rinsing the rice in boiling water, but as he did so he felt a totally unexpected and unaccustomed pang of loneliness. When he came to think of it, it was quite sad that the only real friend he had was Rose Walker, whom he hardly knew at all and who was only friends with him because of their daughters.

So it was in the spirit of friendship that he found himself asking, 'Do you fancy going out for a meal sometime? Just the two of us?'

And he was pretty sure that Rose, after her initial blink of surprise and slightly shocked expression, had said she would love to because she was only being friendly.

So why was his heart thudding at the thought of being on his own with her, without the children?

CHAPTER FIVE

'I feel like a kid truanting from school,' Jason said, and Rose laughed as they stepped inside the pub.

She knew exactly what he meant because she felt the same way herself. It was so rare for her to go out at all, and when she did it was normally with Heidi in tow, or going somewhere where Heidi wanted to go.

'Who's looking after May? Is it your ex-wife?' Rose asked.

'Pamela? Yes, she always has her on the weekend. How about you? Who's babysitting Heidi?'

'My mum. Heidi is sleeping at her house tonight.' Rose wished she hadn't said that. It sounded as though she was telling him the way was open for him to come back to hers for some after-dinner fun.

No doubt it *would* be fun, but it so wasn't going to happen, and she didn't want to give him the impression it would. He wasn't interested in her in that way, despite him asking her out to dinner, (she had the feeling he was lonely) but even if he *was* interested, there was no way she was jumping into bed with him on the first date.

But this wasn't a date, so that was irrelevant. This was just two friends having dinner, wasn't it? And she didn't have any option other than to treat it as though it was, although she did feel a little awkward being out with him. That was mainly because she fancied the pants off him, especially considering he looked delectable in a pair of jeans and a shirt which had the top two buttons undone. He was the epitome of smart-casual, whereas she felt slightly overdressed in a playsuit which she'd bought last year to go on holidays and hadn't worn since, so she thought it was about time it had an airing. She'd felt quite smart and sexy in it whilst standing in front of her bedroom mirror, but now that she was sitting opposite him in a little gastro-pub in the middle of nowhere, she actually felt rather immature wearing it. It was the sort of thing much younger women wore, not mothers in their mid-thirties.

'Have you been here before?' she asked and soon they were discussing food choices, their likes and dislikes, and the places where they had eaten out in the past. Then they moved onto box sets and films, before talking about music. And in between they chatted about the girls, and school, their jobs, and their families, until Rose felt she had got to know him considerably better. He was actually easy to talk to and he seemed genuinely interested in her, unlike some of the other dates she'd been on in the dim and distant past where her companions had only wanted to talk about themselves; which, according to some of her single friends, was quite normal.

Jason, on the other hand, seemed to take a genuine interest, asking her questions and listening to her answers. Once or twice she wondered whether it was a diversionary tactic to avoid having to talk about himself, but whenever she asked him a question he seemed more than happy to reply.

Rose popped to the loo after dessert and before coffee, and while she was reapplying her lip gloss, she quickly checked her phone. Heidi had sent her a goodnight text and had followed it up by saying,

Hope you're having a lovely time. Grandma says she hopes you're behaving yourself.

At least, that's what Rose thought it said, as she tried to decipher Heidi's spelling.

Rose sighed. 'Thanks, Grandma,' she muttered under her breath, knowing Heidi would probably ask her what Grandma had meant by that comment.

For one brief moment, as she slipped back into her seat and caught Jason's eye, she wished she wasn't going to behave herself – but that was silly. Anyway, she wasn't going to have any choice, more's the pity.

Hang on a second, she was back to thinking about him like that again, and it simply wouldn't do. But how could she help it when she was sitting across the table from one of the best looking men she'd seen in a long time, and one who seemed to have eyes only for her?

This just wouldn't do, Jason was thinking to himself as he watched Rose walk across the restaurant and re-join him at the table. She looked gorgeous in the all-in-one thing she was wearing; he wasn't sure what it was, but it suited her. She looked lively and full of fun, and young and vibrant, and he could see other men's eyes following her progress across the room and the swift envious glances of the women as she passed.

She was very attractive, and as she picked up her coffee and pursed her lips to take a sip, a thought flashed into his mind – what would it be like to kiss her?

Well now, he said to himself, back off fella. This wasn't a date, and he hadn't asked her out; this was just a couple of friends sharing a meal without the kids.

Oh, for Pete's sake, who was he kidding? He knew when he'd asked her that it hadn't been out of friendship, no matter what he'd said to himself at the time. He'd wanted to spend some time with her alone without the girls.

And if she hadn't been so adamant that she just wanted to be friends, he would have considered this a date.

He hastily looked away, not wanting her to see how attracted he was to her. She didn't need to know; it would do neither of them any good. But when she licked a little bit of froth from her upper lip, his eyes focused on her mouth and he couldn't seem to drag his gaze away.

'What?' she asked. 'Have I got a foam moustache?'

'No, you're good.' He swallowed convulsively, thinking she was more than good, she was gorgeous.

As he continued to look at her, he saw the faint blush on her cheeks and his heart constricted. What on earth was she doing to him?

It must be because he hadn't been out with a member of the opposite sex since the last time he and Pamela had gone out for a meal, he told himself. The novelty was clearly going to his head. Anyone would think he didn't know how to behave around an attractive woman, but he felt gauche and awkward compared to her confident and easy manner.

Before he could say or do anything further to embarrass himself, he signalled to the waiter for the bill.

He saw Rose reach for her purse, and said, 'Let me get this. I asked you out.'

'Okay, but only if you let me pay for the next meal.' Her eyes widened as she realised what she'd said, and he wondered whether she was regretting coming out with him. 'I mean, if there is a next time,' she stuttered. 'If you'd like there to be. I'd like to have another meal out with you, if you would. Oh, dear.'

He stared at her. 'Can I ask you something? Have you ever been riding?'

Rose stared back at him, then she eventually said, 'Pardon?'

Damn it – did she think he had been about to suggest going out again? Twit, of course that's what she was anticipating, considering they'd only just been talking about it. And then he went and asked a ridiculous question like that.

'Riding, have you ever been?' he repeated, feeling a right plonker.

'Um, yes, I used to ride quite a bit when I was younger.'

'Why did you stop?'

'Boys, pubs, too expensive...' She laughed self-consciously.

'Did you ever fall off?'

'Of course I fell off. Everyone who rides falls off at some point.'

'Were you ever scared?'

'No. Never. Excited and exhilarated, but never scared.'

'Did it hurt?'

'Falling off?' She shrugged. 'Sometimes; it depends. Once I fell off because I forgot to do the girth up and the whole saddle slipped. I landed on my bum. The only thing I hurt that time was my pride. The ridiculous thing was the horse hadn't even taken a step. I broke my leg once, though. That hurt a lot.'

Jason felt a shard of ice jab him in the stomach. The thought of May being injured made his blood run cold. 'How did it happen?'

She gazed at him steadily, for far longer than the question warranted. 'I fell down the stairs at home.'

Jason's mouth dropped open and he closed it again hurriedly. 'It wasn't anything to do with horses?'

'No. I know you want to minimise any kind of risk to May, all parents want to do that, but there's even risk in your own home. I was injured more in my house than I ever was when I was out riding.'

'I can see what you're trying to do,' he said.

'I'm not trying to do anything. I'm just pointing out that bubble-wrapping kids doesn't work. May has found something she loves doing – for now. Like I did, she might very well grow out of it. In fact, she probably will. And yes, riding can be dangerous. But so can gymnastics, skiing, ice hockey, rugby…' She stopped.

Jason got her point. He'd played rugby himself in the past, and if May had been a boy he probably would have actively encouraged his son to play. But maybe not at six years old.

'Those horses are so big compared to her,' he said.

'Yes, but what she's doing at the moment is as safe as riding gets. Tango is a gentle old soul, and I realise May won't be riding him forever and that she'll probably progress to a larger pony soon, but Petra is very careful to make sure the pony matches the rider.' She paused, tilting her head to one side, her gaze intense. 'Why don't we go for a lesson?'

'What kind of lesson?'

'A riding lesson.'

'Are you serious?'

'Totally. We can have a private one, just me and you in the arena, and you can see for yourself what it's like.'

Jason wasn't sure about that. But he had been challenged, and he wasn't the sort of guy to back down from a challenge. 'You're on. When?'

'Before the gymkhana,' Rose said, 'and then you can make a final decision.'

'I've made a final decision.'

'Have you?'

He nodded, but for some reason he didn't think they were talking about gymkhanas anymore.

Rose couldn't believe Jason had agreed to a riding lesson. She felt like fist pumping the air but guessed it wouldn't be a good idea. She was under no illusion that he still might not agree to May taking part in the gymkhana, but at least she had done her best. She could tell that the little girl was absolutely desperate to take part, but Rose was conscious she might be interfering a little.

At least his suggestion had deflected Jason from her assumption that they would be going for another meal. Saying *I'll pay next time*, was just a figure of speech. If she'd been with one of her friends and had said the same thing, she would have thought nothing of it, but she wasn't with one of her friends, was she – she was out with Jason and she couldn't help it if she felt like she was on a date.

His mind was clearly on the upcoming riding lesson (she reminded herself to book it with Petra tomorrow) and he was asking what he should wear.

'What about a helmet?' he asked. 'Pamela bought May's. I don't own one.'

'Petra has got loads of spares,' Rose said. 'I'll have to borrow one of hers, too. And I don't have any jodhpurs either, before you ask. I'll just wear tracksuit bottoms; something stretchy is best, although jeans will do at a push. Make sure they're an old pair, though. But whatever you do, don't wear trainers. You need something with a heel and I'm not talking about a four-inch stiletto.' She glanced across at him to see that he was smiling.

'Why do I need a heel?'

Rose said, 'The last thing you want is for your whole foot to slip through a stirrup. A small heel, say half an inch, will prevent that from happening. If you've got an old pair of work boots, they would be ideal.'

'We're really doing this, aren't we?'

'You can back out if you want,' Rose said, 'but I'm still going to go anyway. It's years since I've been on a horse, and I don't know why I didn't think of riding again sooner.' Then she giggled. 'Oh, yes, I do; it's too darned expensive! Every now and again is doable, but once a week not so much.'

'When were you thinking of going?'

'I'll see when Petra can fit us in.'

'We could leave it a few weeks,' Jason suggested.

'Scaredy cat,' she teased.

'I'm not!'

'I think you are.'

'Okay, maybe I am, but have you seen the size of the beast Petra Kelly rides? Then there's the other one, Midnight I think his name is, the one Faith rides, or is it Charity…or perhaps it *is* Faith – one of the twins, anyway.'

'Don't worry, Petra will put you on an old plodder. And me too, I expect. There's no way she'd put you on something lively the very first time you got in the saddle.'

'Do you think there'll be one big enough to bear my weight?'

They pulled up in front of Rose's cottage but Jason made no move to switch the engine off, although he did twist around in his seat slightly to gaze at her.

Rose made a show of looking him up and down and tutting. 'I don't know,' she said. 'I'm not sure if there's a horse big enough for you,' and then she laughed when his mouth dropped open.

'Cheeky madam!' Jason exclaimed, also chuckling.

'I'll give you a ring tomorrow, shall I, when I know?'

'Okay, I'm looking forward to it.'

'Liar.'

His laugh was soft and did a funny thing to her insides. She shivered.

Jason made no move to kiss her, and as she got out of the car she was ever so slightly disappointed. She hadn't been kissed in a very long time, and she wondered what it would feel like to kiss Jason. She could smell his aftershave, and it was intoxicating.

Rose shut the car door, leaving him and his tantalising scent trapped inside.

He wound the window down and she ducked slightly to look at him.

'I enjoyed myself this evening,' he said.

'I did, too.' She took a breath. 'I meant it when I said I'll pick up the tab next time. If you want to go out with me again, that is.'

'Don't you want to see how rubbish I am on the back of a horse first? You might not want to be seen out with me.'

'I think I will,' she said. There wasn't so much of a hint of flirting in her voice, it was more like a promise.

They gazed at each other for a moment longer, something unspoken passing between them. Then Rose straightened up and began walking to her front door. She hesitated when she reached it and saw he was waiting for her to go inside. With a small wave and a sense of unfinished business, Rose unlocked the door and turned back to watch him drive away.

She hoped Petra would be able to fit them in for a riding lesson tomorrow, because she really wanted to see him again. And soon!

CHAPTER SIX

Jason hadn't expected the riding lesson to be quite so soon. He had no idea why, but for some reason he assumed Petra wouldn't have a slot free for at least a couple of weeks and certainly not until the gymkhana was over. How wrong could one be?

When Rose rang him this morning, he had still been in bed. Admittedly it was only just eight-thirty and he'd been awake for ages lying in bed and thinking, but he was nevertheless surprised to hear from her. When she'd told him their lesson was on for four o'clock that afternoon, he was even more surprised.

He was also slightly panicked. He barely had time to get his head around the notion that he was going riding, and there he was – about to go riding!

In a fit of nervous energy, he leapt out of bed and padded downstairs. He should make himself some breakfast, but his tummy was doing funny things, so he opted simply for coffee.

What was even more disconcerting, was that he didn't think the butterflies were entirely due to the riding lesson itself. He had a perturbing feeling it was because he'd be seeing Rose again.

He liked her a lot. Last night had been great fun and he'd seriously enjoyed spending time in her company. That he was also physically attracted to her was an added bonus.

But it also raised a warning flag – he was starting to get feelings for her, ones he wasn't sure he wanted. Since he'd split from Pamela, it had just been him and May, there had been no one else. Was he prepared for that to change?

Jason gave himself a mental shake. He was jumping the gun here, imagining all kinds, when they hadn't been out on a proper date yet. The meal last night was just food out with a friend. Today was just a riding lesson. Neither events could be described as a date.

Nevertheless, he spent rather longer than normal shaving, and he sprayed on his best aftershave rather than the everyday one he normally wore. He tried to choose his clothes with care but that was rather difficult considering the instructions had been to wear old stuff and work boots. It was only after he'd spent the greatest part of the morning faffing about with his appearance, that he realised what he was doing.

Gah, this was getting silly. He was behaving like a sixteen-year-old on his first date, when he was twenty years older than that and this wasn't a date at all. What the hell was he playing at? But even as he tried to distract himself by doing the laundry (crumbs, his life was so exciting) he still couldn't help thinking about Rose, wondering what she was doing now, and wondering if she was as nervous as he was.

And if she *was* nervous, was it because she would be getting on a horse for the first time in ages, or was it because she'd be seeing him?

Rose felt a little apprehensive, and she wasn't sure whether it was because she was going riding again, or whether it was because she was seeing Jason. A bit of both, she suspected. Then she tried to imagine it was her and Heidi going for a ride, and she realised she didn't feel quite as excited. Dammit, that meant the cause of her being so unsettled was Jason himself.

She shouldn't have suggested seeing him again. And she certainly shouldn't have suggested going riding. But she'd been thinking about May and her obvious disappointment at not been able to enter the gymkhana, and it had just slipped out.

It had nothing to do with wanting to see him on the back of a horse. Or see him again at all, for that matter.

Drat – she had to pull herself together. It wouldn't do to have these feelings for him, especially since he didn't appear to feel the same way about her. But then there was the look they'd shared, the long lingering one where she'd felt sure she'd seen something in his eyes which made her think she might be more than just a friend.

They'd agreed to meet at the stables, and Rose was the first to arrive. She saw two horses tied up outside the barn, then Petra came into view.

'Never thought you'd get that one on the back of a horse,' Petra said, jerking her head out over the rolling fields beyond the stables.

Rose turned to look and saw Jason's car trundling up Muddypuddle Lane. 'Neither did I,' she admitted.

'He must like you,' Petra said gruffly.

'Oh, I don't think so, it's not like that.'

'What *is* it like then, hmm?'

'Jason is just a friend.'

Petra gave her a scathing look. 'If that's what you want to believe, you carry on. But I've seen the way he looks at you, and if a friend looked at me like that I'd be bloody worried.'

Rose froze. If Petra had also sensed there was something between her and Jason, then maybe Rose's inkling about the look they'd shared last night hadn't been too far off the mark. But before she could explore the thought any further his car was pulling into the car park and he was getting out, and she caught her breath. Oh my god, he looked gorgeous. Suddenly she became aware of Petra studying her.

'Looks like you've got the hots for him, too,' Petra said, and Rose shot her an incredulous look.

'I haven't—' she began, then stopped abruptly, and Petra snorted in satisfaction.

'What goes on between you is your business,' Petra said, 'but my Uncle Amos gave me a piece of advice not so long ago. What he told me was, don't leave it too late. Think about it.' Then she turned away and began seeing to the horses and lengthening the stirrups, leaving Rose to mull over what she meant.

'Crumbs!' Jason exclaimed when he was finally in the saddle and looking at the ground. 'It's a long way down.' It made him quite nervous.

'Only if you fall off,' Petra pointed out dryly, and Rose sniggered.

Jason gave the pair of them a sour look.

'It's all right for you,' he said to Rose. 'You've been on one of these things before.'

He didn't even bother saying anything to Petra.

'Right, now you're safely in the saddle, I'm going to show you what to do with your legs, how to sit and how to hold the reins,' Petra told him. 'Rose, I can tell you've ridden before, so I want you to walk around the arena to let me assess your seat.'

Jason didn't like to say anything, but from where he was sitting Rose's seat looked just fine. He looked away when he noticed Petra scrutinising him and he felt a spot of warmth creep into his face. His daughter's riding instructor had just caught him ogling the behind of the mother of one of May's friends. Wonderful. Simply wonderful.

After a brief instruction from Petra, Jason's horse was told to walk on, and he nearly unbalanced when it stepped forward and he was forced to grab the pommel in a desperate attempt not to fall over backwards. To his surprise though, once he got into the rhythm of the gentle sway of the horse's movement, he found it was quite soothing. Gradually, throughout the course of the lesson, Petra had him turning left and right with total ease, and he was amazed at his control over the animal. He had a hint of how May must feel, so small, yet able to control something so large, just with her legs and her hands.

However, trotting was a completely different experience, and one he wasn't sure he was comfortable with. Especially the first few times, when he just slapped up and down on the saddle; he didn't think his undercarriage would ever be the same again.

But with Petra's patient instruction, it didn't take him long to get into the swing of things, and by the end of the lesson he had managed a rising trot, much to his surprise and satisfaction.

However, when he dismounted (far less elegantly than Rose) he had to grab onto the saddle to keep himself upright. His legs felt like quivering jellies, and he was certain he was walking like John Wayne. Jason thankfully unbuckled his helmet and handed it to Petra, who took both horses' reins and led the animals out of the arena.

'What did you think?' Rose asked.

'I enjoyed it,' he said, hearing the surprise in his voice. 'I think you might need to give me a minute though. I don't think I can put one foot in front of the other at the moment.'

Rose giggled. 'What you need is a hot bath, but I must warn you, you'll probably feel worse in the morning. Riding takes a bit of getting used to because you're using muscles you probably haven't used much in the past.'

Jason put his hands on the small of his back and leant first to one side and then the other. 'You can say that again,' he declared. 'I've never been so tense in all my life.' Then he sobered. 'I now know what May sees in it. It was quite exhilarating, and I didn't even manage anything faster than a trot.'

'If you never go riding again, at least you can say you've done it once,' Rose said. 'Did you feel safe up there?'

'Not at first, I didn't, but Petra is very good, isn't she? And so was Beauty. Although I felt she was only humouring me whenever I gave her an instruction. I think she knew what was expected of her.'

'She probably did,' Rose said. 'Petra's horses and ponies are very well trained, and she chooses them carefully for their temperament.'

'So you're telling me that I've got nothing to worry about when it comes to May going riding?'

'No, I'm not saying any such thing. You know as well as I that riding can be a dangerous sport, but then so can many others. Riding in an arena like this is probably as safe as it gets.'

'I should let her enter the gymkhana, shouldn't I?'

'It's up to you. You're her father, you're the one who has to make the decision.'

'But you're letting Heidi enter?'

'You know I am. Horses are the only thing Heidi has ever been interested in. I can't bring myself to not let her ride. It would be something akin to turning down her dimmer switch. Besides, I don't think she'd ever forgive me.'

'I don't think May is quite as committed.'

'She probably isn't, but she is getting a great deal of enjoyment out of it. As I said, it's your decision.'

Jason thought for a moment. 'You're right, it is. I think I *will* let her enter.'

Rose beamed. 'May will be absolutely thrilled.'

He stared at her, her face flushed, her hair slightly wild from wearing the hat, her eyes sparkling, and he knew he wanted to kiss her.

What the hell, he'd already agreed to two reckless things in less than twenty-four hours, he might as well make it three. So he took one small step towards her, bent his head, and kissed her.

For Rose the rest of the world completely disappeared when Jason's lips touched hers. For a split second she was totally taken aback, but the feel of his mouth, the scent of him, the way his arms slipped around her waist pulling her close, drove everything else from her mind until she was completely immersed in him.

She had no idea how long it was before he gently moved away, although his arms still encircled her, and she was filled with regret that the moment had to end.

Trembling slightly, she gazed up at him, those deep brown eyes drawing her in until nothing else, and no one else, existed.

'I've been wanting to do that for a while,' he admitted, his voice soft, his breath warm on her cheek.

'Me, too,' she told him, knowing deep inside how true it was. Stuff this friendship business; she didn't want just his friendship. It would be nice, but she wanted an awful lot more from him, and she sincerely hoped she was going to get it.

They grinned at each other, their noses almost touching, and she was about to go in for another kiss when there was a loud cough from behind.

They leapt apart and for a second Rose was mortified, until her happiness threatened to bubble up and explode.

'Sorry to interrupt your meeting,' Petra said, looking anywhere but at the pair of them. 'I was going to lock up for the day; I've got no more lessons you see, and…' She trailed off, clearly embarrassed.

'We were just about to leave,' Jason said, as Rose tried hard to stifle her giggles.

She felt like a schoolgirl being caught necking behind the bike sheds by the headmistress.

But as she stepped past Petra, the woman caught her eye and smiled.

'I told you he fancied the pants off you,' Petra whispered. 'Glad to see you took my advice.'

It was only when she was outside, Rose realised it wasn't her who had made the first move, it had been Jason, and she wondered what advice, if any, Petra might have given *him*.

It looked like he hadn't wanted to leave it too long, either, and the fact he was prepared to take a chance made her heart sing with joy.

'Where do we go from here?' Rose asked, later that afternoon. Heidi was still at her grandma's and Jason had invited her in for a coffee before she went to pick her daughter up. Rose hoped it didn't sound odd her asking such a forthright question, but she wanted them both to be clear on what was happening between them.

'The beach?'

'What? Now?' The evenings might be long drawn-out affairs, but she had to collect Heidi in an hour or so.

'I was thinking one day after school next week.'

Rose was dubious. Picklewick wasn't anywhere near the coast. It would take them a couple of hours to get there, and with school the next morning…

Her doubt must have shown on her face, because Jason uttered a chuckle

. 'I'm going to bring the beach *here*,' he said.

His statement didn't help soothe her misgivings. 'I'm sorry, I thought you said…?'

'I did.' He rose from his seat at the kitchen table and put his mug down. 'Come here.'

Rose got up and followed him into the garden.

'See that spot there?' he said.

'The one with nothing growing in it?' The garden sloped away from the house, and the lower third had been levelled and was empty of everything but soil.

'That's the one. I've recently cleared it because I was thinking of turning it into the seaside.'

'You've lost me.' Rose sighed with disappointment: he'd seemed so normal, too.

'May loves the beach – the sand, the sea, the little beach huts you get… I'm planning on giving her a taste of that in the garden. I've got some sand and pebbles being delivered tomorrow, along with some old railway sleepers. It'll take a few days for the guys I've hired to complete it, but once it's finished what do you say to helping May and me christen it? Heidi could put that swimming cap of hers to good use.'

'You're serious, aren't you?'

Jason shrugged. 'I've thought about this a lot. May has been helping me plan it, and she's chosen the pool and the summer house. I put my foot down at the donkey she wanted me to buy her, and the Punch and Judy booth she tried to persuade me to get. She also wanted a swimming pool with a wave machine, but we settled on one of those inflatable ones instead.'

'You *are* serious.' Rose was in awe. The theme of her own garden could only be described as neglected dead-swing turf. And the turf bit was debatable.

There was something she and Heidi had that Jason and May didn't though, and after she'd fetched Heidi from her mum's she had a good root around in the attic until she found what she was searching for.

'Heidi? How do you fancy playing with papier mache?'

Jason was delighted with the way his garden was looking. It had been hard graft on his part and there were some finishing touches still left to do, but he'd booked a sneaky day off work and he'd managed to get most of it done.

Rose had offered to fetch May from school and bring her home, and May had been in a state of high excitement since the second she'd woken up, and she'd fretted that the beach hut hadn't been painted, and there wasn't any water in the pool yet, and a hundred and one other things. Thankfully, he hadn't let on he was taking a day off, otherwise he'd have had a devil of a job to get her to school this morning.

He had just enough time to have a quick shower and spruce himself up before Rose arrived with the children, but he couldn't help pausing for a moment to admire his handiwork. The pool was full and even though it wasn't particularly deep, he knew May would have hours of fun in it. He'd created a beach, and he was especially pleased with the pebbles and driftwood to the one side, with a boardwalk leading to both the pool and the beach hut. He'd painted the hut in pink, powder blue and cream, and he'd even had time to hang some bunting and fairy lights on the outside. Everything had been softened by the addition of the grasses he'd planted in any bare areas, and off to one side sat a table and a barbeque.

He'd fire it up shortly, but first he needed that shower he'd promised himself. To his surprise he was just as excited to see Rose again as he was to see May's expression, and it disconcerted him a little. Not since Pamela had a woman affected him this way, and he hoped he wasn't setting himself up for being hurt. He hadn't known how to respond when Rose had asked him where they went from here, which was why he'd blurted out the beach thing. He'd made it sound far more exotic and wonderful than he'd originally planned on it being (he'd had a paddling pool and a sandpit in mind, with the addition of a tonne of pebbles) but it had grown somewhat in the telling and he'd been forced to up his game.

He was pleased he had though, because the previously unloved bottom half of the garden now looked stunning. He'd been debating what to do with it for a while; May had consistently and repeatedly tried to persuade him it was big enough to keep a pony on, but he hoped she'd like this almost as much.

The doorbell ringing alerted him to Rose's arrival a short while later, and May barrelled in, flinging her little backpack and school jumper at him, as she raced through the hall and into the kitchen, her pigtails flying as she yelled for Heidi to follow her.

Hastily Jason stood to the side to let Heidi dash past, leaving him and Rose alone for a second.

'Hi, you,' she said softly.

'Hi, yourself.' She looked delightful in a pair of shorts and a strappy top, her hair gathered up in a ponytail, and her skin glowing.

Uncertainly, he took a step towards her at exactly the same time she moved towards him, and before he knew what was happening he was kissing her hungrily, his arms holding her tight against his chest, his senses awash with the scent of her hair and the taste of her lips.

Girlish squeals of delight rapidly brought him back to himself, and they broke apart a second before the children stampeded back into the house.

'I love it! Thank you, Daddy. Rose, come and see. We're going to build sandcastles, and swim, and have hotdogs and burgers.' May was bouncing up and down.

Jason took the opportunity to leap in when his daughter paused for breath. 'You need to change out of your school uniform first, May.' He glanced at Rose, whose glow had intensified since he'd kissed her.

Rose held up a bag. 'I've brought a change of clothes for Heidi,' she said, passing the bag to her daughter, who thundered up the stairs after May. 'And we've got a present for May in the car, if you can help me with it.'

Wondering what it could be, he followed her outside and his eyes widened when he saw what was in the boot of her car. 'Is that what I think it is?'

'It's not strictly for Punch and Judy, and if you turn it around, you'll see that the other side is a kind of a market stall, but it's been in the attic for over a year, and I thought May could have it.'

Jason carefully slid the wooden puppet theatre out of the car and stood it up. 'It's even got stripey fabric around the bottom, like a real Punch and Judy booth. Did you do that?'

Rose nodded. 'And we made these.' She handed him a bag. Inside were Punch and Judy puppets and a crocodile cuddly toy. 'Heidi and I made the heads out of papier mache. They're a bit rustic, but I hope May will like them.'

Jason was speechless. 'I can't believe you've gone to all this trouble. Thank you so much.'

'May can keep the stand; Heidi hardly played with it. She was more interested in the model stable and horses she was given the same year. It's a pity for the stand not to be used, and if it gives May some pleasure...'

'Are you sure?' When she said the word "pleasure" his stomach fluttered and a thrill shot through him. He badly wanted to kiss her again. That this kind, wonderful, sexy woman wanted to kiss him back was electrifying.

Aware he needed to take things slowly (they both did), he gave her a hug and a peck on the cheek. He had to be mindful that there were other hearts and emotions involved than just his and Rose's, and no matter how much he was falling for her, or how invested he was becoming in having a relationship with her, he couldn't forge ahead without thinking things through. But later, when he saw her sitting on the sand playing with the girls as he took charge of the food, he couldn't help but think how right the scene looked. May had taken to her already, and the children got on extremely well together.

He just hoped he wasn't making a mistake by opening his heart to her. If she broke it, that would be awful enough; but if his daughter's was broken along the way, he didn't think he'd be able to live with himself.

CHAPTER SEVEN

What a wonderful day, Rose thought, as she drove along Muddypuddle Lane with a bouncing Heidi in the passenger seat. It was a glorious summer morning, the sky was an azure blue with not a cloud in it, and the day was already promising to be a warm one.

She got out of the car, Heidi bounding out ahead of her, the child hardly able to contain her excitement, and took a deep breath of fresh country air. There was a vague smell of horses, but the overriding scent was that of the meadow on the other side of the car park which was filled to bursting with wildflowers. A chicken scratched in the grass near the fence, making soft clucking noises to itself, followed closely by the cockerel, Frederick, who was strutting about as if he owned the place which, to be fair to him, he probably did.

The cat, Tiddles, was basking in the sun surrounded by her kittens, who now had their eyes open and were able to toddle about. Their mewling cries carried on the breeze, and she could also hear the sound of a goat bleating.

The gymkhana was being held outside and, as she'd drove up the lane, Rose had noticed various cones and poles all neatly arranged in one of the fields. When she walked across the yard, several horses' heads poked over the tops of their stalls and she could see they were already tacked up. She wasn't quite the first to arrive; she was close to it though, because she'd had immense difficulty in containing Heidi's excitement and the child had been itching to get to the stables.

But within a few minutes of them arriving the compound had filled up and the squeals of excited children rang in the air.

The horses and ponies could also sense the excitement and they tossed their heads and whickered to each other in their eagerness to be released from their stables. Petra had managed to transport the stage seating from the arena, and it had been erected in the field, along with a barrier to contain the spectators. There was also a refreshment van in the form of an old caravan which someone had converted, and she could smell the enticing aroma of coffee, doughnuts and frying onions, and she knew what she was having for lunch.

Automatically her eyes scanned the adults, looking for Jason.

It was less than a week since they had shared their first kiss, but they'd achieved several more since then, most noticeably the evening of the beach barbeque as she'd come to refer to it in her head, although finding opportunities for sneaky kisses hadn't been easy with the two girls around. Neither child had commented on it, but Rose was sure Heidi suspected something.

Rose didn't care. She'd made a promise after she and Ben had split not to be one of those women who introduced her child to lots of uncles, and this was the first time she had entertained the idea of any man being a part of her and her daughter's life. It was early days yet, very early, but she felt good about this.

Every time she thought of Jason her heart fluttered and her tummy turned over.

There he was! She waved, rather too enthusiastically she realised, as a couple of the mums from school saw and nudged each other.

What the hell? She wasn't ashamed of the way she felt, and apart from being discreet around Heidi, she didn't see why she should hide it. They were both single and both consenting adults. It was nobody else's business, and if some of the other parents wanted to gossip, then so be it.

Jason made his way over and, to her delight and in full view of everyone, he gave her a quick kiss on the lips. It looked like he wasn't ashamed either.

'Fancy a coffee?' she asked. 'It should be starting soon, so if you find a seat I'll go and fetch us a couple of drinks.'

As she walked over to the refreshment van, she couldn't help thinking that to anyone who didn't know them they appeared to be a couple, and a feeling of contentment stole over her. She was happier than she had been in ages, and it was such a lovely uplifting feeling that she smiled widely as her heart filled with elation.

Jason leapt to his feet, cheering wildly and shouting, 'Go, May, go!' as his little girl re-enacted the scene from the other Thursday when she'd ridden her pony between a series of upright poles with little flags on the top. She was racing against another child, and she was going to win. Whoever won this heat automatically went through to the next one, and he was practically hopping up and down at the thought of her winning.

'Yay, well done, May!' he yelled, then turned to Rose. 'Did you see that, did you? She won, she's through to the next round.'

'Well done, May,' Rose called, then turned to Jason. 'You must be so proud of her.'

Jason nodded vigorously. 'I am, I most certainly am. She rode that pony like a pro.' He beamed, and saw that Rose was just as pleased for May as she would have been if it had been Heidi. The knowledge made his heart sing.

He watched his daughter as she walked the pony over to the holding-area and dismounted. Two more children were to go next, and the winner of that round would compete with May in the semi-finals. He gave his daughter a wave and her face wreathed in smiles.

'I won, Daddy,' she mouthed at him, and he gave her a double thumbs up.

He wouldn't have believed watching a few children dash up and down a field on ponies would be so much fun, but he was having the time of his life. Not only were some of the antics hilarious, like the egg and spoon race for instance (which he had no idea could be done on horseback) but there was also the more serious and competitive show jumping.

His heart had been in his mouth, as he watched the older children and some adults competing in the show jumping arena, and he'd almost lifted out of his seat every time a horse took a jump. He could feel Rose shaking with laughter next to him, but he didn't care.

The most exciting part for him, though, was when May was competing. It was all a bit of fun, but he was taking it almost as seriously as if she was in The Horse of the Year Show.

He sat back down and drew in a breath. 'That was tense,' he said, and Rose shook her head at him.

'You really are competitive, aren't you?' she joked. 'And to think you weren't going to let her enter.'

Jason was about to agree with her, when a shout went up. His eyes automatically searched for May. She was exactly where he'd seen her a few moments ago, in the holding pen awaiting her next go.

Relieved to see she was okay, he looked for the source of the commotion. One of the girls, he couldn't remember her name but he thought it might be Jane's daughter, was practising leaping into the saddle and jumping off again in preparation for one of the other games, and it looked like she'd missed and had slid off to land on the ground in a squealing heap.

The girl's pony, alarmed at all the commotion, suddenly swung his back end around, catching May and knocking her off her feet.

Tango danced out of her way, straight into the other animal's hindquarters. The creature bucked, his back hooves lashing out, and caught Tango a glancing blow. Tango, to Jason's horror, shied in response.

One of his hooves came down on May as he landed, and her scream of pain filled the air.

Jason was out of his seat in a heartbeat. Oh my god, oh my god, was the only thing he could think. Please don't let her be hurt. *Please!*

'I'm coming, May, I'm coming!' he called, running headlong, oblivious to anyone or anything in his way.

He reached her at the same time as Petra, and he had dropped to his knees by her side and was cradling her head before Petra had a chance to check her over. May was crying and holding her arm.

'Are you okay, May? Speak to me! Where does it hurt?' he yelled.

Petra pushed him away. 'Let me see, and can someone please grab that horse?'

Reluctantly he moved to the side. Please let her be okay, he prayed, his heart pounding, his mouth dry. But when Petra touched May's arm and his daughter shrieked, he knew without being told that it was probably broken.

He looked up when he heard Rose say, 'Should I call an ambulance?' and anger surged through him. He knew he shouldn't have allowed May to take part, he *knew* it; yet he'd allowed himself to be swayed by a riding lesson and a pretty face.

But Rose's expression when he said frostily, 'No, thank you, I'll take her to the hospital myself in my car,' was something he knew he wouldn't forget in a hurry.

'Will May be all right, do you think?' Rose asked worriedly, and Petra shrugged.

'Of course she will. It didn't look too bad a break. In fact, her arm mightn't be broken at all, but it's better to be safe than sorry.'

Rose had just watched Jason carefully pick his daughter up and stalk off, the crowd parting like the Dead Sea to allow him through. She'd wanted to run after him, knowing he needed all the help he could get, but from the expression on his face the last person Jason wanted to see right now was her.

Why, oh why, did it have to happen to May? Just when Rose thought he was coming to accept his daughter's love of riding, the little girl had an accident. It could have happened to any of the children. But it had to be her. Poor little thing; she'd sounded as though she was in a great deal of pain, and Rose prayed she'd be okay.

Alongside his concern about his daughter, was the way Jason had looked at Rose when he'd rejected her suggestion of ringing for an ambulance – he'd looked as though he hated her.

And Rose had a horrible suspicion he blamed her for May's accident.

CHAPTER EIGHT

'May has had an accident.' Jason's voice was clipped as he spoke to his ex-wife on the phone. 'She's most likely broken her arm – it's not serious, but it could have been. And guess how she did it?' He didn't give Pamela a chance to respond. '*Riding*,' he spat.

'I'll be there soon as I can,' Pamela said, and he heard the worry in her voice, but that didn't make it any better. His daughter was hurt, and as far as he was concerned it was Pamela's fault for letting her go riding in the first place.

It was also Rose's, for being so blasé about it, and encouraging him to allow May to take part in the gymkhana.

But most of all, it was his own fault. Jason blamed himself for his daughter being injured. He should have put his foot down. He knew how dangerous horse riding could be, but he'd let it go. Actually, he'd done more than let it go; by allowing her to take part in the gymkhana, he'd actively encouraged it.

How could he have been so reckless?

Now he was in A & E with his little girl, who had most probably broken her arm.

He just hoped the break wasn't too bad and that it could be easily fixed with a cast, because if it was anything more serious he didn't know how he'd ever live with himself.

'How is May, Mum?' Heidi asked when the gymkhana ended, clutching her rosette.

Rose took it from her absently and popped it into her bag. Heidi had won an event but Rose wasn't sure which one, because she'd been too busy worrying about May and Jason. The distance in his face lingered in her mind, chilling her heart and freezing her thoughts.

'I don't know, sweetie. He hasn't replied to my text.' Or her phone call. She hoped it was because he had no signal, or no charge, and not because May was being rushed into surgery, or something equally awful.

Of course, he could be ignoring her, and deep down she didn't blame him. If she hadn't taken him riding, if she hadn't encouraged him to let May enter the gymkhana, his daughter wouldn't be in this position.

'I'm worried about her,' Heidi said. 'Do you think she'll be all right?'

'I'm sure she will be. People break arms all the time. She'll probably have to have a cast on for about six weeks, and have to do some exercises afterwards to help strengthen it, but in no time at all she'll be back to normal.' Unless she had to have surgery and metal pins and—

Rose pushed the thought away. She needed to think positively. May was going to be all right, she had to be.

'Rose?' a voice called, and Rose turned to see Petra hurrying towards her. 'Any news?'

'Nothing yet.' Rose pulled a face. 'I'm sure Jason will be in touch when he knows something.'

'It's not your fault,' Petra said astutely. 'You can't go blaming yourself. Accidents happen.'

'Yes, but if I hadn't—'

'He's a grown man. He made the decision to let May have riding lessons.'

'But that's the thing – I think he was railroaded into it by his ex-wife.' Rose glanced around, wondering how much she should say in front of Heidi, but Heidi had moved off a little and was chatting to one of the other girls. 'Jason didn't want May to have riding lessons in the first place, and he seriously hadn't wanted her to enter the gymkhana. I persuaded him to let her.'

'He could still have said no,' Petra pointed out, 'but I see where you're coming from. You can't blame yourself. No one is to blame. As I said, accidents happen. She could just have easily have fallen off the slide in the park, or tripped over the pavement.' Petra's eyes bored into her as Rose wrung her hands.

'Do you think he has a point?' she asked. 'Should I pay more attention to Heidi's safety?'

Petra shrugged. 'It's up to you, of course. Life isn't without risk, and forbidding Heidi from riding will negate some of that risk, but how unhappy will it make her?'

'Mum! You can't!'

Rose looked around to see Heidi's stricken face, and her heart dropped to her boots. Great, her daughter had overheard the conversation and now she'd have to deal with the fallout.

'You can't stop me riding. You wouldn't be so mean!' Heidi's eyes filled with tears. 'It's the only thing I've ever wanted to do, and you're going to stop me doing it. I hate you!' She whirled around and ran off.

Rose wasn't sure what she should do. The thought of Heidi with a broken arm made her blood go cold. The thought of Heidi with a worse injury absolutely terrified her. Yet riding and being around horses was the only thing her daughter was passionate about. Could she honestly take that away from her? And if she did, would her daughter ever forgive her?

She guessed she'd already lost the man she loved – was she prepared to lose her daughter too?

* * *

The ringing of his doorbell jerked Jason out of his thoughts, and he glanced at the time. It was gone eight o'clock, and he guessed it was probably Pamela. He'd expected her hours ago.

'Where the hell have you been?' he demanded.

'I was away for the weekend; you knew that. How is she?'

He opened the door wider to let his ex-wife in. 'She's in bed, asleep. I would appreciate it if you didn't wake her.'

Pamela glared at him. 'I wouldn't dream of waking her. But she's my daughter too, and I want to see for myself that she's okay. Where's the break?'

Jason rubbed a hand over his face. 'It's not a break, it's a sprain. No thanks to you.'

'What the hell is that supposed to mean?'

He kept his voice as low as Pamela's, so as not to wake May, but he felt like shouting.

'Do you know how dangerous riding is?' he growled.

Pamela sighed and rolled her eyes. 'Not this again.'

'Don't you care that she could have been killed?'

'Aren't you exaggerating? I rang Petra at the stables, so I know what happened. I'm going upstairs to see my daughter. When I come back down, we'll continue this conversation.'

Jason shook his head in despair. Pamela hadn't been there; she hadn't seen their daughter knocked off her feet and trampled on. She hadn't had to sit for hours in the hospital, waiting for a crying May to be examined by the doctor. She hadn't had to wait anxiously for the results of the X-ray, and she hadn't had to soothe May off to sleep.

She hadn't had to witness their daughter's pain.

There was something else he was glad Pamela hadn't witnessed and that was May begging to be allowed to go riding again. Just before his daughter had drifted off to sleep, she'd pleaded with him with fresh tears in her eyes. If Pamela had seen that, she would definitely have promised to allow May to continue riding.

That was never going to happen. Jason would do everything and anything to prevent his daughter from being hurt again.

Rose sighed and picked up the phone. She put it down, only to pick it up once more. She was desperate to hear how May was, but she'd sent Jason a couple of texts and had called him twice, and he hadn't responded. Why would she think this time would be any different?

She had to try though; she couldn't just let it lie. For one thing, she was genuinely concerned, and for another she just wanted to tell him how sorry she was that it had happened.

She was listening to the ringtone with half an ear, not expecting him to answer, so she nearly jumped out of her skin when he said, 'Hello?'

'Hi, Jason, it's…um…Rose.' He'd taken her by surprise, and she was stammering.

'I know.' He sounded very distant.

'How is May?'

'It's a bad sprain, not a break.'

Rose could almost hear him say *no thanks to you*. 'Thank goodness for that,' she said. 'How is she in herself?'

'Exhausted. In pain. What you'd expect really.'

'I'm just glad it wasn't anything worse,' Rose said.

'So am I.'

Rose thought she might as well take the bull by the horns. 'I don't expect she'll be going riding again,' she said.

'That's correct. The next time she'll go anywhere near a horse it will be over my dead body.'

Rose heard someone mutter in the background, 'If that's what it takes,' and she froze. The voice belonged to a woman, and she took an educated guess that it was Pamela.

'Well, good, I'm glad she's okay. Tell her Heidi was asking after her, won't you?' Rose said.

'Will do,' he replied, then ended the call without saying goodbye and Rose was left listening to a dead line.

That told her, she thought. At least she wouldn't have to see him again if May wasn't going riding. Heidi would be a little upset, but she'd get over it, she had plenty of other friends and she could still see May in school.

Rose, on the other hand, was incredibly unhappy to think she'd never see Jason again, apart from around the village occasionally. In the short time they'd been seeing each other, she'd managed to fall in love with him.

More fool her. She should have known better. Jason Halligan had too much baggage, and she wasn't talking about his daughter. May was an absolute delight, and both Rose and Heidi enjoyed spending time with her, but she didn't think Jason was emotionally equipped to be in another relationship just yet, especially since childcare was split so equally between him and his ex-wife. Prior to this, Rose had had reservations about how any relationship with him could work, but when she'd taken things a step further and imagined the four of them living together (more than a step further, more like a giant leap) she couldn't imagine how things would work when May would be at her mum's for half the week, and Heidi would be there all the time.

It wouldn't work, would it? Resentment would bound to develop, despite their best efforts.

So, in a way, this was probably for the best, although she wished May hadn't been hurt in the process. May, however, would recover soon enough.

Rose's recovery, on the other hand, would take a little longer, because she had fallen head over heels for Jason Halligan and her heart was sorely broken.

'Was that Petra?' Pamela asked as Jason ended the call.

'No. I've already texted her to say May is okay.'

Pamela folded her arms across her chest and leant against the door frame. 'If it wasn't Petra, I'm guessing it was Rose,' she said. 'May has told me all about her and Heidi.'

'I don't know what she's said, but there isn't anything to tell.' Jason knew he was getting defensive, but he didn't want to discuss Rose with Pamela right now. Or ever. He and Rose were over. But even as he thought it, there was an awful ache in his heart, and his stomach twisted.

He grunted in annoyance. Yes, he felt something for her, but he'd get over it. Time and distance always worked. He just had to make himself believe that.

'I hope you didn't wake May,' Jason said.

'No, I didn't, she was still awake.'

'She was fast asleep fifteen minutes ago,' he pointed out.

'Actually, she wasn't. She was just pretending to be because she wanted you to leave her alone.'

'Why on earth would she want me to do that?'

'Because she doesn't like you very much at the moment.'

'She told you that, did she?'

'As a matter of fact, she did.'

'I'm her father, I don't care if she doesn't like me.' Even as he said it, he knew it wasn't true. He wanted his daughter to like him, but sometimes he understood that it simply wasn't possible when you were a parent and you had to make tough choices and difficult decisions. 'My job is to keep her safe, not to be her friend,' he said.

Pamela narrowed her eyes at him. Their split might have been amicable but that didn't mean to say they hadn't had their moments of carping and scoring points off each other. He'd thought they'd moved past all that, but this riding business brought it all to the forefront again.

'Are you accusing me of not keeping our daughter safe?' Pamela's eyes narrowed and she folded her arms across her chest.

'You're not.'

'She's sprained her arm, Jason. She could have done something similar ice skating or in the playground at school, or climbing a tree.'

'For one thing, she doesn't go ice skating and for another, she doesn't climb trees.'

Pamela tilted her head to one side. 'She went ice skating for a friend's birthday, and yes she does climb trees. Admittedly, they're not very tall ones, but we have trees in our garden, and I've seen her on the lower branches a few times.'

'Why didn't you stop her?' he demanded.

'Because she's a child, and children have to explore. Didn't you climb trees when you were a child?'

Jason huffed. 'That was different.'

'How so? Because you're a boy?'

'That's not it at all. It's because I'm older now and I can see the dangers.'

'That's the problem,' Pamela said. 'You're not prepared to take a chance on anything.'

'If you're talking about our daughter's safety then, no, I'm not.'

'Actually, I was talking about you.'

Jason blinked. 'Excuse me?'

'May has told me all about Rose.'

'May doesn't know what she's talking about.' Suddenly Jason was aware of a little face peeping around the door behind her mum. 'May, what's up?'

'I *do* know what I'm talking about, Daddy,' May said with a sob. Her tear-stained face was stricken.

'Oh, poppet, have you been crying? Does your arm hurt?' Jason closed the distance between them, but May backed away, shaking her head.

Jason glared at his ex-wife. 'Is this anything to do with you?' he asked. 'What did you say to her?'

'Nothing controversial, and nothing you wouldn't approve of. Don't bring me into this. This is between you and May. And Rose.'

'Leave Rose out of it,' he commanded.

'Try telling that to our daughter. She thinks Rose is very much in it.'

'Please don't shout at Mummy,' May cried. 'Mummy stop being mean to Daddy. I hate it. I hate it, hate it, hate it!'

Pamela knelt down so she was at eye level with May, and held out her arms. May rushed into them, and buried her face in her Mum's neck, sobbing loudly.

Jason was mortified. 'I'm sorry, poppet. I didn't mean to shout at Mummy. It's just I worry about you; you know I do.'

May sniffed loudly and looked at him from under her lashes, wiping the back of her hand across her nose.

Jason automatically reached into his pocket for a tissue and handed it to her.

'I worry about you too, Daddy,' May said.

Jason's eyes widened. 'Why are you worried about *me*?'

'Because you don't have anyone. Mummy has Craig, but you only have me. Rose only has Heidi.'

Jason gazed at Pamela. 'Is she matchmaking?' he asked, incredulously.

Pamela smiled up at him. 'I think she might be.'

'Well, I never. May, I like Rose a lot. But not in the way that Mummy likes Craig.'

'Mummy loves Craig, and you love Rose.'

'I think I'd know if I love Rose,' Jason pointed out.

'You look at her the way Craig looks at Mummy. Craig loves Mummy, so that means you must love Rose.'

Jason didn't know what to say to that, other than to protest.

But before he could gather his wits together and come up with something that sounded plausible, May carried on.

'You're cross with Rose because I got hurt riding, but it wasn't Rose's fault.'

'I still don't like the idea of you being on the back of a pony,' he said as gently as he could. It was breaking his heart to see her so upset about not being able to go riding anymore, but he sincerely believed it was for the best.

'I won't ask to go again,' May vowed, 'if you make friends with Mummy and Rose.'

Pamela shook her head. 'If you've fallen out with Rose over the gymkhana, then you're an idiot. You've got a chance to make a new life with someone, why mess it up?'

He was about to tell her it was because Rose had talked him into allowing May to enter the gymkhana, when he realised how pathetic it sounded. He'd made the decision; *him*, not Rose. He'd already accepted he was to blame, so why was he trying to deflect it onto someone else? Especially someone he loved. There, he'd admitted it.

His ex-wife stood, then bent down and lifted May into her arms. 'Okay,' she said. 'You win. If you're so worried about May going riding, I won't take her. Let's not fall out over this. May, I'm sorry sweetie, but your dad and I think it's for the best if you don't go again.'

May's chin wobbled, and her eyes filled with fresh tears.

'Before I go, I want to say one thing,' Pamela continued. 'Rose sounds lovely. Isn't it about time you took a chance on love?'

'I'll think about it,' was all he was prepared to say.

He might have fallen in love with Rose, but it was just too complicated, particularly since he wasn't prepared to let May go riding and Heidi would continue to, which was going to cause conflict between the two girls going forward. It simply wouldn't be fair on May.

Not just that, May only lived with him for half the week. Heidi lived with Rose all the time. Would May feel resentment because Heidi saw more of Jason than she did? It was certainly something to be considered.

With an increasingly heavy heart, Jason made his decision. He and May were fine as they were, and he intended for them to stay that way. The least disruption to May the better because she'd already had enough of that in her short life.

But when Pamela came downstairs after tucking May back in and assuring him that this time their daughter really was asleep, she said something that turned his whole world upside down yet again.

'Jason, we need to talk,' she began.

CHAPTER NINE

Even though Rose hadn't expected Jason and May to be at the stables the following Thursday, she was disappointed nevertheless. Apart from that one phone call on Saturday evening, she hadn't tried to contact him again. There didn't seem any point. Both of them were aware the relationship had ended – not that it had been much of a relationship to begin with. They'd hardly declared their undying love for each other, and she'd been pretty certain Jason wouldn't allow May to go riding again now that she'd been knocked over, even if the little girl hadn't sprained her wrist.

Rose sat in her customary seat in the viewing area, and watched Petra put her clients through their paces. Every lesson began this way, with a reminder of how to control the ponies, legwork, footwork, posture and so on. Rose tuned out a little, so she was rather surprised when someone slipped into the seat next to her.

It was Jane. 'Petra told me May suffered a sprain, not a break. I bet her father was relieved.' The woman was at it again, fishing for information.

'He was. I think we all were, including Petra.'

'Do you think she'll come riding next week?' Jane asked. 'Fleur wants to say how sorry she is. She feels partly responsible because it was her pony that made Tango shy.'

'I doubt it,' Rose said.

'Won't it all be better by then?'

'I doubt it,' Rose repeated.

'It must have been some serious sprain,' Jane said, and Rose realised she'd been talking about May's arm, not about her and Jason's relationship.

'It's not that. Jason doesn't like May riding. He thinks it's too dangerous, so I doubt we'll be seeing them again.'

'That's a pity. Will you pass a message on to him? Will you tell him Fleur is sorry, and that we all miss May?'

Rose said she would, knowing she was telling a fib even as she said it. She wouldn't be seeing Jason anytime soon. Maybe she'd spot him at the school gates now and again, but that would be it. She didn't even know whether she'd go and talk to him. These past five days had been awful, and it was going to take her some considerable time to get over him. Perhaps it was for the best that May wouldn't be coming to the stables any more. That way Rose could avoid Jason and give her broken heart time to heal.

Blinking back unexpected tears, Rose sent Jane a vague smile, then concentrated on Heidi. It was just the two of them once more. They'd survived it once, they would survive it again.

Jason helped May out of the car, even though her wrist was more or less healed and she didn't need any help from him whatsoever. His daughter was beaming, full of suppressed excitement, but all Jason could think about was whether he was doing the right thing.

'Hello, May, how's your wrist? Petra told me you'd sprained it.' Faith was smiling down at May. 'We didn't expect to see you this week,' she added. 'Are you here to ride? Or just to watch?'

'Ride, please,' May said. 'My wrist is all better.' She waved it in the air. 'See?'

Faith said, 'I'll go and fetch Tango for you. The lesson has already started – you've missed about half of it.'

Jason would have been happier if May had missed all of it. He'd still been uncertain whether to bring her or not, but she had been so terribly sad that he'd finally given in. He and his daughter had reached a compromise: May could continue to have riding lessons, but not enter any more gymkhanas.

May had agreed, but she had added a proviso of her own which had made Jason chuckle. She'd told him she would only go riding if he made friends with Rose again. He'd agreed willingly. Although their relationship had been of a short duration, he couldn't believe how much he missed her. And Pamela was right, he did need to start taking some chances. He intended to start with Rose.

The seat next to Rose was empty, and Jason walked over to it and sat down.

She didn't even glance up and his heart sank. She was ignoring him, and he totally deserved it. He'd treated her shabbily, and he supposed the first thing he needed to do was to apologise.

He leant closer and said quietly, 'I'm sorry.'

Then he jumped back in his chair as Rose let out a small squeak.

She turned a shocked face towards him and hissed, 'I thought you were Jane.'

'Nope, I'm Jason.'

'I can see that now,' she said in a normal voice. Then a slow smile spread across her face. 'You came. I take it you've brought May?'

'Her wrist is better. It's not entirely back to normal, but my daughter can be a very persuasive little madam when she wants to be.' He inhaled deeply. 'I owe you an apology.'

Before he could say anything further, Rose jumped in with, 'I should be the one apologising to you. I shouldn't have talked you into letting May enter the gymkhana, and I certainly shouldn't have taken you riding.'

'May isn't your responsibility. She's mine. I didn't have to go riding; you didn't make me. And you didn't force me to allow May to go to the gymkhana. That was all down to me. Those were my decisions, not yours. Please don't blame yourself.'

'Yes, but if I hadn't—'

'I can't wrap her in cotton wool, I realise that now. I think I might have been a bit over-protective. May and I have come to an agreement – she can continue to have lessons indoors once a week, as long as she doesn't take part in anything like a gymkhana. At least, not until she's a little older.'

Rose nodded slowly. 'That sounds sensible.'

'There's another reason why I decided to let her continue with her lessons,' he said.

'Oh?'

'It wouldn't be fair to May if Heidi keeps having lessons when she can't.'

Rose's eyes widened as she realised what he meant.

Jason continued, 'If we keep seeing each other, and I hope we do, May is going to make my life a misery if she can't go riding and Heidi can. Although, I understand if you don't want to see me again,' he added hastily.

'Why wouldn't I want to see you again?' Rose's voice was soft and a smile played about her mouth.

He stared at her lips, wishing he could gather her up and kiss her soundly. 'Because of the way I acted and…' He hesitated. 'There is something else.' Jason paused, wondering whether what he was about to say was going to make any difference to their blossoming relationship. It would certainly put them on a more equal footing.

'Go on,' she urged a bit too loudly and earning herself a shush from Petra in the arena.

Jason explained, 'It's about Pamela. She was away last weekend when May had her accident. When I phoned her it took her hours to return home. She and Craig were in Inverness. He's been offered a new job and he wants her to go with him.'

'To Inverness?'

Jason nodded.

'Will she take May with her?' Rose asked.

'No, she doesn't think it's right to take May away from all her friends and her school, and they'll probably only be there a year. Pamela is leaving May with me.'

'How does May feel about it? Is she okay?'

Jason's heart swelled with love for the woman sitting next to him. Her first reaction had been concern for May, and not about their relationship. And he knew that whatever happened, Rose Walker would put his daughter's interests before her own.

'She's a little upset,' he said, 'but I think coming to the stables has helped. We'll visit Pamela in Scotland as often as we can, and I assured May her mum would fly back once a month to see her. I know it's not the same as seeing Pamela several days a week, but this is the arrangement we came up with.'

'It can't be easy for Pamela, either,' Rose commented, and Jason put a hand on hers.

'I doubt if it is, but she said something to me that struck a chord. She told me you have to take chances in life. And that's what she's doing. It's what I want to do, too, if you let me. I want to take a chance on you, on *us*, because after all, life doesn't stand still and one day the girls will be grown and flown, just like the swallows in the barn when they fly south for the winter, and then it will just be you and me. If you'll have me.'

He hesitated, his eyes boring into hers, trying to gauge whether this was what she wanted. But she deserved to know the truth, so that's what he told her.

'I'm in love with you, Rose,' he said, 'and I'm taking a chance you feel the same way about me.'

Rose's heart was so full she thought it might burst. There was only one way she could respond – he was being honest with her, and she had to be honest with him.

'I'm in love with you, too,' she told him, and watched the worried expression disappear from his face, to be replaced by a wide grin.

'You are? You've just made me the happiest man in the world!' Jason exclaimed, and threw his arms around her. Before she could draw breath, his lips were on hers and he was kissing her so soundly that for a moment she forgot the rest of the world existed.

She was brought back to the present by the sound of whooping, cheering, and the stamping of feet, and they pulled apart to discover that everyone in the arena was smiling at them and clapping.

Even Petra looked pleased for them, and when she saw that Rose had noticed her, she gave her a big thumbs up. The only people who didn't seem to be amused were the ones having the riding lessons. Most of the children looked a little grossed out, and Heidi was pulling faces at her mother.

Rose didn't care. Jason was right; life *was* about taking chances and making hay while the sun shone – and this summer it was shining very brightly indeed.

AUTUMN

CHAPTER ONE

Timothy crossed the road, stepped onto the pavement and took a deep breath. He felt so nervous that his stomach churned. Interviews weren't his strong point (he tended to get a bit tongue-tied and flustered) and he was dreading this one, more than any other. Possibly because he wanted the job so badly.

The email inviting him for the interview had instructed him to go to the staff entrance and press the buzzer, but when he located it around the side of the building, he paused for a moment, vainly trying to compose himself.

It was no use – he was more nervous than a turkey at Christmas. Deciding to simply get it over with, he held his thumb on the buzzer and tried not to hold his breath.

The door was answered by a lady in her fifties who smiled warmly at him.

'You must be Timothy. I'm Celia, one of the reception staff. Come through, they're waiting for you.'

Timothy gulped and followed her, yanking at his tie as though it were a hangman's noose around his neck, which if he was truthful, was exactly what it felt like.

'If you'd like to wait in here, Tina and Brandon will be with you shortly,' Celia said, showing him into a spacious office.

Timothy thanked her and headed for a seat, but changed his mind at the last moment. It wouldn't look good if he'd made himself at home; not only that, he also didn't want to be at a disadvantage by having to leap to his feet when they came in.

Thankfully, his wait was a short one. In less than a minute the door opened and the two partners (husband and wife team, he assumed from their joint surname) greeted him.

'I'm Tina…'

'And I'm Brandon.'

He shook hands with them both, expecting them to sit down behind the desk, but was surprised when Tina handed him a white coat.

'We thought we'd leave the formal bit until later. I know we're looking for a large animal vet, namely equine, but how do you feel about having a crack at what's in the waiting room?'

'Er, fine, yes, okay, I'd love to,' he stammered, hastily removing his suit jacket and shoving his arms through the sleeves of the overall.

'We've got a full waiting room by the looks of it,' Brandon said, and Timothy bit his lip.

Being a vet meant being put under pressure on a daily basis, but not this kind of pressure. He felt as though he was sitting his exams all over again. However, as soon as he stuck his head into the waiting room and saw the dogs, cats and other assorted creatures in pet carriers and cardboard boxes, he immediately snapped into professional mode.

'Who's first?' he asked his interviewers out of the corner of his mouth.

'Penny Shanklin. French Bulldog,' Tina replied. 'I'll be your nurse today if you need one,' she added.

Timothy called the dog's name and its owner brought the little black animal into the consulting room.

'What seems to be the problem today?' he asked, as the elderly gentleman scooped the dog up and popped her on the table.

'Are you the new vet?' the animal's owner asked.

'No, but I hope to be,' Timothy replied with a smile, holding his hand out for Penny to sniff. Her nose was cold and wet, and she snuffled his fingers. 'What can we do for you?'

'Booster,' Mr Shanklin said. 'And she needs her nails clipped.'

'I'm sure we can manage that,' Timothy said, picking up a small black paw and seeing that the claws were indeed rather on the long side.

In a little over ten minutes the dog had received her booster and had been given a manicure; she had also been weighed, and Timothy had checked her eyes, ears, and teeth, and had listened to her heart and lungs.

Penny was now hoovering up her reward of several dog treats for being such a good girl, and as soon as she'd left the consulting room Timothy was on to the next patient – a cat, this time, who had an unexplained cough – and then the next.

Five dogs, three cats, one rabbit, one hamster, a gecko, and an extremely large and hairy tarantula later, and the waiting room was finally empty.

'Fancy castrating a llama?' Brandon asked, just as Timothy assumed the hands-on part of the interview was done.

He considered his new suit trousers, new white shirt and polished loafers, and his heart sank. 'Great!' he said enthusiastically. 'What's the background?'

'Just kidding,' Brandon said. 'We've seen enough. Let's have a cup of tea first, then a quick chat. Do you like Penguins?'

'Only if someone holds their beaks while I examine them,' Timothy replied seriously, as he was invited to take a seat in the office. Although he liked all animals, birds weren't his favourite. He preferred bigger and more solid creatures, such as horses.

'Oh, ha, ha,' Brandon chuckled, and it was only when Celia brought in a tray of drinks and a packet of Penguins that Timothy realised the vet had been referring to the chocolate biscuits and not the birds. Thankfully, Brandon thought he'd cracked a joke, and Timothy wasn't about to set him straight. He took a sip of tea, feeling nervous once more.

'I see you're currently a locum,' Tina said, getting down to business. 'Is that why you applied to Picklewick Veterinary Practice?'

'Yes, I've been covering a maternity leave,' he explained.

'I take it you're willing to relocate. Would that be a problem?'

'Not at all. My brother lives in Picklewick, so I'll move in with him.' Not that he'd asked Harry yet, or had even told him he was applying for a job here.

'Would that be Harry Milton, by any chance?' Brandon asked. 'We did wonder when we saw the surname.'

'It would.'

'He's a good bloke.' Brandon nodded his approval.

Timothy agreed. His brother was one of the best; although how he'd react if Timothy actually landed this job was anyone's guess. The main reason for Harry moving out of the family home in Cheltenham and buying the farrier business in Picklewick had been to give Timothy his independence. Yet here Timothy was, planning on getting a job in the same village as his brother and expecting to move in with him.

A solid half-hour grilling later, and the interview was finally over. Timothy hoped he'd done enough to impress the partners, but all he could do now was wait.

Feeling slightly sick – he'd been too nervous to eat breakfast this morning – he left his car in the practice's car park and decided to grab a sandwich before he headed home. He supposed he should also drop in and see Harry before he left. He didn't want his brother to find out about his job application second hand. From what Harry had told him, the village wasn't very big and word might soon get around.

Picklewick had a main street with some quaint little shops such as a florist, a baker, a butcher, and a convenience store. There was a small church, a community centre, a care home, and a pub called the Black Horse. Timothy hoped it was a good sign, because horses were his specialty.

Deciding against paying the pub a visit this early in the day – after the morning he'd had he might be tempted to sink a pint or two and, as he had to drive home, he thought he'd better not – he came to a halt outside a cafe and peered inside. It looked nice enough so he pushed the door open and went in, feeling thankful his interview ordeal was over and praying Tina and Brandon wouldn't take too long to get back to him.

Charity Jones checked the time before deciding she could pop into Blake's cafe for a take-out sandwich and a coffee without being late for her shift. Falling asleep earlier hadn't been part of her plan for today, but she'd been up since the crack of dawn mucking out stables, so when she'd squished down on the sofa intending to read for half an hour she had ended up having a two-hour nap. She'd woken up groggy and disorientated, and had forgotten to make a sandwich for work.

The wonderful smell of fresh coffee hit her as soon as she stepped inside, and she fished her reusable cup out of her bag. A double shot of caffeine would hopefully wake her up enough to get through the following eight hours.

There was a bit of a queue, so she stood patiently in line and studied the selection of sandwiches and baguettes in the chiller. Should she go for tuna and mayo, or spicy chicken, she wondered.

Automatically, she texted her sister to see what she would plump for.

Faith's response was immediate. ***Ham***
Had ham yesterday.
Tuna. Everything okay this morning?

Charity thought back; this morning seemed such a long time ago. She shuffled forward a place as someone was served, and almost bumped into the guy in front. He turned to look at her and she mouthed 'Sorry' at him.

He smiled, a dimple appearing in each cheek, and she couldn't take her eyes off them. She hadn't seen him before, and wondered who he could be. Picklewick was a small village, where everyone knew everyone else, more or less. But it had its fair share of visitors to the area, so he was probably only passing through.

He was seriously good looking, about her age, with sandy blonde hair, and twinkly blue eyes. She looked away quickly when she realised she was staring at him, and glanced back down at her phone to reply to her sister.

Yeah, fine, Midnight was a pain
In what way?
He was being unruly, Charity messaged. *You need to ride him more*
Haven't got the time. I'll take him for a quick ride when I go to the stables later.

Charity let out a small sigh. It wasn't just time that was Faith's problem; it was a steadily declining interest. The sisters had ridden since they were small, and for the past ten years or so they'd been lucky enough to have their own horses. They kept them at the stables on Muddypuddle Lane in exchange for helping out with things like tacking up, taking classes, accompanying people on hacks, and doing many of the other things necessary to keep a riding school running smoothly. Petra, the stable's owner, was more than happy with the arrangement, as were Charity and Faith, but lately Faith was more interested in her boyfriend than her horse, Midnight.

A worm of worry worked itself into Charity's heart. She could sense change in the air, but she had no idea what she could do about it. It was only natural that Faith, the more outgoing of the sisters and the one who'd had loads of boyfriends and who relished going out and socialising, would one day meet the man of her dreams. Which subsequently meant she had less time for her horse, and presently she had even less inclination. Charity was relieved to know Faith was going to the stables later, because unfortunately she'd be at work, so she wouldn't be able to.

With another sigh she dropped her phone into her bag, then went to fish it out again when the ringtone sounded, before belatedly realising it wasn't *her* phone that was ringing. It belonged to the guy in front. That they both had the theme tune to *Black Beauty* as their ring tone made her smile.

He was next in the queue, and as they shuffled forward once more Charity began tapping her foot, wondering why this was taking so long. She needed to get going if she wasn't going to be late for work.

'*What?*' the guy in front cried, his phone to his ear, and Charity shot him a look. He was rather on the loud side, and for a second she wondered if he was one of those people who wanted the whole world to hear his conversation, before she realised he was genuinely shocked as his face broke into the widest smile she'd ever seen and his eyes lit up.

'Really? That's wonderful. Yes, yes of course. I've left my car in your car park, so I can be there in about ten minutes, if that's all right? Brilliant, just brilliant! Thank you ever so much. You won't regret it.'

He stared at his phone for a second, his face

shining. Then he turned around and made to leave, clearly not wanting to wait any longer in the queue. Charity was pleased he was going because it meant she was one step closer to getting her tuna baguette and coffee.

Suddenly she felt the guy grab her arms and swing her around, then he planted a smacker of a kiss on her cheek as he declared, 'I've got it, I've got the job! Woohoo!' He did a little dance, swinging her round again, and she couldn't help but smile at him even though she should have been appalled that a strange man would do such a thing.

'Congratulations,' she said.

'I can't believe it, I honestly can't believe it.' Then he must have realised he had hold of her, because he suddenly let her go and his face was a picture of contrition. But underneath she could tell he was still sparkling with excitement.

'Sorry,' he said. 'I didn't mean to...' The grin broke out again.

'It's fine,' she said, laughing at his obvious elation.

'I must dash, I've got to sign something or do something, or...I don't know.' He shrugged, his happiness so palpable that Charity couldn't help be pleased for him.

'Just out of curiosity,' she said, 'what job did you get?'

'I'm the new vet in Picklewick.'

Charity cocked her head to the side and studied him. That was interesting – she used Picklewick vets for her own horse, as did Petra. 'No doubt I'll see you around,' she said.

'I hope so.' He made a squeaking noise and hopped up and down on the spot. 'I can't believe I've got the job,' he cried again. 'I'm the practice's new equine vet. Did you hear that? *Me!* I'm going to be the equine vet for Picklewick Veterinary Centre. I can't believe it. Wow!'

Wow indeed, thought Charity. She couldn't believe it, either. Not only was this guy attractive and friendly, he also seemed to share her love of horses.

Abruptly Charity wasn't sure whether she actually did need a coffee to perk her up, because the perking had already been done.

CHAPTER TWO

Timothy dashed out of the cafe without waiting to be served, because he didn't want to waste one single second before returning to the practice. He couldn't believe they'd made the decision so quickly. It was barely an hour since he'd shaken their hands and slung his jacket in the car as he'd loosened his tie and removed it, relieved to feel a little more casual. Formal attire wasn't his thing. He was far happier in jeans and a tee shirt, and he hoped his discomfort in having to wear a suit hadn't shown.

He hadn't recognised the number when it came up on his phone, and he had been in total shock when he'd heard Tina's voice on the other end. His initial thought was that he'd forgotten something, but when she'd said he'd got the job, he had been so excited he'd grabbed the girl standing behind him in the queue and he'd kissed her.

It was inexcusable and he shouldn't have done it, but he'd been so damned happy and he'd wanted to share it with someone. Thankfully, she didn't seem to have been too upset, so hopefully he hadn't alienated her. She might well live in the village, or nearby, and the last thing he wanted to do was to start off on the wrong foot.

Obviously, she'd been taken aback at first, but then she'd smiled at him and for a few moments all thought of his new job was eclipsed by the most beautiful smile he'd ever seen.

However, he'd better concentrate now, because he had paperwork to complete and things to sort out – namely, his future.

It was another hour before he'd signed everything that needed to be signed and the various details had been hashed out, and he was free to go. Timothy now had a bullet to bite, and he suspected it would be a hard one; so it was with some considerable apprehension that he phoned his brother to give him the news. At least it was a fait accompli and not just a "by the way I've applied for a job in Picklewick and I thought I'd better tell you before someone else did" conversation which was what he'd originally been preparing for.

'Hi bro,' he began airily when Harry answered.

'Hello, Timothy, to what do we owe the pleasure—? Hang on a sec, Petra wants me.' Harry's voice became muffled and Timothy guessed he'd put a hand over the phone.

He could hear Harry replying to Petra, and while he waited he formulated what he was going to say to try to soften the blow.

It was hardly a blow, though. More of a shock. Hopefully a welcome one. Timothy wasn't proposing to invade Harry's space, just rent a bit of it for a while until he found somewhere to live. Although, it did seem rather daft to rent somewhere when there was a perfectly good room in his brother's cottage going spare.

'Sorry about that,' Harry said, coming back on the line.

'Are you at the stables?'

'Yes, why?'

'Just wondered.' Maybe it would be better to speak to Harry in person, with Petra there to diffuse the situation.

'Did you ring for a chat?' Harry asked. 'Because if so, can I call you back? Petra is having a problem with one of the horses.'

'Okay, no worries. I'll speak to you later,' Timothy said, and with that he got in his car and drove out of the village towards Muddypuddle Lane.

He'd visited the stables once before, back in the summer, curious to meet the woman who'd stolen his brother's heart. Before Picklewick, Timothy had begun to suspect Harry was a confirmed bachelor as he recalled Harry having had very few girlfriends, and it made him feel guilty to think Harry had sacrificed so much for him over the years, including his own chance of becoming a vet.

Harry had been in his second year of vet school when their parents had been killed. Timothy had just turned eleven. And for the past fourteen years, Harry had put his life on hold to parent Timothy. He'd given up his dreams and his youth. He'd tried to be both mother and father to a boy who'd had his world turned upside down and inside out, when he was barely more than a teenager himself. He'd fought to give Timothy as normal a life as possible, whilst putting his own on the backburner and struggling to keep a roof over their heads.

Now though, Harry had a thriving business after training to be a farrier, and had fallen in love with the prickly Petra, who wasn't half as cactus-like as she'd first appeared. It had been a love of horses which had drawn them together – that and Harry no longer having his little brother to hold him back.

Harry had told Timothy he'd moved out of the family home in order to give Timothy space and room to grow. He didn't need his older brother breathing down his neck, Harry had said. So as soon as Timothy had graduated and landed his first job, Harry had bought an established business shoeing horses and had moved to Picklewick, leaving Timothy to spread his wings.

Timothy, however, had done enough wing-spreading whilst he'd been in university. And he might still be young (although twenty-four, nearly twenty-five, wasn't *that* young) but he felt it was now time to settle down. A new job and a new place to live would enable him to do that. Their home in Cheltenham, the one left to them by their parents and which he and Harry owned jointly, held too many memories. Within its walls he still felt like a little boy, lost and grieving.

He had already been looking for another job because the one he currently had was only a locum position, and he had been open to the possibility of relocating to anywhere in the UK, when he'd seen the advert for an equine vet in the same village his brother lived in.

He told himself it was fate, and ignored the very real worry that Harry had escaped Timothy as soon as his conscience would allow.

As Timothy drove the short distance from the village to the stables on Muddypuddle Lane, he pushed the worry to the back of his mind and thought about handing in his notice, putting the house in the hands of a letting agent, and a hundred and one other things, instead.

He pulled into the car park and got out, scanning the empty yard as he did so, and wondered where Harry could be.

Amos, Petra's uncle and the chap who owned the stables, would probably be in the house, so that was where Timothy headed.

'Amos? Petra? It's Timothy,' he called as he walked across the yard, adding, 'Harry's brother,' in case anyone had forgotten.

'I know who you are, sonny,' Amos said, coming out of the tack room and wiping his hands on an old rag. He looked guilty and Timothy wondered what he'd been up to.

'They're down the bottom field,' Amos said. He glanced behind him nervously, then looked back at Timothy. 'Don't mention I was in there when you see Petra,' he said. 'She'll only tell me off, and what she don't know can't hurt her.'

'Why, what were you doing?'

'Best you don't know either, so you can't blab.'

Timothy tried not to smile. He should say something to Petra really, but he didn't want to cause any more waves than he was about to, and the elderly gent looked healthy enough. Harry had told him Amos suffered from angina and that Petra refused to let him do anything physical around the stables, so they employed a bloke called Nathan for the heavy work. Amos was relegated to doing the paperwork and the cooking, with the most energetic thing being to fork up the carrots in the veggie patch when they were ready for eating.

'I won't say anything,' he promised, earning himself a nod from Amos in return.

'It's lucky you showed up,' he said, and Timothy followed the direction of his gaze to see Harry and Petra walking up the field hand in hand. 'She'd have caught me, otherwise. Tell them I'm brewing a pot of tea if they're interested.'

Timothy strolled over to the fence at the edge of the stable block, rested his arms on it and stared out over the rolling countryside. The fields had lost their summer lushness and were turning pale gold, the colour triggered by the encroaching chill of the autumn air and the shortening of the days.

It was a beautiful spot: although it was just two miles from the village it felt as though the stables were in the middle of nowhere. The only habitation he could see were a few farms in the distance. The air was clean and fresh (if he ignored the aroma of horses) and the only sounds were the lowing of cows in a distant field and Petra's dog uttering the occasional bark as she nosed about in the undergrowth.

Harry and Petra were deep in conversation and Timothy was reluctant to make his presence known just yet, so they were almost in the yard before they noticed him. When Harry saw who it was, he did a comical double-take.

'What are you doing here?' he asked, releasing Petra's hand and pulling Timothy in for a hug. Petra patted him on the shoulder as she walked past, heading for the house.

'I've got some news,' Timothy said.

Harry stepped back. 'Oh?' He looked wary.

'I've got another job.'

'That's fantastic! Who with?'

Harry, Timothy realised, was assuming that Timothy would be working for one of the several veterinary practices in and around Cheltenham.

'Picklewick Veterinary Practice,' Timothy said.

'I'm sorry, I thought you said Picklewick.'

'I did.'

Harry froze. His expression was inscrutable and Timothy's already churning gut clenched. 'Why?' his brother asked eventually.

All the reasons Timothy had thought of when he debated what to say to Harry ran through his head and straight out again, until he was left with the only one that truly mattered. 'I miss you.'

'Aw, Tim…'

'I know, I know…I'm sorry.' He felt like crying. 'I'll tell them I've changed my mind. It's not too late, I haven't handed my notice in yet or—'

'Stop. Why would you do that?'

'Because you came here to get away from me and—'

'You silly sod!' Harry pulled him into another hug. 'I did *not* come here to get away from you,' he said indistinctly, his face buried in Timothy's hair.

'But I thought…'

'You thought wrong. I *told* you why.'

'I know what you said, but—'

'Do I ever say what I don't mean?' Harry leant back and grasped him by his upper arms.

'No?' Timothy felt as though he was a teenager again.

'Well, then. I moved to Picklewick so you didn't have me breathing down your neck.'

Timothy fell silent. It was true, that's what Harry had told him. 'You aren't mad at me?'

'Not at all. Now, tell me about this job of yours.' Harry slung an arm around his shoulder. 'And, more importantly, where are you going to live?'

'I thought I could move in with you for a while?'

'Now I really am mad at you. You do realise you'll be cramping my style?' his brother teased.

As Harry led him towards the house a weight lifted from Timothy's shoulders, and he buzzed with happiness. He simply knew he was going to love living in Picklewick.

***

'Is it cold outside?' Brian asked, when Charity wandered through the reception area heading towards the staff room to stow her bag and coat.

'It's fresh, but not too chilly. A typical autumn day,' she replied.

'I'd like to go for a walk.' The old man stared out of the window.

'Have you asked April?' April was the manager on duty today.

He shook his head.

'Would you like me to ask her for you?'

'If you wouldn't mind? I don't want to be any bother.' His expression was hopeful, with a hint of worry behind it.

Charity gave him a hug. 'It's not any bother. You must ask if you want something. We mightn't always be able to help, but if we don't know what you want we definitely *can't* help.'

'You're all so busy,' he pointed out.

'Busy trying to make everyone as happy as we can,' Charity said, smiling at him. 'And if going for a walk makes you happy...?'

'Can *you* take me?'

'I wish I could, but I have to be on reception. Tell you what, if it isn't possible for anyone to take you out today, I'll come in early tomorrow.'

'You're a good girl. Can we take my dog? He'd love a walk.'

Charity's heart went out to the old man. Brian's dog had been re-homed at the same time as Brian. The old man's family had suspected he'd been suffering from dementia for a while, and when he'd had a nasty fall and had to be hospitalised, their fears had been confirmed. Unable to look after himself any longer, he'd moved into the care home. Brian had been upset about his dog, but increasingly he forgot the little animal now had a new owner.

'I'll see what we can do,' she replied gently, not wanting to break his heart all over again by telling him he no longer had a dog. It was kinder this way, and by tomorrow he might well have remembered for himself.

'You're a good girl,' he repeated, and she felt tears prickle at the back of her eyes. Maybe she could ask Petra if she could borrow Queenie for a couple of hours? The spaniel loved people, and was soft-mouthed and gentle. Petra had brought her in before, and many of the residents enjoyed petting her. Thinking of Petra led Charity to think of the stables and the horses and ponies who lived there, and before she knew it she was thinking of Picklewick's newest vet.

Initially, she'd been shocked and rather perturbed at being accosted by a strange man, but he'd been so excited and so happy that she'd forgiven him immediately. No doubt she would see him around, and the knowledge had made her feel a little lightheaded.

Don't be silly, she told herself, as she settled in her chair behind the desk, her eyes running down the list of jobs she needed to do. He wouldn't be interested in her. A good-looking guy like him was bound to have a girlfriend. Charity had happened to be in the right place at the right time, that's all. If Brian had been standing behind him in the queue in the cafe, the guy would have done the same to him. Nevertheless, the attraction she'd felt refused to go away, and she wondered what his name was, where he lived and when she might see him again.

Cross with herself for wasting brain time on him, she tackled the first task on the list, and was soon on the phone confirming a delivery of supplies for the kitchen. Yet she still couldn't get him out of her head.

She tried telling herself he was far too exuberant for her taste, too confident and outgoing, more suited to Faith's personality than hers. Charity tended to go for shy, introverted men; not that she'd had many boyfriends, shy or otherwise, probably because both parties were too shy and introverted to ask the other person out. Besides, she didn't have a great deal of time for romance.

Storm, her horse, kept her busy, especially since Charity paid for the animal's board and lodge by helping out at the stables. What with that and working at the residential home, it was tantamount to having two jobs.

'How's that horse of yours?' Olive asked, shuffling slowly through reception on her way to the lounge. Olive used to ride, Charity had discovered, and now relived her days in the saddle through Charity's stories of going on hacks or helping out with the riding lessons.

Olive stopped for a chat, and soon Charity had the old lady in stitches when she told her how Princess, the goat, had eaten one of Harry's favourite socks, and Petra had been on poop watch to make sure it came out of the other end of the goat and didn't cause the creature internal discomfort.

'You ought to have seen Harry's face when Petra asked him if he wanted the sock back,' Charity chortled.

Petra had mellowed considerably since Harry had arrived on the scene, and although she still generally preferred horses to people, she was now far more light-hearted and easy-going.

Charity hoped she could find a man like Harry one day – solid, dependable, grounded, kind, and rather attractive, too. Petra was a lucky woman.

A stab of envy caught Charity unawares, and she blinked at the unaccustomed emotion. For some reason, she found herself wishing she had someone special in her life, and she wondered what had brought that on. Not even loved-up Faith had made her feel she was missing something, yet here she was dwelling on love and romance.

What had gotten into her?

Unbidden, the face of Picklewick's newest vet swam into her head...

CHAPTER THREE

'Is this the last of it?' Harry asked, dumping the box none too gently on the floor of the spare bedroom.

'There's one more.' Timothy had been unloading the car and putting the assorted bags and boxes in the living room, and Harry had been helping by taking them upstairs. The pair of them were standing in what was now Timothy's bedroom and staring at the mess.

'You forgot something,' Harry said, shaking his head.

'What?' Timothy was pretty sure he'd packed everything he needed.

'The kitchen sink.'

'Ha, ha, very funny. You'd better stick to shoeing horses, because your stand-up comedy sucks.'

'I'll fetch whatever is left in the car,' his brother said. 'You make a start on this lot.'

Easier said than done, Timothy thought, putting his hands on his hips and blowing out his cheeks. Maybe he had been a bit excessive?

When *was* he going to have a kick about with a football? He hadn't played footie in a park since he was about eighteen, so what made him think he was going to do so now? And he was never going to listen to his old collection of CDs, was he? He didn't even like that kind of music anymore and neither did he have anything to play them on. He'd been so focused on getting the house cleared of anything personal, valuable or sentimental in order for it to be rented out, that he'd blindly packed anything he didn't intend to leave.

'Blimmin' heck, I reckon this one *does* contain the kitchen sink,' Harry said, letting a rather large box slip to the floor with a thud.

Timothy stared at it. 'That's Mum and Dad's stuff.'

'Ah.' Harry fell silent, and Timothy recalled the two of them going through their parents' things, trying to decide what to keep and what should be given to the charity shop.

Timothy had cried at the time, but Harry had remained stalwart. It was only later, long after Timothy had gone to bed that he'd heard his brother sobbing.

'Do you want to keep it in here?' Harry asked after a while. 'Or should I put it in the attic?'

'Attic,' Timothy said.

'Righto.' Harry clapped his hands together and set to work.

'I feel like we're the brothers in *All Creatures Great and Small*,' Timothy said sometime later, when Harry had taken yet another box up to the attic, tutting as he did so. 'I'm Tristan and you're Siegfried.'

'I hope you're *not* like Tristan,' Harry said. 'He was an irresponsible so and so. And don't you go playing around. Picklewick is a small place, and the female population doesn't need you trying to get into its knickers every five minutes.'

'I'm not like that!' Timothy protested.

'How many girlfriends have you had?' Harry countered.

'I can't help it if women find me irresistible,' Timothy said, then ducked when Harry threw a trainer at him. 'Seriously, I won't embarrass you,' he added, putting the trainer in the bottom of the wardrobe and wondering what had happened to its twin. 'I'm not a student any more.'

'I know. I can't believe you're all grown up.'

'I can't believe you're so old,' Timothy teased.

Ah, here it is, he thought, as he dodged another flying missile in the form of his trainer's mate.

'It's Tina and Brandon I feel sorry for,' Harry said. 'They don't know what they've let themselves in for.' And Harry chuckled as the trainer flew back across the bedroom.

'Stop being so childish,' Harry said.

'You started it.'

'No, I didn't.'

'Yes, you did,' Timothy argued.

Oh, this was going to be so much fun, Timothy thought. Away from Cheltenham and the family home which was now in the hands of a letting agent, his brother seemed lighter-hearted, more carefree. And he didn't think it was solely down to Harry relocating – if that's what being in love did for a fella, Timothy wouldn't mind finding the woman of his dreams, either.

An image of the girl in the cafe popped into his mind and he wondered whether he'd meet her again. He thought it was quite likely, especially if she had a pet.

Now that he'd officially moved to Picklewick, it might be a good idea to start getting to know the area and its residents. He had a couple of days before he had to report for work, so maybe he could pay a visit to Petra's stables. Riding was a great way of getting about, and he'd see far more from the back of a horse than he would if he drove, and he could cover more ground than if he walked. Besides, he loved riding and he hadn't done enough of it lately.

'Do you think Petra would take me on a hack?' he asked.

'I'm sure she would. Give her a ring.'

'Couldn't you ask her for me?'

Harry narrowed his eyes. 'How old are you – ten? Ask her yourself. She doesn't bite.'

'I don't like to impose.'

'You aren't. You're family as far as she's concerned.' Harry flattened a box, then looked at him.

'Will you two get married, do you think?' Timothy asked.

'Possibly. I'd like to think so.' Harry was thoughtful. 'I've been on my own for so long, that being in a relationship is taking a bit of getting used to. Both for me and for Petra.'

'I'm sorry.'

'For what?' Harry's expression was perplexed.

'For holding you back. I should have gone to live with Aunty Emma and Uncle Colin.'

'Don't be daft. You didn't hold me back. When Mum and Dad died, I wanted to look after you. I still do.'

'I don't need looking after,' Timothy objected, rolling his eyes, and once more the mood lightened.

He'd made the right decision in accepting the job and moving in with Harry, Timothy thought with a contented sigh. It was wonderful to see his brother so happy, and Timothy had a feeling he was going to be happy living here, too.

'Hi,' Timothy said warmly. He recognised the woman at once as the one from the cafe, and he felt a glow of pleasure. He'd only moved in a couple of days ago and he'd been hoping to bump into her. Surprised and pleased to discover she worked in the stables, he smiled broadly.

She returned his smile but there was no recognition behind it.

'I'm the new equine vet,' he said, hoping to prod her memory. 'Timothy Milton. Harry's brother,' he added in case she didn't make the connection.

'Hi, Timothy, nice to meet you. I'm Faith.'

'Actually, we, um...' He'd been about to remind her that they'd already met, but he decided not to bother. It hadn't been one of his finer moments, leaping on a total stranger. And he hadn't realised he was so forgettable either, and the knowledge knocked him down a peg or two; he was unused to such indifference from the opposite sex, although he did notice her look him up and down. He settled for, 'Nice to meet you, too.'

'If you wait here, I'll go fetch the horses,' she instructed, and left him loitering in the yard.

He watched her walk away, her hips swaying, her back straight, her hair stuffed underneath her riding cap to reveal the column of her soft white neck...Man, she was cute. Although, she seemed a little different to the woman he'd leapt on in the cafe, sharper somehow. He'd got the impression she was the typical sweet girl-next-door, but now he hastily revised his opinion. This woman was aloof, confident, spikier than he remembered. That would teach him to make assumptions about someone who he'd had only a fleeting contact with.

He could hear Petra's voice coming from the indoor arena and he guessed there must be a lesson going on, but of his brother and Amos there was no sign.

However, Nathan, the guy who was employed to do much of the heavy work, was driving a tractor up the lane, and he nodded at Timothy, who nodded back. The man was in his mid-to-late forties and as reticent as the vehicle he was driving, but Harry had told him he was a sound bloke and his actions spoke louder than words. Nathan might not say much, but he got the job done (whatever it might be) with the minimum of fuss.

'Petra tells me you've ridden before,' Faith said, coming around the corner leading two horses. One was a sizeable black gelding, the other a more delicate-looking thoroughbred mare. He assumed the gelding was for him.

'I've done a bit of riding, yeah,' he said, not wanting to blow his own trumpet. When his parents were alive, he used to compete most weekends.

'You won't need a leg up, then,' she said, handing him the mare's reins and going around the side of the gelding to lengthen the animal's stirrups.

'Let me do that,' he offered, wanting to make sure the length was right for his legs.

'You can do your own,' she told him, gathering the reins, sticking her foot in the stirrup and bouncing as she swung herself into the saddle. The gelding tossed his head and crabbed to the side.

Timothy looked at the mare, who gazed back at him impassively. She was an altogether calmer proposition.

'Are you sure you want to ride him?' Timothy asked Faith, as she shortened the reins even further to prevent the gelding from dropping his head. The horse pranced in annoyance at being thwarted.

'I think I should, considering he's my horse,' she replied with a smirk.

Timothy groaned inwardly – he was making assumptions again. Saying that though, the horse she was riding suited her.

'Walk on,' she told the horse, not waiting for him to mount up, and he found himself hopping on one leg as the mare began to move off before he'd managed to swing himself into the saddle.

Shaking his head at her, he pulled his horse to a stop, mounted, then followed the gelding. Soon they were on the open moorland above the stables with a chill westerly wind in his face, and he started to relax, contentment seeping into his heart as he felt himself gel with the mare and move with her gait.

There was only one small cloud on the blue sky of his horizon, and that was the rider in front of him. Clearly she wasn't into him at all – which was a pity, because for some reason she'd stuck in his mind and he'd been looking forward to getting to know her better.

Charity uttered a deep sigh as she gazed out of the window. Petra had phoned her earlier to ask how she was fixed for going on a hack later today, but she had been getting ready for work, so she'd suggested Petra asked Faith, as it was her twin's turn to be at the stables this afternoon.

She really wished she didn't have to go to work. Although she enjoyed her job, the day was a lovely crisp autumn one, and she would have loved nothing better than to have taken Storm out. She'd visited the stables this morning to muck out and clean some tack, but she hadn't had enough time to go for a ride.

Never mind, there was always tomorrow. Maybe she'd get up extra early, so she could get her chores done and saddle up her horse. She tried to ride her every day, but it wasn't always possible.

At least the latter half of the afternoon shift tended to be less busy than the mornings, and by the time seven o'clock arrived and she was on her break in the staff room, Charity had worked her way through her to-do list and was looking forward to a calm evening.

She had just made herself a hot drink and had settled down with her sandwiches when her mobile rang. It was her sister.

'How was the hack?' Charity asked before Faith had a chance to say anything.

'Oh, um, good. Harry's brother is a bit of a dish,' Faith said.

'When did you see *him*?' Charity had heard he'd moved in with his brother and the grapevine had also informed her he was due to start work at the vets shortly, but she had yet to bump into him.

'This afternoon. He was the guy I rode with.'

Charity's mood dimmed. She would have loved to have gone on a hack with Timothy. Work had got in the way, she thought grumpily, then she felt incredibly mean when she saw Mrs Routledge shuffling forlornly along the path leading from the outside seating area to the residents' entrance, and Charity made a note to sit with her for a while. The old lady had moved in only last week and she was feeling the loss of her home and her independence keenly.

'If I wasn't madly in love with Dominic, I'd fancy him myself,' Faith was saying. 'As well as being seriously good-looking, he's really friendly and he's smart.'

Everyone, especially men, responded to Faith in the same way, probably because of her outgoing personality. People tended to be more reserved around Charity, which was undoubtedly a reflection of her shyness. How could she expect a man to have a scintillating conversation with her, when she could barely look him in the eye?

Charity would bet her last penny that if Timothy was going to fancy anyone in Picklewick it would be Faith. Unluckily for him, Faith was smitten with Dominic so she wouldn't look at the new vet twice.

'Too friendly, I thought,' Faith was saying. 'I was a bit standoffish, though. I didn't want to give him any ideas.'

'What's he like as a rider?' Charity asked.

'Trust you! Here's me saying that a good-looking chap has rocked into town, and all you can think of is how well he rides.' Faith chuckled down the phone. 'He's pretty good, actually. Decent seat, and I'm not referring to his backside, although he did fill out his jodhpurs nicely.'

Heat stole into Charity's cheeks as she thought about Timothy's behind. She'd caught a glimpse of it as he'd dashed out of the cafe the day he'd found out he had the job, and even in a pair of suit trousers it had looked rather trim.

'He rode Storm and handled her like a dream,' Faith said, and Charity's blush deepened as she thought about him sitting astride her horse. Then she fanned herself with her hands and blamed it on the heat in the care home. It was usually warm, and Charity was often glad she was based in reception, as the doors to the main parking area were always opening and closing, letting in a constant stream of fresh air.

'Midnight was a nuisance, though,' Faith added. 'I should have swapped horses and ridden yours. Midnight could do with a firm hand, and this guy seems to know what he's doing.'

'I'll look forward to meeting him,' Charity said, muttering, '*Again*,' under her breath. For once, Charity hadn't shared everything with her sister. For some reason she'd not told Faith about him kissing her in the cafe. She tried to tell herself it was because she hadn't had the opportunity, but that was a lie; as was the excuse that it had slipped her mind – it hadn't.

She'd thought about him a lot as the weeks passed and the date for his arrival in Picklewick grew closer. She'd daydreamed and played what-if, envisioning their next meeting, and how delighted he would be to see her again.

In reality though, she guessed he would have totally forgotten her, and even when he was reminded he'd still be none-the-wiser. Besides, he'd met Faith now, and what man wouldn't prefer the more outgoing sister.

Charity emerged from her reverie to discover there was an unaccustomed silence on the other end of the phone, and suddenly her senses were on high alert. Something was wrong – there was an atmosphere which hadn't been there a second ago.

'I need to tell you something. It's the reason I phoned.' Faith sounded sheepish and hesitant. Not like her usual confident self at all.

A horrible feeling welled up inside her, and Charity desperately didn't want to hear what Faith was about to say. She felt sick, her half-eaten sandwich resting heavily in her stomach. This wasn't going to be good – she felt it in her bones.

'Dominic has asked me to move in with him,' Faith said.

Was that all? Relief surged through her: trust her to get worked up over nothing. Charity wasn't surprised at the news. 'You practically live at his house already,' she said, 'so it makes sense.'

'He's got a new job.'

Something in her sister's voice sent a shiver down Charity's spine. Why should a new job matter?

'It's in Norwich,' Faith continued. She sounded upset, and the shiver turned into a tremor. Was Faith distressed because she didn't intend to move halfway across the country with Dominic, and therefore their relationship was over? Or – and this thought made Charity's blood run cold – was Faith anxious because she *did* intend leaving Picklewick and her family, and things would never be the same again? Charity began to well up and she chewed at her lip.

Faith said, 'I'm sorry to land this on you over the phone, but he only just rang me and told me about the job. I simply had to speak to you *now*.'

'What are you going to do?' Charity asked, sniffing, her eyes stinging with unshed tears. She understood why Faith hadn't wanted to wait to tell her face to face. If the shoe had been on the other foot, Charity would also have wanted to share the news with her twin immediately.

'I love him,' Faith said, and the simple sentence told Charity everything she needed to know.

'Then you have to go with him. I would.'

'Would you?'

'I would.' Charity nodded emphatically, even though her sister couldn't see her. She wasn't being strictly truthful, but Faith didn't need to hear her doubts and reservations; her twin needed to follow her heart. There *was* one thing Charity wanted to know, though. 'If you don't go, would Dominic leave Picklewick anyway?' she asked.

'No. He'll stay.'

'Is it a good job? One worth moving for?'

'Definitely. He's been dreaming about a job like this ever since he left university.'

'He must love you very much,' Charity observed.

'He does.'

'So the question you should ask yourself is, do you love him as much?'

'I do – I really do.'

'Then you must go. You'll easily get another job – it's not as though you're wedded to the one you've got,' Charity observed.

'I don't want to leave you,' Faith cried.

And Charity said the hardest thing to ever pass her lips. 'Faith, my darling, you already have.' She was thankful Faith couldn't see her face, because she was falling apart inside. 'I'm so pleased for you,' she said, gulping back tears and hoping her distress couldn't be heard over the phone.

'Thanks. Shit!' Faith's voice was strangled. 'I said I wasn't going to cry.' She let out a sob which immediately set Charity off, and she put the rest of her unwanted sandwich to the side and staggered over to the sink for some kitchen roll to stem the flow.

When the sobbing had reduced to sniffles and Charity could speak again, she said, 'Have you told Mum?'

'Not yet. I wanted to speak to you first, to see what you thought. There wasn't any point in upsetting her, if I decided not to go.'

Charity felt tearful all over again; to think if she hadn't been so supportive Faith might have decided to remain in Picklewick, where she wouldn't be happy without the man she loved.

'I'll talk to her and Dad this evening,' Faith promised. 'I know they'll be pleased for me.'

As am I, Charity thought. And she *was*. Faith deserved every ounce of happiness in the world. 'How long before you leave?'

'Two months, maybe? I think Dominic will be starting his new job in January.'

So soon? Charity felt lost, as though her anchor had been pulled up and she was drifting out to sea, alone and rudderless.

What was she going to do without her sister? She had always been one half of a pair, but now the other half was aligning herself to someone else and Charity didn't know how she was supposed to bear it.

'Smile lovey, it might never happen,' Brian said, as she emerged from the staff room, red-eyed and shaking some time later.

'Actually, Brian, I think it already has,' she told him, earning herself a confused glance as he hurried off to find someone more cheerful to talk to.

CHAPTER FOUR

Charity adored dressing up, and Halloween was as good a reason as any. She had bought her costume and that of her horse ages ago, and had been looking forward to it, but the news that Faith had dropped on her had driven all thoughts of the party out of her mind.

Faith wasn't as keen on fancy dress, and Charity wondered if it had something to do with their different personalities. Charity enjoyed hiding behind her costume and mask: Faith didn't appear to need to, so what her sister wore tended to be more sexy vamp than a bandaged mummy, which is what Charity had dressed up as last year for the Halloween party. It hadn't been her best look, she admitted, and the bandages had been far too hot and restricting.

This time she was going as a skeleton, with an all-in-one stretchy suit which made her look like she was nothing but bones in the dark (the white parts of the fabric were slightly luminous) and Faith had done her make-up for her, so her face now looked like a skull. She thought she was the epitome of Halloween. It also suited her bleak mood perfectly.

The party was being held at the stables; it was mainly for the younger ones, but she always dressed up for it and she knew many of the parents would be in costume too. She'd even painted white bones on her horse (somewhat inexpertly) so Storm, who was a very dark bay, looked like a skeleton horse if she squinted and the light was poor – which it would be in the arena later. The place had been kitted out with battery-operated lanterns in the shapes of pumpkins, skulls and other assorted Halloween-y things ready for the scary ghost stories at the end of the evening.

Charity, Faith and Petra had taken ages to decorate the arena, and that was after Petra and Nathan had done the hard work of humping bales of hay around and setting up the indoor games. Amos had provided a buffet in the viewing gallery, out of the reach of whiskery noses and equine curiosity. It was shaping up to be a great evening.

Storm was still in her loosebox, so Charity went to fetch her, and giggled when she saw the mare's long-suffering expression. The horse didn't look particularly pleased with being painted, and as Charity saddled her, she kept glancing around at her rump as though she couldn't believe what she was seeing.

'Come on, girlie,' Charity murmured, 'You'll enjoy yourself – you always do. And Amos has baked some horsey treats for you.'

Storm's ears pricked up and not for the first time Charity had the impression the animal understood what she was saying.

Faith was already in the arena, supervising the arrivals, Midnight tethered to a post by her side and contentedly munching on some hay. The other ponies had been brought out and had been "dressed" for the occasion, and the space was filling up with excited children and their parents.

Before Petra allocated each child a mount, the first competition took place, which was the best costume, followed by the best parent and child costume, then the funniest outfit, plus several more, until each child had a small prize. Harry had been roped in to judge and he was resplendent as a wizard, complementing Petra's witchy outfit.

Faith, Charity noticed, had slipped away soon after, having done her duty by showing her face. Charity felt slightly resentful: it was yet another sign that Faith was gradually distancing herself from the stables. What worried Charity was the fear that Faith was distancing herself from her, too. They'd always sworn no man would ever come between them, but Faith was in love, and Charity, to her shame, felt left out. The fact that Faith was disappearing off to Norfolk next weekend for a couple of weeks in order to sort out accommodation and to attend an interview or two, didn't help Charity's glum mood.

Deliberately pushing her negative thoughts away, she plastered a smile on her face and determined to be as cheerful as possible this evening for the children's sakes. They didn't deserve to see her miserable face, and neither did Petra. After all, Charity admonished herself silently, it wasn't as though she wasn't pleased for her sister – she was thrilled to bits for her. It was her own fault she was feeling so down; she relied on Faith too much and Charity had been guilty of being content to live her life vicariously through her twin.

It was time Charity made more of an effort with socialising, and it was probably a good idea if she paid less attention to her horse and put more energy into finding a boyfriend of her own, then perhaps she wouldn't feel so left behind.

Petra was about to start the games, beginning with a spooky egg and spoon race where riders balanced a plastic eyeball on a spoon whilst steering their ponies around a line of poles, when Charity spotted a familiar face. Timothy, the new vet, had come dressed as the Grim Reaper. The cloak and the cowl suited him, and she noticed he had let his beard grow a little. To Charity, he looked as though he belonged in Middle Earth, and to her consternation she came over all giddy.

Thanking her lucky stars he was too busy watching the first game to notice her and her furious blushing at how attractive she found him, Charity checked that the stables' version of ducking for apples was ready to go. The apples hung at face height (if you were astride a horse, that is) and it took skill for the children to grab the apple with their mouths, whilst keeping the horse still and not falling off. Last year, Parsnip, a creamy coloured cob, had managed to sink his teeth into the apple before his rider had a chance, leading to much hilarity.

Charity was hoarse from shouting encouragement by the time the final competition was over, and her sides ached from laughing. She loved these events, seeing the shining faces of the children and the pride of their parents, but this evening there was an extra zing to the atmosphere, a zing no one but her could feel, and that was because of Timothy.

He'd finally noticed her underneath all the paint, and had sent her a smile which she'd returned, glad that the black and white make-up hid her blushes.

She didn't think it could hide the confusion she felt about him though, and she hastily looked away, hoping he couldn't tell how much she was attracted to him. But she couldn't help glancing back at him again, only to find he was still watching her, and it made her quite light-headed – until she realised he probably thought she was her sister. Her outgoing, confident, sparkling sister.

Her spirits suitably dampened, Charity grabbed hold of the reins of the nearest pony and took him to his stable to be bedded down for the night.

My word, that was fun, Timothy thought when the games drew to a close with a hunt-the-spider event which was the same as an Easter egg hunt but without the chocolate goodies and with a great deal more squealing.

Petra's ponies were patient creatures, well used to the antics of the children who rode them, and hardly flicked an ear when their riders shrieked at the sight of a plastic spider.

'I can't touch it, Daddy,' cried one little girl, and Timothy hurried over to help her.

'I'm Timothy and I'm a vet, so I'm used to picking up spiders,' he told her, smiling at the child's father. 'What's your name?'

'My name is May, and this is Tango. He's older than me but he doesn't like spiders, either.'

Timothy reached up to remove the plastic spider from the top of a pole and popped it into the basket Petra had given each child. Tango, despite the little girl's conviction that the pony didn't like spiders, didn't bat an eyelid.

'How many have you got?' he asked her, and she counted.

'Seven.'

'That means seven sweets. Well done!' Petra, rather than hide sweets in the arena where any forgotten ones might be discovered by Queenie, her spaniel, or by one of the ponies, had hidden loads of fake spiders around the place, which would be exchanged for sweets to eat after the buffet.

Thinking of the buffet made Timothy's stomach growl. He'd come straight from work and was starving. He'd only had time to change into his Death costume, complete with scythe which he was unduly pleased with because he thought it gave him an edgy look, before he'd hightailed it to the stables.

As soon as he'd entered the arena (which was wonderfully decorated) he had been accosted by a cacophony of children's voices, the smell of hay and horses, and by the sight of Faith.

He'd spotted her within the first few seconds, and he thought how sexy she looked dressed in a figure-hugging skeleton costume. She'd painted her face to look like a skull and her long dark hair was piled loosely on the top of her head. She'd even painted a horsey skeleton on Storm, although why she was riding the mare and not Midnight flummoxed him for a moment until he realised the gelding might be too flighty.

He'd smiled at her and she had smiled back, then she'd looked away, before glancing back at him again, which had made him wonder if she was flirting with him. He thought she might be, but he wasn't convinced; if she was, he didn't appreciate the hot and cold approach. He decided to give her the benefit of the doubt, though – maybe she had her reasons for being so distant the other day.

Finally, the games were over and it was time to eat, and he was about to head to the viewing gallery when he realised Harry, Nathan and Petra were leading the ponies out of the arena, and Faith had already left. Guessing she was seeing to Storm, he helped May dismount from Tango, lifted the reins over the animal's head and led the pony outside.

'Where does this one go?' he asked, meeting Faith as she was walking back to the arena. Hopefully she'd bring another pony out and they could unsaddle them together, but when he glanced over his shoulder he realised there were no more mounts left inside.

'Fourth stall from the end,' she said, and he noticed she gave him only a swift look before averting her eyes.

'Thanks,' he said, convinced she was definitely flirting when he took a step in the direction of the row of stalls, and he saw her peep at him again.

By the time he'd unsaddled Tango, brushed him down, and had made sure the pony had a hay net to munch on, the buffet was in full swing.

Timothy grabbed a plate and piled it with food, and as he did so the main lights overhead went out, leaving only the lamps for illumination. Most people were sitting on a pile of bales in one corner which had been arranged in a semi-circle around a single point, and it was to the figure sitting on her own that his attention gravitated.

Faith had an open book in her lap, and she began to read.

Drawn to her like one of the moths fluttering around the lanterns, Timothy perched on the edge of a bale, his food forgotten as he listened to her weaving tales of ghouls and ghosties and things that went bump in the night.

Mesmerised, he gazed at her without embarrassment, and as he did so he realised he was more attracted to her than he'd ever been to any other woman he'd met.

He just hoped she was attracted to him, too.

***

'The End,' Charity whispered and closed the book with a snap that made her avid listeners jump, then giggle. She waited a moment for the children and their parents to gather themselves, then she nodded to Petra to switch on the overhead lights.

Blinking owlishly at the abrupt brightness, she stretched and got to her feet. It might be time for most people to leave, but she'd stay to help Petra tidy up. Even though the horses were safely tucked up for the night, there was still a great deal to do, from putting away all the poles and returning the bales to the barn, to clearing away the paper plates, and raking the arena so it was fit for lessons tomorrow.

Technically, she wasn't expected to do any of it, but she wanted to. She had nothing to rush home for and she'd only be scrunched on the sofa with a book if she left now. Besides, Timothy was still there, and at this very moment he was hoisting a pole and Petra was showing him where it lived.

Reaching for a black bag to put the rubbish in, Charity began collecting up plates and cups, and as she was doing so she was acutely conscious of

Timothy – where he was, what he was doing, how gorgeous he looked dressed as the Grim Reaper, how the short beard suited him…

All through her reading, she'd been acutely conscious of his eyes on her, making her glow from the inside out, making her heart race and her fingers tingle. He'd kept his attention on her the whole time, and she'd had to fight not to lose her place in the story. The goosebumps which had sprung up on her arms didn't have anything to do with the scary tale, and had everything to do with the way he was looking at her, until she was reluctant to lift her head from the book as she read, in case he realised the effect he was having on her.

'It was a good evening,' he said, materialising at her elbow and making her jump. Clearly she'd not been as in tune with his whereabouts as she'd thought she was, letting him creep up on her like that.

'It was,' she agreed, keeping her gaze downwards as she searched for more rubbish.

'Hold the bag open,' he instructed, and when she did as he asked and he popped the core of an apple into it, his hand brushed hers, sending desire surging through her veins.

It was so unexpected and so unlike her, that she gasped, and he snatched his hand away.

'Sorry,' he muttered.

'It's okay, you made me jump, that's all.' As explanations went, it was a poor excuse for one and he shot her a curious glance.

'How long have you worked here?' he asked, falling into step next to her as she trailed around the arena.

'I don't actually work here,' she said. 'I stable my

horse in exchange for mucking out, teaching the odd lesson, and so on. I work in the care home in Picklewick as a receptionist.'

'I bet it's rewarding,' he said.

'Sometimes. It's hard when you lose a resident though.'

'I hate losing patients too.'

'How are you settling in?'

'Great, thanks. The practice is fab, and I love my work. Harry's not a bad landlord either, when he remembers not to leave his dirty socks on the bathroom floor.'

'Oi! I heard that, and those socks, my friend, were yours,' Harry chuckled.

'Were they?' Timothy scratched his chin. 'I could have sworn they were yours.'

Harry bumped Timothy's elbow as he walked past. 'I'm going to check on the horses with Petra and then I'm going to turn in for the night. Make sure you lock up when you get home.'

'I take it you're spending the night here?' Timothy asked.

'Yep. See you tomorrow, little brother. Night.'

'Night,' Timothy called, as Charity gave Harry a small wave. 'Are you off home, too? Can I give you a lift?'

'I've got my car, but thanks anyway,' she told him. 'I have a few more things to do here, so you might as well get going. Thanks for your help.' She nodded at the almost full rubbish bag in her hand.

'If you're sure…?' He paused. 'I really enjoyed the hack the other day,' he said.

'Good.' Her tone was non-committal, but her heart dropped to the soles of her riding boots. Great

– he was sounding her out about Faith. That was why he was hanging around.

'Do you think we could go out again?'

'You'll have to ask Petra,' Charity said.

'I'll do that,' he said. 'No doubt I'll see you around?'

'No doubt,' she replied stonily, disappointment oozing from every pore as she watched him leave.

And when Petra locked the arena doors a short while later and said goodnight to her, Charity's fears were confirmed when Petra said, 'Timothy wants to go on another hack – I take it he's okay to ride Storm again?'

Numbly Charity nodded. It made no difference that Faith was in a relationship and that she wouldn't look twice at him – the fact that he was interested in her sister and not her, was the issue. Which was a pity, because she really fancied him and for a while she'd got the impression the fancying was mutual.

Down in the dumps and feeling rather sorry for herself, Charity made her way home, thinking that the closest she was ever going to get to Timothy was sharing her horse with him.

How sad was that?

CHAPTER FIVE

Because the Black Horse was the only pub in Picklewick, it was usually busy, especially on Friday nights and at the weekend. On this particular Friday the twins were enjoying a drink together because Faith was about to depart for Norwich tomorrow for two weeks and this might be their last chance to catch up for a while.

They might both still live at home, but lately it had been a technicality on Faith's part as Dominic was renting a place of his own, so Faith spent most of her time there.

Of course, the sisters phoned and messaged each other constantly, but it wasn't the same as one of them popping into the other's bedroom before they went to bed, or chatting over a bowl of cereal at breakfast, or exchanging gossip as they helped their mum make dinner.

In fact, Charity was having difficulty remembering the last time they'd done anything like that, because Faith was hardly ever at home these days.

They used to be so close they knew what the other was thinking, more or less living in each other's pockets, but gradually as their jobs led them in different directions, and then as Faith began to fall in love with Dominic, they saw less of each other. And it didn't help that Charity worked shifts, and they took it in turns going to the stables, so their paths crossed less and less.

Sometimes Charity thought that if it wasn't for the fact they were identical twins and she saw Faith's face staring back at her whenever she glanced in the mirror, she would have forgotten what her sister looked like.

Okay, maybe she was exaggerating, but Charity couldn't help feeling sad that Faith was moving on with her life and leaving Charity behind. And now she was also physically moving halfway across the country…

Crumbs, Charity couldn't even find herself a boyfriend, and her envy at the love her sister and Dominic shared made her feel sad, unloved, and unwanted, especially since the only man she'd been attracted to in a very long time had the hots for her sister.

'How did the Halloween party go?' Faith asked, sipping a bright blue cocktail through a straw. 'When I left, it was just getting started.'

'It was a great evening. The kids loved it and I think the parents did, too. Petra was pleased, so that's the main thing.' Petra worked her socks off to keep the stables solvent, and even though the party had been hard work to arrange, it had been worth it.

'That's good. Did she get you to read a story like she did last year?'

Charity nodded, tucking her long dark hair behind her ears, her mind flitting back to when she'd sat on the bale of hay with the lights low and with Timothy's unwavering gaze caressing her face.

At least, that was what she would have liked to believe. The reality was, he'd more than likely had been imagining it was Faith in front of him, not Charity.

'Did Petra arrange for you to go on another hack with Timothy?' Charity asked, surmising she hadn't when Faith's expression went blank for a moment.

'Timothy? Oh, Harry's brother?' her sister said. 'No, was she supposed to?'

'She said he wanted to go for a ride.'

'She hasn't mentioned anything to me and I'm off to Norwich tomorrow. That's another thing to be sorted – the stables. As things are at the moment, I'm only just managing to fit in my normal duties, and to be honest it's all getting a bit much. I love Midnight to bits, but…'

'…you're not taking him with you,' Charity supplied, her heart plummeting. She'd been anticipating this, but knowing it was coming didn't make it any easier to deal with.

'I still love riding him, you know I do,' Faith continued. 'But I can't take him to Norwich. I can't afford to stable him for one thing, and for another—'

'—you've got other things to occupy you,' Charity finished, sympathetically.

Now that she and Dominic were a couple, Faith's priorities had understandably shifted, but it didn't prevent Charity from feeling upset and strangely hurt. The stables and their horses had been a part of their lives for so long, that Charity couldn't imagine Midnight not being there, or her sister not helping out anymore. They were undeniably drifting apart, even though she knew it was inevitable to a certain extent. She might well feel the same way if she had a lovely boyfriend like Faith had, and an image of Timothy popped into her mind.

She pushed it away.

Faith put her arm around Charity's shoulder and hugged her. 'I can't see Midnight and the stables in my future,' she said. 'Sometimes you have to choose. I've done a lot of soul searching, and I really do think it's time I sold Midnight; even if I wasn't about to move, I can't give him the attention he deserves and it's not fair on him.'

Charity felt like crying. Once upon a time she and Faith had been inseparable, but now their paths were diverging. Faith was ploughing a new furrow, one which didn't involve their once all-encompassing love of horses and riding.

Saddened and upset, Charity couldn't help feeling lost and out of sorts. She was on the cusp of change, and she had an awful feeling she wasn't going to like it.

Timothy girded his loins and walked into the Black Horse. It wasn't as though he was a total stranger to its hop-scented interior because he'd been there before, but Harry had been with him in the past and this evening Timothy was on his own and feeling a little lonely. Harry was with Petra, and Timothy mused that his brother was spending far more time up at the stables than in his rented cottage, so Timothy wouldn't be surprised if Harry moved to Muddypuddle Lane soon.

'A pint of ale, please,' he said, when the landlord asked him what he wanted.

He paid and took a deep draught, then licked his

lips, trying to ensure there was no foam left on his beard. He scratched it thoughtfully, debating whether to shave it off. He was still getting used to it, and he couldn't decide whether it suited him.

'How are things. Are you settling in?' the landlord asked, and Timothy rooted around for the man's name.

'I am, thanks, Dave.' Pleased he'd remembered, he tipped his glass at him. 'Can I buy you a drink?'

'That's very kind of you. I'll have it later, if you don't mind. How's that brother of yours?'

'He's good – not that I see a great deal of him.' Timothy might as well be renting the cottage by himself, and he was hoping he'd be able to take over the tenancy if Harry moved in with Petra.

They continued to chat, and as they talked (Dave breaking off to serve now and again), several people smiled at Timothy and nodded, and he realised his face was beginning to be recognised around the village.

At one point when Dave was serving a succession of customers, Timothy turned around to lean his back against the bar, and his gaze wandered around the room as he tried to put names to familiar faces.

When his gaze came to rest on a certain woman he was awfully attracted to, he straightened, then froze. Faith was with someone, and for a second Timothy wondered if his drink had been spiked.

There were *two* of her!

Not believing what he was seeing, he peered at them, resisting the urge to rub his eyes.

Damn, one of them had noticed him, and he saw her nudge the other, so he hastily turned around again as he processed the information.

He hadn't been expecting *that*.

Faith had a twin, and from this distance they looked identical. That might explain things. But the question was, which one of them had he shared his enthusiasm on hearing about his new job with, and was it the same one who had taken him on a hack, or the same one who he'd gazed at like a love-sick teenager during the Halloween party? Because that was the one he wanted to speak to. Or had he been talking to the same one all along?

Unable to decide whether he should speak to them, he ordered another pint instead.

Charity spotted Timothy at the bar long before Faith nudged her in the ribs. She'd seen him walk in looking rather nervous, and she'd noticed how the stiffness of his back and shoulders had gradually eased as he'd taken a deep drink of his pint and began chatting to Dave.

Occasionally he'd glance around and nod at a few people, but she and Faith were sitting in the far corner near the door, and he'd have to turn towards it in order to see them. Charity was quite happy for him to remain oblivious to her presence, especially since she was able to study him (the back of him, at least) to her heart's content.

'There he is, Harry's brother,' Faith hissed. 'See what I mean about him being a dish? Don't look, he's seen us.'

'I thought you wanted me to look?'

'I do, but not when he can see us gawping at him. I don't want him to get the wrong idea. Did I tell you he was very friendly when I took him riding – too friendly, if you ask me.'

'He probably didn't realise you've got a boyfriend,' Charity pointed out. Something was niggling at her and it took her a moment to realise what it was. 'Did you tell him you had a twin?' She'd assumed he knew, because everyone in the village did…but perhaps he didn't.

'I assumed he knew; it didn't occur to me to mention it.'

'I don't think he did know until this evening.' He had done a comical double-take and his eyes had widened. Then he'd turned around as though he was embarrassed.

'Ha! No wonder he looked surprised when he saw us pair sitting here,' Faith chortled.

'I met him when he came for his interview at the vets,' Charity said, her attention still on him. 'He kissed me.'

'*What?* I thought you said you hadn't met him?' Faith turned to her in astonishment. 'There was I telling you what a dish he was, and you'd already snogged him! You kept that quiet.'

'It wasn't like that,' Charity said, and told her what had happened.

'That explains it,' Faith said, finishing her drink. 'He must have thought I was you when we went for the ride. I'd forgotten that used to happen. We don't get it so much anymore. People in Picklewick are used to us and most of them can sort of tell us apart, so they don't get us mixed up.'

'Looks like he did.'

'Does it matter?' Faith asked.

Oh, yes, Charity thought – it mattered a great deal, indeed. But the question was, which twin had caught his eye and which twin did he want to get to know better? 'I quite like him,' she admitted

'You do?' Faith appeared to be surprised, then a grin spread across her face. 'Are you sure?'

Charity nodded. She was blushing again, and felt all hot and bothered.

'Why don't you go and talk to him?' Faith suggested.

'I don't think so!' Charity was horrified. She didn't do that kind of thing. Faith was the forward one.

Abruptly Faith rose to her feet. 'I'm off to the loo. Why don't you get a couple more drinks in?'

Charity hesitated. Faith had that look on her face, the one which told Charity she was up to something. Not wanting to go to the bar, she sat there for a while, hoping Faith would return soon and save her the bother. However, it was Charity's turn to buy the drinks and knowing Faith, her sister wouldn't return to their table until Charity had done as she was asked. Faith could be stubborn, especially when she had an agenda. Honestly, Charity thought, this is ridiculous. Would she be as reluctant if Timothy wasn't there? Of course she wouldn't.

She was being silly; Picklewick was a small place and avoiding him would be impossible. She might as well get this over with.

Taking a deep breath, she walked over to the bar and stood next to Timothy, hoping Dave would serve her soon so she could flee back to her seat, mission accomplished.

'Two grapefruit gins, please,' she said, when Dave

noticed her. 'One with ice and one without.'

Timothy glanced to his right, spotted her, and gave a start. 'Faith, right?'

'Charity.'

'Where's hope?'

'Ha, ha. We've not heard that before.' Sometimes Charity felt like having stern words with her parents; what on earth had they been thinking?

She watched him process her reply, wondering if he'd be offended, amused, or indifferent, and as he gave her a wide smile, she realised he was none of those things, and she smiled back.

He really did have a lovely smile…

'Are you the nice twin or the evil one?' he asked, and he could have kicked himself as her face fell. She'd seemed so happy to chat with him, too…Embarrassed, he studied the ale in his glass.

'It depends on your perspective,' she retorted. The smile hadn't reappeared, so he wasn't sure if he'd annoyed her or not.

'Do you remember meeting me in the cafe down the road? I sort of, um, kissed you?'

'I remember.'

'Sorry about that. I was so happy and excited I'd got the job, that I had to share it.'

'Would you have shared it as enthusiastically if it had been Amos standing behind you in the queue?'

Timothy pulled a face. 'Probably not.' Then he laughed as the penny dropped. 'Ha! That means you're not Faith.'

'I thought we'd established that.' She was frowning, but she made no move to pick up the drinks she'd paid for and return to her seat.

'What I'm saying is, you didn't accompany me on the ride last week.'

'No, that was my sister.'

It felt odd that he'd thought her name was Faith when her real name was Charity all along. It was nice. It suited her – softer, somehow. But at least it explained why the woman who had taken him on the ride hadn't recognised him.

'And which one of you was at the Halloween party at the stables?' he asked.

'We both were, but Faith left early to meet her boyfriend.'

He felt she was trying to tell him something; that Faith was out of bounds, perhaps? He didn't care, it was Charity he was interested in. More than interested…

There was Faith now, walking towards them, and he felt deflated that Charity would go back to her table. He would like nothing better than for her to stay at the bar and keep him company.

The two women were incredibly alike he thought, inspecting them whilst trying not to let either of them see. Apart, he'd most definitely have trouble knowing one from the other – it would be a fifty-fifty guess, but when they were standing next to each other as they were doing now, he noticed subtle differences. The main one was that Charity appeared more reserved than her sister. However, there was a way of telling them apart when they weren't together, he saw – Charity had a small scar on her cheek, and he filed the information away for future reference.

He also now knew which twin it was he'd been staring longingly at during the Halloween party, and he was relieved to discover it had been Charity.

He watched Faith lean in close, cup her hand around Charity's ear and whisper, and he noticed how Charity looked panicked for a moment, before she inhaled and nodded.

To his surprise, Faith sauntered towards the door, swinging her bag and waving goodbye, leaving her sister at the bar.

He waited for Charity to gather herself before he asked, 'Is your sister coming back?'

She bit her lip and shook her head.

'I'd offer to buy you a drink, but you already have two in front of you and I don't want you to think I'm trying to get you drunk,' he joked, but when he failed to elicit a response he said, 'I'm going to sit down. Would you care to join me?'

She narrowed her eyes, then appeared to come to a decision as she picked up both drinks and made her way to the table she'd not long vacated.

Timothy sat next to her, in the same seat her sister had. He put his drink down and prepared to do battle. He had a feeling it was going to take more than his usual charm to break down Charity's barriers, and he very much wanted to get to know her better.

'How long have you worked in the care home?' he asked, and was gratified to see she was pleased he remembered.

And as she told him, and they began to discover more about each other, Timothy realised that for the first time in his life he was smitten. It was a rather pleasant sensation, and he was disappointed when Dave announced last orders a couple of hours later.

'Gosh, is that the time?' she said. 'I have to go – I've got an early start in the morning.'

He drained what was left in his glass and stood up, and the two of them made their way to the door, but once outside, he felt at a loss. 'I'll walk you home,' he offered, assuming she lived close enough to walk. She certainly hadn't driven to the pub and she wasn't making any move to order a taxi.

Her smile was shy. 'I only live around the corner.'

'I'd like to make sure you get home okay, if that's all right with you?'

'If you're sure. I live in the opposite direction to Harry's cottage.'

Timothy wouldn't have cared if she lived at the North Pole. 'It's no bother,' he assured her.

They fell into step side-by-side, and he felt his heart race as her arm brushed against his. It seemed only natural he should reach for her hand.

He felt Charity begin to pull away, but then her fingers curled around his and his stomach somersaulted with desire. Her hand was soft and warm, snuggling into his like a baby rabbit. Actually, that was what she reminded him of, a shy, nervous bunny. It made him feel all protective and masculine.

Walking in silence, Timothy cast about for something to say, before realising there was no need to say anything. He was perfectly content to stroll along the quiet streets of Picklewick without needing to talk.

'This is me,' she said quietly, as they halted outside a terraced cottage.

Suddenly, he felt awkward and uncertain. He so badly wanted to kiss her, but he couldn't tell whether she'd be amenable or not.

Should he ask her? Or would he look a prat?

He'd ask her.

Timothy became aware of Charity gazing at him with a bemused expression, and he also became aware he was still holding her hand.

'Can I kiss you?' he blurted.

Her eyes shone luminously in the streetlights, and she paused for such a long time he was convinced she was going to say no. But finally she nodded and, still clasping her hand, he dipped his head towards her.

She lifted her chin as he brought his mouth down to hers, her pupils large and dark as she locked her gaze on him. As their lips met and he felt her soft breath on his face, her eyelids fluttered closed and she let out a soft sigh.

Tentative at first, he kissed her gently, delicately, feather-light in his delight. But as she responded and her mouth opened, passion sparked through his body and he had to hold himself back for fear of scaring her with his urgency.

He deepened the kiss, then eased slowly away. He was breathing hard and his heart pounded, and he'd never felt so lost in a woman as he had just now. It was exhilarating and frightening at the same time.

Slowly, tantalisingly, Charity opened her eyes, her expression unfathomable. Wanting to kiss her again, Timothy held back. It might be a good idea to give himself some time to reflect on what had just happened before he risked further physical contact.

'Have you got any plans for tomorrow?' he asked. His voice was gruff, and he cleared his throat.

'I'm in work until four.'

'What about the evening?' He felt on safer ground now, as his pulse dropped to more normal levels and his unruly emotions were brought under control.

'Bonfire Night. There's a display in the park. It's only a small one.' She seemed as flustered as he was.

'Oh, yes, I'd forgotten about that.'

'There'll be hotdogs and toffee apples. You should go.'

Timothy frowned. Fireworks weren't Harry's thing and Timothy didn't want to go on his own. 'I might,' he said, doubtfully.

'Okay, I might see you there, then.'

'Would you like to go with me?' he blurted.

'I'd love to. My sister and I usually go together, but she's off to Norwich tomorrow.'

'So you'll settle for accompanying me instead?' His tone was wry.

Charity laughed and the atmosphere lightened a degree or two, although the kiss they'd shared continued to hover in the air between them. 'I'll meet you by the hotdog stand – six-thirty?'

Timothy didn't think about what he was going to say next, until he'd said it. 'We can go for a drink afterwards, if you like.'

Her shy smile and the way she peeped up at him from underneath her lashes told him that she *would* like.

'Can I have your phone number?' he asked and when she gave it to him, he immediately rang her. 'There, now you've got mine, too. I'll see you tomorrow.' He trailed a finger down her cheek, then cupped her face. 'Nice meeting you properly,' he said.

As he walked away, heading for home, he felt her gaze on his back. It was a wonderfully pleasant sensation.

Timothy slumped onto the sofa, a glass of water in his hand. He hadn't bothered to turn the telly on even though he was too wired to go to bed yet. His mind swirled with thoughts of Charity, and he couldn't stop smiling. Every now and again he'd chuckle when he recalled turning around, seeing a double image of Faith, and wondering if his drink had been spiked.

When he thought about that glorious kiss, his heart missed a beat. He had never felt this way about a girl before. It was so new to him and he couldn't wait to see her again.

The sound of the front door opening made him jump and in turn Harry let out a yell when he saw Timothy.

'Why are you sitting in the dark?' his brother cried, turning on a sidelight. 'You nearly gave me a heart attack.'

'I didn't expect you home tonight,' Timothy said.

'Petra had to come into the village to pick Amos up from the pub, so I thought I'd sleep in my own bed for a change considering I've got to be up and out at the crack of dawn tomorrow.'

Timothy remembered Harry saying something about promising to visit a stable several miles away, where three of their mounts had lost shoes, and who were all due to be ridden tomorrow. Harry tried not to work weekends, unlike Timothy who was frequently on call, but this was an exception.

Not for the first time Timothy wondered if he was cramping Harry's style by moving in with him. With Amos, Petra's uncle, living at the stables, Timothy suspected Harry and Petra used to spend time at the cottage in order to be alone. However, that was now denied them, because of him.

'I might look for somewhere to rent soon,' he said. 'You and Petra need a place you can be together.'

Harry yawned and stretched, his fingers touching the living room ceiling. 'This isn't it,' Harry said. 'She would never spend the night at the cottage – it's too far away from her horses.'

'But if you ever want me to make myself scarce, just say.'

'By the moony look on your face, it's me who should be making myself scarce.'

'I've not got a moony look on my face.'

'Yes, you have.' Harry smirked. 'Is it anything to do with Charity Jones?'

'I don't know what you mean,' Timothy retorted, loftily.

'You were with her most of the evening.'

'How do you know that?'

'Amos. He was in the snug playing darts. He saw you together and said you looked like a fella who'd lost a penny and found a pound.'

Amos was right – that was exactly how he felt!

For once Faith wasn't spending the night at Dominic's place, wanting to be at home for her last night in Picklewick for a couple of weeks, and when Charity crept into the house expecting everyone to be in bed, she discovered her sister had waited up for her.

'Well?' Faith demanded, as soon as Charity cleansed her face and slipped into her pyjamas. Faith was already snuggled up in Charity's bed, and she scooted over to make room for her.

'Well, what?' Charity feigned ignorance, but when Faith whacked her with a pillow, she couldn't stop the huge smile spreading across her face.

'Are you seeing him again?' Faith wanted to know, and Charity nodded.

'I'm meeting him at the firework display tomorrow.'

'Go, you! You like him a lot, don't you?'

Charity was thankful it was dark so Faith couldn't see her blush, but her sister knew her only too well.

'I'm pleased for you,' Faith continued. 'It's about time you had some love in your life, so don't be embarrassed. From the little I saw, he seemed to be into you, too.'

Charity certainly hoped he was.

'Did you see his face when he realised there are two of us?' Faith chortled. 'I'd forgotten how much fun it was.'

'No, you can't play a trick on him,' Charity warned, knowing what her sister was like. It had been her favourite thing to do when they were younger.

'Spoilsport.' Faith dragged the duvet over her. Charity dragged it back. 'Did you kiss?' Faith asked, and when Charity failed to answer, she cried, 'You did! You kissed him. What was it like? Is he a good kisser? Were there tongues?'

'*Faith!*' Charity and her sister had always shared everything (almost everything – things had changed since Dominic had arrived on the scene) but Charity wanted to keep the details of their kiss to herself.

It was too precious to be shared.

And she did keep it to herself, bringing it out only when Faith had retired to her own bed, leaving Charity alone with her thoughts and her dreams.

She'd had boyfriends before but none she'd felt such a strong attraction to, and it had nothing to do with Timothy being so good looking. It ran much deeper. She knew it was daft and far too soon to be thinking like this (they hardly knew each other) but she felt as though she'd known him forever.

When she finally drifted off to sleep, it was with his image in her mind and the taste of him on her lips.

CHAPTER SIX

Charity was still in bed when she heard Faith get up, and she rolled over for an extra five minutes of blissful snoozing. Eventually though, she had to force her reluctant body out of bed and get ready for work. Tired didn't begin to describe how she felt this morning; she was exhausted from having a fitful restless night. And every time she'd woken, Timothy's face had swanned into her mind and had refused to budge.

She kept seeing his smile, the way his mouth twisted slightly unevenly giving him a wickedly sexy air, the single frown line between his eyes when he was concentrating on something she'd said, hearing his infectious laugh… She also kept reliving the moment when his lips had touched hers, and the cascade of emotions that had poured through her and the way her heart had stuttered made the blood sing in her veins.

After visiting the stables extremely early this morning, coming back in time to wave Faith off and make her promise to message her as soon as she got to Norwich, Charity made her way into work, her thoughts about Timothy interspersed with her worry about the stables. She couldn't stop thinking about Faith having to sell Midnight. Her sister had owned the horse since she was fourteen and he was six. It was a long time, especially in equine years, but Charity knew deep down that Faith wasn't being fair to him, even if she didn't intend to leave Picklewick. He needed to be ridden far more frequently than Faith could manage. He was a big lad and spirited, so was totally unsuitable for the vast majority of riders at the stables. Petra took him out now and again, but she had her own horse, Hercules, who needed to be exercised. Charity rode Storm, wanting to ensure her horse was fit, so that only left Harry, who sometimes saddled up and went for a ride, or Nathan, who was the stable's handyman. Nathan occasionally accompanied Petra on a ride, and Charity had gone out with him once or twice. But Midnight still didn't have enough exercise, and he was starting to become a little unruly.

Maybe Timothy could ride him, Charity mused, but that didn't address the issue of the arrangement the twins had with Petra; both horses were liveried for free in exchange for the sisters' help around the stables. Over the past few months Charity had found herself picking up some of Faith's slack, and she'd been fine with that – all that mattered to Charity was that Faith was happy. But Charity simply didn't have the time to ride both horses herself, as well as doing everything else.

As usual, Charity stowed her coat and bag in the staffroom, said hello to Rose who was the office administrator, and spoke to a few of the residents before she began work. Most of them were either still in bed, or were in the process of getting up, which could be a long-drawn-out affair for some of them, involving a couple of staff members and a hoist.

Charity could smell bacon, and her stomach

growled. Honeymead Care Home lived up to its name, in that it cared for its residents very well indeed, and the food it provided was no exception. There was always a decent range on offer for breakfast, and Charity would have loved to eat a bacon sandwich right now, having skipped breakfast.

'Smells nice, doesn't it?' Olive said, as she tottered past. 'Want me to save you a slice?'

Charity gave the air a final sniff. 'That's very kind of you, Olive, but I've already eaten,' she lied, not wanting to give the old lady any excuse to smuggle food out of the dining room. She was a bit of a madam for stuffing half of what was on her plate into her pockets. Lena, Olive's daughter, was worried that hoarding food might be a sign of dementia, especially as the care home offered three substantial meals, plus home-made cakes, crisps and biscuits in the cafe area for residents to help themselves.

Charity knew the reason for Olive's penchant for secreting food about her person, but Olive had sworn her to secrecy. She was feeding a stray cat, who lingered in the garden outside her room every morning and evening. Charity wasn't convinced cats liked roast potatoes, though.

'Do you need me to bring in any more cat food?' Charity asked.

'I've still got some, but I've had to put it in the safe,' Olive said. 'I don't want anyone to find it, you see. They might ask questions.'

Charity shook her head. 'The safe is for your valuables,' she reminded her. Every resident had their own safe in their rooms, much like a hotel room.

'That's okay,' Olive said cheerfully. 'I haven't got any.'

At least if Olive was feeding the cat proper food, then she wasn't smuggling half a roast dinner out of the dining room, and Lena wouldn't worry about her mother as much.

'You look tired, my girl,' Olive said, waving her walking stick at her. 'Have you been out partying?'

'I don't like parties, although I am going to watch the fireworks tonight. You should have a good view of them from the terrace.'

'Bah, noisy things. I like the colours though, so perhaps I'll watch from inside. Do you have a nice young man to accompany you?'

Charity smiled. 'I think I do. It's the new vet.'

'Ooh, a new vet? Do you think he'll take a look at Marigold?'

'Marigold?'

'The cat.'

'I thought his name was Rambo?'

'That was when I thought he was a him. Now I think she's a her.'

'I see. I can ask him. She might be a bit difficult to catch, if she's semi-wild.'

'What's this fella of yours like? Is he handsome?'

Charity nibbled on her bottom lip. 'I think so.'

'Does he treat you well?'

'Tonight will be our first proper date. He walked me home from the pub last night, though,' she confided.

'I wish I was your age, and knew what I know now,' Olive said. 'If you like him, don't hang about. And make sure he puts a ring on it. That girl on tv, the one who shakes her tail feathers, has got it right.'

'Beyonce?'

'That's the one. Marvin took three years to propose to me. I was getting jolly fed up, I can tell you.'

'It's too soon to think about that,' Charity said, relieved when the main door buzzed and she had to hurry away to let someone in, leaving Olive to make her way into the dining room.

It was Lena, Olive's daughter.

'Your mum is about to have her breakfast,' Charity informed her. 'Why don't you have a coffee while you wait?'

'Good idea,' the woman said, and Charity had no sooner made one for her and one for herself, when the door buzzed again.

This time it was Amos, and he'd brought Petra's black Cocker Spaniel with him.

'That's so kind of you to bring Queenie,' Charity said. 'Brian especially, will love to see her. He misses his dog dreadfully. Take a seat and I'll make you a hot drink, then I'll tell Brian you're here.'

'Thanks, my lovely,' Amos said, easing himself into the chair next to Lena, who was fussing over Queenie. The dog was lapping up the attention. 'I'll have a tea, if you don't mind. I saw you and Timothy in the Black Horse last night. The pair of you looked quite cosy.'

'Would Timothy be the new vet?' Lena asked, scruffling Queenie's silky ears.

'It would. Nice lad is Harry's brother,' Amos said.

'Harry's nice, too,' Lena said. 'How is he getting on with Petra? Any sign of wedding bells?'

Charity left them to chat and retreated to her desk. What was this fascination with marriage today, she wondered. It was all anyone seemed able to talk about. There was more to life than getting wed, although she strongly suspected her sister didn't think so, and once again Charity felt the breeze of change blow through her mind.

But this time, it carried an image of Timothy with it.

Timothy, shirt off, lathered up his hands and forearms using antibacterial soap, and prepared to do battle. His opponent was a cow who was having difficulty calving, and he knew the next half an hour or so wasn't going to be pretty. It would be dirty, strenuous, and hard work, and was definitely the less glamorous side of being a vet. But hopefully, there would be a healthy mother and baby at the end of it.

As he put on a plastic apron and donned a pair of arm-length plastic gloves, Timothy was in his element. He preferred horses, but a vet in a general practice couldn't choose his clients. If an animal was in trouble it needed to be helped, and this poor creature wouldn't be able to give birth without assistance.

Grimacing, he examined her. 'I can feel a leg and a nose,' he said to the farmer. 'Hand me the calving rope, I'm going to have to bring the other leg forward before I can pull the calf out.'

It was a good half an hour before he was finally able to stand back and watch the new mum lick her black and white calf clean.

'He's a decent size,' the farmer said happily, as Timothy stripped off the plastic apron and gloves, and gave himself another wash.

Calving was a mucky business.

'He certainly is,' he agreed, satisfied he'd done a good job. He loved assisting at births when there was a good outcome, and he smiled as the baby shook his head and blinked. In a few minutes it would struggle unsteadily to its feet and take its first drink of milk. Timothy would wait until that happened, then he'd make his way to his next client.

Suitably dressed again, he put his things away and tidied up after himself.

'Settling in all right?' the farmer asked. 'Brandon told me he had a new vet on his staff.'

Timothy nodded – he was settling in just fine, and with each passing day he felt more at home. He'd made the right decision in moving to Picklewick. He enjoyed working at the practice, and he loved living in the village. Harry didn't seem to mind having him around, so that was a bonus, but he still intended to get his own place eventually. He'd have to save a bit first for a deposit, unless…?

He and Harry owned the house in Cheltenham between them, having inherited it when their parents died. What if they were to sell it? Timothy had put it in the hands of a letting agent so it was bringing in some income for the pair of them, but he guessed Harry had no intention of ever living in it again, and now Timothy had left he didn't believe he would return to the family home either. Picklewick was a fresh start for both of them.

Timothy said goodbye to the farmer, plugged his next client's address into the Satnav and trundled off up the track, wincing at each pothole. Relieved to reach the tarmac road, he pulled onto it and was soon on his way, letting the soothing electronic voice guide him as his thoughts turned to fresh starts and new beginnings. He hoped one of those new beginnings would involve Charity. She'd managed to get under his skin, which was a first, and he was astonished at how much he was looking forward to seeing her again. He couldn't wait for this evening, although he wasn't entirely sure whether it was a date or not.

What he was sure about though, was his desire to kiss her again, and to keep kissing her until she'd fallen for him as deeply as he'd managed to fall for her.

'I hate Bonfire Night,' Petra muttered for the tenth time. She said the same thing every year, and for good reason. Horses, like most animals, hated sudden loud noises, and there had been whistling explosions for the past few days as people set off the odd rocket or two prematurely. The fireworks had been known to go on for days afterwards, too. 'Sodding fireworks,' she added, sourly.

Charity understood where Petra was coming from, because even with the stables being so far out of the village, the noise of the fireworks carried, and the official display would be twenty minutes of incessant loud noise and lights in the sky. The horses would absolutely hate it, which was why Charity had popped up to the stables immediately after work to help Petra bed them down for the night. At least if they were in their stalls before the madness began, they would be less likely to panic and injure themselves. And, of course, Petra would be there to reassure them.

On the other hand, Charity loved Bonfire Night and always had done. The smell of woodsmoke from the bonfire itself, the scent of cordite (was it? she was never sure), the sparklers, the lights illuminating the sky for the briefest of moments, then falling back to earth…the whole thing was magical and catapulted her firmly back to her childhood. Then there was the huge bonfire, and the astonishing heat which radiated from it, the hotdog and burger stands with the delicious aroma of frying onions. And tonight there would be the added excitement of seeing Timothy again.

Last night had been wonderful. They'd talked for ages, and it was as though she'd been speaking to an old friend. She had so much to learn about him, yet she felt like she'd known him her whole life. It was a most extraordinary thing.

Then they had kissed and her world had shrunk to that incredibly wonderful meeting of their lips and the sensations swirling through her.

'Charity?'

'Huh?'

'You were miles away,' Petra said. 'In a proper daydream you were. Would that lovesick look on your face have anything to do with Harry's brother, by any chance?'

Good lord, did everyone in Picklewick know her business? Petra normally didn't bother with matters of the heart, but she was certainly taking an active interest in Charity's love life.

'No comment,' she replied haughtily, and stuck her nose in the air.

Petra was right though, Charity *was* all dreamy.

She couldn't stop thinking about Timothy, and she hugged herself in delight.

She was falling for him, and it felt absolutely wonderful.

CHAPTER SEVEN

Timothy sniffed the air appreciatively, the aroma of fried onions bringing back memories of half-forgotten Bonfire Nights from his childhood. Times like this were bitter-sweet, as he remembered being taken to the display in Cheltenham by his parents. After they'd died, Harry had gone with him, but Timothy had quickly grown out of being escorted by an adult (which Harry was, as his legal guardian) and preferred to go with his friends instead.

Picklewick's Bonfire Night celebrations were an altogether smaller affair and as he walked through the crowd searching for Charity, he saw many familiar faces. He might not be able to put names to them all, but nods and smiles were exchanged, and occasionally he was stopped by someone whose animal he had treated and he had a quick chat.

The bonfire hadn't been lit yet – apparently that would happen after the fireworks – and most people were gathered behind a line of barriers, beyond which shadowy figures carrying torches could be seen doing last minute checks.

Timothy stopped and scanned the field, his gaze flitting over faces, seeking out one in particular. Then he spotted her near the hotdog stand, talking to an older woman, who he guessed might be her mum as the two women shared similar features.

Hastening over, he came to a halt in front of Charity and smiled broadly. Gosh, was she a sight for sore eyes! She wore a bobble hat which framed her face, and was bundled up in a scarf and a thick winter coat, and had sturdy boots on her feet. Her breath misted the air and as she blew on her hands his gaze came to rest on her puckered lips and he longed to kiss them.

'Hi,' he said, shuffling from foot to foot, feeling absurdly nervous, before turning his attention to the woman next to her. 'Hello.'

The woman held out her hand. 'You must be Timothy, the new vet. Pleased to meet you. I'm Valerie, Charity's mum.'

He shook her hand, conscious of her scrutiny of him, and he hoped she approved of what she saw. 'Pleased to meet you too,' he said.

She held his gaze for a moment, then said to Charity, 'I'll go and find your father. No doubt he's near the beer tent. I just hope he's not got his hands on any sparklers. He nearly set his hair on fire last year,' Valerie told Timothy, with an eye roll and a deep sigh.

Charity watched her mother leave, her eyes warm and soft. 'It might not seem like it, but they love each other to bits,' she said. 'They are my benchmark – I want to have a marriage like that one day.'

An image of his own parents drifted into his mind. They'd been happy and he wondered, as he often did, what they would have been like now if they'd lived. And what would Harry's life have been like? Vastly different without having his younger brother to take care of, Timothy knew. He'd have become a vet, for one thing. But Timothy recognised that Harry was happy now. He had a job he loved and a woman he loved even more. Harry seemed more settled and contented than Timothy could remember him ever being, and he was so pleased for him.

Timothy was also happy, and he'd be happier still if the woman by his side was to become his girlfriend. To test the water and to make sure last night wasn't a one-off, he put his arms around her, gratified when she lifted her chin for a kiss.

He kept it brief, mindful her parents were nearby and there were loads of children around, but the taste of her made his heart race, and her perfume had his head spinning with longing; and after he'd pulled away he was desperate to kiss her again.

He had no idea what was happening to him, or how to make sense of the emotions surging through his mind and his body, but he knew he liked it. He liked it very much indeed.

Charity would have been happy for the kiss to have gone on all evening, but they were in a very public place and her parents were close by; she didn't want them to have to witness her snogging the face off the new vet.

Giggling, she wondered how long people would continue to refer to Timothy as the "new vet". Years, probably.

'What are you laughing at?' he asked her, dropping a swift kiss onto the end of her cold nose. His lips were incredibly warm, and she glowed at his touch.

When she told him, he laughed. 'Probably until Tina and Brandon employ another vet,' he said. 'Then I'll become the "not-so-new" vet.'

He was about to say something else but a blast of music drowned him out, and she realised the firework display was about to start, so she caught hold of his hand and dragged him over to the barriers. Charity would have liked to continue to hold Timothy's hand, but he pushed her forward into a space, and took up position behind her. She hoped he'd be able to see over the top of her head, but as for herself she didn't care about watching the fireworks. All she could concentrate on was the man standing behind her. He was so close she could feel the solidity of his chest against her back, and she shivered with the anticipation of being kissed again later.

Possibly thinking her shiver was from the cold, he wrapped his arms around her and pulled her into him, his mouth near to her ear. She wished he'd nibble it, so she tilted her head slightly to the side, feeling incredibly brazen. His breath fanned her cheek, and she snuggled deeper into him as his arms tightened around her.

They stayed that way all through the display, their faces lifted to the sky as they became immersed in the lightshow overhead. And when it was over, he kissed the skin below her ear, and she shivered again as a tingle of desire shot through her.

'Shall we warm ourselves by the bonfire?' he asked.

Charity felt hot enough already. Any additional heating might result in her bursting into flames. However, she was happy to wander over to the pyre and feel the warmth on her face and sniff the aromatic smell of burning wood. The crackle of flames and the snap of burning branches replaced the music which had played during the display, and gradually people began to make their way home, many of them with sleepy children in tow.

Content to stand and watch the flames, the flickering light casting dancing shadows across the grass, Charity uttered a deep sigh of happiness. The night was perfect – a clear sky, an autumn chill to the air, velvety darkness beyond the reach of the light from the fire – and she was spending it with a man she felt a strong attraction to, who was just as attracted to her if the passion in his kisses was any indication. Beneath the building excitement they generated in her was a euphoria she hadn't experienced before, and during one of their subdued clinches she'd caught herself fast-forwarding several years to marriage, a home of their own, and a baby in a nursery.

Laughing inside at herself (she'd even tried out Charity Milton in her head, to see how it sounded), she was brought back to the present with a jolt when she heard her mother's voice.

'There you are!' Valerie exclaimed, as she walked towards them, hand-in-hand with Charity's dad. It was so cute the way they still held hands after all these years, Charity thought.

Charity beamed at her parents then introduced Timothy to her father. The poor guy, she thought – he'd already met her parents and he wasn't even her boyfriend yet. However, in a village like Picklewick it was hard not to get to know everyone, so she supposed it was going to happen sooner rather than later.

After the two men had been introduced and had found some common ground discussing sport (with an eyeroll from Valerie), Charity linked arms with her mum as they strolled across the field and into the village.

'How is it going with Timothy?' her mother asked. 'You seem very loved up.'

'He's gorgeous,' Charity murmured, not wanting to risk Timothy overhearing.

'I'm so pleased for you.' Valerie gave her arm a squeeze.

'Don't go putting the cart before the horse,' Charity warned. 'Technically, this is only our first date. He hasn't even mentioned seeing me again.'

'He will.' Her mum sounded positive. She stopped walking to allow the others to catch up, and said, 'I wonder if Timothy would like to come to lunch tomorrow? Your dad has bought the most enormous chicken – I don't know how we're going to fit it in the oven, let alone eat it all. We're going to need some help.'

Charity noticed Timothy's shocked expression out of the corner of her eye, and she hoped her mum wasn't putting him in an awkward position.

Oh dear, it had all been going so well until now…

'I'd love to, Mrs Jones,' Timothy replied, delighted to have been asked, but concerned what Charity might think of the invitation. 'I'm going to have to decline though, because I might have to dart off. I'm on call, you see.'

Mrs Jones looked at her daughter and then back at him. 'It's perfectly fine,' she said. 'We don't mind, and I have a feeling Charity might have to get used to you being on call. Please call me Valerie – Mrs Jones is so formal.'

Timothy had been planning on shoving a pizza in the oven. He had an open invitation to eat at the stables (Amos did most of the cooking and was rather good at it), but he didn't want to intrude on Harry and Petra. Harry didn't need his little brother hanging about, especially when he had a girlfriend.

On glancing at Charity to make sure she was happy with the situation, he was thrilled to see she was beaming.

'In that case, I'd be delighted,' he said.

'Alan, let's leave these love birds to it,' Valerie said to her husband, and moved away leaving him and Charity standing on the pavement.

'It's still early,' Timothy said. 'Fancy going to the pub?' He didn't really want a drink, but neither did he want to say goodnight.

She sighed heavily. 'I'd suggest you came back to mine for a coffee, but I still live at home.'

'Harry is at the stables, so how about a nightcap at my place?' His heart was thumping at the thought of the two of them being alone.

He had no intention of dragging her off to bed (although he would like nothing better than to make love to her) but being able to kiss her whilst sitting on a comfy sofa in a warm room would be something of a novelty; and he was acutely aware of how new this relationship of theirs was.

There were so many firsts ahead of them and he wanted to savour every single one. Which was exactly what he did, as the coffee he'd made sat untouched on the side table, for the next hour of delicious kissing and cuddling. And when he escorted her home, anxious not to let her out of his sight any sooner than he absolutely had to, his heart sang and he was so happy he wanted to tell the whole world.

'I had a great time,' he said when they reached her house, and he turned to kiss her again. He couldn't get enough of those delectable lips.

'So did I. Are you sure you want to come to lunch tomorrow? You don't have to.'

'Don't you want me to?'

'That's not what I said.' She dropped her gaze. 'It's not easy getting to know someone, is it?'

He placed a finger under her chin and raised her head. 'No, but it's good fun, and I want to get to know you an awful lot better. I want to know you inside and out, even if it takes me a lifetime to do it.'

Charity giggled softly. She sounded nervous.

'Too fast?' he asked.

'Just a little.'

'We can take things as slowly as you want.'

'This is only our first proper date,' she pointed out.

'I know, and I've loved every second of it.'

'Me, too.' She looked away, and he realised this was as new to her as it was to him.

'Until tomorrow.' He kissed her again. It lasted quite some time. If it was up to him, it would have lasted all night, and then some.

Finally, he released her, although she seemed as reluctant as he to end the embrace, and he knew he was utterly smitten. It might be early days and they'd hardly known each other long, but he was looking forward to seeing where their relationship would lead.

As he dawdled home, an image of Harry entered his mind and he fervently hoped he would find with Charity what Harry had found with Petra.

If the loss of his parents had taught him one thing, it was that life was incredibly short and love was all that ultimately mattered.

'You're back then? I was about to send out a search party,' Valerie joked.

'Very funny. Not.' Charity slung her coat on the back of a chair and took her hat and scarf off.

'Oi, put that away,' her mother instructed.

'I was going to.' Crumbs, living at home could be a trial sometimes. She adored her parents but they continued to treat her like a kid, and if she was honest she continued to act like one on occasion. She'd noticed Faith was the same when she was at home, and Charity thought back to the peace and solitude of Timothy's house.

He was in the same boat to a certain extent, because he was sharing a house with his brother who was also a father figure. It must have been dreadful for them both when their parents died she thought, her heart going out to the brothers. Timothy had told her the story, and she'd heard the grief in his voice and had sensed a deep well of sadness in him, which she guessed would always be there. It made her own heart ache for him, and she would have loved nothing more than to be able to ease his pain.

She hung her coat up in the cupboard under the stairs and put her hat and scarf away, then slumped onto the sofa.

'Did you enjoy the fireworks?' Valerie asked.

'Hmm.' Charity knew what her mum was fishing for, and it had nothing to do with the fireworks in the sky and everything to do with the fireworks in her chest. Her heart kept skipping a beat and her tummy turned over each time she thought of Timothy – which was every other second. He was so gorgeous—

'You didn't mind me asking him to lunch, did you?' Her mother broke into her thoughts, and Charity wished she'd gone straight to bed and avoided the third-degree questioning which she simply knew she was about to be subjected to.

'Not at all,' she replied. 'It was kind of you to invite him.'

'I've been thinking about Faith and Dominic…' Valerie said. She looked wistful.

'What about them?' Charity was thankful the conversation was moving away from her and Timothy.

'I wouldn't be surprised if there are wedding bells in the next year or so.'

The very same thing had occurred to Charity. It was a scary thought. Throughout their lives, the twins had relied on each other first and foremost – parents, friends and boyfriends had always had second billing. Then Dominic had arrived on the scene and things had slowly changed. It was only natural for Faith's priority to be the man she loved, but Charity had felt hurt, all the same.

Now, though, she felt a glimmer of what Faith must be feeling, and a new understanding of what her sister was going through crept into Charity's mind.

One day, Charity herself might feel the same way about someone. She sincerely hoped so.

Maybe that man would be Timothy?

Timothy's mouth was watering as soon as he walked into the hall of the Jones's house the following day, as the glorious aroma of roasting chicken assaulted his nose.

'Smells nice,' he said, sniffing appreciatively.

Charity's arms snaked around his neck, and he dipped his head towards her.

'So do you,' he added, then he kissed her, wishing he didn't have to stop.

'Come into the living room,' she said. 'Drink?' She showed him into a spacious room with two large sofas and a set of patio doors leading out to a generous garden. It was empty, but he heard noises coming from the kitchen so he assumed her parents were in there.

'A soft one, please. I'm on call, don't forget.'

She fetched him a cold drink from the kitchen, then sat next to him.

He felt rather awkward and Charity smiling nervously at him didn't help, so he decided to try to break the tension.

Leaning in close, he whispered in her ear, 'Do they bite?'

She giggled and any inhibitions dissipated. 'Only on weekdays,' she whispered back.

'What are you two whispering about?' Valerie asked, appearing in the doorway. 'Hi, Timothy, how are you?'

Timothy made small talk whilst helping Charity lay the table, and as he did so he felt as though he was getting to know a little more about Charity herself. He could see where her personality came from – her dad was quiet and reserved, her mum was far more lively and talkative. Her parents were opposites and she seemed to follow her father.

Come to think of it, he and Charity were opposites too, Timothy thought. He had always been up for a laugh and ready for fun, most of it noisy and exuberant. He was much more outgoing than Charity, he realised. Maybe it was part of the attraction between them – she was ying and he was yang. Or the other way around. Whatever…they fitted together as though they were two halves of the same person. Like Charity and Faith. Like Valerie and Alan.

There was a gentle, easy atmosphere between Charity and her parents, and a stab of pain caught him in the chest. Would his parents have been like this with him? Would they have welcomed Charity as warmly as Valerie and Alan had welcomed him? He was certain they would have done, and he felt their loss more keenly than usual.

Timothy had just finished the last morsel of chicken, having used it to mop up the smidge of gravy on his plate, and had placed his knife and fork down with a replete sigh, when his phone rang.

Taking it out of his pocket, he smiled apologetically. 'Sorry, I'll have to take this,' he said, and got to his feet.

His heart sank when he discovered he had a patient to see to. After promising to be there as soon as possible, he returned to the dining room to deliver the news.

'I've got to go,' he said. 'Thank you so much for inviting me. It was absolutely delicious.' He turned to Charity. 'Sorry,' he said. 'I'll give you a ring later?'

'You'd better had.' She got up and accompanied him to the door.

'Hopefully this won't take long,' he said, mentally crossing his fingers, and he bent his head to kiss her.

His joy when she slipped her arm around his neck and pulled her down to him, was only tempered by the knowledge that her parents might hear and could probably guess what they were doing. But as he left, he felt a warm glow of happiness which kept him going throughout the rest of the afternoon.

Charity dashed to the door when she heard the bell ring later that evening and opened it to find Timothy hiding behind a bunch of flowers.

'These are for your mum,' he said. 'To say thank you. Do you think she'll mind I bought them from the garage? The supermarket wasn't open.'

'She'll be thrilled you even thought of it,' Charity said. 'Come in and you can give them to her yourself.'

'Oh, you shouldn't have!' Valerie exclaimed as soon as she saw them, and she buried her nose in the colourful petals, inhaling deeply. She ran some water into the sink and popped the flowers into it. 'I've got a vase around here somewhere,' she muttered, opening and closing cupboards. She stopped searching and turned to him. 'Would you like a cup of tea?'

Charity leapt in before he had a chance to say a word. 'Thanks, Mum, but if it's okay with you, we'll nip to the pub for an hour or so.' Lunch had been lovely, but she wanted Timothy all to herself, and even the thought of having to put up with the other customers was better than sitting there with her mum and dad, being subjected to their knowing looks. Her mum hadn't stopped talking about how nice Timothy was, and dropping not-so-subtle hints that he was a keeper.

'Was your call-out okay?' she asked, as she pulled her front door closed behind them, and took hold of his hand. It seemed like the most perfectly natural thing to do, and she relished the feel of his palm on hers.

'Not really. A sheep had been worried by a dog. I stitched her up, but I doubt she'll last the night.'

She listened sympathetically. It wasn't easy losing an animal. She'd witnessed a fair few losses at the stables, from chickens to a cat, and on one awful occasion an old horse that had been put out to pasture years ago but who Petra still loved and cared for had died suddenly in the field.

'What was that?' she cried, when a loud bang made her shriek and set her heart racing. Timothy jumped too, and let out a cry.

'Dear god!' he exclaimed. 'Someone is setting off their own fireworks. Sales of them to individuals should be banned.' He grimaced. 'I sound like a right old fogey,' he said, 'but people don't realise how much distress they cause to animals. Harry was saying that Queenie spent most of Bonfire Night hiding under the stairs, and the stables are a fair distance away from the village.'

'I hope Storm is okay.' Charity chewed on her lip, imagining how scared her horse must be at the loud noises. And poor Queenie – the dog hated Bonfire Night, but for the fireworks to keep being set off for days ahead and for days afterwards was irresponsible.

'Do you want to drive up to the stables?' Timothy asked, as they reached the pub.

She shook her head. 'I'm being silly. If there was anything wrong, Petra would phone me. And if there was anything *really* wrong, she'd call *you*.'

'That's what I'm here for,' he said. 'Are you sure you don't want to give Petra a call?'

'I'm sure.' She stepped inside. 'Let's talk about something more uplifting.'

'How about…I think Harry will move in with Petra soon,' Timothy said, after he'd bought a couple of drinks and they found a free table.

'You do? She won't move in with him? I'm thinking of Amos and their lack of privacy.'

Timothy took a long swallow and leant back in his seat with a sigh. 'She won't leave the stables. Besides, if it isn't Amos getting in the way of the love-birds at the stables, it will be me in the cottage,' he said.

'What will you do if he does move in with her?'

'The lease on the cottage is due up in a couple of months – I'll renew it, if possible.'

'You're thinking of staying in Picklewick for a while, then?'

'Permanently. I love it here. My job is fab, the village is lovely, and my clients are great. And I've met you…' He waggled his eyebrows at her, in what he must have thought was a suggestive way.

'Stop it,' she laughed, tapping him on the arm. 'That's creepy.'

'You've hurt my feelings. I thought I looked sexy.'

'You do, when you're not using your eyebrows like a demented Sean Connery.'

'Ah, so you *do* think I'm sexy?'

Charity forgot where she was for a moment as she inched closer and wrapped her arms around his neck. 'You're *incredibly* sexy.' Her lips parted and she readied herself for a deep kiss when someone laughed on a nearby table, reminding her where she was. 'Later,' she promised, excitement coursing through her, making her all breathless and trembly.

She had no intention of sleeping with him yet, but the anticipation was excruciating and the touch of his hand in hers almost sent her into orbit.

When the landlord of the Black Horse finally announced time and urged his customers to drink up and be on their way, Charity didn't want the evening to end. She'd had a thoroughly glorious time getting to know Timothy on a deeper level, but there was no way she could invite him back to her house to continue their conversation: not with her mum and dad there. Once again, she thought it might be time she found a place of her own.

'I'll walk you back,' Timothy said, holding her coat out so she could slip her arms into it.

'That'll be nice. I'd invite you back for coffee, but…' She worried at her lip, hoping he hadn't taken her meaning the wrong way. Even if she had the house to herself, her invitation would be for nothing more than coffee and some serious snogging.

'We could go back to mine,' he said, then he grimaced. 'For coffee, I mean. Just coffee.' He shot her an apologetic look, and Charity was amused that he was worried she might think he was suggesting something more nefarious.

She was definitely thrilled at the idea, but not yet.

'Just for coffee,' she agreed, and she felt the tension leave him, only for it to return a half an hour later, after an enthusiastic and passionate embrace on his sofa.

'Goodness,' he murmured, panting slightly when they eventually surfaced.

Charity was trembling with desire and her own breathing was fast and shallow. 'Goodness, indeed,' she agreed, her voice hoarse and ragged.

Their coffees sat on a nearby table, cold and untouched. A fire spat and crackled in the hearth, and the room was warm enough for her to have shed a few items of clothing if she'd had a mind to. Soft music swirled around them, a soothing backdrop for her heightened emotions.

'Shall I take you home now?' he asked gently, his breathing returning to normal. Charity wished hers would, and her heart rate along with it, because her pulse was thudding in her ears.

'I think you'd better had,' she said, 'before things get out of hand.'

His smile was wry. 'I wouldn't complain if they did.'

Neither would I, Charity thought, before she gave herself a stern talking to. But the thought stayed with her all the way home and for a very long time afterwards.

Harry was at home when Timothy returned, which he was surprised about.

'I thought you were staying over at the stables tonight,' Timothy said. Thank god Charity had decided to go home when she had, otherwise Harry might have walked in on them. Not that they'd been naked or anything, but still…

'I had to come back for the van in the morning, and Petra was back and forth to the stables like a yo-yo all evening, checking on the horses. Some idiots have been letting off fireworks at the other end of Muddypuddle Lane and scaring the animals half to death.'

'I heard. I didn't realise the noise was coming from there – I thought it was coming from the village.'

'Kids, I expect, and when I say kids, I mean youths. Anyway, where have you been? It's gone midnight.'

'The Black Horse, with Charity.'

'Have you been snogging on her doorstep again?'

Timothy narrowed his eyes at his brother. 'We were here, actually.'

'You were? Do I have to give you the birds and the bees talk?' Harry laughed, ducking as Timothy threw a cushion at him.

'I think you gave me that talk a good few years ago. It was excruciatingly embarrassing.'

'Yeah, well, I had the talk off Dad; that was worse.' Harry stopped and stared at Timothy. 'I wish he had been here to give you yours.'

'Me, too.'

'I'm sorry I haven't been home more, Tim.'

'Hey, don't be daft. I didn't take this job so I could live in your pocket.' He twisted his lips into a wry smile.

Harry studied him. 'Are you okay about me and Petra?'

'Hell, yeah! I didn't think there was a woman out there who was prepared to put up with you!' Timothy paused. 'Can I ask you something? Can I take over the lease when it's due up?'

'If you want, or we can put it into joint names.'

'I think you'll move to the stables soon.'

Harry snorted. 'I might as well considering I spend so much time there, but we haven't talked about it. She's got to ask me first, and if you hadn't noticed, Petra is incredibly independent.'

'Talking about asking, would you ever ask her to marry you?'

Harry was silent for a while. 'Definitely, at some point. But not yet.'

'How did you know she was the one?'

'I just did. She fits into my life as though she's meant to be there, and when I tried to imagine life without her, I couldn't.'

It was Timothy's turn to fall silent for several minutes.

Eventually he said, 'I really like Charity. A lot. Did I tell you about when I went on my very first ride at the stables? Faith took me out for a hack and I thought she was Charity. I didn't realise they were twins.'

'And I never thought to mention it. How did that work out?'

'I thought she was awfully stuck-up until I found out I'd been trying to chat up Faith instead of Charity.'

'Ha! Bet that didn't go down well – she's all loved up with a guy who lives in the next village.'

'So I discovered.' Timothy chuckled, his thoughts turning to the stables. 'I wouldn't mind taking up riding again. It's bloody expensive, though.'

'Is that because of Charity? She's almost married to her horse.'

'Not at all.' Timothy drew in a long reflective breath. 'I miss it. Remember when we used to go riding with Mum? Then after they died how I used to beg for rides whenever and wherever I could? I miss the freedom, the feeling of being at one with the horse.'

'There's nothing stopping you from helping out at the stables in exchange for a free ride or two. I hear Faith is leaving Picklewick, so Petra will need someone.'

'I wish I could, but I don't really have the time.'

'You've got time to canoodle with Charity,' Harry pointed out with a laugh.

'That's because I really, really like her.'

There was that look again, as though Harry was examining him. 'I'm pleased for you. She's a lovely woman.'

Timothy blew out a breath. 'It's early days, but I think she likes me too.' And with that, he took himself off to bed, praying he was right.

CHAPTER EIGHT

Charity was in the tack room, performing the weekly chore of cleaning the bridles and saddles. It was a job she didn't particularly enjoy but one which had to be done, and everyone took turns, even Amos and Nathan, and Harry had also been known to lend a hand on occasion.

She wondered if Timothy might be roped into cleaning – according to her sister, he was a decent enough horseman, and she could envisage sitting in the tack room with him occupying her sister's chair, contently sharing the same tub of saddle soap.

It felt strange to be at the stables and knowing Faith was miles away. It was something they usually tried to do together, and they used to love chatting and giggling as they worked. Faith had been gone for eight days, and Charity missed her badly. How was she going to cope when her sister was gone for good?

The day was overcast and dull, with a raw northwesterly wind whipping over the hills, causing lips to chap and eyes to water by the time she finally finished her chores and was able to mount up and go for a ride. Storm pranced and tossed her head, trying to turn her backside to the weather, but once she'd trotted to the end of the lane, the mare settled down and Charity could relax.

It was a bittersweet ride for Charity, as she spotted Midnight grazing in a field next to the lane and guessed he might not be at the stables for much longer. And thinking about his empty stall made her want to cry. She and Faith were coming to the end of an era, and although the future was bright and rosy for Faith, and Charity wanted nothing more than for Faith to be happy, Charity couldn't help feeling sad for herself.

'Snap out of it,' she muttered crossly, then spent the rest of the ride trying to enjoy it and failing miserably. And for the first time ever, she was glad to return to the stables and the warmth of the house.

'Thanks, Amos.' Petra's uncle handed her a mug of piping hot cocoa as soon as she stepped inside, and Charity sipped gratefully, hoping it would ease the chill in her bones and her heart.

Harry was at the sink peeling potatoes, looking incredibly at home, and Charity all of a sudden felt shy and tongue-tied. His features were so similar to Timothy's, it was like gazing at an older version of the man she was falling for, and her tummy flipped over. Would she and Timothy still be together in ten years' time? It would be nice to think so. She could look back on today and remember thinking this very thing...

'Is something wrong?' Harry asked, and she hastened to wipe the glum expression off her face.

'Oh, you know...life...' she replied, the heat of the mug seeping through into her hands.

'Faith?' he guessed.

She nodded.

'Change isn't easy, is it?' he said, and she felt guilty for being so sad about Faith moving away from

Picklewick when he and Timothy had suffered a far more devastating blow.

'I need some time to adjust, that's all,' she said. 'We've always done everything together until—' She stopped abruptly, realising how churlish she sounded.

'She fell in love?'

'Are you reading my mind?' she half-joked.

'Not at all; I felt the same way about Timothy to a certain extent. I had to let him go, too.'

'Until he followed you to Picklewick,' Petra said smiling as she strode into the kitchen and headed for the fridge. 'Faith will always be your sister,' Petra said to Charity. 'You might be twins, but you are two separate people, with your own lives to lead. Harry's situation is different; he had to be a parent as well as a sibling. But he's right, you have to let her go up here.' Petra tapped her temple.

Charity knew Petra was right. The days of dressing the same, liking the same things, and finishing each other's sentences weren't exactly gone, because there would always be that unique connection that twins had, but it was time for them to be their own people. Faith was already some way ahead of her on the path.

'I'm going to get my hair cut,' she announced, and Harry blinked at the apparent change of topic. Petra got it though, and she nodded.

Filled with enthusiasm Charity finished her drink and headed back to the village. The hairdresser might be able to fit her in today, if she was lucky.

On the way, she passed Timothy's cottage and her thoughts kept coming back to him. His car was on the drive, and when she imagined him inside the house, her heart predictably skipped a beat. That he was capable of making her heart bounce around and her tummy play host to a hundred butterflies was comforting, because suddenly she knew she wouldn't feel as alone when Faith left as she would have done if Timothy hadn't come into her life.

Maybe, just maybe, she'd find her own happily ever after, too.

'What do you think?' Charity asked, turning her head from side to side.

'It suits you,' Timothy replied, meaning it. She looked more confident, more sophisticated, and the sleek shoulder-length bob highlighted her heart-shaped face. 'You look beautiful.'

'Do you mean it?' Charity frowned.

'I wouldn't say it if I didn't,' he assured her. 'I'll never lie to you.'

'What would you have said if you didn't like it?' She was teasing him, and her eyes twinkled.

'I would have said something like "it's really shiny". Or, "at least I'll not mistake your sister for you again". What does Faith think about it, now you no longer look identical?'

'I haven't told her I've had it cut, and I've asked Mum and Dad not to mention it when they speak to her. I was going to send her a photo but I want to see her reaction first-hand, not when she's had time to filter it. I'll be able to tell straight away if she hates it or not.'

'She won't hate it,' Timothy said. 'Not when you look so gorgeous.'

'We've always worn our hair the same, though,' she said, looking worried.

'New beginnings call for a new hairstyle,' he said. 'At least, that's what they say, isn't it? I'm sure she'll understand.'

'Talking of new beginnings, I'm also looking for somewhere to rent,' she told him. 'It's time I stood on my own two feet. I can't live with my parents forever. I'm never going to move on if I don't move out. I wonder if Dominic's place will become available? I must remember to ask Faith.'

'Harry is moving into the stables,' he said. Harry had informed him only last night.

'You thought he might,' Charity said, snuggling on the sofa next to him. He draped an arm around her shoulders and pulled her close.

'I'm taking over the lease for the next six months, then I might look for somewhere to buy.' He debated whether to offer for her to live with him, but even if it was only a platonic arrangement in that she would have one of the bedrooms and he would have the other, he didn't think that would end up being the case, or that Charity would view his offer in the spirit it was intended. They'd known each other for all of three weeks (not including their first encounter in the cafe) so it was far too soon to take their relationship to the next level, no matter how swiftly his feelings for her were growing.

'Harry has shifted a lot of his stuff already. I'll give him a hand with the rest tomorrow.'

'I must admit, he was looking very much at home when I saw him up at the stables earlier. He was peeling potatoes.'

'I hope I haven't driven him away,' Timothy said. He'd been fretting about it all last night and most of today, in between patients. 'I feel that no sooner I've moved in, than he's moving out.'

'Does he love Petra?'

Timothy was startled. What a question! 'Most definitely.'

'There's your answer.'

Reflectively, he considered what she'd said. Charity had hit the nail on the head. Harry had tried to reassure him on several occasions, but it had taken someone else to make him see the truth of it.

'Thank you,' he said, twisting around to face her. 'I've been going around in circles and beating myself up over it, but you're right. Harry's motive is love, not a desire to escape from his annoying little brother.'

'You're not annoying.'

They were nose to nose, his mouth inches from hers. 'I'm not?'

'I don't think so.'

'What am I?'

'Stop fishing for complements,' she murmured, 'and kiss me.'

He didn't need asking twice.

And when their kisses deepened, passion sweeping over them, and she asked, 'Are you expecting Harry back this evening?' he understood what she meant, especially when she grasped his hand and led him upstairs to make him the happiest man in the world.

Charity yawned hugely, and briefly closed her eyes. She was so tired she could sleep for a week. The past few days (or should she say "nights") had been notable for the lack of sleep, amongst other things. It was thinking about the *other things* that made her blush this morning.

'Are we keeping you up?' Brian asked, and she jerked awake.

Blimey, fancy falling asleep at her desk! It was lucky it was a resident who'd noticed, and not William, the care home manager.

'Sorry,' she muttered, but she couldn't prevent a smile from taking over her face as she thought of the main reason she was so exhausted lately. It was all Timothy's fault. If he wasn't so irresistible…

'You look like the cat what's got the cream,' Brian said. 'It's bound to be a fella.'

It certainly was! Charity had never been as happy. She had been on cloud nine since she and Timothy had made love, and she couldn't stop smiling. He had a particular knack of making her feel she was the most special person in the world, and when they slipped between the sheets she felt so very loved and cherished – as well as totally satisfied.

Loved and cherished…hmm. He hadn't said he loved her yet, and he might never utter those three little words, she conceded, but she got the feeling he cared deeply for her.

She more than cared for him. She'd completely fallen for him. It might not be the most intelligent thing she'd ever done and making love with him had only exacerbated her feelings, but she'd been unable to prevent the avalanche of emotions sweeping through her.

Nevertheless, she was hopeful he felt the same way, and every day that went by cemented her certainty. In the short amount of time she'd known him, she felt as close to him as she did to Faith. He completed her, filling a hole in her heart she hadn't been aware was there. She could so easily and thoroughly fall in love with him. In fact, she suspected she was halfway there already.

'He'd better be worth it,' Brian said, and she realised he was standing right next to her and had been watching her for the last couple of minutes.

'He is,' she sighed. 'He most definitely is!'

On impulse, she leant towards the old man and gave him a quick peck on the cheek.

Brian flushed and a smile lit up his face. 'You've made my day,' he told her, and she grinned as he slowly walked away.

Fizzing with happiness, she could fully appreciate what Faith had been experiencing. Charity was finding it hard to concentrate on anything other than Timothy. He seemed to have pushed everything else out of her head. Everything except Storm and the stables, but even when she visited Muddypuddle Lane, half her mind was on what Timothy was doing, and hoping he was thinking about her as much as she was thinking about him.

It was hard fitting it all in, she acknowledged, feeling sympathy for Faith. Her job took a large chunk of her time, and although she loved working at the care home, she would have loved being in bed with Timothy more. The same went for her responsibilities at the stables, especially since she was also doing Faith's share of the work. It wasn't fair for it to fall on Petra's shoulders – Midnight was still being housed at the stables and Charity couldn't expect Petra to do it for nothing. She had a business to run, after all, and lots of mouths to feed. Faith had promised Charity she'd make it up to her, and Charity intended to hold her twin to her promise; she was looking forward to spending more quality time with Timothy as soon as Faith got back.

Which was any minute now, Charity saw, when her phone vibrated and she read Faith's message. Faith was coming home a day early because she and Dominic had finalised everything, and Faith was anxious to sort things out in Picklewick. She was popping into the village to pick up a few things, then Dominic would drop her at their parents' house. Charity smiled drily, betting the sole purpose was to get her washing done.

Charity couldn't wait to see her sister, and she squealed with excitement. They had so much to tell one another, so much to share, and finally Charity didn't feel as though she was being left behind. She felt as though she was starting a whole new chapter.

Life was looking pretty good for both of them, and Charity hugged herself with elation before messaging Faith to tell her she'd missed her and couldn't wait to see her.

If it was Timothy's day to be in the practice he normally walked to work. There didn't seem much point in starting his car's engine for a two-minute journey. And if he was called out to an emergency, he used the company's SUV.

Today had been a typical day of skin rashes, booster shots, a cat off her food, a retriever with an evil-smelling ear, a cockatiel whose beak needed trimming, and a German Shepherd with arthritis. All in all it had been a good day: no upsetting diagnoses, no end of life discussions. He'd operated in the afternoon, and the two spayings and the removal of an abscess from a rather large rabbit had gone without a hitch. He'd finished sooner than he'd scheduled, so he was able to head off home slightly earlier than usual.

He let the staff door click shut behind him and he took a deep breath of fresh air and stretched to ease the kinks out of his back before he began his walk to the cottage. If he called into the corner shop on the way, he might be able to pick up a pumpkin (he'd noticed some the other day when he was in there) and he'd have a go at making pumpkin soup for when Charity got home. His home, not hers. She was spending more and more time in the cottage and Timothy was loving it. It was almost as though they were living together, and he hoped one day she would actually consider moving in with him.

Ever since she'd taken him to bed (he'd teased her that she'd seduced him, and she didn't deny it) she had become the focal point of his life. He thought about her constantly, and whenever he did, his heart filled with joy. It had been totally the right decision to relocate to Picklewick; everything was falling into place and had done from the moment he'd seen the job advertised. Not only did he love his job and the village, he'd also fallen head over heels for the most wonderful woman, and to top it all off, the house in Cheltenham was on the market and the estate agent was hopeful of an offer in the not too distant future. As soon as the house was sold, he could think about using his share to put a deposit on a place in Picklewick, and by then he and Charity would have known each other long enough that his suggestion they live together wouldn't seem so silly.

He was acutely conscious their relationship was incredibly new, but he was also confident it would last. They were made for each other. Timothy couldn't imagine being with anyone else, and if what he felt was love, then so be it. Coming to Picklewick and meeting Charity was fate.

Coming to a halt outside the corner shop, he checked his pocket for his wallet. Did he need to get any money out?

Undecided, he glanced across the road to the hole-in-the-wall to see if there was a queue, and blinked when he spotted Charity.

He thought she was supposed to be at work; the care home was only on the other side of the village however, so she might have nipped out for something. She wasn't wearing the black tailored trousers that were part of her uniform, though; she was wearing jeans and a colourful top, and he wondered if she'd finished early for some reason. He put his hand up to wave, but her back was to him, her bobbed hair swinging around her face as she concentrated on the instructions on the screen, so he let it drop to his side.

Timothy was about to cross the road for a sneaky kiss, but a lorry trundled past and by the time the road was clear, she'd finished her business at the cashpoint and had walked towards a car parked at the kerb. She opened the door and got in.

Then she leant towards the driver and gave the man behind the wheel a long kiss on the lips, her arms entwined around his neck. Even from this distance, she looked as though she was enjoying herself.

Timothy's jaw dropped.

He wasn't sure whether his eyes were playing tricks on him, or not. Could it be Faith? He shook his head, trying frantically to process what he was seeing. It couldn't be Faith. Faith had long hair. The woman in the car had the same sleek bob as Charity, so it had to be her.

He watched as Charity eased back into the passenger seat, and the man tucked a strand of hair behind her ear. It was the same gesture he himself had performed numerous times.

His heart splintering into a thousand pieces, he reached for his phone, hardly taking his eyes off the scene in front of him. He simply couldn't believe she was being so open about it. She was seeing someone else, and she didn't care who knew it.

Dear god…

He swallowed, gathered his courage, and with a shaking hand he sent a message to the woman he finally admitted to himself that he had fallen in love with.

I never want to see you again, it said. ***I saw you kissing that man.*** Then he turned his phone off.

When he saw Charity bend her head to her phone and begin to read, he turned around, tears building behind his eyes, and walked away, agony in his heart, disbelief in his mind and emptiness in his soul.

Charity Jones had broken his heart and he didn't know how he'd be able to live with the pain.

'What on earth?' Charity read the message for a second time, then a third, her mind lagging behind what her eyes were telling her.

Why would Timothy send her such a thing? What was he talking about? *What man?* He couldn't have meant Brian, could he?

She checked the message again, making sure the number definitely was Timothy's, her heart sinking when she realised it most definitely was. There was no mistake – the message was from him.

What had he thought he'd seen? And *who* had he thought he'd seen her kiss?

Confused and more than a little upset, she tried calling him, but he must have switched his phone off. A horrible thought occurred to her – had he blocked her number?

What had she done? Or, more to the point, what did he *think* she'd done?

Whatever it was, his reaction had been over-the-top. Extreme, even. He wasn't giving her a chance to explain, although she was bewildered as to what explanation she could possibly give him considering she didn't have a clue what he was on about or what she'd done wrong.

Tears gathering in the corners of her eyes, she tried his number again, with the same result, and she understood he had no intention of speaking to her.

Her heart aching and her tummy in knots, she shakily tried calling him from Honeymead's phone, in the hope he wouldn't recognise the number and would answer her.

On hearing the same recorded message, she admitted defeat and left a garbled one of her own. Then she put her head in her hands, gulping back tears as she wondered what on earth was going on. Desperately wanting to speak to him but having to remain at work until the end of her shift, she tried to compose herself. She had a job to do, and it wasn't fair on either visitors or residents if she wasn't totally professional. However, she couldn't prevent a tear sliding down her cheek, no matter how hard she tried, and it was just bad timing that William happened to be heading off home for the day when he spotted her.

'What's wrong?' he asked. And that was all it took for her to begin to cry in earnest.

Little fazed her manager, and unfortunately tears were an all too frequent occurrence in a place such as a care home (although Charity didn't often cry in work, except when a resident passed on), so he gently guided her away from the reception area, whilst asking Rose to cover for her.

'Can I do anything?' he asked when she was safely tucked into his office and away from curious gazes. 'Do you need me to phone anyone?'

The one person she wanted to speak to was Timothy, but he was blanking her.

'Do you mind if I call Faith?' she asked, realising the only other person she wanted was her sister. Faith would know what to do and what to say. 'I'll try not to be long.'

'Of course I don't mind. Take all the time you need. In fact, why don't you knock off now? There's not long to go until your shift ends.'

'Thank you,' she whispered, grateful for his kindness. She'd give Faith a call, then try to do something about her stinging eyes and red nose before she went home. She didn't need her parents asking questions when she didn't have any answers to give them.

'Stay there, I'll come and get you,' Faith said immediately, as Charity sobbed down the phone. Her sister didn't even ask what was wrong. That was what having a sister like Faith was all about – if Charity had told her she'd killed someone, Faith wouldn't ask questions; she'd just turn up with a shovel and her unshakeable belief that whoever it was that Charity had done away with, must have had it coming to them.

Charity had attempted to make herself presentable, although holding a wad of wet tissues to her reddened eyes had done little to make them less red, and was sitting sadly in William's office watching through the window for her sister to arrive when Faith hurried through the main gates.

What Charity saw when she clapped eyes on her sister almost made her smile, and it would have done if she hadn't been so upset.

Faith had been to the hairdresser and she'd also had her hair cut – *into a sleek, shoulder-length bob!*

CHAPTER NINE

'You should talk to him,' Faith said to Charity, for about the tenth time that week. It had been five days since Timothy had accused her of kissing another man. Five days since he'd jumped to the wrong conclusion and hadn't given her a chance to defend herself.

'No way. If he was the last man on earth I'd walk past him and keep going.' Charity's breath clouded around her head as she stomped down the lane towards the field containing Storm and Midnight, plus an older mare. The sisters were bringing them in for the night. It was only during the warmer spring and summer months, did the animals stay out overnight.

'But look at you – you're as miserable as a wet weekend in January.' Faith was puffing and panting behind her as she tried to keep up.

'I like January. Snowdrops flower in January and the days start getting longer.'

'You know what I mean.'

Charity knew perfectly well what Faith meant, but she didn't care.

'How dare he not even give me the opportunity to explain. He should have asked me first, not jumped to conclusions.'

She'd said the same thing countless times.

'I agree, but in a way I can see where he was coming from. I did give Dominic a proper sucky-face snog.'

'Ew.' Charity paused at the gate, slid the bolt back, then held it open for Faith.

'And he wasn't to know I'd had my hair cut in the same style as you.'

'Copycat,' Charity said. 'We've been over this. Let's just lay it to bed and move on, okay?'

'But you're miserable.'

'Yes, I know. I'll get over it.'

'When? How? You're skulking around the village, worried in case you'll bump into him. You can't go on like this. Besides, when he sees me, he'll know he's made an idiot of himself.'

'Duh, he'll think you are me.'

'I'll soon set him straight.'

'Don't bother. If that's the kind of person he is, I've had a lucky escape. I don't want a man who gets jealous and is in my face all the time.'

'He had a good reason. I would have reacted in the same way if I'd caught Dominic in a passionate clinch with another woman. If you won't speak to Timothy, then let me.'

'Don't you dare! I forbid you to speak to him – I can fight my own battles, thank you, and if anyone is going to confront him, it will be me.'

Charity clicked her tongue at Storm and called the horse to her. She was grateful for Faith's concern and support, but she had to stand on her own two feet. They might be twins, but they were separate people, and soon her sister would be gone and Charity would have to learn to deal with things on her own.

'I should have told you I'd had my hair cut,' Faith said yet again. She'd been lamenting the fact she hadn't ever since Charity had told her what happened.

'Yes, well. I didn't tell you, either.' Charity said. She'd felt incredibly strange after she'd had it cut to think that she and Faith no longer looked quite as alike. How wrong could she have been? If she'd only had known it, Faith had given herself the new hair, new beginnings talk too, which had resulted in her paying a hairdresser a visit and emerging with the exact same style as Charity.

When their mother had seen Faith's new hairstyle, all she'd done was roll her eyes and repeat the story of Faith falling out of the tree at the bottom of their garden, and Charity, who had been in the living room reading a book at the time, crying out in sudden pain and clutching her leg. Valerie finished her tale by saying, 'Nothing about you two surprises me.'

A loud bang made Storm startle and shy away, her tail held high as she whirled on her haunches and trotted across the field, Midnight following close behind her. Mabel, an older horse and one which was only ridden occasionally, stared after the younger animals with what could only be described as an amused expression. She calmly flicked an ear and went back to cropping the grass.

'Stormy,' Charity called, as the mare who was doing a circuit of the field with Midnight hot on her heels, came closer to the gate. 'Look what I've got.' She held out half an apple in the hope it would entice the horse to have a lead rope attached to her halter. 'Damned fireworks – someone has been letting them off for weeks. It's not even dark properly yet, so I don't see the point.'

'There are some really stupid people about,' Faith agreed, but before Charity could say anything further, a tremendous explosion sounded almost directly overhead, and she ducked instinctively.

'Bloody hell,' Charity swore, as Midnight squealed in alarm and tore past her, only missing her by inches and catching Faith on the shoulder.

Faith staggered, was spun around and almost lost her balance. Charity shot a hand out to steady her. 'Are you okay?' she asked, keeping her eye on Storm who was galloping around the field with her ears back and her nostrils flaring.

'I'm fine.' Faith rubbed the top of her arm. 'But we need to catch the horses before they do themselves some mischief. Oh, no! *Midnight!*'

Charity tore her gaze away from the mare, to see Midnight aiming directly for the fence. Terrified he was going to attempt to clear it, Faith screamed, and at the last possible moment, he skidded to a halt and tried to turn, but his speed was too great. Charity watched in dismay as he ploughed into the fence. The top section of wire came away with a twang, bringing a length of wood with it. Then to her horror, it snapped back and it's sharp, splintered end pierced the horse in the chest.

Midnight squealed and reared up, hooves flailing, his yellow teeth bared and the whites of his eyes showing. Faith shrieked and dodged to the side as he spun on his hind legs, leapt forwards and charged past her.

Charity thought fast.

'Grab Storm, if you can,' she shouted to Faith, as she ran towards Mabel who had spooked at the sudden noise but had settled down again.

Charity didn't often ride bareback and without reins, but she could when she had to, and this was one of those times. Almost without breaking stride, she vaulted onto Mabel's back and grasped her mane.

Urging the elderly mare forward with her legs and her voice, Charity persuaded her into a trot, and she aimed the horse at a spot where she anticipated Midnight to be in a few moments if he carried on doing wild laps of the field.

Keeping low on Mabel's back so as not to upset Midnight more than he already was, Charity urged the mare into a canter and for several strides the two animals ran side by side, with Charity edging Mabel ever closer to the gelding, trying to use the fence on the one side and the mare's body on his other to slow him down.

It seemed to take forever, but it couldn't have been very long because Petra had only just reached the field when Midnight slowed to a trembling uneven walk, and Charity was able to stretch across and attach the lead rope to his halter.

Feeling sick and shaky herself, she guided Mabel to the gate, where she gladly handed Midnight over to Petra.

'There, there,' Petra murmured, soothing the gelding, running her hands over his body and legs to check for damage. Midnight, still trembling, tolerated her ministrations. He was blowing hard, the whites of his eyes still showing, and he twitched and shook, but at least he didn't try to bolt.

'Call the vet,' Petra said, her voice low. 'Tell them we've a horse with a puncture wound to his chest. It's not very big, but I can't tell how deep it is.'

Charity got her phone out of her pocket, surprised

to find she hadn't lost it in the mayhem.

'Are either of you hurt?' Petra asked, continuing to stroke the gelding.

Charity raised her eyebrows at Faith and her sister shook her head. 'No,' Charity replied.

'What about the other horses?' Petra asked.

'They're fine.' Charity swallowed hard, her limbs still shaking.

'Bloody fireworks,' Petra muttered. 'Come on, boy, let's get you in your stall and see what's what.' Never once taking her eyes off the horse, she said to the twins, 'Are you okay to bring the others in? Harry and Amos are rounding up the ponies in the top field. I can send Harry down when they've finished, if you want.'

Faith didn't say anything, and Charity's gaze met Faith's wide eyed and shocked face. She was clutching Storm's lead rope with white-knuckled hands, her mouth opening and closing but nothing was coming out, so Charity answered for them both.

'We can manage.'

'Good work, ladies.' Petra's smile was grim. 'If you hadn't had acted so quickly, we could have had a disaster on our hands. Right, I'm taking Midnight up to the stables. Don't forget to ring the vet.'

Faith didn't look capable of speaking to anyone, so it was down to Charity. She didn't bother with calling the practice; instead, she phoned Timothy. No matter how she felt about him personally, he was a darned good vet. There was no one she trusted more with a horse.

It was just a pity she didn't trust him with her heart.

Timothy's heart nearly leapt out of his chest when he reached for his mobile and saw who was calling him.

Charity!

'Um… hi?' he answered, not daring to hope, but hope flaring deep inside him anyway.

'It's me, Charity. Can you come to the stables? Midnight is hurt.'

Without thinking, his professionalism took over. This wasn't a social call. 'Of course. What's the problem?' He was still in the surgery, and he was shucking off his lab coat as he spoke.

'He's got a puncture wound in his chest from a length of wood.'

'On my way,' he said, hanging up and shouting to Celia to tell her where he was going. Used to having the vets dash off at a moment's notice, she nodded and made a note of his whereabouts.

His thoughts were in turmoil at the prospect of seeing Charity again. He'd not spoken to her or even caught a glimpse of her since he'd accused her of being unfaithful. Harry had tried to reason with him, saying there could be a perfectly acceptable explanation, but as far as Timothy was concerned there could be absolutely no excuse for her to play tonsil hockey with another man when she was supposed to be his girlfriend. Hell, he'd even been considering asking her to live with him when the time was right.

It looked like the time was most definitely *not* right, and never would be. And neither did he accept Harry's argument that a kiss didn't mean she had been unfaithful. As far as Timothy was concerned it meant precisely that, and he'd refused to discuss the situation any more, even going as far as sticking his fingers in his ears and singing la-la-la loudly when Harry had tried to talk to him about it again.

His brother had given him a stern look, then had thrown his hands in the air and stalked off. Timothy had taken his fingers out of his ears and had caught the tail end of what Harry was saying – something about Timothy finding out for himself. 'I give up,' had been Harry's parting shot.

Since then, he'd heard little from Harry, and if he was honest Timothy was glad to put a little distance between him and his brother's well-meaning interference.

With his heart hammering, he pulled into the yard and switched off the engine. Now was not the time to be thinking of Charity: he had an injured horse who deserved his full attention.

Climbing out of his vehicle, he saw Harry waiting for him. 'How bad is it?' he asked.

'It's difficult to tell. I suspect not too bad, but the horse has had a fright and he's in a bit of a state.'

Petra was holding Midnight's head when he entered the animal's stall, stroking the soft nose and blowing gently into the horse's dilated nostrils. The horse was trembling, his skin twitching as though a swarm of insects were irritating his skin, and he rolled his eyes and tossed his head when he saw Timothy.

'It's okay, boy, it's okay,' he crooned, slowly sidling into the stall and being sure not to make any sudden movements. Charity was standing behind Petra and he gave her a brief nod, his swift glance taking in the worry on her face and her tear-filled eyes.

He frowned: something wasn't right.

Suddenly Midnight thrashed and pawed the ground, churning up the deep hay, and Timothy snapped his attention back to the horse, which was where it should have been in the first place.

'Everyone out,' he instructed. 'Let's give him some space. Petra, can you stay and hold his head while I examine him?'

He took a slow step towards the animal, and Midnight flicked his tail and his ears went back. 'There's a good boy,' he said, trying to ignore Charity as she sidled past him.

It was impossible.

His eyes jerked towards her, and he let out a gasp.

The woman who he'd assumed was Charity, was *Faith*.

Midnight crabbed sideways, banging against the side of his stall, and once again Timothy dragged his mind back to his patient.

'What happened?' he asked, scrutinizing the animal.

'Some idiot let off a sodding firework in the lane,' Petra said, anger oozing from her. 'Midnight bolted and tried to plough his way through the fence. A piece of wood splintered and caught him in the chest. I don't think it's serious or deep, but just in case…'

The horse was sweating profusely, his black coat sodden, so it was difficult to tell if he was still bleeding, but Petra had blood on her hands and a smear of copper on her cheek.

It took some time and a lot of comforting for the horse to calm down, but once he did and Timothy examined him, cleaned the wound and gave him a shot of antibiotic, both Timothy and Petra were satisfied the animal didn't need stitches.

'You'll be fine, won't you, lad?' Timothy patted the horse on the neck, glad to see he was nosing at his hay net. Midnight began to nibble at it with soft mobile lips, and Timothy left him to it. 'I don't need to tell you to stable him for a day or two, and keep an eye on him.'

'No, but you did anyway,' Petra retorted.

Timothy didn't take offence, knowing Petra well enough to realise relief was making her cranky. 'You'd better tell Faith her horse is okay. She looked terribly upset.'

'She was. You probably aren't interested, but Charity was an absolute star. If it wasn't for her, Midnight might have done himself a great deal more damage.'

'Of course I'm interested.'

'You've got a funny way of showing it.'

He took a breath and blew it out slowly. 'I thought Faith was Charity just now.'

'Huh, can't you tell them apart yet?' Petra gave him a scornful look.

'The last time I saw Faith, she had long hair. I didn't realise she'd had it cut. It's in the same style as Charity, so I think it was an easy mistake to make.' His eyes widened. '*When* did she have it cut?' he asked slowly.

'When she was in Norwich. Neither of them was aware the other had changed their style until Faith came home. I laughed my socks off when I found out they'd gone for the same one, so they look almost identical again. Doing something like that is a twin thing, apparently.' She stopped talking and bit her lip, a smirk growing around the edges of her mouth. 'You didn't know.'

He shook his head. It was now glaringly obvious to him what had happened

'You're kidding, right?' Petra was incredulous, as well she might be, and she barked out a laugh. 'Oh, my god, that's priceless! No wonder you thought Charity had been kissing another bloke. It was Faith, all along.'

So that's what Harry had been trying to tell him, that Faith had the same haircut; but Timothy had been childishly chanting la-la-la and had refused to listen. What a dipstick he'd been.

'I'd better go and talk to her, hadn't I?' he said, feeling a total fool, but behind the embarrassment a faint flame of hope had fanned into life.

If he explained, maybe she'd forgive him.

Or maybe not. All she'd needed to do was to tell him what had happened, but she hadn't. Had he burned his bridges and driven her away?

Petra snorted. 'You'd better had. If I was her, I probably wouldn't want to speak to you ever again, though. Muppet,' she added, under her breath.

Her assessment was an accurate one. He really had behaved like a muppet. In his defence, it was only because he had such deep feelings for her that he'd reacted the way he had. If Charity had been any other woman, he'd have simply shrugged and walked away, never to think about her again.

But she wasn't any other woman, and he *had* been thinking about her. Constantly. He hadn't been able to get her out of his mind, and he'd never felt so miserable in his life.

He lifted his chin and squared his shoulders. It was time to tell her how he felt.

All he hoped was that she felt the same way, and she could find it in her heart to forgive him.

Charity had been hoping to keep out of Timothy's way until Faith was ready to go home, or until Timothy left the stables.

It wasn't to be.

She'd taken herself off to the kitchen and had one of Amos's famous hot chocolates to soothe her ragged nerves. She was still shaking from the drama of the evening, and was worried sick about Midnight, and those two things would have been enough on their own, but having Timothy so close was too much, and it had brought her to tears.

Amos had put his arm around her and given her a hug, then in his practical way he'd made her a hot drink and let her get on with sorting herself out.

She'd just finished the last sip and was wondering whether it was safe to return to the stable and find out if Midnight was okay, when a figure loomed in the doorway and she knew without turning her head that it was Timothy.

'I was hoping to catch you,' he said.

Charity hadn't hoped for anything of the sort. The last person she wanted to see was him. He'd caused her enough pain and she wanted some distance between them for a while to try to put her feelings for him behind her. It wasn't going to be easy avoiding him, but she'd been doing all right so far.

'What do you want?' she asked woodenly, then she had a terrible thought. 'Is Midnight okay?'

'He's fine. He's scoffing his supper as we speak.'

'Thank goodness.' She slumped back in her chair, suddenly feeling weak and giddy, despite the hot sweet drink.

'I'll…er…go and see if Petra needs any help,' Amos said, sidling past her as though she was a snake ready to strike. He gave Timothy a nervous smile, then legged it.

Charity watched him go with regret. She'd have preferred him to stay to act as a buffer between her and Timothy.

'I've come to apologise.' Timothy walked over to her and knelt by her chair.

She refused to look at him, knowing if she did, she might burst into tears.

'I thought Faith was you,' he continued.

'Clearly.' Tell her something she didn't know.

'I didn't realise she'd had her hair cut the same as you. It was an easy mistake to make.'

'Agreed. But you didn't give me the chance to defend myself, or to explain.'

'I know, and I can't apologise enough.'

'Agreed,' she repeated. No amount of saying sorry would make up for his lack of trust.

'Would it help if I told you I wouldn't have reacted like I did, if I didn't care about you as much as I do?'

No…Maybe…Heck, she didn't know. She glanced at him. He looked awful. There were dark circles around his eyes and she thought he might have lost some weight.

He gazed at her pleadingly. 'It might be too soon to say this, and you might not want to hear it anyway after the way I treated you, and I know we've only known each other for a few weeks, but when I try to imagine you not being in my life, I can't. I'm falling in love with you, Charity.' He stopped and took a breath, his eyes downcast.

Charity hadn't been expecting that. A profuse apology, perhaps. Even a grovelling one. But not a declaration of love.

It was utterly unexpected. And utterly wonderful.

Joy cascaded through her and she couldn't catch her breath with the force of it.

As she watched his expression turn from hopeful to despairing, she forced herself to speak.

'I'm falling for you, too,' she squeaked, her voice several octaves higher than normal. This wasn't how she'd imagined a man telling her he loved her. She'd envisaged dinner and candles, and wine. Definitely wine.

Before she could say anything further she felt herself being enveloped in his arms as he rained kisses over her face.

Laughing, she captured his mouth, her lips seeking his as she melted into him, her heart filled with love and her soul filled with happiness.

He might be right – they hadn't known each other long, but she felt she'd known him forever, like he was a part of her that she hadn't known was missing until he'd come into her life.

'I love you,' he said, breaking away for the briefest of moments. 'Just in case I didn't make myself clear. I don't want any more misunderstandings.'

'Are you sure you're kissing the right sister?' she teased.

'I'm sure. I've never been so sure of anything in my life.'

'Oi, you two!' Petra made them both jump. 'Stop canoodling and put the kettle on. I could do with a cuppa. Bloody fireworks. They should be banned.'

Petra was right, they should be banned. Charity caught Timothy's eye and grinned; who needed actual fireworks when there were enough emotional fireworks between them to last a thousand Bonfire Nights.

And when he kissed her again, all she heard was Petra muttering, 'Bloody fireworks,' as her love for this wonderfully handsome, thoughtful, silly man burst into everlasting flame.

WINTER

CHAPTER ONE

'You're giving this to me *now*?' Megan Barnes stared at the card and the words written on it, and shook her head. She was trying to hold back tears and so far she was succeeding, but she didn't think she'd manage it for much longer.

Richard winced. 'It was what Jeremy wanted and I've never deviated from his instructions; you know that.'

'But it's December – far too cold to go horse riding.'

'Look,' her brother-in-law said. 'I didn't have anything to do with this. Or any of the other—' he cleared his throat '—gifts.'

'I used to ride when I was a girl,' she said, sitting down abruptly. They were in her living room, the place where Richard usually handed her the envelopes Jeremy had left for her since he'd died. And every time Richard did so, it was as though her heart was being torn from her chest and she was losing Jeremy all over again.

Richard, who was Jeremy's brother and the executor of his will, said, 'If it's any consolation, this is the final one. There are no more.'

'Thank goodness for that. I don't think I can take any more.' The last one had instructed her to go diving. She and Jeremy had intended doing it when they went on holiday to Turkey, but the holiday had to be cancelled. In the end, Megan had dived without him, off the coast of West Wales. It had been a far chillier experience than the one they'd planned. But during those brief minutes on the seabed, she'd felt closer to her husband than ever. Megan gulped, wishing he had been with her; he would have loved it. But this last and final gift wasn't *their* dream. This one belonged to her and her alone.

'How do you feel about it?' Richard dropped into the chair opposite and nodded at the card she was holding in her hand.

'Horse riding in the snow?' she mused. 'I did that once, when I was fourteen. It was magical.'

It was so sweet of Jeremy to have remembered. She recalled what they'd been doing when she'd shared the memory with her husband. Except, he hadn't been her husband then. He'd been a man she'd fancied rotten and it was their third date. He'd taken her to a repurposed lighthouse somewhere in North Devon for a meal. It must have cost him a fortune because there had only been five tables in the room at the top where the light would once have shone, and it was rather exclusive. She'd known then that she wanted to marry him.

She'd got her wish.

Her only regret was that he'd died so young. Forty-three was no age. He hadn't reached his prime yet. But cancer had snatched him from her with grim and deadly determination.

Megan let out a shaky sigh. 'Hit me with it,' she instructed.

The card told her the bare minimum. Jeremy had undoubtedly left more details with Richard, which her brother-in-law always followed to the letter.

'Five lessons, and the last one is to be a hack – I think that's the word – in the hills when it snows.'

'This one can't have been easy for you to arrange,' she said, and when he gave her a puzzled frown she added, 'Arranging for it to snow on the very day I am to go riding.'

'Very funny,' he said, shaking his head at her. He hesitated. 'It's nice to see you crack a joke again.'

Is that what she'd done? It had been so long since she'd found anything remotely funny, she'd assumed her humour had gone for good, that it had died along with the love of her life.

'Don't read too much into it,' she warned. 'I probably won't do it again.'

'It's been nineteen months.'

'So? Does grief have an expiry date?'

'Of course not, and I feel his loss as keenly as you, but you can't mourn him forever.'

'Who says I can't?'

'Jeremy.' Richard reached into his jacket pocket and put another envelope on the coffee table.

'What does it say?' Megan was scared to read it. She could guess what was in it, and she wasn't ready. She didn't think she ever would be.

'Read it,' Richard said, getting to his feet. He gave her shoulder a squeeze. 'Life is for living. Jeremy knew that – he wants you to know it, too.'

Wants…not *wanted*. That was the problem with her husband speaking to her from beyond the grave – both she and Richard had a tendency to refer to him as though he were still alive.

'Take care of yourself,' her brother-in-law said as he always did on parting. To be fair to him, he tried his utmost to make sure she was okay, but he had a wife and children, and a demanding job. He had enough on his plate without her and her steadfast and inconsolable grief.

'I'll try,' she replied, as she always did.

Taking care of herself was a hit-and-miss affair, with eating regularly being the major issue. When she looked in the mirror, she didn't recognise the skeletal pale wraith staring back at her. At least the horse wouldn't have a sturdy burden to carry. She had lost nearly a third of her body weight since Jeremy died, but she consoled herself with the knowledge that she'd had a fair bit of padding to spare, so it looked more dramatic than it was.

Richard, however, was convinced she was fading away.

She wished the letter sitting on the table in front of her would do exactly that. She wished Richard hadn't given it to her. She wished Jeremy hadn't felt the need to write it. But he'd known her better than she knew herself – he'd anticipated her desolation, and the gifts had been his way of helping her cope.

This last dream wasn't his, though. It had been hers, and the symbolism of doing something purely for herself, something he'd had no interest in, wasn't lost on her.

Taking a deep breath and with tears trickling unnoticed down her face, Megan reached for the letter.

Nathan never knew how to behave around crying women. Was he supposed to give them a hug? Pretend it wasn't happening? Make them a cup of tea?

In the end he settled for muttering a trite, 'There, there,' and patting Charity Jones on the arm, whilst wishing he was anywhere but here.

The stables on Muddypuddle Lane and the surrounding countryside was usually his favourite place to be. Except for today.

'Why don't you see if Timothy will buy him?' Nathan suggested.

'He'd love to, but he's not got the time to look after him, and Midnight needs to be ridden more often than Timothy can manage. You know how the horse gets when he isn't ridden enough.'

Nathan sighed. He did know. Midnight could be a right pain in the rear end. 'Do you want me to deal with this fella?'

'Do you mind?'

Nathan minded a lot, but he minded Charity's tears more. He shrugged. 'I suppose not.'

He completely understood her distress, even though Midnight wasn't her horse. Midnight belonged to her twin sister, Faith, and the two girls had stabled their animals here for years. But Faith was moving to Norwich to live and she couldn't take the beast with her. And neither could she afford to continue to keep it at the stables because the horse had lived here free of charge in exchange for Faith's labour. Charity had the same arrangement with her mare, Storm.

And that was where Charity's tears stemmed from – Faith was selling Midnight, and nothing would be the same again. Nathan got that, he really did. But he still felt uncomfortable being around Charity while she was so upset, and neither did he particularly want to get involved in the sale of the horse. But what else could he do? She was in no fit state to deal with the man who was coming to look at the animal, and besides which, she was rather on the young side, being only twenty-five (he was allowed to call her young because he was forty-seven) and he didn't want anyone to take advantage of her.

Charity said, 'Faith had asked Mum to deal with it, but Mum's got enough to do with Grandma. She's going to have to see about her going into Honeymead soon.'

'At least it's local,' Nathan said. 'And your grandma will see you almost every day.' Charity worked in the care home in Picklewick, so she'd be able to keep an eye on her grandmother. 'Why can't Faith see this fella herself?' He didn't think it right she'd asked others to do what she should be doing herself.

'She can't face it,' Charity said.

Nathan almost replied, *and you can?* but he held his tongue; there was no point in him rubbing in the fact that she couldn't face it, either.

She thanked him profusely and he watched her walk across the yard. Both Charity and Faith were lovely young ladies, but Charity was probably his favourite of the two. She was quieter and more introverted than her twin, and if he'd been lucky enough to have had kids he would have loved to have had a daughter just like her.

It was his one big regret in life that he and Lynnette had never had children. The time had never seemed to be right, and suddenly it was very wrong indeed and they had ended up getting a divorce. She'd gone on to have two children with her new partner, whilst Nathan hadn't even entertained the idea of having a relationship with anyone else.

It was too late now, of course. Even if he managed to find someone who'd be willing to put up with him, he didn't fancy having kids at his age. He was too set in his ways for nappies and sleepless nights.

He was happy as he was, with only himself to answer to. And his boss Petra, of course. She owned the stables along with her uncle, Amos, and she ran a tight ship. But that's the way he liked it. A person knew what was what with Petra; she didn't pussyfoot around – she told it like it was. And as long as he did his job, she let him get on with it.

The arrangement suited them both; she trusted him to know what he was doing, and he was happy not to have anyone breathing down his neck.

Ah, this must be the fella, Nathan thought, as he saw a car trundling up the lane, bouncing over the potholes. Come the spring he'd have to fill those in; some of them would put a moon crater to shame, they were that deep. However, winter wasn't the best month to try laying tarmac.

'Luca, is it?' Nathan asked as the car drew to a halt and a man got out. 'Here about buying a horse?'

'That's me.'

Nathan gave him a quick up-and-down glance. Mid-thirties by the look of him, slim, athletic, not bad looking. Those white jodhpurs were a bit over-the-top, and his helmet looked brand new, but all Nathan hoped was that he knew his way around a horse. Midnight could be a bit of a handful, and wasn't suitable for an inexperienced rider.

Oh, well, best get this over with.

'He's happy to give the full asking price,' Nathan said to Petra after Luca had left. 'So you'd better let Faith know she's sold her horse.'

'When will he come for him?' Petra was sitting on a small stool in the barn, busily milking Princess. It was a scene reminiscent of a bygone era, a rural pastoral idyll, with the goat contentedly munching on some vegetable peelings, and Petra with her breath misting above her head as she milked the animal by hand. All that was needed to complete the scene was for her to be wearing a long dress and a pinafore, and maybe a frilly cotton cap on her head.

Nathan scratched his chin. 'Ah, now, that's the thing. He wants to know if he can leave him here. He'll pay livery fees.'

'He better had. I'm not feeding that brute for nothing.'

Nathan knew she didn't mean it. Petra loved all the animals at the stables, and she might curse them herself, but woe betide anyone else who did.

'I've left his number in the office,' Nathan said. 'He'll be wanting a vet to check him over before he signs on the dotted line.'

'Fair enough. Does he want to bring his own vet in, or will he be okay with using the practice in Picklewick?'

'No idea,' Nathan replied, chirpily. He'd done his bit, the rest was up to Faith, Petra and Luca to sort out.

'Can he handle him?' Petra asked.

'I think so.' This new fella didn't have too bad a seat on him, Nathan had thought as he'd watched him put the horse through its paces. He'd seemed confident enough and he hadn't put up with any nonsense from Midnight. He'd even got the animal over a few jumps, and not a bad height at that. The man had clearly done some jumping in the past.

Nathan was about to get back to work when the phone rang, echoing through the barn, sounding shrill and tinny over the loudspeaker.

Petra glanced up. 'Do you mind getting that? Amos has gone to the supermarket and if I leave Princess half milked, she won't be happy.'

Princess, when she was unhappy, was a right madam, so Nathan nodded and trudged over to the office, glad of a chance to be in the warm for a few minutes. Winter had its own special beauty, but that didn't mean to say he was a fan of the cold.

'Muddypuddle Stables,' he said gruffly, picking up the handset.

The person on the other end was a woman. 'Hello, I, um, I've been gifted some riding lessons with your stables, five to be exact. Well, four, the fifth is meant to be a ride in the snow.'

'In the snow,' Nathan repeated woodenly. 'Is that right?' He didn't know Petra was doing snow rides, or sunshine rides, or any weather rides. As far as he knew, you booked a ride and you took pot luck when it came to the elements. The most common weather was overcast, or rain. You didn't get to choose.

'Yes,' the woman continued. 'Was it arranged via yourself?'

'Nope. With Petra, I expect. Or Amos.'

'Oh, I see. Could you check for me, please?'

'Wait there.' Nathan put the handset on the desk and went back to the barn. 'There's a woman on the phone saying you can make it snow,' he said, chuckling to himself.

'Pardon?' Petra stopped milking and she straightened up. Princess, cross at the cessation of service, bleated loudly and pawed at the pile of hay she'd been working her way through.

'A woman on the phone has been given four lessons and a ride in the snow,' Nathan said, pulling a face. 'I think that's what she said.'

Petra frowned for a moment, then her forehead cleared. 'Ah, I remember. Her husband – he's dead now, by the way – arranged for her to have a few lessons to refresh her riding skills, then a hack on a day when the snow is down.'

'I see.'

'Don't give me that look,' Petra said. 'I can't guarantee it'll snow this winter, but it usually does. Book her in for me, would you? Thanks.'

Nathan stomped back across the yard and returned to the office to resume the call. 'Amos is out and Petra is busy,' he said, 'but she's told me what's what, so I'll book you in for your first lesson.'

'I don't need a lesson, as such. I can ride, although it's been a good few years since I was on the back of a horse.'

'You said you'd been given four lessons?'

'That's right. And a hack.'

'Then that's what you'll have. What day were you thinking of?'

'Oh, um…Friday?'

Nathan grabbed the diary and a pen, and flipped to the correct page.

'What time? I'm assuming this lesson is a private one?'

'It is,' the woman confirmed. 'I'm free all day, so whatever suits you.'

'Two o'clock?'

'That's fine. Um, I take it you have a helmet I can borrow? I've not ridden for quite a few years.'

'So you said. It's a good job you'll be having some lessons,' Nathan retorted. 'Yes, we've got hats. What's the name?'

'Megan Barnes.'

'Right, we'll see you on Friday at two,' he said, snapping the diary shut.

'Yes, Friday. Two pm. I'll be there.'

After he'd come off the phone, he thought she'd sounded nervous, and he recalled what Petra had said…something about a dead husband buying her lessons. He couldn't have died all that long ago, Nathan surmised, then felt a little guilty for being so short with her.

Oh, well, he said to himself, it wasn't as though he'd have to speak to her again. Petra would be taking the lesson, whilst he got on with whatever jobs needed doing.

He didn't like being around crying women, and he liked being around grieving ones even less.

CHAPTER TWO

The weather forecast said there might be a white Christmas this year, but Megan wasn't holding her breath. They were barely into December, and she didn't have faith that anyone was able to accurately predict more than a day or so ahead. Sometimes they couldn't even manage to get today's weather right she grumbled to herself, when it began to drizzle as she pulled into the lane leading to the stables. It was supposed to have been fine all day, if overcast, but at least the riding lesson was indoors. Long gone were the days when she'd happily go out in all weathers. When she was a girl, the only thing she'd cared about was being on the back of a horse, and in those days she'd been too full of youthful enthusiasm and zest for life to feel the cold. But neither had she had to sort out sodden clothes and muddy boots, because her mum had done that for her.

Thinking about her mother made Megan recall her latest visit, and her mum's reaction when she informed her of Jeremy's final gift. Her mother had sniffed and pulled a face, more intent on showing her disapproval of a woman of Megan's age risking climbing onto the back of a horse, than appreciating the romantic and incredibly sad gesture.

Her mother's condemnation had only served to push Megan into making the decision to phone the stables and book herself in for her first lesson.

She knew it was childish, but it typified their relationship.

Now though, Megan was beginning to regret the whole thing, beginning with the terse manner of the man on the other end of the phone when she rang the stables to book the lesson, and ending with her conviction that her mum was probably right, and she was probably too old to go riding. Jeremy, bless him, still used to think of her as the young woman he'd married. He'd never seemed to notice her ever-growing number of grey hairs, or the deepening lines around her eyes. If he could see her now though, she thought he might be shocked. She'd aged about ten years since he'd passed away, and when she looked in the mirror Megan didn't recognise herself. She was forty-two but looked a decade older. His death had taken its toll on her, emotionally, mentally and physically.

It was only to be expected. It was impossible to lose the only man she would ever love and come through it unscathed. To her credit, she looked better now than she had in the months immediately after he'd died, when her skin had been pallid and grey and she'd moved like an invalid, slowly and carefully. The blow it had dealt to her soul had been reflected in her body, and she'd almost welcomed it as a physical sign of the absolute grief she'd felt.

The grief hadn't gone away and she suspected it never would, but she was learning to live with it, absorbing it into herself, allowing it to become part of who she was rather than having it draped over her like a heavy cloak, weighing her down.

Sighing deeply, she switched the windscreen wipers off and sat in the car for a moment, relishing the warmth, because she had a feeling it was going to be bitterly cold outside.

And she was right, she discovered as she clambered out, ungainly in her haste to retrieve her old coat from the back seat and grab her brand-new riding boots. She'd debated the wisdom of buying them, but unlike the helmet which she intended to borrow, wearing someone else's riding boots wasn't an option she fancied, and she didn't have anything suitable that she was prepared to ruin; mud and horse poop wasn't going to do her usual footwear much good.

After slipping her trainers off and changing into her boots, she was as ready as she ever would be. Spotting a sign that said Reception, she headed towards it and hoped she wouldn't bump into the man she'd spoken to on the phone. When she'd questioned Richard, he'd informed her that when he'd helped Jeremy set up the lessons, it had been through a woman. But that was nearly two years ago, and staff might have changed. Megan had been surprised anyone had remembered and was going to honour the pre-paid lessons.

'Hello?' she called, entering the side of the large metal structure and finding herself in a corridor with an office to the right, a toilet to the left and a viewing gallery set out with hard plastic chairs directly in front of her. Beyond it, she could see an arena and guessed that was where her lesson would take place.

'You must be my two o'clock,' a female voice behind her said, and Megan jumped in alarm.

'Goodness, I didn't hear you,' she said, clutching a hand to her throat. 'Yes, I'm she.'

'I've put you on an old lady called Mabel,' the woman told her, 'just to see how you get on. If I think you can cope with a less steady horse, I'll put you up on a different one next time.'

'Oh, right, um…I have ridden before. Quite a bit, actually.'

'When was that? My name is Petra, by the way. Petra Kelly. I run the place.'

'Nice to meet you, Petra.' Megan held out a hand and Petra's eyebrows twitched. She shook it though. 'Um, when I was a teenager,' Megan admitted.

'That's got to be a couple of decades ago.'

'And the rest.' Megan smiled, appreciating the woman's tact.

'Horse riding is a bit like riding a bike,' Petra said. 'You don't totally forget but it does take your body a while to get used to it again, and regain your confidence. But horses aren't bikes and they can sense when you're nervous. Mabel won't bat an eyelid – she's as steady as a rock.' Petra looked her straight in the eye. 'I was beginning to think you weren't coming. But I remember the man I spoke to telling me it might be a year or so, two even…My condolences,' she added.

Megan inclined her head, grateful the woman didn't do the sympathetic head-tilt that so many people did when faced with the recently bereaved. Except, it wasn't so recent any more – two years sounded an awful lot longer than twenty months.

Petra cleared her throat. 'Shall we get on? You told Nathan you needed a hat?'

'That's right.'

'Come through and you can try some on.'

Megan followed Petra into the office and saw the shelves of helmets stacked along one wall, and as she tried a couple on she filed Nathan's name away for future reference if she had the misfortune to speak to him again.

'How many horses do you have here?' she asked when, hat-fitting done, Petra showed her into the arena and the gentle old mare waiting for her.

'Three for customers to use, plus another three, one of which is mine and the other two which belong to the girls who work here. Then there are seventeen ponies, a donkey and a goat. No one rides the donkey. Or the goat, for that matter.'

Megan laughed. She had a vision of a small child perched on top of a goat. 'How long have you been here?' She stroked the animal's nose and the mare gazed back at her with doe-soft eyes. Megan had forgotten how lovely and whiskery a horse's nose could be, and she smiled as the fine hairs tickled her palm.

'All my life, on and off. My aunt and uncle owned the place and I used to visit every chance I could. Then Aunt Mags passed away and Amos needed the help, so I moved in when I was eighteen. Been here ever since. Wouldn't want to be anywhere else.' This last was said with a hint of belligerence, as though she'd been questioned about it in the past.

'If you find what you like doing, you should stick with it,' Megan said. 'I envy you – I still don't know what I want to do when I grow up.'

'What do you do, if you don't mind me asking? Here, let me sort the stirrups out and I'll give you a bunk up.'

Megan stood to the side to let Petra lengthen the stirrups. 'I work in HR.'

'From the tone of your voice you don't sound as though you like it,' Petra observed astutely.

'I don't,' Megan replied. Then her eyes widened. She'd not said that out loud before, but the thought had been lingering in the back of her mind for a while, without her being totally aware of it. Gosh…

Petra pulled a face. 'So don't do it. Here you go – stick your foot in there and I'll shove your backside.'

Megan did as she was told and found herself sitting astride the horse in one smooth movement.

'Gather the reins and ask her to walk on. A circle around the arena, should do it. You've paid for five sessions in all – if you're as competent as I hope you are, the final ride will be in the snow. The one before that can be a hack out onto the hills so you can get a feel for being outside on the horse. This one is to gauge where you are, so the other two will depend on what happens today. Is that okay with you?'

Megan nodded; she had a feeling Petra wasn't asking for her opinion or her input. She was simply telling her what was going to happen. The woman was almost as gruff as Nathan. Maybe it was a horsey thing.

As Megan and Mabel made their way to the far end of the arena and back again, Megan asked, 'Is Nathan your husband or partner?'

'I'm not married, and he's not my partner in any sense of the word. He's a good bloke, though. I couldn't run the stables without him. Try trotting; I expect to see air between you and the saddle,' Petra warned.

Ouch, Megan had forgotten how hard on the thighs a rising trot was. Her leg muscles were screaming at her before she'd done a single lap, and she made a promise to herself that she'd do some squats at home before her next ride.

All too soon though, her hour was up and despite aching more than she'd ever ached in the past, she realised she'd had a fab time. Being on horseback had dredged up so many childhood memories, and she recalled how happy riding used to make her.

As she slid rather inelegantly from the saddle, she sent a silent thank you to her husband. She'd enjoyed herself immensely and couldn't wait for next week.

'Before I go, do you mind if I have a look around?' she asked.

'Be my guest. Just be careful about putting your fingers too near Princess's mouth, else she'll try to eat them. Princess is the goat.'

Megan took her hat off and shook out her hair. 'Shall I pop this back in the office?' She held up the hat.

'That'll be a help, thanks. When do you want your next lesson?' Petra was shortening the stirrups and sorting out the reins.

'Same time next week?'

Petra wrinkled her nose as she thought. 'When you go into the office check the diary on the desk. If two o'clock is free, write your name down.'

Megan blinked. That was very trusting. She wasn't sure she'd want anyone messing with her diary. Oh, well, if it worked for Petra who was she to criticise she thought, as she left Petra to see to the horse.

'Oh, hello.' Megan hesitated in the office doorway. She'd been about to enter when she'd spotted a man standing at the opposite end to the shelves of hats.

He had his back to her and was staring at a whiteboard filled with scribbled writing.

He put a tick next to one of the items, nodded to himself, then turned around. 'Hello, who are you?'

'Megan Barnes. I was just putting this back.' She held up her helmet and as she did so, she could have sworn she heard the man mutter, 'Bugger.'

It took her a moment to guess why that was and when she did, she tried not to smile. If she wasn't sorely mistaken, the man was none other than Nathan, who she'd spoken to on the phone. And he looked rather dismayed to see her.

Good.

※

The last person Nathan wanted to see was Megan Barnes. He knew she was booked in for a lesson today because he'd booked her in himself, but he'd thought he was safe enough in the office. Clearly, he was wrong.

'Petra told me to put myself down for another lesson next week,' Megan said, hesitating before adding, 'If that's okay?' She glanced at the diary on the desk, then turned around to put her helmet back on the shelf.

When she turned back to him and he got a proper look at her, he was surprised at how attractive she was. He guessed her to be a few years younger than him, but it was difficult to tell. He'd never been very good at women's ages. This one could be anywhere between thirty and forty.

She had longish hair, falling past her shoulders, in a glossy brown with the odd grey hair showing at her temples. It seemed she didn't colour it, and he quite liked that. He much preferred the natural look, and she didn't appear to be wearing any makeup either, so that was a plus as far as he was concerned. Her cheekbones were quite prominent, and she had a generous mouth which was made for smiling, but from the haunted expression in her eyes he didn't think she did much of that.

She stared right back at him, her gaze steady and direct.

Nathan coughed and bent his head towards the diary. The book was dog-eared and well used. 'What day?' he asked.

'Same day, same time, please.'

He used a slightly grubby finger to flick to the correct week then he ran it down the page until he came to the right day. 'I'll write you in,' he said, picking up a pen and scrawling her name across the page with 2 p.m. next to it. 'There – all done.'

'Thank you.' She paused, and for a moment he thought she was going to say something, but she didn't. All she did was smile politely and walk to the door.

He waited for her to leave and watched her walk into the yard. Expecting her to drive off, to his consternation he saw her heading in the opposite direction from the car park and he hastened after her, wondering what she was up to.

She glanced over her shoulder as she heard his footsteps and came to a halt, looking nervous. 'Petra said it was okay if I had a look around,' she said. She gave him a small smile that didn't reach her eyes. 'I've already been warned about Princess.'

Nathan saw her gaze travel around the yard. He had already brought some of the animals in from the fields because it was starting to get dark. None of the horses or ponies were left out overnight in the winter, so there were several equine heads peering over the half-doors, their ears pricked, waiting for their supper.

'He's a handsome fellow,' Megan said, as her gaze swept around the loose boxes and came to rest on Midnight, the horse that had just had a new owner.

In fact, there was the chap now, Nathan saw, as another car pulled into the car park.

Luca got out and gave him a nod. 'Everything all right?' he asked as he came closer.

'Couldn't be better,' Nathan said. 'I've brought him in for the night.' He jerked his head towards Midnight. 'He's got a fresh hay net, but I haven't given him any grain yet.'

'That's okay, I can do that.' Luca sauntered across the yard, heading straight for his horse. Megan's eyes followed him, then she caught Nathan watching her and she dropped her gaze.

Nathan wondered if she was in the market for a new husband. Luca was good-looking, and despite the outward confidence and slightly brash air, the brief contact Nathan had had with him revealed him to be a pleasant enough chap. He didn't mind getting his hands dirty, and he mucked out his horse's stall willingly enough even though the fee he paid Petra for continuing to house his animal at the stables included everything except for shoeing.

Anyway, it was none of Nathan's business who Megan looked at. As long as she didn't bother him, he didn't care what she did. 'I'd better get on,' he said.

'I've got the rest of the ponies to bring in.'

Luca said, 'I'd give you a hand but I can't stay long. I just thought I'd pop in for half an hour so we could get acquainted.' He patted Midnight's neck and the horse tossed his head.

Nathan grunted. He would have appreciated the help. An extra pair of hands around the place would come in handy. Faith and Charity used to do this between them, but now that Faith had sold Midnight, she was no longer obliged to help out at the stables. It was therefore down to him to bring the horses in if Petra was busy and if Charity was at work. He wondered if Petra was planning on hiring someone to replace Faith. He certainly hoped so, because his workload had increased quite a bit. Petra had even asked if he'd be willing to take a hack out if needed, but so far he hadn't had to, thank goodness.

'*I* can help, if you like?' Megan said, and Nathan was taken aback.

'Er, thank you, but I can manage.'

'It's no trouble,' she said, seeming rather insistent. 'I don't have anything to rush home for.' Stopping abruptly, she bit her lip.

Nathan winced; he hoped she wasn't going to mention her recent loss. He was sympathetic to her situation, but that didn't mean to say he wanted to be drawn into a discussion about it. Or worse – what if she began to cry? He shuddered, then felt guilty and prayed she hadn't noticed.

'How many of them are left to bring in?' she asked. 'Gosh, I haven't done anything like this since I was a girl.'

She suddenly looked more animated, and he didn't have the heart to repeat that he could manage on his own. What harm would it do? He usually brought the horses and ponies in two at a time, but with this woman to help he'd be able to bring in the last four without making two trips to the field.

'Go on, then,' he said. 'But if you get your foot trodden on, I'm not taking responsibility.'

Megan blinked at him. 'No doubt the stable has insurance,' she said.

'It does, but as I was saying, you offered to help, so if something happens it's on your own head.'

'Noted.'

'And you're going to get those mucky.' Nathan stared at her boots.

Megan looked down at them. 'That's what they're there for.'

They looked very new and rather shiny to him, but if she wanted to muck them up it was up to her. 'I'll fetch the lead ropes,' he said, and stamped off to the tack room, feeling rather out of sorts.

Nathan was mostly a taciturn man. He'd freely admit it. But rarely was he such a grouch, and he wondered why he was being so curmudgeonly now. For some reason Megan Barnes was bringing out the worst in him, and he couldn't understand why. He'd only spoken to her once on the phone, and he'd just met her in person today. His acquaintance of her added up to all of five minutes. But there was something about her that made him uneasy, and he couldn't put his finger on what. Was it because she was recently bereaved? Was he worried she might collapse into hysterics?

Possibly – Nathan halted in the act of lifting a couple of lead ropes off the hook, as he suddenly realised what was wrong. He was attracted to her.

The newfound knowledge didn't help his mood one little bit. He didn't want a woman in his life and he had no need of one; he was perfectly fine the way he was without the added complication of romance and relationships. He had his job, his friends and his little Jack Russell to keep him company and to keep him busy. And on the odd occasion he felt lonely, he'd give himself a good telling off and take the dog for a long walk.

Nathan snatched the lead ropes off their hooks in a fit of angst and clumped back to where he'd left her. But Megan was no longer there, and for a second he felt quite put out as he wondered whether she'd changed her mind and had gone home.

To his immense annoyance, his heart lifted when he spotted her in Midnight's loose box holding the animal's head whilst Luca checked his hooves, before his heart plunged to his boots as he realised a woman like her wouldn't look twice at a man like him. Luca was more her type.

He whirled on his heel, heading for the lane, eager to put a bit of distance between her and his wayward feelings, when he heard her call, 'Wait up,' and there was the sound of her footsteps hurrying behind him.

'Here,' he said, thrusting two of the lead ropes at her when she caught up. Megan took them without a murmur, but the look she gave him was enough. She clearly wasn't impressed with him. Nathan wasn't impressed with himself either, for that matter.

He knew he was behaving badly, so in an effort to appear less sullen, he asked, 'How was your riding lesson?' then shot her a quick look out of the corner of his eye.

She raised her eyebrows at his sudden friendliness but she answered readily enough. 'It was good, thanks. Petra was very patient with me. And so was Mabel.'

'Aye, she's a good 'un,' he said.

'Petra or the horse?'

It was Nathan's turn to raise his eyebrows, and to his surprise he chuckled. 'Both,' he said, and he saw her smile. 'Mabel is as calm and steady as they come, Petra not so much. But she's a damn fine horseman, and she's a good teacher, too.'

'Petra was right, riding isn't like riding a bike. You do lose some of your confidence. Mabel looked after me though.'

'She's good like that. Getting a bit long in the tooth now though, so she doesn't get ridden much these days. She'll be put out to pasture before long.'

'I expect you and Petra will miss her.'

Nathan shook his head. 'She's not going anywhere. She'll live out her days at the stables. Petra keeps all her animals, no matter how old or sick they get. Once an animal arrives at the stables it stays here until it's carried out in a box. Me included. Oh dear…'

Nathan wished he hadn't said that. He pulled a face and prepared to apologise, but when he risked glancing at her he saw that Megan's expression was calm and she didn't seem to have taken offence from his careless and unthinking remark.

'You're not that old, surely?' she asked him.

'Coming up for fifty,' he said. 'Although I suppose that's not old these days. In my grandad's day, you retired at sixty-five and you thought you were past it. You had maybe another five or ten years before you kicked the bucket.'

Dear god, he'd done it again. What was wrong with him? He didn't seem able to stop sticking his foot in his mouth.

'It's okay,' Megan said, seeing his embarrassment.

And he *was* embarrassed, very embarrassed. See, he said to himself, this was why he didn't like talking to people. Because he tended to put his foot in it and make an idiot of himself.

'It's funny how our language is littered with references to death,' Megan said, and Nathan drew in a deep breath.

Here we go, he thought. Thank god the gate to the field was only a few yards away and he could use the excuse of catching the ponies not to have to listen to her.

'You can't get away from it,' she was saying, 'so please don't restrict what you say because of me. I won't get upset and I won't take offence. Only yesterday I said to someone at work that I should have put on a thicker jumper because I was going to catch my death.'

Nathan felt a little better. 'Did you really?'

'No, I didn't.' She smiled at him. 'But I could very well have done, so please don't feel awkward. I'd hate for anyone to feel uncomfortable when they were talking to me.'

'It can't be easy,' Nathan said not wanting to get into a discussion, but feeling he had to say something. 'How long has it been?'

'Since my husband died? It's okay, you can say those words. Twenty months.'

Nathan jerked to a halt, one hand on the bolt, the other on the top bar ready to pull the gate open. 'Oh, I thought it was more recent.'

'Some days it feels very recent,' she said. 'Other days it feels like a lifetime. Jeremy, my husband, in cahoots with his brother, booked these riding lessons for me before he died. He arranged for me to do a few other things too, and Richard, that's my brother-in-law, has been doling them out to me on a regular basis. Riding in the snow is the last one.'

'That's um…' Nathan was lost for words. He wasn't sure whether it was a lovely thing to do, or an awful thing. It certainly kept her husband's memory alive for her, but on the other hand it also might stop her from moving on. Heck, what did he know? He'd never lost anyone; both his parents were still alive and so were his two siblings.

'Bizarre?' she said, completing his sentence for him. 'Some people have said so, and others have said how lucky I am. To be honest, the jury is still out on that one. Some days it's a tremendous comfort to know he was thinking of my future without him. Other days it's unbearable, because I feel like he's still here when I know he isn't.'

Yep, that was more or less what Nathan had been thinking. Wisely he didn't say that. Instead, he said, 'That one there and that one are the easiest to catch,' pointing to two of the ponies. 'The chestnut is Tango, the cream one is Parsnip. If you call them, they'll probably come to you.'

He left her to it, whilst he carried on trying to catch the terrible twosome – a pair of Shetland ponies who refused to go anywhere without the other. They weren't keen on being brought in for the night either, and Nathan sometimes wondered what they got up to when they were left outside during the warmer months.

Eventually he caught one of them and, knowing the other would follow, he made his way back to the gate where Megan was waiting for him with her charges.

'Everything okay?' he asked.

'They were as good as gold.'

'That's because they're greedy, and they know they're going to get a bucket of warm mash.' He frowned, thinking she might think he was referring to mashed potato. 'Mash is a mix of grains and warm water, and other stuff like carrots, beets and apples.'

'I remember,' she said. 'The stables where I used to ride when I was younger fed their ponies the same sort of thing.'

'There you are!' Nathan exclaimed as Patch, his Jack Russell, scurried down the lane towards them. Out of the corner of his eye he saw Megan stiffen, and he hastened to reassure her. 'He's very friendly and the ponies are used to him, so there's no need to worry.'

'I'm not. Hello, boy.' She crouched down and the terrier almost leapt into her arms in excitement. He tried to lick her face and she laughed. 'What's his name?'

'Patch.'

She glanced up at him and Nathan caught her amused smile.

'It's because he's got this brown bit over his eye,' he explained. 'I know it's not very original.'

'Who cares?' she said. 'As long as you're happy with it, that's all that matters. We were going to have a Jack Russell,' she said, her tone wistful. 'We even went as far as making an appointment to see some puppies, but Jeremy became ill and...' She sighed. 'In some ways I wish we'd gone ahead and bought one, but it wouldn't have been fair on the dog.' Another sigh. 'It must be nice having him to come home to.' She gave Patch a final cuddle and put him on the ground.

'It is,' Nathan said. 'But he usually goes everywhere with me.'

'What about shopping?'

'I get everything delivered.'

'Meals out?'

'I have pie and chips in the Black Horse now and again, and they allow dogs, so…'

'What about visits to the barber? The dentist? The doctor?'

'I take him with me to the barber, he sits in the car when I go to the dentist and I can't remember the last time I went to the doctor. I'm never ill.'

She looked at him sharply. 'Let's hope you never are.'

'How long was your husband ill for?'

'Long enough.'

'It must have been tough.'

'It's been tougher since he died.'

'I expect it has. Are you going to get yourself a dog?'

'I can't; I'm at work all day.'

'Best you don't, then,' he agreed. 'You can always borrow this one.'

'You mean, like walk him?'

'If you want. He doesn't need much walking, though – he gets plenty of exercise around the stables. You ought to see him and Petra's dog playing together. It makes me tired just looking at them.' They reached the yard and he added, 'Tango goes in this stall here, and Parsnip in that one.'

He watched to make sure Megan was okay, then he turned his attention to his own ponies, grateful for a chance to be on his own for a few minutes. He couldn't recall the last time he'd chatted to a total stranger as much as he'd talked to Megan. But it wasn't his garrulousness that concerned him – it was the way she made him feel. Unsettled, uncertain, uneasy – and probably a whole lot more words beginning with *un*, if only he could think of them. One word did spring to mind, one which he knew he had to heed, and that was the word *dangerous*. Because he was in danger of liking her – and that would never do, would it?

By the time all four animals had been bedded down it was fully dark and had begun to rain heavily. Megan, water glistening in the strands of hair surrounding her face, hoisted her hood up over her head, shouted, 'Goodbye, see you next week!' and made a dash for her car.

To his astonishment, Nathan was sorry to see her go.

'Dangerous,' he muttered to himself, calling Patch to heel. But despite the risk to his equanimity, he couldn't help looking forward to next week's riding lesson.

'How did the riding lesson go?' Richard asked Megan the following Monday when he phoned her at work. As always when Megan heard his voice her heart twisted with renewed pain; he sounded so like Jeremy that some days it hurt to speak to him.

'It was incredibly enjoyable,' she said, glancing into the corridor to check no one was listening to her conversation. She had an office of her own, but her open-door policy meant her door was usually ajar. The rest of the department was open-plan, and the illusion was enhanced by the use of large windows instead of walls. Sometimes she felt as though she was working in a fish tank.

'Petra, the woman who runs the place, is lovely,' she continued. 'She put me on this gentle old mare, and to be honest I was a bit put out because I thought I could handle something with a bit more spirit. But she was right – I haven't ridden in such a long time that it took me a while to regain my confidence.'

'I take it I won't be seeing you in The Horse of the Year Show any time soon?' His chuckle stole her breath and she swallowed, reminding herself it wasn't Jeremy on the other end of the phone.

'I used to dream of that when I was a girl. Now all I'm dreaming about is being able to sit down without groaning – I'm still aching! I could hardly get out of bed the next morning. It was fun though. I'm glad I went.'

'Good.' She heard the relief in his voice and knew it hadn't been easy for him. As the executor of Jeremy's will he must have dreaded handing her those envelopes and witnessing her grief all over again, as her husband reached out to her from beyond the grave. Richard had his own mourning to endure.

'How do you feel about this being the last envelope?' he asked.

'Abandoned, relieved, sad…when *don't* I feel sad?' she joked ruefully. 'I get why Jeremy organised them, but I'm not sure they helped. In fact, I know they didn't; I miss him as much today as I did the day he died.'

'You were going to miss him, regardless. Would you like me to come over after work?'

Megan would dearly like him to, but she didn't *need* him to. And that was the difference between those early days of inconsolable grief and today. She'd probably have a little cry when she got home (she often did) but she now had ways of coping, and she had learnt not to rely on Richard so much for emotional support.

'Thanks for the offer but I'll be fine. I'm going to make myself some pasta and contemplate what I want to do with the rest of my life,' she said.

'That…um…some evening. Are you *sure* you don't want me to pop in?'

'I want a dog.'

'Okaaay…' Richard drew the word out and she heard the concern and bewilderment in his voice. He must think she was becoming unhinged, when actually she was seeing clearer than she'd done for years.

'When I was at the stables last week, I realised I don't enjoy my job and I haven't for a while,' she told him.

'What's that got to do with getting a dog?'

She could tell by his tone that he was baffled. 'I'm not *getting* a dog. I *want* a dog – there's a difference.'

'We don't always get what we want,' Richard said.

Didn't she know it. 'I know I have to work, so having a dog would be out of the question, but it made me think what I would do if I had a different job.'

'Get a cat; they're less hassle. You don't have to walk them, for one thing.'

'You're missing the point.'

'Which is?'

'What the hell am I going to do with the rest of my life?'

CHAPTER THREE

'We've only just had Bonfire Night,' Petra grumbled, 'yet here we are, nearly halfway through December. I swear the years are going by faster.'

'That's what happens when you get older,' Nathan said. 'Although you shouldn't be saying something like that at *your* age.'

Petra snorted. Some days she felt like a teenager and others, like today, she felt ninety. 'I'm getting too old for this,' she said, sweeping her arm over the boxes of Christmas decorations.

'You're never too old for Christmas,' Nathan said, and Petra barked out a laugh.

'So says the man who could give Scrooge a run for his money when it comes to festive cheer.'

'I've got plenty of festive cheer,' her handyman said. 'I just don't show it.'

'Humbug,' she retorted. 'Last year you complained constantly about the Christmas songs.'

'They were bloody everywhere,' he said, making her laugh. 'On the telly, on the radio, in the shops, and even—' he glared at her '—in the arena. Did you have to play *Mistletoe and Wine* every five minutes?'

'You can blame Amos for that. If it was up to me, I'd have played *Fairytale of New York*, but Amos wouldn't let me.'

'I can see why. It's not suitable for kids, is it?

Where do you want this?' Nathan pointed to the rather large pot containing a rather large tree.

'In the gallery, please.'

'If you've got to play something, I prefer a good old-fashioned carol.'

'Like what? Give me an example.'

'*Away in a Manger* would be nice. Or *Little Donkey*.'

'Good one,' Petra chortled. Nathan might come across as dour, but he had a wicked sense of humour beneath his slightly grim exterior.

Petra had always been ambivalent about Christmas to a certain extent. When she was a child, all she'd wanted for Christmas was a pony. Needless to say she'd never got one, and she'd found it hard to pretend to show enthusiasm for the presents she did receive. It had been ungrateful of her and she realised her parents must have been hurt, but she couldn't do anything about the way she felt – they were unable to give her the only thing she truly wanted, and they knew it. The one shining light of any Christmas was when the family paid a visit to the stables on Muddypuddle Lane, and she was able to get her fix of all things horsey.

Then when she'd moved in with Amos and had taken over the running of the stables, Petra had realised that in some respects Christmas Day was like any other, in that the animals still had to be cared for. Horses came first; unwrapping gifts and having a glass of eggnog or mulled wine came second. And she did mean only one glass, because the animals also needed seeing to in the evening. Besides, trying to deal with a tetchy goat or a pony with an attitude when you had a hangover on Boxing Day wasn't much fun.

She watched Nathan manoeuvre the tractor into position and ease the tines of the forklift attachment away from the pot. It was a delicate job, and needed some muscle at the end to wiggle it into position. Petra was glad Nathan was there to do it. She was perfectly capable of driving a tractor and had moved the Christmas tree into the arena in the past, but this year if Nathan hadn't been around, she didn't think she could have faced it. Maybe next year they'd leave the damned thing where it was and buy a smaller tree.

Satisfied it was in position, she stood back to admire it. 'I feel like leaving it au naturale this year,' she said, not relishing the thought of getting the ladder out and climbing up and down it numerous times in order to decorate it.

Oh, well, it was for the kids and their parents. They expected it, and she had to admit that when it was done it did look lovely. She wanted to finish the trimming up by Thursday afternoon, ready for the weekend classes, and she ran through a mental list of what she had on for today and tomorrow: two beginner classes this evening, and a private lesson tomorrow afternoon with Megan Barnes, followed by a showjumping class an hour afterwards. It should give her enough time to get it all done, especially if she roped Charity into helping. But then, Charity was needed for other things.

Petra acknowledged she needed to employ someone else, but just before Christmas wasn't the best time to advertise a vacancy. Nathan had mentioned it again last week, when Megan had given him a hand to fetch the last of the ponies in after her lesson had ended. Petra had teased him about it because he was never normally as friendly with the clients, and he'd become even more close-lipped than usual, which had led her to wonder if she'd touched a nerve. For most of the parents who brought their children to the stables, he faded into the background. She'd never noticed him speaking to any of them unless he had to though, so it was a surprise to see him happily chatting to Megan.

Did Nathan like her? If so, he wasn't letting on, and Petra wondered how Megan felt about him. He wasn't the most talkative of men, and people often found him rather distant, but Megan seemed to be getting on all right with him.

Petra thought back to the conversation she'd had with Megan's husband nearly two years ago. He'd been direct and lacking in self-pity when he'd told her what he was planning and why, and she'd assured him that no matter how long it took for his widow to book her lessons, she'd honour the payment. It hadn't occurred to Petra that it would take two years, so when Megan Barnes had arrived for her lesson, Petra had assumed her husband had managed to hold out for longer than he'd anticipated, even though Jeremy Barnes had told her he didn't have more than a few weeks to live.

It looked like he'd been right.

His wife was still grieving, but was two years enough to think about having another relationship? And if so, would the woman think of Nathan in that way? Petra would like nothing better than to see Nathan fall in love – as long as the love was reciprocated.

With a huff at her silliness, Petra forced her mind away from matters of the heart (she blamed it on being so loved-up herself, and she simply couldn't imagine being without Harry now), and tried to focus on the task at hand, which was decorating this ridiculously tall tree.

She really didn't feel like it; what she felt like was a nap.

Blimmin' heck, she must be getting old if she was wishing she could take a nap during the day. Maybe she should start taking supplements, or something? Admittedly the last couple of months had been hectic, what with the Halloween Party, then Harry moving into the stables and Faith no longer helping out, but she was only in her early thirties for goodness' sake. As soon as the festivities were out of the way, she'd put an advert in the paper, because the sooner she had another pair of hands around the place, the better!

As Petra began to dig around in one of the many boxes of baubles and tinsel, her thoughts kept returning to Megan, and she wondered if the woman had any regrets about falling in love with a man she was to lose far too soon. Was it better to have had such love in her life, or would she have preferred to have never met him?

Petra pondered her own circumstances as she carefully decorated the tree, and she came to the conclusion that by the time she had realised she was in love, it had been too damned late to do anything about it. All she hoped was that she didn't lose Harry, because now he was in her life, she didn't know how she'd carry on if he disappeared out of it.

'The decorations look great,' Megan said as she did a lap of the arena on a gorgeous horse called Sherbet. Petra was standing in the middle, turning slowly on the spot and giving the occasional reply between issuing instructions.

'Ask her to canter. You'll have to keep her on a short rein, because she might be a bit keen,' Petra advised. 'It took two days to decorate the place. Good, watch your seat, you're starting to get sloppy, and keep those elbows in. That's better.'

Megan tried to maintain an upright posture, but it was far too easy to lean over the animal's neck, which Sherbet interpreted as a request to go faster. Sitting up straight again, Megan gently pulled the horse back, using her hands and her legs, until the canter was more of a rocking horse gait, than a potential headlong rush.

'You are lucky you knew you always wanted to work with horses. I need a change,' Megan said. 'Do something different with my life.' She didn't know why she was confiding in Petra, but for some reason she felt she could talk to her.

'What were you thinking of doing?' Petra asked.

'No idea.' Megan sounded cheerful, but inside she was anything but. Changing jobs would be the last big upheaval in her life for a while, and one which she now recognised was long overdue. If Jeremy hadn't fallen ill, she probably would have taken this step three years ago. But once the cancer was diagnosed, nothing else mattered. And by the time it was all over, she was just grateful she had a job she could slot back into without any fuss. She knew her role inside out, and although it helped keep her occupied during the day and was challenging enough to stop her from dwelling on things (and she'd been very glad of that at the time), she didn't enjoy it any more. When she peered into the future, she couldn't see herself working in the same place in twenty years' time.

The problem was, she didn't know what else she wanted to do instead. Whatever it was, she'd more than likely have to retrain, unless she intended to swap HR for another admin job, which would be pointless. But returning to full-time education was out because she still had bills to pay, and although they weren't extortionate, being without an income for however long it took to complete a course wasn't an option.

'It's going to be tricky to find something else, if you don't know what you want to do,' Petra said, stifling a yawn. 'Sorry, I'm exhausted.'

'Too many late nights?'

'Too many early mornings. The damn cockerel wakes me up at five-thirty every morning.'

'I thought they were supposed to crow at dawn? It doesn't get properly light until eight.'

'I don't think he got the memo,' was Petra's dry response. 'Okay, how do you feel about walking over some poles?'

'Can I?' Megan's eyes lit up. Walking over poles was the first step towards jumping.

'We're not talking about five-foot fences here,' Petra said, going across to the far corner of the arena where all kinds of poles and jumps were kept. She lifted one of the poles and carried it to the middle and dropped it on the ground. 'Ouch!'

'Are you okay?' Megan asked as Petra rubbed the side of her chest.

'Caught myself in the boob,' she said. 'They're bloody sore, too. Who'd be a woman, eh? Men don't know how lucky they are not to have periods.'

Nathan had just opened the door and stepped inside, when he caught the tail end of Petra's grumble, and he promptly did an about-face. 'Oh, I'm out of here!'

Megan grinned. Jeremy never had an issue discussing periods, but some men were averse.

'Come back and help me with this pole,' Petra shouted after him, and after a second his head appeared around the door.

He looked positively terrified.

'Can you set up three poles on the ground, five paces apart? Thanks.' It didn't seem as though Petra was going to take no for an answer.

Megan smiled at him apologetically and mouthed, 'Sorry.'

He shrugged. Then he smiled at her and Megan blinked. Crumbs, he should do that more often. It had transformed him from a slightly po-faced bloke into a man who was rather handsome in a rugged, outdoorsy kind of way.

Nathan was another person who seemed happy in his job, and she envied him. Working at the stables wasn't high-powered and it was hardly likely to make him rich, yet he seemed happy, despite his outward grouchiness.

'Megan was saying she's thinking about changing jobs,' Petra said to him, as he carried the next pole and measured out the correct number of paces before he dropped it in position.

'Oh aye? We could do with a hand here,' he said, giving Petra a pointed look. 'We're a body down.'

Megan saw him wince at the word "body", and she shook her head. It seemed he was unable to avoid mentioning things to do with death. It didn't bother her, but it seemed to bother him.

'I don't think that's the kind of thing Megan had in mind,' Petra said.

'You mean be a stable hand? I'd love to!' Megan giggled when she saw their faces. 'Or I would if I was twenty years younger. I'm not cut out for humping bales of hay around, or for being outside in the cold and the wet.'

'Fair-weather rider,' Nathan teased.

'Guilty as charged, and I don't mind admitting it. I hate being cold.'

'Yet you want to ride in the snow?'

'It does seem incongruous, doesn't it?' Megan agreed. 'But it's a cherished memory of mine, and one I would love to repeat. Jeremy understood that…' She became pensive, then abruptly snapped out of it. 'Sorry, I didn't mean to kill the mood.'

She saw Nathan wince again. He needed to get over his worry about her feelings she thought, as she first walked Sherbet over the poles, and then trotted her over them.

By the end of the lesson she was aching again, but once more she'd thoroughly enjoyed it and she felt lighter than she'd felt for a very long time. Jeremy, bless him, had known what he was doing. All of the gifts he'd given her had been designed to lift her spirits, or to push her so she didn't get stuck in a rut of grief and longing. This last one, she understood, was a farewell…

She wasn't yet ready to let him go, but she was getting there. He'd always be a big part of her, the best part, but it was nearing the time for her to move on. Life was too precious to waste it in sadness and heartbreak, and she was now beginning to feel able to face it again.

The hard part was almost over – compared to what she'd been through. Deciding what she wanted to do with the rest of her life would be a piece of cake.

Cake? Ah, now, there was a thought…

CHAPTER FOUR

Megan was on her hands and knees, with her head in a cupboard which was crammed with all those things she'd kept because they might come in handy one day but she'd probably never use again if she was being truthful.

Yet today she *was* going to use something from out of there, if only she could find it.

There it was, her cake decorating box. It looked like a toolbox but held everything the budding cake decorator needed.

Although, Megan wasn't so much budding, as lapsed. Years ago, she used to balance the demands of her job by the creativity of designing cakes. She also used to go running, but that wasn't something she was planning on resurrecting any time soon. She didn't think her knees could cope.

Stiffly and with a considerable amount of groaning and pulling herself up by hanging onto the worktop, she got to her feet. Riding had certainly highlighted how unfit she was, and although she was aching slightly less than last week, her muscles continued to protest at the unaccustomed exercise.

Opening the box, Megan broke into a sad smile. She vividly remembered baking Jeremy a cake for his thirtieth birthday and how pleased she'd been with the result. He loved old cars, and she'd made a kind of road out of grey fondant icing which curled around the sides of the cake and across the top. And in the centre of it, she'd modelled a Triumph Spitfire. At least, that was what it was supposed to have been. Anyway, he'd loved it, and she'd gone on to make loads of other cakes over the years for friends and family. Then life had become so much more difficult, and she had slipped the toolbox into the cupboard and it had sat there ever since.

The first thing she needed to do was to bake a cake, and for a while Megan couldn't think what sort, but as Christmas was looming she decided to make a festive one. If it turned out okay, she'd take it to work and let her colleagues devour it.

She'd dropped into the supermarket on the way home from her riding lesson yesterday and had picked up flour, butter, eggs and anything else she needed, so she set about making a simple Victoria sponge with orange-flavoured buttercream filling. It had taken her a few minutes to firstly find her cake tins (under the stairs), rinse and dry them, then remember the quantities of each ingredient. Eventually though, the cakes were rising in the oven and with the delicious aroma wafting up her nose, she thoroughly washed and sorted all her cake decorating equipment before she decided how she wanted to decorate it.

Remembering she had several books on the subject, Megan eventually found them in the attic. She'd put them up there, along with a great many other things when their living room had been repurposed as a bedroom for Jeremy in those final few weeks before he'd died.

Megan hadn't bothered to bring any of it back

down, and she'd become used to only seeing the bare bones of the three-piece suite and a few other bits of furniture. It had suited her mood.

Now though, she brought an armful of books down with her, dusted them off, and popped them on the almost empty shelves of the bookcase, which had once held an astonishing and disturbing array of medical equipment and medicines.

The cake decorating books looked lonely all by themselves, and she vowed to return the bookcase to its proper function soon. Now, though, she had a cake cooling on a wire rack and she had to decide what she was going to do with it.

Flicking through the first book she picked up and loving some of the cakes in its pages, she sadly came to the conclusion that she needed to start simple and work her way up to a more complicated design. So she chose a snowman's face for this attempt. It was rather childlike, but she realised she had a better chance of making it look decent, than if she tried a more complex one.

The next two hours were spent happily rolling out sheets of fondant icing to cover the whole cake (white for the snowman's head and face) then messily colouring the rest of the icing to make a green and red hat, which she patterned using the tines of a fork to make it look like woollen material. Then she added a red scarf around the side, and black blobs for the eyes and mouth. She finished it off by using some orange icing which she'd fashioned into a cone shape to represent a carrot for the nose.

It wasn't the most professional cake she'd ever seen, but it wasn't hideous either, and she carefully put it to one side ready to take to work on Monday.

Reluctant to pack everything away – because she had nothing else to do for the rest of the day – she had a go at making some fondant roses, which were more difficult than she remembered, and then she whipped up a batch of royal icing and had a go at piping.

Hmm…that was trickier than she remembered too, she decided, as she stood back and surveyed the designs she'd tried to create.

They weren't the best, she acknowledged, and she wondered if she'd ever been very good at royal icing decorations or whether she was misremembering. Admittedly, she was better with fondant – it was more forgiving and somewhat like modelling with playdough.

Wanting to be good at both and realising it might not be a simple case of practice makes perfect, Megan cleaned up the quite considerable mess she'd made then dug out her tablet.

Always one for recognising the benefits of training, she searched the websites of local colleges and was delighted when she found a ten-week cake decorating course starting after Christmas which took place in the evenings. Not only would she learn new things, but it would also get her out of the house for a few hours.

Megan now had something else in her life to look forward to, and she was starting to feel renewed hope for the future.

But even with a subdued excitement about her new venture slowly starting to build, her thoughts kept returning to the stables on Muddypuddle Lane and the man who had unwittingly piqued her reluctant interest.

Nathan strolled into the Black Horse, sniffing the aroma of beer and chips. It was a heady combination, and he thought he might treat himself to pie and chips to go with his pint of real ale. He'd opened the fridge when he'd got home from work, stared balefully at its contents, then closed the door again. Nothing had appealed to him, so he'd gone to the pub instead. He'd fed Patch of course; the dog ate better and more regularly than his master did, and no doubt he'd cadge a bit of pie from Nathan's plate.

Being the only hostelry in the village, the Black Horse was usually busy, especially on a Saturday evening and tonight was no exception.

'All right, Nathan? How's tricks?' Amos was already there, propping up the bar, a pint of Guinness in front of him and a set of darts in his hand. 'Fancy a game?'

'You know I can't play for toffee. Besides, I need food first.' He signalled for Patch to sit, then attracted Dave's attention and ordered a pint and his dinner.

'You're not that bad. I've seen you throw a decent dart. And you should have eaten with us – there was plenty to go round. We had sausage and mash, and the onion gravy was the tastiest I've made yet, even if I do say so myself.'

'Maybe I should have,' Nathan replied, not meaning it. He loved the stables, he loved Petra and Amos, and he'd taken quite a liking to Harry, but that didn't mean he wanted to live in their pockets. And he was pretty sure they didn't need him hanging around all the time.

He felt a clap on his back and he turned to see Harry squashing in between them. 'Amos is right, his gravy is the best,' Harry said.

Nathan gave him a rueful smile. He'd forgone the offer of an evening meal at the stables (Amos always offered and Nathan nearly always refused) so they didn't have to put up with him after work, yet here they all were in the pub together. Except for one person.

'No Petra tonight?' he asked.

'She didn't feel like it,' Harry said. 'I'm only here because Amos needed dropping off, and I'll only have the one pint so I can pick him up later. I'll finish this—' he nodded at the half-empty glass on the bar '—then I'll go home and spend a couple of hours with Petra. She'll probably be asleep though,' he added regretfully. 'I wish she'd get a move on and employ someone else; she's like the walking dead at the moment with all this extra work.'

'Tell me about it,' Nathan grumbled.

After he'd ordered his meal, he left Amos and Harry at the bar and took a seat at a free table. He was just about to take his second sip of ale, when he noticed who was sitting at the table next to him.

'How is Midnight?' Faith asked. She was cuddling up to her boyfriend Dominic and happiness was shining out of her.

Mind you, he thought, her twin, Charity, looked equally as happy. Timothy, Harry's brother, had his arm around her and was holding her close. They made a lovely couple. To his shame, Nathan felt a little envious – oh to be so young and in love. If only he had his time over again…

'Your horse is fine,' he assured her.

'He's not my horse any more,' she reminded him, her face sad. She clicked her fingers and Patch got up to allow her to fondle his floppy ears.

'He'll always be your horse in here,' Nathan said, and tapped his chest.

'That's a lovely thing to say,' Charity cried. 'I'll have to remember that when one of the residents is upset about the loss of their pet. Brian was upset again today because he remembered his dog has had to be rehomed. He's got dementia,' she explained, 'and some days he thinks he still owns the dog and other days he remembers that he had to give him up.'

'Aw, bless,' Faith said, and Nathan saw the genuine sympathy in the girl's eyes. He knew it must have been hard for her to sell Midnight, but horses weren't like dogs – as long as their owners were good to them, most of them didn't seem particularly bothered who they belonged to.

He felt for Brian even though he'd never met him. He'd be devastated if he had to give Patch up. The dog was a huge part of his life and as far as Nathan was concerned anyone who didn't like his dog wasn't welcome.

Abruptly, an image of Megan crouching down to gather Patch into her arms popped into his mind and his stomach did an odd roll. Flippin' heck, he should have eaten before he came out. He was starving and Patch, who was lying at his feet, whined as though he sensed his master's mood.

'What do you think?' Charity asked him.

'Sorry, what?' He'd been so lost in his thoughts he had no idea what she was talking about.

'About taking Gerald to the care home.'

Nathan blinked at her. 'Did you say, *Gerald*?'

'Yes.'

'To the care home?'

'That's right. I'm sure the residents would love to see him, especially on Christmas Eve. You're okay with that, aren't you, Amos?'

Amos nodded. Harry appeared bemused. Nathan didn't blame him: he was rather bemused himself.

'Donkey poo and carpets don't mix,' Nathan pointed out.

'He can come as far as the reception area – that has wooden flooring. We should be able to fit everyone in, if we squash the chairs together. Amos can lead him in and we can have panniers on him for the presents.'

'Panniers.' Nathan was close to speechless. 'Where on earth are you going to get panniers from?'

'I'm sure we can make some.'

'Good luck.'

'I'll help,' Timothy said, and Faith piped up, 'So will I.'

Nathan pursed his lips. 'You'll have to run it past Petra,' he said, and he wasn't certain she'd agree. It was one thing taking a small dog into a care home, but it was another thing altogether to take a donkey for a visit. Still, it was a lovely idea and would make Christmas Eve quite magical for the residents, so he vowed to do everything he could to help make it happen. 'If she says yes, count me in,' he said.

Charity leant across the space between his table and hers, and planted a big kiss on his cheek. 'I knew I could count on you.'

'Get off,' he grumbled, but secretly he was pleased. It was nice to feel useful and it was even nicer to feel appreciated. But even as he mulled over the practicalities of getting Gerald from the stables to the care home, his thoughts kept returning to Megan and the sadness in her eyes.

CHAPTER FIVE

Megan used to adore Christmas. Even as little as three years ago, she used to love immersing herself in the festivities and she enjoyed everything about it, from carefully choosing and wrapping each present, to baking mince pies and making her own mulled wine. Then there were all the parties and the socialising, plus visiting their respective families, and afterwards winding down with cosy nights in front of the TV drinking mugs of hot chocolate and stuffing their faces with marshmallows.

Until it had all changed; and now she dreaded Christmas. There were only eight days to go until she would wake up on Christmas morning filled with indescribable sadness and an ache in her chest, which wouldn't leave until everyone was back at work and life had returned to normal. Or what passed for normal now that Jeremy was gone.

Megan didn't anticipate that this second festive season without her husband would be any better than the first. If anything it might be worse, because she knew what to expect.

At least she'd have something to take her mind off it this year for a while, because when she was making and decorating cakes she was fully immersed in what she was doing. So far, she'd made three cakes and had also created a complete nativity scene out of fondant icing. What she was going to do with it, she had yet to decide. But she had brought one of the cakes with her to the stables to give to Petra and the others. Megan would never eat it all by herself and it seemed a shame to waste it. This one was the best so far, and she was rather proud of it. Three rotund reindeers in decreasing sizes sat on the top, roped together with a harness, and pulling a sledge with a sack of presents on it. The presents were small and had been fiddly to make, but now they were done they looked quite good, she thought.

But when she stuck her head around the door to the arena to let Petra know she'd arrived, she was taken aback to see Nathan readying the horses, especially since he had a helmet on and was wearing proper riding boots and not the steel toe-capped footwear he usually had on his feet.

'Hi, I, um, brought you a cake.' She held up the box. 'Not you personally, you understand: it's for everyone at the stables. The human occupants, I mean, ha ha.' She was rambling. No wonder Nathan was staring at her oddly. 'Shall I put it in the office? I'll get a helmet while I'm there.' She hesitated. 'Are you going out for a ride?'

'I am.' He turned away to check the girth on a chestnut thoroughbred stallion, who looked to be a bit of a handful.

'That's nice.' As much as she'd enjoyed her lessons in the arena, she longed to be outdoors – there was something very uplifting about riding across fields and hillsides. 'I'll get my helmet and wait for Petra, shall I?' Her lesson was due to start any minute, so she knew Petra wouldn't be far away.

'No need, I'm taking you out today.'

'You're taking my lesson?'

'No, I'm taking you out for a hack.' He glanced around at her and noticed her shocked reaction.

'You are?'

'Which bit are you unsure about? Me taking you out? Or going out at all? Petra said you were ready for a gentle ride up onto the moors, but if you don't want to—'

'I want to!' Excitement surged through her, and she couldn't wait to mount up. Hastily she hurried into the office, popped the cake on the desk and scribbled a note, then grabbed her hat.

She was back in the arena in a trice.

Nathan was standing at Sherbet's head. 'Do you need a hand getting on her? I can take her over to the mounting block, if you want.'

The mounting block was a large lump of chiselled rock in the shape of two steps, and Megan was tempted, but what she really wanted to do was to try to get on by herself. She'd been doing all kinds of stretches to aid her flexibility and she wanted to see if they were working.

'I can manage,' she said, taking the reins from him and putting her left foot in the stirrup. One bounce, then another, and she hoisted herself into the saddle, ignoring the way the mare turned to look at her ungainly antics with a curious stare.

'Yes,' she cried, and earned another curious look, this time from Nathan.

As soon as she was settled, Nathan came around to the side of her horse and checked both stirrup lengths. Megan moved her leg to allow him better access to the straps, but when he accidentally brushed her shin with his hand, a surge of heat shot up her leg.

She bit back a gasp; it was a very long time since a man had touched her. Her father and Richard didn't count, neither did her doctor or dentist. Nathan was a relative stranger, and although he was simply doing his job, she felt weirdly embarrassed. Her reaction didn't help, either.

'Try them now,' he said, stepping back, and she was pleased he hadn't noticed how weirdly she was behaving.

She slid her feet back into the stirrups and raised herself out of the saddle. 'They're fine,' she said, eager to get going so he didn't see the blush spreading across her cheeks.

'Good.' He walked over to the stallion and mounted up. 'Ready?'

'Absolutely.' She urged Sherbet forward and the mare fell in behind the other horse. 'Where's Patch?' she wondered.

'Sleeping in front of the fire – him and Queenie both. They're not daft.'

Megan wondered whether Nathan thought she was daft for wanting to go riding on this cold, glum day. She gazed at his back, straight and tall on the back of his horse. 'What's the horse's name? Is he yours?'

'He's Petra's horse and his name is Hercules. She doesn't let anyone else ride him, apart from me and Harry.'

'I'm not complaining or anything, but I just wondered why Petra isn't taking me out.'

'Christmas.'

'Ah, I see. It's a busy time of year for everyone.'

It used to be a busy time of year for her too, but not any more.

Megan hadn't gone to a party since Jeremy's diagnosis, and neither had she gone out for a meal, or for drinks after work.

Nathan gave a noncommittal grunt, and she suddenly got the feeling it wasn't a very busy time of year for him either.

'Do you work much over Christmas?' she asked, wondering if he got any time off at all.

'I have to – the animals don't look after themselves.'

'Petra relies on you a lot, doesn't she?'

Megan saw his shoulders lift in a shrug. 'Running a riding school is a lot of work for one person. Amos does his best, but he's got to be careful because of his angina. He helps in other ways, like keeping the house going and doing all the paperwork.'

'Do you like your job?' she asked, as he angled his horse sideways up to a gate and lifted the latch. What was it with her need to know if other people enjoyed their jobs? Was she trying to justify what she was thinking of doing, or was she trying to give herself a reason to stay in a job she disliked – hoping if no one else was happy in their work there would be little incentive for her to change career.

'I love my job,' he said, asking Hercules to back up so he could open the gate.

Sherbet walked through, and Megan pulled her up to wait for Nathan. His answer didn't surprise her; she'd already got the impression he liked what he did.

'Harry loves his, too,' Nathan said, passing her to lead the way.

Megan took a deep breath of extremely chilly air, glad she'd worn an extra fleece under her coat and hadn't left her scarf in the car. At least it didn't look like rain, as the sky was cloudless, the weak sun low in the sky. The shortest day would soon be upon them, and dusk wouldn't be far off by the time today's ride was over.

'You've got to love animals to be able to work with them,' Nathan was saying as the path widened and he slowed to allow her to walk alongside.

She asked, 'Did you always want to work with horses?'

'I'm from farming stock,' he said, 'so I've grown up with sheep and cows, dogs and chickens. I've worked on farms all my life. My brother and his family still run the family farm.'

'Didn't you want to run it?'

'We don't rub along too good. I'm better off working for someone else. Besides, he's got his own family – my nephews are grown up now and they help run it with him.'

'What about you? Do you have a family?'

'Wife and kids? No.' His voice was terse, and she wondered what had happened to him in the past. 'Have you got any kids?'

'No. We always meant to, but it wasn't a driving ambition, and then when Jeremy became ill it went off the radar completely.'

They rode in silence for a while, and she sarcastically congratulated herself for being able to kill the mood.

'What do you do for a living?' he asked after a while.

'I work in HR.'

'Do you like your job?'

'Not really.'

'Why do you do it?'

'I sort of fell into it after university. I'd been doing some admin work for an agency to gain some experience, and saw a vacancy in the HR department of the council, and it all started from there.'

'Why do you do it?' he repeated, and she gave him a sharp glance.

'I know my job inside out – I could probably do it standing on my head – and the money is good. To be honest, staying there was the easiest thing to do.'

'What about now?'

Megan shot him another look; he was incredibly astute. 'I don't know,' she admitted.

'I'm not the best person to be giving career advice,' he said, 'but all I can say is, life's too short to stay in a job you don't like. You spend the biggest part of your week at work…'

'I want to make cakes,' she blurted.

He glanced at her. 'So why not do it?'

'It's easier said than done.'

'No, it's not.'

'You don't understand; I've got bills to pay, a car to run.'

'Haven't we all? But you cut your coat according to your cloth.'

Megan frowned; this ride wasn't turning out to be as relaxing as she'd hoped. But he did have a point, and hadn't she been thinking the exact same thing herself, otherwise why was she asking people whether they liked their jobs, and why had she signed up for a cake decorating course. Deep down she knew she wanted it to be more than a hobby.

So what was stopping her?

Her own fear, that's what.

Yet, Nathan was right. She didn't have a mortgage (they'd saved hard to pay it off) and she had some savings. And she could certainly trim quite a bit off her monthly outgoings. She didn't need the satellite TV package she was currently paying for (she always switched the TV on every evening, but if anyone asked her what she'd watched she wouldn't be able to remember). She could sell her car and buy a smaller one which was cheaper to run. She had no inclination to go on holiday (on her own? no thanks!), and she had more clothes than she could possibly wear. So did she need such a well-paying job?

'I'm looking forward to trying your cake,' Nathan said.

Megan grimaced. 'Please be honest with me. If it's awful I prefer you to tell me.' She leant forward in the saddle, putting most of her weight onto the horse's front legs to help the mare stumble up a particularly steep and rocky section of the path. It was instinctive and she was pleased she'd remembered to do it without having to think about it.

He nodded slowly. 'Just as long as you don't get upset.'

'I promise I won't.' She probably would, but she'd do her utmost not to show it. 'I used to bake and decorate cakes all the time, but life got in the way.'

'It has a habit of doing that.'

'I've signed up for a cake decorating course at the college, starting in January. If that goes well, maybe I'll have a serious think about my future.'

'It sounds to me like you've already had a serious think.'

It was true. She had. She just needed to see whether she had the skill to make beautiful cakes, and whether anyone would want to buy them. For a while she could do the cake decorating alongside her day job, because she had nothing else to occupy her time in the evenings and at weekends. Maybe nothing would come of it, but she decided to give it a go. She would only regret it if she didn't.

'My husband should have bought me a cake decorating course instead of riding lessons,' she said, and was bemused when Nathan firmly shook his head.

'Did Jeremy ride?' he asked.

'No. I don't think he'd ever been on the back of a horse.'

'I suspected as much. I think he gave you the perfect gift – for *you*.'

She smiled. 'You're biased.'

'I might be, but the lessons are for you and you alone. They weren't because it was something the two of you enjoyed together, and your husband was reminding you of it. He was reminding you of what *you* loved to do. Look, I never knew Jeremy, but please don't shout at me if I suggest he bought you the lessons in order for you to reconnect to who you used to be before…'

'He died?'

'Yes.'

Maybe he had, at that. For some reason being on the back of a horse had not only reminded her of the past when she was young and free and heartwhole, it had also made her think of the future, and how she was going to live it without Jeremy in it. But her thoughts weren't panicked, desolate ones, and she now found herself more open and willing to move forwards.

It was a scary and daunting thing, and she didn't just mean her potential career change. She was referring to finally facing a future without Jeremy and opening her heart and mind to new possibilities.

'I'm sure you're right,' she said. Trust Jeremy to have been so thoughtful, and for him to know what she needed even though she hadn't known it herself until now.

She just had to get through Christmas, then she'd attack her future head on.

Sherbet kicked a loose stone, bringing Megan back to the present. Here she was, out on her first real ride in twenty-five years, and she was so far in the past that she wasn't enjoying the present.

Hercules stopped and her mare halted. Nathan pointed down into a little valley cut out of the rock by a small fast-flowing tumbling brook running through the bottom of it. She'd been so engrossed in her thoughts she'd hardly been aware of her surroundings, but when Megan looked to where he was pointing, she inhaled sharply in wonder.

'Oh,' she breathed, her eyes wide in awe, because where the water had eaten into the ground it had left a bank of overhanging rock, soil and grass, and dangling from the overhang were hundreds of icicles. Some were as tall as she, others were less than an arm length, but all of them were totally unexpected and utterly magical.

Once again she thanked Jeremy, but this time she was also grateful to another man, a man who had come into her life unwanted and unbidden but one whom she wanted to get to know on a much deeper level – if only she'd let herself.

Her eyes brimming with unshed tears at the beauty before her, she caught Nathan's eye, and when the burst of attraction cascaded over her, she welcomed it. Maybe she was ready to embrace life again, and maybe, just maybe, Nathan might be the man to help her do it.

Nathan's phone pinged in his pocket and he scrabbled around for it, smiling when he read the message, and announced, 'Amos says he's got a pan of hot chocolate on the go, and a slice of your cake for when we get back. I'll see to the horses while you go into the house and have a warm.' He didn't feel the cold much because he was used to it, but he reckoned Megan must be freezing. It was bitter out on the bare hillside without any trees to deflect the bite of the wind.

'Oh, I don't know,' she said. 'I ought to go home.'

'It's a tradition,' he told her. 'Anyone out on a day like this gets to warm up with a hot drink beside the Aga before they leave.'

'If you're sure?' She still sounded doubtful.

'I'm sure.'

'What about you?'

'I'll have a slice later.'

'You must be frozen, too.'

'I'm not so bad. Anyway, the horses need seeing to before I can think about my own comfort.'

He glanced back at her to see her chewing her lips, which were reddened by the cold and starting to look chapped. He nearly offered her his lip balm, but he thought it was too intimate. If she had been Petra or Charity, he wouldn't have hesitated – needs must, and all that. But he didn't know this woman well enough, and he thought she might take it the wrong way. After all, sharing lip balm wasn't exactly hygienic, although to be fair it was in a small tin and not the stick variety.

'Can I help?' she asked. 'Two pairs of hands make light work.'

'I couldn't ask you to do that.'

'You didn't ask. I offered.'

It was his turn to hesitate. When Petra had asked him if he'd mind taking Megan out for a ride, his heart had missed a beat. Scared of his reaction at the thought of being alone with her for a whole hour, he'd almost said no. Now his hesitation was because he so desperately wanted to say yes; it would mean at least another twenty minutes in her company without anyone else around.

But he was also fearful of his growing feelings towards her. Having no idea how to control them, spending more time with her than was strictly necessary probably wasn't the best idea.

'Okay, then,' he said, and frowned. That wasn't what he'd intended to say, but the words had slipped from his lips without any input from his brain.

With a clatter, the horses trotted up the lane and into the yard, heading eagerly for their stalls, and Nathan slid from the saddle almost before Hercules came to a halt. He hurried over to Sherbet and took a hold of her bridle, guessing Megan's fingers would be frozen.

'If you open that stall there and this one here, we'll get them inside before taking their tack off.'

Megan dismounted, her movements stiff, and she hobbled towards the first loose box and slid the bolt across, then opened the other one.

'Take Sherbet,' he said, handing her the reins. 'There's a brush already in there – you only need to do where the saddle was – and her rug is there, too.'

He watched to make sure she was okay, then he turned his attention to Hercules. Having had far more practice, Nathan was done before Megan, so he called to tell her he was making up a couple of buckets of feed. By the time he'd done that she had finished her task.

For a brief moment they watched the horses tucking into their supper, then Megan shivered and he hastened to get her into the house and out of the increasingly cold wind.

'Blimey, it's bitter out there,' he announced as he showed her into the kitchen. Patch leapt up and jumped into Nathan's arms, his backside waggling with the force of his waggy tail as he uttered little whimpers of joy.

Amos was stirring a saucepan full of brown liquid and the enticing smell of chocolate hovered in the air. Petra and Harry were also there, mugs in hands, and so was Timothy.

Nathan made the introductions, even though he felt it wasn't his place to do so, and once everyone had said hello, he buried his nose in his dog's warm coat and cuddled him close.

'They reckon we might have a spot of snow before Christmas,' Amos said.

'It's cold enough,' Timothy said. 'I was on a farm doing TB testing this afternoon, and I swear the temperature has dropped about ten degrees.'

Petra pulled out a chair for Megan and indicated she should take a seat. With a wink at Nathan, Petra pulled out the one next to Megan and dared him to refuse to sit down.

Aware of everyone's eyes on him, Nathan carefully kept his face blank as he dropped into it, still holding onto Patch, who immediately jumped down and clambered onto Megan's lap and demanded attention.

'Would you like marshmallows in yours?' Amos asked Megan.

'Yes, please.'

'You'd better take your coat off, else you won't feel the benefit of it when you go outside,' Petra said. 'Same goes for you, Nathan.'

Nathan shrugged off his coat, and when Megan removed hers he held out his hand for it, using the act of hanging it up on the rack by the door as an excuse to move away from her. As well as the smell of hot chocolate, he'd detected a heavenly scent of perfume and it was making his head spin. Or was that due to the heat of the kitchen? With the Aga going and so many people crammed into it, it was stifling, and he felt his cheeks growing warm.

'Thank you.' Megan took the mug Amos held out to her, wrapped her hands around it and took a sip. 'Mmm, this is delicious.'

'Have a piece of your cake,' Amos said. 'Sorry, but I've already cut into it. Petra couldn't wait to try it.'

'Did you make this?' Harry asked, looking at it.

Megan nodded.

'It's very good, and I love the reindeer.'

Petra grinned at her. 'Thanks for bringing it, it's lovely. You ought to go into business.'

Megan's face glowed, and Nathan thought she

might be embarrassed by the compliment, although she looked pleased, too. 'I might just do that,' she said, not meeting anyone's eye.

With his mouth full, Timothy said, 'It's the best cake I've had for ages. Is it too late to order one for Christmas?'

Megan reddened. 'Oh, I don't—'

'You *do*,' Nathan interjected, and Megan stared at him in surprise for a moment. Then her eyes widened and she nodded slowly.

'Erm, no, it's not too late,' she said. 'If you give me your email address, I can send over some ideas, or you can let me know what you want?'

Timothy took out his phone and once they'd swapped numbers, he sent her a message with his email address. 'I'm going to give it to Charity's mum – she's invited me for Christmas lunch.'

'I thought you'd be having lunch with us?' Amos said. 'Harry is, and so is Nathan.'

'I am?' Nathan wasn't surprised – he had Christmas lunch at the stables every year – but he'd yet to be formally invited, so he hadn't taken it for granted he would be this year, especially now Harry had moved in.

'You are,' Amos said, his voice firm.

'Anyway, nice as this is, that's not the reason I called in,' Timothy said. 'I just wanted to warn you that there's been a spate of horse thefts in the area, and to be extra vigilant.'

'Petra is always vigilant, aren't you Petra?' Harry said. 'Petra?' He nudged her. 'Petra.'

'Hmph?'

'You were fast asleep,' he said, with a loving smile. 'You're going to have to place an advert for a stable hand soon because you're burning the candle at both ends. I'm not sure how much longer you can keep this up.'

Petra yawned and stretched. 'I didn't realise how much I relied on Faith. Charity's brilliant too, but she's having to do extra shifts at the care home because there are so many staff off with colds, so we're almost two people down, not one. I suppose I'm going to have to pull my finger out and get something sorted. Should I put an ad in the post office window? And what should I say in it?'

'I can help, if you like,' Megan said, and everyone turned to look at her. This time she didn't blush, and Nathan assumed it was because she was on firmer footing with this type of thing, and more confident of her abilities.

Petra stared at her. 'Of course, you're in human resources.'

'That's right. I've placed more adverts than I've had hot dinners. I can help you write it and suggest where you should advertise it. I assume you have a job description?'

Petra's eyes were wide and she shook her head. 'Should I have?'

'It helps. You'll also need to consider hours of work, salary, holiday entitlement, and so on.'

'Yikes.' Petra glanced at Nathan. 'I didn't give you a job description.'

'You don't give me any holidays, either,' Nathan joked. 'It's lucky I know you so well.'

Petra sighed. 'Okay, thanks Megan. It looks like I'll have need of your services.'

'Have a think about what the hours are, et cetera, and let me know, and I'll put an advert together for you. What start date are you thinking of? I doubt you'll get anyone this close to Christmas, and anyway, you need time to interview and to obtain references.'

'I've never interviewed anyone in my life. Is it strictly necessary?'

'You'll want to make sure they fit in at the stables,' Harry pointed out.

'And it doesn't have to be anything formal,' Timothy added. 'A big part of my interview at the vet practice consisted of dealing with that morning's surgery. Someone brought in a tarantula.'

'What was wrong with it?'

'Dehydration.'

'Really?'

'Yep. He was lethargic and shrivelled.'

Megan visibly shuddered and Nathan felt like doing the same. He didn't mind spiders, but tarantulas were too big for his liking.

'The advert could go out immediately after Christmas, with the aim of interviewing the second week of January,' Megan said, and Nathan was pleased she was taking charge. He had a feeling that left to her own devices, Petra would struggle along, getting more and more worn out because she didn't like the non-horsey side of the business.

'I can't believe it's only a week to Christmas,' Nathan said, thinking this might be a golden opportunity to bring up the subject of Gerald and the care home. 'I, erm, that is… Charity…'

'Gerald?' Petra interrupted.

'You know?'

'Amos told me there was something afoot. Or should I say, ahoof?'

'You don't mind?'

'As long as you're the one who accompanies him, and you clean up his poo; and make sure he doesn't knock anyone over because I don't think I'm insured to take donkeys into care homes.'

Nathan caught Megan's confused expression. Timothy also looked mystified, so Nathan explained. 'Charity thought it might be a nice idea to take Gerald, the donkey, along to the care home on Christmas Eve. Amos dresses up as Santa every year, and there's usually a cheery festive atmosphere.'

'What a lovely thing to do,' Megan enthused.

'You're going to need some help,' Petra said to Nathan. 'I would lend you Harry, but if both you and Amos are going to be in the village, I'll need a hand here.'

Timothy pulled a face. 'I'm on call over most of the Christmas period,' he said. 'I could help but there's no guarantee I'll be there for the whole thing.'

'I don't mind giving you a hand,' Megan offered.

'Great idea. That's settled. Megan can help with Gerald,' Petra declared.

Nathan shot Megan a sharp look. The eagerness in her voice had made him pause, and he was startled to see her glowing. He didn't think it was solely to do with the warmth of the kitchen and neither did he think it was due to embarrassment. He was astonished at how different she now looked, compared to the drab withdrawn woman he'd met three weeks ago. Along with the colour in her cheeks, there was a bit of life about her.

When his heart missed a beat and his stomach did a slow roll as desire surged through him, he was abruptly glad Christmas was fast approaching and he wouldn't see her for a couple of weeks. It was best he put some distance between them, because he wasn't interested in having a woman in his life, and he was pretty sure she didn't want another man. Not just yet anyway. But the thought of her being with someone else gave him an unaccustomed pang of jealousy.

That's enough, he said to himself. He needed to keep his distance. Once Christmas Eve was out of the way he needn't see her again. Petra would no doubt take her for the remaining two lessons, then that would be the end of it. He vowed to stay out of her way until her last lesson was done and dusted, because she was far too disturbing for his peace of mind.

Megan wasn't at all sure why she had offered to help with the donkey on Christmas Eve, or what help she could possibly give, apart from some moral support, and she wondered what possessed her to offer. She'd already offered her HR skills, so hadn't she done enough? It wasn't as though she owed the stables anything.

But she had felt included and part of something whilst she was in Petra's kitchen, and when she'd returned home and had a chance to mull things over as she sat quietly in her living room with a glass of wine in her hand and soft music playing in the background, she realised what it was – she'd felt as though she belonged. Which was ridiculous, because she'd only met them less than a month ago.

The strange thing was, she felt like she'd known Petra for far, far longer, and Nathan, too. Despite the shortness of their acquaintance, she was beginning to feel as though they were old friends. Heck, she'd told both Petra and Nathan about her misgivings about her job, and she'd even confided in them her desire to make and design cakes. Not only that, but she'd also given them one of her attempts. And they'd all appeared to enjoy it.

Not that she'd thought anyone at the stables would be so mean as to say they didn't like it (she might ask Petra to be brutally honest with her sometime in the future – although not yet) and Harry's younger brother, Timothy, had even asked her to make a cake for him. Jeremy would have been so proud of her.

She wasn't sure how she felt about baking and decorating a cake for a stranger – nervous, excited, apprehensive… Things were moving too fast: one minute she'd been grumbling about her job and wishing she had the courage to do something else, and the next minute she was signed up for a course and had her first commission.

When Nathan stepped in just as she was about to protest that she didn't make cakes for other people and he'd told her she did, she'd felt a rare pride and confidence that she could do this. His simple 'You do,' had given her the courage to say yes to Timothy. Now though she didn't know whether to be grateful to him or annoyed.

She did know one thing however (and it terrified her more than being paid to bake a cake for someone she didn't know) and that was she felt an increasingly strong attraction for Nathan. After her initial disquiet about him accompanying her on the ride in place of Petra, Megan had soon felt glad and, as the hour had ticked by, she'd not wanted the hack to end. So much so, she'd prolonged it by offering to help him put the horses to bed, and then sharing a hot chocolate with him and the others in the stable's kitchen.

She had to admit she liked Nathan a lot. Far more than she wanted to, or felt she should. Not only did she feel she was betraying Jeremy – and that was awful – but Nathan hadn't given her the slightest hint he viewed her as anything more than a client.

Feeling suddenly deflated and lost, she slumped back in her armchair and wished with all her heart she could speak to her husband. Her longing for the man she had vowed to spend the rest of her life with rose up like a tidal wave and crashed over her.

'Why did you have to leave me, Jeremy? Why?' she whispered into the still air, grief clawing at her with sharp talons.

Knowing that the best thing to do was to ride it out and not try to fight it, she nevertheless couldn't stop herself from phoning Richard, because the sound of his voice was the closest she was going to get to hearing her husband's.

'Oh, hi, Sonja, I, um, is Richard there?' Megan adored Richard's wife and the two women got on well, but it was Richard's voice she needed to hear.

'Hi, Meg, he's out, sorry. Is there anything I can help with, or did you just ring up for a chat?'

Disappointed, Megan tried to lighten up, not wanting her dismal mood to drag Sonja down. 'I was at a bit of a loose end, so I thought I'd ring for a chat.'

'Will I do?'

'Of course, you will,' Megan cried, not wanting to be rude. 'Are you ready for Christmas?'

'Nope. I never am – you know me, I'll still be running around like a headless chicken on Christmas Eve. Are you sure you won't come to us? We'd love to have you.'

'I know, and thanks for the offer. I would love to come to you, too, but I'm going to my parents. They're flying out to Spain for a couple of months immediately after Christmas, so I won't see them for ages. Lucky things.' She suspected they would have gone at the beginning of December but for her, and she felt guilty she was inadvertently spoiling their plans. Then a wave of self-pity engulfed her for being so pathetic and needy, which meant they felt they couldn't leave her on her own over the festive season, even though she would have preferred to forget Christmas was happening. How could she celebrate it without Jeremy? This Christmas, like last year, was something to be endured until it was over.

Sonja said, 'Lucky things! I wish I could disappear off to the sun for a couple of months. Come see us on Boxing Day, instead.'

'Definitely. I'll look forward to it.'

'Liar.'

'Sonja…' Megan was dismayed that her sister-in-law could see through her so easily and she worried she'd upset her. It was the last thing she wanted to do after all the support she'd given her.

'You don't have to pretend,' Sonja said. 'I understand how hard it is for you. It's hard for Richard, too. But we love seeing you.'

'Even when I'm a miserable cow?'

'Even then.' Sonja's soft laughter carried over the airwaves.

They chatted for a bit and Megan enthused about her riding lessons. But maybe she'd mentioned Nathan's name once too often because Sonja abruptly said, 'You like Nathan, don't you?'

'No! Whatever gave you that idea?'

'I don't know – female intuition? And don't sound so shocked. It's a perfectly normal thing to do.'

'No one can replace Jeremy.'

'Of course they can't. But that doesn't mean to say you need to be on your own for the next forty years.'

'Gosh, that sounds so depressing.' That Megan might live one half of her life like Queen Victoria – in a perpetual state of mourning – was a sobering image.

'That's what might happen if you don't give yourself permission to love again,' Sonja said. 'Does he like you?'

Megan said, 'He hardly knows I exist, so it's all hypothetical. Anyway, even if he did fancy me, I can't betray Jeremy.' The guilt she felt at having even the tiniest of feelings for another man was already crippling. Imagine how much worse it would be if she kissed him.

'Would you feel like that if it was you who had died and Jeremy was the one left on his own?' Sonja pointed out.

'That's too awful to contemplate. I'd hate for him not to be happy again.' Megan was adamant. She ignored the stab of pain she felt as the words in his final letter to her slipped into her mind. He'd said the same thing to her – that he hoped she'd move on and find love and happiness again. But how could she?

Echoing her thoughts, Sonja asked, 'Don't you deserve to be happy?'

'But what if I fall in love and he dies?' The thought escaped her before she'd fully formulated it. It wasn't something she'd consciously considered, but now the idea had been spoken she realised how true it was. Was that the real reason she was holding back? She'd been telling herself it was too soon, that she'd lost the love of her life and would never find another, that she would be fine on her own – but were all these things mere excuses because she was terrified she would fall in love again and risk heartache for a second time?

'He *will* die – that's a given. We all will. But it shouldn't stop you from loving someone,' Sonja argued.

'I couldn't keep Jeremy alive,' Megan wailed, the ache in her chest so fierce she thought she might die from it.

'Oh sweetie, no one could.'

'But what if I'd noticed he was ill sooner?' I should have realised—'

'Stop! You can't go on torturing yourself like this. What happened to Jeremy was tragic and awful, but you have to stop blaming yourself.'

Megan was unable to say anything, the words catching in her throat and choking her.

'This Nathan has got you in a right tizzy, hasn't he?' Sonja asked, after a moment.

Sonja was more perceptive than Megan gave her credit for; Nathan *had* got her in a tizzy. She wasn't sure she liked it, but her sister-in-law was right. She didn't want to spend the rest of her life in hopeless despondency.

Maybe she *could* allow herself to love again? To have a relationship? It wouldn't be with Nathan, but at least she could stop beating herself up over finding him attractive and enjoying his company.

She could consider it a trial run for getting out in the world again and one day, when she was finally ready, perhaps she *would* fall in love again.

CHAPTER SIX

Nathan usually felt ambivalent about Christmas Eve. On the one hand, he used to think it was the most magical part of the festive season, especially when he was a child, and sometimes he was able to recall his intense feelings of excitement and joy. On the other hand, it highlighted his aloneness like no other time of the year.

Today, when he'd finished at the stables and he and Patch had returned home, he felt a deep sense of anti-climax when he opened his front door only to be confronted by a cold, dark house and the silence within. As always, he immediately lit a fire and turned the lights and the telly on, so his cottage was soon warm and cosy, but he was unable to dispel that initial impression.

Suddenly, he was glad he was going out tonight. He liked a bit of carol singing even though he was tone deaf, and it would be nice to be around people for a change. There was something about Christmas that disturbed his usual acceptance of being alone.

Nathan had returned to the stables to collect the donkey and he'd just given Gerald a good brushing down and was making sure his halter was sitting right when he heard a car drive up the lane, and a frisson of anticipation ran down his spine.

'Give over,' he muttered, cross with himself. Megan wasn't coming to see *him* – she was here to help with the donkey, and possibly because she'd be on her own too. He didn't know what made him think that, because she'd mentioned family briefly when they'd been on their ride so he knew she wasn't alone in the world, but he got the impression she was lonely nevertheless.

His heart went out to her, and to Amos, as well. This time of year wasn't easy if you'd lost someone you loved, and both of them had lost their spouses. Nathan remembered Amos's wife as a warm, giving lady, and he knew Amos must be feeling her loss even after all these years.

Nathan heard Megan's car door slam and the sound of her quick footsteps across the yard, and he took a moment to compose himself before he ventured out of Gerald's stall. Patch had raced on ahead, eager to greet her. The little dog, although friendly with everyone, had taken a particular liking to Megan.

'Hi,' she said when she saw him, and he was struck anew by her prettiness. Good cheekbones and clear skin, combined with a spring in her step made her appear younger than she was. Although only five years older than her, Nathan felt ancient in comparison. Even if she was ready to "put herself out there", Megan wouldn't want to do so with him. What could he offer her?

'All right?' he replied. 'Amos is just fetching the horsebox, then we can load the donkey into it. You might as well wait in the warm.' He jerked his head towards the house.

'I'm okay to wait out here. We'll probably be glad of some fresh air by the time we're done at Honeymead. It looks lovely. I drove past it on the way here. They've pushed the boat out with the decorations.'

'As care homes go, it's a pretty good one,' Nathan said. 'Charity is forever singing its praises.'

The noise of an engine ended the slightly stilted conversation, and Petra's battered but perfectly serviceable Land Rover trundled into view. It was towing a horse trailer, and Nathan watched Amos expertly manoeuvre it into position.

As soon as it came to a halt, Nathan opened up the back of it and lowered the ramp. 'You can bring Gerald out, if you want,' he said to Megan. 'Have you loaded anything into a horsebox before?'

'This is a first for me,' she said.

'He'll load okay. He's as good as gold.' The donkey was a sweet old thing, and was utterly placid – Petra wouldn't risk taking him to the care home if he wasn't bombproof.

However, Nathan wasn't about to let Megan do this by herself, although he did try to stand back and only offer advice when it was needed, until the donkey was eventually settled into the trailer, and he and Megan were free to climb aboard the Land Rover.

'Come, Patch,' he called, and the dog leapt into the footwell, where he turned in a circle and curled up in a ball.

Although this wasn't the first time Nathan had seen Amos in his Father Christmas glory, he couldn't help laughing out loud. The man was the epitome of Santa Claus, although maybe not quite as rotund as was traditional. His crinkly eyes peered at Nathan from above a surprisingly realistic beard, and Amos was also sporting some white bushy eyebrows.

'Are those caterpillars above your eyes?' Nathan chortled. 'Or did you raid Petra's stash of cotton wool?'

'Cheeky beggar, these are my own. I've sprayed them with some white stuff to make them look more authentic.'

'Have you thought about trimming them?' Nathan was trying to hold back his laughter and failing dismally.

'Let me see?' Megan said from the backseat, and Amos turned around and waggled them at her. 'Oh, my,' she said, flinching. 'They are rather full.'

'Full? They could have a postcode all of their own.' Nathan slapped his thigh, his laughter ringing out.

Amos said, 'As for you, you grumpy git, I didn't think you had a laugh in you.' He glared at Nathan, but Nathan could tell he didn't mean it. Amos gave him a final stare, then turned the volume on the radio up to drown out Nathan's chuckles.

For some reason, Nathan was feeling lighthearted and almost (not quite) in a festive frame of mind, and this feeling was heightened when they pulled up outside the care home and he saw the lights festooning the outside.

It was a two-storey, sprawling building, shaped along three sides of a square, with the open side featuring a courtyard, well-maintained gardens and glorious views of the surrounding hillsides. The open side was hidden from the front of the building and the car park, and this was where they were headed, Nathan discovered, when Charity, bundled up against the cold in a padded coat with a fur hood, dashed across the tarmac to meet them.

'We thought you could come in through the French doors via the garden, rather than simply appear in reception.'

Nathan caught the question on Megan's face and he explained that the cafe was more of a meeting place between the two wings of the home, where visitors and residents alike could help themselves to drinks and a variety of cakes and snacks. 'It serves as the focal point of the care home,' he said. 'It's almost like being in a real cafe, but you don't have to pay.'

'I'll unlock the side gate for you,' Charity said, 'and the panniers are over there, along with a couple of sacks of presents. They're all labelled,' she told Amos, 'But when you call the names out you may have to shout, although there are plenty of staff on hand for those who can't hear so well, or aren't as able to join in.'

The donkey walked down the ramp without any fuss as soon as the horsebox was opened, his ears swivelling from side to side as he took in his surroundings. He didn't object when the unfamiliar panniers were put on his back, although he did bray loudly once, just in case there happened to be any other donkeys nearby.

Plodding behind Nathan and Megan as they led him through the gate, Gerald seemed perfectly happy, especially when Nathan produced half an apple from his pocket and fed it to him. Patch walked obediently at heel, and stayed close to his master.

The sound of *Away in a Manger* being sung by a multitude of quavering voices (and one or two more strident ones) reached them as they rounded the corner, and when Nathan saw the large tree in the centre of the garden gleaming with fairy lights, and the row of expectant faces through the window, he was glad Charity had thought of the idea.

'It must be hard being in a care home at this time of year,' he murmured in Megan's ear, as Amos strode forward, a huge smile on his face and crying, 'Ho, ho, ho.'

Megan whispered back, 'I'm so glad you're doing this – look at their faces.'

Nathan scanned the lined faces of the residents, and his heart sang. Bless them, they looked so hopeful and excited, like children, and they all wore smiles. One old lady was banging her fists on her wheelchair in excitement, and another kept trying to get out of her seat but was gently held back by one of the staff. It was best if everyone stayed seated whilst the donkey was on the premises, Nathan thought; he didn't want to risk any delicate toes being trodden on, or Gerald tossing his rather hard head and bumping into someone.

As Amos cheerily handed out the presents from the panniers, Nathan kept his attention on the donkey – most of the time, because he kept having to drag his gaze away from Megan, who was helping the residents open their presents (some people wanted to save theirs for the morning) and chatting away to them. And everywhere she went, Patch was right there with her.

She knelt next to chairs and patted gnarled hands. She smiled and kissed wrinkled cheeks, and had a word to say to everyone. He noticed how good she was with them, how patient and kind, and how she offered to bring them cups of tea, glasses of eggnog or sherry, or mince pies, and how they responded to her. And even though he could guess how hard this time of year must be for her, her smile appeared more open, and she seemed freer and less uptight as the evening wore on. So maybe this was doing her as much good as it was the elderly people she was spending time with?

'I want you to sing my song,' Amos declared, once all the presents were distributed.

'What song is that?' asked William, the care home manager, with a wink.

'Why, *Jingle Bells*, of course!' Amos clutched his belly and ho, ho, ho-ed again, to gales of laughter and raised glasses.

'I'm surprised they allow alcohol,' Megan said to Nathan, coming to stand next to him and Gerald, who was half-asleep with one small hind hoof cocked and his head hanging down.

'I've been told it's one of the better care homes,' Nathan said. 'Not only is there this cafe, but they serve three courses at lunch and dinner, and wine if anyone wants it. There's a gym, a spa and a hairdresser, a library and a games room. And there's a full list of activities every day.'

'Crumbs, it's like a hotel!' she said, putting her mouth next to his ear as she tried to make herself heard over the enthusiastic warbling and the plinking of piano keys.

'It's not cheap,' he replied. 'But it's worth the money if you can afford it; they do take great care of their residents.'

'I can see that. Thank you for letting me come with you. I've enjoyed myself.'

So had Nathan. It made a pleasant change from lolling in front of the telly and feeling slightly sorry for himself, which was what he usually did on Christmas Eve. Christmas was just a bit too in your face, he thought. It could often highlight what you hadn't got as much as what you had; and he hadn't got anyone apart from Patch. And the stables. But then, he wasn't a member of the family as such. He couldn't forget he was an employee, for all that Petra and Amos went out of their way to make him feel included, valued and liked.

He supposed he could have taken some holiday leave and spent a few days with his mum or his siblings. But as much as he loved them, he always got itchy feet after a couple of hours and was glad to go back home. He'd never manage a whole day, and certainly not three or four. No, he was better off staying put, and enjoying his lunch tomorrow at the stables – after he'd helped turn the horses out into the fields and muck out, that is!

Nathan's social battery was running low by the time he loaded Gerald back into the horsebox. There was only so much socialising he could tolerate, and he was grateful for Megan coming along to take some of the attention off him. He'd not smiled as much in ages, and his cheeks ached as a result. He hadn't made a fool of himself and neither had he been too grumpy he thought, pleased with how well the evening had gone. Gerald had behaved himself impeccably, and so had Patch, who'd been a great hit with those folks who liked dogs. Amos had brought good cheer (and presents), but the star of the show, Nathan felt, had been Megan. The residents had loved her, and when she'd waved goodbye her ears must have rung with all the pleadings for her to come back and visit them soon.

She'd promised she would, and Nathan believed her. He didn't think she was the type to make a promise if she didn't intend to keep it.

After they'd put a bemused Gerald back in his stable and closed the door, Amos yawned hugely and invited them in for a nightcap before they went home, then wandered into the house, leaving Nathan and Megan alone.

Nathan glanced across the yard, golden light from the windows spilling out onto the old cobbles. He could see Amos enter the kitchen, and Petra turn to speak to him.

'I'd best be getting off,' he decided, calling Patch to heel. The terrier had been rooting around in the straw of the donkey's stall, but as soon as he heard his name, he leapt up at the half-door and scrabbled over the top of it to drop down to the ground.

'Well I never!' Megan exclaimed. 'If I hadn't seen him do that with my own eyes, I wouldn't have believed it.' She bent to pet him. 'You are so bouncy for a little dog,' she crooned. 'Yes, you are.'

Patch lapped up the attention, leaning against her leg in bliss as she ruffled his ears.

'You were marvellous with the old people,' Nathan said.

'I enjoyed talking to them,' Megan replied. 'And I think they had a good time. As did I.'

'Me too.' He stared at her awkwardly, wondering what to say next. 'Um, Merry Christmas.' He cringed, guessing that was probably not the most sensitive thing to say to her under the circumstances.

'You, too.' She hesitated, then stepped towards him, and to his dismay and delight her arms came around him and she pulled him into a hug.

Oh, my, it felt amazing to be held by her, however briefly, and he inhaled her perfume and closed his eyes for a second, relishing the feel of her as he hugged her back.

Without meaning to, and certainly without any conscious thought, Nathan kissed her on the cheek. His lips encountered soft skin and it was all he could do not to kiss her again, but this time it wouldn't be on her cheek. He wanted to taste her lips, to feel the heat of her mouth—

Bugger.

His heart was racing so fast he thought he might pass out, and he hastily released her and backed away.

'Er, see you after Christmas,' he said, not daring to look at her for fear of what he might see. She was probably as appalled as he. What had possessed him to do such a thing? He was the least touchy-feely person he knew. He'd never been a hugger, and for him to have hugged her back so enthusiastically had shocked him. And then he'd *kissed* her…

He remained motionless as she wished him Merry Christmas again and walked towards her car. He stayed where he was as she got in and started the engine, flashing her headlights at him as she reversed, and then drove off.

He was still standing there five minutes later, long after her taillights had disappeared.

Nathan felt like giving himself a stern talking to, but it was impossible while his lips tingled and his heart throbbed, and an unexpected elation made his pulse race and his stomach turn over. And all he was able to do was to ask himself how come he could feel happy and glum at the same time.

***

Megan didn't expect to enjoy Christmas in the slightest, but when she woke on Christmas morning to see a fine blanket of snow on the ground, her spirits lifted. However, it wasn't long before they plummeted again as she contemplated the fact that she wouldn't be able to go riding in it. Only for them to lift again, because it meant she still had two more riding lessons to look forward to. Anyway, the white stuff didn't hang around for long and by the time she arrived at her parents' house it had all but gone.

It didn't stop her wondering how the horses were faring, though. Had they been let out to play in it, or were they going to spend the day in their nice warm stables? And how was Gerald feeling after his visit to the care home last night? She must remember to take him a little treat next time.

Thinking of the animals inevitably led her to thinking about Nathan. He'd seemed out of his comfort zone yesterday and she could tell he didn't enjoy being around so many people, but hats off to him for going regardless. She had to admire him for that.

Oh, who was she kidding? He hadn't *just* popped into her head – she'd been thinking about him all night. He'd lodged himself in her mind as soon as his arms had reluctantly gone around her as she'd impulsively hugged him, and she'd felt his solid body against hers, and felt the strength of his embrace, and smelt his outdoorsy scent that was a mixture of washing powder, shower gel, and the almost imperceptible aroma of horse and leather. It was intoxicating and she'd breathed him in, letting the scent of him wash over her and through her.

And then he'd kissed her.

Okay, so it was a maiden aunt kiss on the cheek and he'd certainly not meant anything by it, but the brief feel of his warm lips on her skin had shocked her. In a nice way.

Or maybe not. She hadn't been at all prepared for the way she'd reacted, and it had left her out of sorts for the rest of the night. And today, too.

What shocked her the most was the way she'd wanted to turn her head and feel his mouth on hers. She'd wanted him to kiss her properly, the way lovers kiss. And the knowledge had both appalled and excited her.

That he didn't feel anything for her had been evidenced by his awkwardness when they were saying goodbye.

Without warning, a longing to see him engulfed her, and she simply didn't know how she was going to get through the next few days of forced Christmas jollity, and the pity and concern of her parents.

Nathan wasn't a whistler. He disliked whistling and never did it. So why was he whistling now? He'd caught himself, lips puckered and a toneless high-pitched noise emanating from his mouth, and he'd immediately stopped making such a dreadful racket.

Even Patch was looking askance at him, and Hercules had given him a thoroughly disgusted glare when he'd gone to take him to the field.

Thankfully, only the animals had heard him, so there was no one to ask him why he was so chirpy. Because if someone had, he wouldn't have a clue what to say to them.

And he didn't have a clue what to say to himself. There was no reason for him to feel cheerful. No reason at all.

Maybe if Megan had reacted in a positive way to the kiss he'd given her, he might have a reason; but she hadn't. In fact, their goodbye had been embarrassing and awkward, and he'd be surprised if she didn't go out of her way to avoid him in future.

So there was absolutely no reason at all for him to be so jaunty.

Reining himself in, he finished all the jobs he'd set himself, then went to the farmhouse to wash his hands and change out of his work clothes. He'd brought a clean pair of jeans with him and a checked flannel shirt, and in no time at all he was looking presentable. He probably could have done with a shave, but a bit of stubble helped keep his face warm this time of year. His hair could do with a trim, too. And was that a new wrinkle running down the side of his nose to his mouth? He had another one on the other side, he noticed, peering into the speckled mirror of the downstairs loo and shower room.

Meh, so what? He was getting older, and he should expect his face to show his age.

Megan looked younger than hers though, he mused. She was forty-three but he remembered when he'd first set eyes on her that he'd estimated her to be anywhere between thirty and forty.

He wondered what she was doing now. Was she thinking about him?

No, of course she wasn't. Stop being so daft, he told himself. He'd kissed her on the cheek, in the same way she'd kissed many of Honeymead's residents last night. It had meant nothing to her.

But it had meant something to him, and he still wasn't sure what had possessed him to do it.

He couldn't stop thinking about it, though: he couldn't stop thinking about *her*. The way her arms had snaked around him, the way she'd felt so delicate, yet so soft and yielding. Her perfume, the smoothness of her skin, her luminous eyes.

'Are you okay in there?' Amos yelled outside the bathroom door.

'Eh? Er, yeah, I'll be out now,' he called, then muttered, 'Pull yourself together, man,' and grimaced. His reflection snarled back at him. That's more like it, he thought. All that smiling didn't sit well on his face.

Thankful he'd got his wayward emotions under control, he settled down to enjoy the sumptuous lunch which Amos, Petra and Harry had prepared between them. Roast turkey with all the trimmings, pumpkin soup to start, and Christmas pud with brandy sauce for afters, it was a feast for a king, and by the time Nathan forced the last spoonful of pudding into his mouth, he was so full he thought he might pop.

Everyone else at the table had also made a good fist of their lunch, but there were loads left in the tureens, which Amos began to decant into a huge pan ready for the traditional Boxing Day meal of bubble and squeak.

Petra groaned. 'I'm stuffed.' She made to get up.

Nathan put out his hand. 'Stay where you are, all of you. I'll clear away and stack the dishwasher. It's the least I can do – that was stunning. I don't think I'll eat for a week.'

'I take it there's no point in me wrapping up some turkey for you to have for supper?' Amos teased.

'Go on, then. I might be able to manage a bite or two later.'

As he was dealing with the saucepans, Nathan caught himself mid-pucker and realised he was about to whistle again, so as a distraction he stuck his head into the living room to ask if anyone wanted a cuppa. They'd shared a bottle of wine during lunch, and Amos had treated himself to a small sherry beforehand, but Nathan guessed a cup of tea would go down better than alcohol considering the horses would have to be brought in later.

He almost barked out a laugh at the sight of Amos and Petra fast asleep, Amos with his mouth open, Petra with her head on Harry's shoulder. All three were still wearing the party hats that had come out of the crackers, and they looked so comical Nathan chuckled. Petra's had slipped down over her ears and the paper hat covered most of her face; Amos's was balanced on the top of his head, and the cat was trying to bat it with a paw.

Nathan left them to it and finished tidying up, and when he was done he whispered goodbye to Harry, who was watching *The Wizard of Oz* through half-closed eyes.

Despite having enjoyed himself, Nathan was relieved to return to his own house, and he plodded down the lane in the encroaching darkness, his faithful dog at his heels and a foil-wrapped packet of turkey in his pocket. He'd spent enough time with people over the past day or so, and he desperately needed some solitude.

Yet when he opened the door to his cottage and stepped inside, the silence hit him like walking into a wall. There wasn't a sound; not even a creak or groan from the pipes, and without warning he was overcome by a feeling of loneliness.

Is this how it is for Megan, he wondered? He couldn't imagine feeling like this all the time, and he shuddered. It was rare for him to feel lonely, but he guessed that for Megan it was commonplace. Pity gripped him, and he wished he could do something to help her.

She was right not to get a dog, but maybe a cat would help? At least it would be someone to come home to after a hard day in the office he mused, clutching Patch to him and giving him a cuddle, grateful for the warm little body snuggling into him.

She was probably right to think about changing jobs too, and an image of her expression as she waited for the verdict on the cake she'd made swam into his mind. It sounded as though she only had her job in HR in her life, and if she didn't enjoy it, then she needed to seriously think about changing careers.

He knew it was easier said than done, but he couldn't think of anything worse than spending eight or more hours a day in a job he disliked. It must be soul-destroying.

Thankfully he loved his, and as he'd said to Megan, it might not make him rich but as long as he had enough money to live on he didn't need any more.

Although Petra was his boss, she let him get on with stuff, and if there was anything to be done, she wrote it on the whiteboard in the office and he ticked the job off when he'd completed it – it was as good as being his own boss but without the headache.

But almost without his noticing, loneliness stole over him again and he began to wonder if, like Megan, his life was also missing something.

Nathan tried to ignore the odd and unsettling feeling, but it kept invading his thoughts throughout the rest of the evening, and although he tried, he couldn't shift it, especially when Megan slipped into his mind once more.

CHAPTER SEVEN

'Over here,' Nathan called as Megan got out of her car and headed towards the arena, and she stopped and turned at the sound of his voice. It made her heart lurch, but she tried not to let it show. He didn't need to know she was starting to get a bit of a crush on him.

'Did you have a good Christmas?' she asked, walking towards him. He was saddling Hercules, and Sherbet was patiently standing next to the stallion, her saddle already on her back.

'Yes, thanks. You?'

She pulled a face. 'It was okay, considering…' She let the rest of the sentence hang, knowing he'd get what she meant.

'I'm sorry,' he said.

'For what?' The brief brush of his lips on her cheek? She hadn't been able to stop thinking about it all over the festive season.

'For your husband passing on. You must miss him.'

Megan blinked at the unexpected comment. 'Yes, I do,' she replied honestly.

Nathan studied her, then he nodded slowly before turning back to his task, leaving her to wonder what all that was about.

'Are you taking me out today? I assume we're going on a hack,' she asked.

'Is that okay?'

'You or the hack?'

'Either? Both?'

'I want to ride out onto the hills today, and I'm perfectly happy that it's you who will be accompanying me.'

'I thought we'd take the same route we'll be taking when it snows,' he said, and Megan felt a momentary pang. This was her penultimate ride. The next one was weather dependent, and when that was done, her visits to the stables would be over.

Unless…?

She could always make hacking a regular feature. Her rediscovered love of riding didn't have to end on the next snowfall. There was nothing stopping her from booking herself in for more rides.

Or was there?

She glanced across at Nathan, who was sitting astride Hercules and adjusting the stirrup length. More rides meant she'd see more of Nathan, possibly on a regular basis, and she didn't intend to put herself in a position where she might fall for a man who didn't think of her in that way.

On that basis, it was probably better to knock the horse-riding on the head as soon as Jeremy's final gift was completed.

His final gift…

She felt incredibly sad to think there wouldn't be any more envelopes with her name on and his handwritten card inside. It was as though he was severing his last link with her, as though he was pushing her away. Which was ridiculous, but she couldn't help how she felt or the thoughts that flitted through her mind.

Megan mounted up and without being asked Sherbet fell into line behind Hercules, leaving Megan free to dwell on the implications of no longer having this last link with Jeremy. It was both frightening and liberating, and she wasn't sure how to deal with it.

Sherbet breaking into a trot pulled Megan out of herself and forced her to pay attention to the here and now or risk an injury. A rising trot could do that to a person, as a loss of concentration could mean a hearty smack on the backside as one's behind slapped onto the saddle. Not only was it uncomfortable (probably for the horse as well as the rider), but she'd also feel more amateurish than she already felt. It didn't matter that Nathan was ahead of her and wouldn't see her incompetent horsemanship – she'd know, and that was enough.

When they reached the gate leading to the path onto the hillside above the stables, Nathan edged Hercules to the side so he could open it and Sherbet walked through, swishing her tail provocatively at the other horse and crabbing to the side.

'We'll have none of those shenanigans,' Megan told the mare firmly, catching Nathan's eye and pouting her displeasure at him.

'Is she playing you up?'

'Just being a bit flirty. Sherbet, not me.' Maybe the pout hadn't been the best facial expression to use. She didn't want him to think she was being coquettish.

'I didn't think otherwise,' he said.

That told her! If she had been flirting it would have gone over his head anyway, which reinforced her view that he wouldn't look at her twice.

And who could blame him? She was damaged goods. Not the having been married part, but the grief part. Who'd want a widow who had yet to move on from the premature death of the only man she would ever love.

Oh, and yes, that "only man she'd ever love" was a stumbling block, both for her and for any man who fell for her. Because although she was coming around to the idea of at some point in the dim and distant future having a relationship, she didn't for one second believe she'd love as deeply again.

'Oh, my, look at that view!' she exclaimed as the horses emerged onto an expanse of moorland. Below there was a patchwork of rolling fields, meadows, and pockets of woodland, interspersed with farms, and in the distance she could see Picklewick itself. She could make out the square turret of the Norman church, which seemed incredibly small this high up.

For January the afternoon was relatively bright, and although it was too soon to see any lengthening of the days, there were hints of the spring to come in the tiny buds on the hedgerows, and fresh green growth on either side of the rugged track. The air was incredibly fresh and sharp, its chill almost painful on her skin and in her lungs, but she breathed deeply, letting nature flow through her and chase away any dismal thoughts.

Nathan drew Hercules to a halt and twisted slightly in his saddle. 'Have you not been up here before?' he asked.

'Yes, but not for many years,' she replied. 'Jeremy and I always kept meaning to bring a picnic up here, but we never got round to it. I'd forgotten how lovely it is.'

Dragging her eyes away from the view, she gazed around at the golden grass, all its goodness sucked back into the roots. It rippled in the keen wind, and she stared at it mesmerised, until her attention was drawn to the rowan trees with their bright red berries poking through the russet bracken. A blackbird was perched on the uppermost branches of the nearest stubby tree, picking the berries off one by one and gulping them down. Sheep dotted the hillside, little white blobs busily searching for any grass worth eating, and high above a red kite circled, with its unmistakable forked tail and high-pitched cry.

She watched its flight for a moment, then her eyes tracked beyond it to the grey lowering clouds, and she shivered.

'It's definitely a cold one,' Nathan observed, blowing on his hands.

Even though Megan wore thick gloves, her hands were freezing, and she wondered how he could stand it. He was certainly made of hardier stuff than she.

'I reckon we're going to get that snow you want before too long,' he observed.

'There isn't anything forecast,' she said.

'There might not be, but the animals know. See those sheep?' He pointed to the distant hillside. 'If you watch them for long enough you'll see that they're all slowly but surely heading downhill. They'll be seeking out more sheltered places, ready to hunker down. The snow might not come today, and probably not tomorrow, but I reckon it will be here soon. The signs are there if you know what to look for,' he added.

'Can I ask you a favour?' She peered at him hopefully. 'Will you give me a call if it starts to snow;

enough to go out for a ride in, I mean. I'd hate to miss a good opportunity, and my main concern is that if I leave it until it's snowing in the village, I won't be able to get to you, or it would be too dangerous to take the horses out.'

'Of course I will.'

'Can I ask another favour?'

He raised his eyebrows. 'Depends on what it is.' His tone was deadpan but a smile lingered around his mouth, and Megan couldn't help staring at it.

He had nice lips, well-shaped, and he didn't seem to have shaved for a couple of days. The stubble was coming through more grey than brown, unlike the hair on his head which was only greying at the temples. It made him look sexy.

Oh my God, is that what she thought?

That was a kind of step up from finding him attractive, or was it all the same thing? She honestly didn't know, but what she did know was that she felt a pull towards him deep in her gut, and he was in her head, too.

She put a hand up to her cheek where he'd kissed her the other day, before she realised what she was doing and let it drop again, resting it on the pommel of the saddle.

'Well?' he asked. 'What is the favour?'

'Oh yes, I…um…do you think you could take me on my last ride? I'm sure Petra has got lots of other things she can be going on with.'

'And I haven't?' He was grinning at her to show he was teasing.

'I expect you have, but I'd like you to join me.' She knew she was playing with fire, and the only one who would get burned was her, but for goodness sake this was only a hack, nothing more. It would be just as magical if Petra were to accompany her, but for some reason she wanted it to be Nathan.

She almost snorted at herself. *For some reason* indeed! There wasn't any "some" about it; she knew exactly what the reason was, she fancied him and she wanted to spend a bit of time with him.

But so what? She wasn't hurting anyone, and there was nothing wrong with indulging in a little bit of fantasy even though she had absolutely no intention of making any moves to fulfil it. This was just a part of the healing process. She was starting to come alive again, just like nature around her. She'd gone through a long, dark, emotional winter, and now she felt the first stirrings of her own spring in her heart and in her soul.

Megan was under no illusion that this gradual return to life she was about to embark on would be plain sailing, and just like those new shoots that were trying their best to poke through the frozen soil, she'd have her setbacks. Those shoots might soon have a covering of snow, and no doubt she'd have her own internal snowfalls to deal with along the way. But snow melted, and she realised the chill which had engulfed her heart since Jeremy left her, would also thaw.

'We'd better get a move on,' Nathan said, interrupting her thoughts. 'We've got some way to go yet.'

'Where are we heading?'

'There's an old derelict farmhouse about four miles in that direction. I thought next time I'd bring a flask, and we can stop and have a hot drink before we turn around and come back down again.'

'That's a lovely idea. I'll bring a slice of cake. I've got my first class this evening, so no doubt I'll have more cake than I'll know what to do with.'

'Good luck,' he said. 'Although I'm sure you won't need it. As for cake, we'll eat all the left-over cake you can send our way. Timothy said the one you did for him was absolutely delicious. Mind you, he only managed to have a small slice, because Charity's family dived in before he had a chance. It went down a storm, he said.'

Megan smiled. Timothy had sent her an email to thank her and had informed her that the cake had been very well received, but it hadn't lasted long, and he'd thought Charity's father might have polished off three slices all by himself. She was delighted with the compliment, and it had been a great boost to her self-esteem.

She was looking forward to this evening, and she couldn't wait to get started. She kept telling herself it was only a ten-week course, and the fact that she was taking it didn't mean she had to resign from her job and start up a business of her own. But deep down that's what she was secretly hoping might happen.

Telling herself it was far too early to start making those kinds of plans, she nevertheless wondered whether it might be possible to renegotiate her hours at work. Perhaps she could drop down to part-time, which would give her the best of both worlds.

'Do you really think I could make a go of cake decorating?' she asked abruptly, although Nathan probably wasn't the best person to chat to about this.

'I don't see why not,' he said. 'But I think you'll probably need to get some professional advice. I like a nice bit of cake, but I'm no expert.'

'I'm considering going part-time. What do you think?' She didn't know why she was asking him this, apart from that he seemed sensible and wouldn't pander to her, or humour her. She sensed he would tell her straight, even if it was something she didn't want to hear.

'It's a good solution. It gives you a safety net.'

'That's what I was thinking. But I won't do it just yet. I want to complete the course first, and get some more experience under my belt. I'm also going to have to come up with a business plan. I've got an awful lot to do and to think about before I take the plunge. And anyway, it's not as though I've got any other distractions in the evenings or the weekends. I can carry on working and make cakes side by side.'

'Will you carry on with the riding?'

Megan caught him looking at her out of the corner of his eye, and suddenly she had a feeling her answer was important. 'I had considered it,' she replied slowly.

She might. Then again, she might not, and she was leaning more towards the might not than the might. She was enjoying this ride and she'd most definitely enjoy the next one, but that would be the end of it. She would have indulged herself enough. This final gift of Jeremy's would have served its purpose.

As she listened to the steady plod of the horses' hooves as they climbed up the path, the old farmhouse growing gradually closer, she tried to imagine Jeremy by her side – but all she could see was Nathan, a man who was very much here, very much alive, and very much in her thoughts. And she'd never felt so conflicted or uncertain in her life.

'You go on into the house and get warm,' Nathan said, noticing how cold Megan looked as they rode into the yard. 'I'll see to the horses.' Déjà vu, but this time instead of insisting on helping him, she handed him Sherbet's reins, gave him a small smile, and went inside.

Her car was still in the car park by the time he was done, so he didn't linger after he'd finished for the day. Instead, he collected Patch who had sensibly been snuggling in the warm, and headed off home, his thoughts consumed by her.

Cross with himself for letting anyone upset his composure, he clattered around in his kitchen preparing a hot meal, and ate it in sullen silence.

He'd known it would have been better not to have taken Megan out for a trek, but Petra was looking so peaky he hadn't had the heart to refuse her.

Never mind, he told himself, only one more ride to go, and that would be the end of it.

A part of him (a bigger part than he was prepared to admit) was sorry, and he felt a strange ache in his chest at the thought of never seeing Megan again, but it was for the best. She wasn't ready, and when the time came for her to move on with her life, he was not the man she'd choose. He knew that. What could he offer her? He was a solitary, grumpy, middle-aged fellow, who barely had a penny to his name and spent most of his time repairing fences, shovelling manure or driving a tractor.

Clearly, Megan was used to far better than the likes of him.

But however much he tried to turn his thoughts away from her, she invaded his mind, and Nathan had a niggling feeling she was invading his heart, too.

'That's it, we're done,' Megan said, putting her mug on the table and getting to her feet.

Petra felt relief wash over her. She hadn't been looking forward to hashing out the details of creating and placing an advert, but when Megan had stayed on at the stables after her ride in order to help with the recruitment process, she'd been a godsend. Okay, she'd asked questions Petra hadn't known how to answer (holiday entitlement being one of them – and she still had to speak to Nathan about his, because the man rarely took a day off), but with Megan's calm and sure guidance, the advert was finally done and posted online. She'd also printed it out so Petra could ask shops in the village if they'd display a copy for her.

Hopefully, there would be some interest; after all, Picklewick was in a rural area where agricultural and farm jobs were commonplace, so there was a talent pool available. And although she hadn't said as much to Megan, Petra was only interested in whether applicants had an affinity with horses and whether she felt she could get on with them. Petra also made a note to have Nathan sit in on the interviews – he had to get on with the new person too, because he'd be working quite closely with him or her.

Petra blew out her cheeks and got to her feet. 'Thanks for that,' she said. 'Let me pay you.'

'Don't be daft! It's a pleasure.' Megan waved her hand.

'How about a couple of rides, instead? After your snow one? Maybe a few in the spring when the weather breaks?'

'I don't know…'

'Haven't you enjoyed your rides?' Petra frowned. She could have sworn Megan had thoroughly enjoyed herself. Had something happened to make her change her mind?

'I've enjoyed them very much. It's just…' Megan sighed. 'I understand why Jeremy bought them for me and I truly appreciate it and the sentiment behind it, but…' She sighed again. 'I'm not sure I'm ready to put myself out there again.'

Petra was thoroughly baffled. 'It's a couple of rides, not a marriage proposal,' she began, then she stopped and her eyes widened. 'Is it Nathan?'

'Not at all.'

Petra noted the twin spots of colour on Megan's cheeks. *That's the way the land lies, is it,* she mused, never expecting that the still-grieving woman who had arrived at the stables a little over a month ago was beginning to have feelings for Nathan. And Petra wondered what Nathan felt about that – or whether he actually knew. Knowing him, he was probably oblivious.

'It's not like that,' Megan insisted.

'Like what?' Petra asked, innocently.

Megan took a deep breath and drew herself up. 'Thank you for the offer, but I don't think I'll be doing any more riding. It's been lovely, but I can't see a future in it.'

As Petra thanked Megan again for her help and showed her out, she reflected that "see a future" was an odd thing to say in response to the offer of a couple of hacks, and Petra got the distinct impression Megan was referring to something else entirely – something to do with Nathan.

Petra vowed to take a closer look at what was going on between the two of them: she loved Nathan like a brother and she wanted him to be happy, and from what she'd seen of Megan, the woman was ready to embrace life and love again.

Petra, smiling wickedly, had never considered herself to be a matchmaker, but if there was any possibility these two might find love together, she'd do her utmost to make it happen.

'Hi, Megan, it's Petra.' Megan automatically glanced out of her living room window, but she knew Petra wasn't phoning because it was snowing and there was a hack to go on. It was dark outside, for one thing, and for another it was gone eight o'clock in the evening.

'Is everything okay?' A trickle of worry entered her mind.

'It's Nathan—'

The trickle turned into a torrent. 'Oh god, is he all right? Has he had an accident?' Horses could be dangerous, everyone knew that. They had hooves and teeth, and were so large and heavy—

'If you'd let me finish, I was just about to say that it's Nathan's birthday on Saturday, and I was hoping you'd make a cake for him. We're having a little do in the Black Horse.'

Relief made Megan weak and she sagged back in her armchair.

'Yes,' she managed to get out, ashamed of her outburst. 'When do you want me to bring it to the stables? Saturday morning?'

'I was thinking you could bring it with you when you come to the pub.'

'What pub?'

'The Black Horse – keep up.' Petra huffed down the phone.

'You want *me* to go to the Black Horse?'

'You'll have to if you want to help Nathan celebrate his birthday. Either way, it seems pointless you driving all the way up to the stables with the cake, only for me to drive it all the way back to Picklewick again. Are you coming, or not? There'll be a buffet, and I'll even buy you your first drink. What do you say?'

'I'm surprised Nathan has agreed to a party – he doesn't seem the party type.'

'He is when you get to know him,' Petra replied breezily. 'Look, I've got to go. I'll leave the design up to you. He likes a nice Victoria sponge with raspberry jam.'

'Thanks for the—'

Too late, Petra had hung up, leaving Megan bewildered. One moment she'd been scared out of her wits at the thought of Nathan being thrown or trampled, and the next she was being advised of his cake preferences.

So much for her decision to have nothing more to do with the stables once she'd ridden her last hack.

However, she hadn't done that yet, so technically she wasn't going back on her decision. Plus it would be another opportunity to get one of her cakes in front of more eyes than just her fellow students on the course. And she didn't want Nathan to think she'd been invited and had refused. He didn't deserve to be snubbed like that. Another plus would be that the cake could be her present to him, and she wouldn't have to figure out what he might like. Buying for men was always tricky, and she used to struggle with ideas of what to get Jeremy for Christmas and birthdays.

She'd do it, she decided. She could pop into the pub with the cake, stay for a drink, then head off home. Once she'd shown her face she would have done her duty and no one would miss her if she sloped off early.

Her excitement for Saturday made its presence known in the clenching of her tummy and she frowned at herself before she realised she was bound to be excited – this was a great opportunity to showcase what she could do in terms of cake creation.

And she had the perfect cake in mind!

'Saturday, you said?' Nathan shot Amos a look out of the corner of his eye as he stretched the hen's wing out to check her feathers. She'd been off-colour lately and Nathan wondered if she was being picked on by the other birds. 'I haven't played darts for years. There must be someone else you can call on?'

'Can't think of anyone. We've asked all those who are any good.'

'Thanks a lot!'

'You know what I mean. We just need you to make up the numbers. It's the semi-final.'

'Why can't Scouse play?'

'He's had to go to Liverpool. Family emergency. I told you that.'

'So you did.' But Nathan had a feeling something was up, and he didn't know what. Amos's story didn't ring true. He put the bird on the ground, and it dashed off with an indignant squawk. 'Hen-pecked,' he said.

'Scouse? *Is he?* Crumbs!' Amos shook his head in disbelief.

'The *hen*.'

'Oh, I see. What about it, then? Are you up for it, only they won't let us play if we're a man short.'

'Have you asked any of the women? Or does it have to be a man?' Nathan was only teasing, but Amos looked shifty all of a sudden.

'You're our last hope,' Amos insisted. 'I'll treat you to supper and a pint.'

'Make it two pints,' Nathan said.

'Done!' Amos held out his hand and the two men shook on it.

'Just one thing – I thought darts were always on a Friday?'

'Er, yeah, but not this week.'

Nathan sighed. He didn't particularly like darts, but he supposed it would give him something to do on Saturday night, other than sit at home and stare at the telly. It was his birthday, too, so it would be nice to get out even if no one remembered.

Ah, that was it!

Amos *had* remembered, which was why he was so insistent Nathan went to the Black Horse on Saturday. Knowing how Nathan hated a fuss, Amos had come up with the story that he was needed for the darts match in order to buy him a pub meal and a couple of pints.

If that was the worst Amos would do (aside from Petra buying him a card and a bottle of something malty and mellow), Nathan could deal with that.

In fact, he was looking forward to it.

Megan was thrilled with the cake she'd made for Nathan, even if she did say so herself, and she hoped he'd be as pleased.

She'd toyed with a horsey theme because of his connection to the stables, but in the end had gone with her instinct that he'd appreciate a Patch cake instead. Which was why she was walking up to the door of the Black Horse and carrying a box, inside of which was a cake in the shape of a Jack Russell terrier, complete with a dark brown patch over the dog's eye. It looked the spitting image of Nathan's furry friend.

She was concentrating so hard on not dropping it and trying to hold an umbrella aloft which was wedged between her elbow and her body (the snow had yet to materialise, although what was falling from the sky this evening was more sleet than rain) that she nearly walked into a person who was also hurrying towards the door.

'Oops, sorry,' she said, almost poking the man in the head with her umbrella.

He pushed the hood of his parker back and her eyes widened as Nathan stepped in front of her and opened the door. 'After you.'

Megan slipped into the porch, grateful to get out of the dreadful weather and Patch trotted in behind her. Not knowing whether the cake was to be a surprise to be brought out at the end of the evening, her smile was more of a grimace, and she hoped she hadn't been rumbled.

'I'll just, erm…' she said, nodding towards the door to the main bar and hoping she'd spot Petra.

'Is that a cake?'

'Erm, yes. Someone ordered it. I'm meeting them here.'

'Can I buy you a drink?'

'Shouldn't I be buying you one? Happy birthday, by the way,' she added as he also opened this door for her.

'How do you know it's my—'

'Surprise!' a chorus of voices yelled and Megan jumped, almost dropping the cake box.

Nathan looked stunned. And not particularly happy.

Megan saw Petra sitting at a table with Harry, Amos, Timothy and a load of other people, and she shot across the room. 'Here's the cake,' she cried, thrusting it at Petra.

Petra took hold of it and passed it straight to Harry before leaping to her feet and darting to the door. Megan turned in time to see Nathan hastening out of it.

'He hates fuss,' Amos said to her. 'I had to get him here under false pretences.'

'He didn't know about the party?'

'He wouldn't have come if he had. Leave Petra to sort him out, take off your coat and have a drink. What's your poison?'

'A white wine, please. But I won't stay long.'

'You'll stay for the buffet, won't you? Dave, the landlord, has put on a lovely spread in the back room.'

'Um, okay. I can manage a sandwich.'

Harry said, 'I'll just take this out the back, then I'll go to the bar.'

Megan shuffled out of her coat and draped it over the back of a vacant chair, before sitting down. Oh dear, this wasn't going so well, was it? The birthday boy didn't appear to appreciate his surprise party and had done a runner, and she worried he might lay an equal amount of blame on her shoulders for being party to the deception.

Eventually, though, Nathan came back in with Petra (she had a firm grip on his hand and was towing him behind her) and he was persuaded to take a seat and drink the pint put in front of him.

Megan sipped her wine and gradually relaxed. She knew everyone at their table, and although many people came up to wish an embarrassed Nathan a happy birthday, she didn't feel out of place.

That Nathan was sitting next to her and kept giving her reassuring glances, went some way to her growing enjoyment of the evening.

Nathan was well-liked and, although he was shy, by the time he'd finished his third pint, she could tell he was beginning to mellow and might even be enjoying himself.

Telling herself she was going to leave as soon as the cake was unveiled (or unboxed, as the case may be), Megan accepted another glass of wine, and vowed to do her best to enjoy the occasion; this was the first time she'd been to a party since Jeremy died, and she knew that if she was to fully immerse herself in her life there would be many more firsts to come.

But after the buffet had been well and truly tucked into, and the cake had been presented to a scowling Nathan and Happy Birthday had been sung, Megan was still rooted firmly in her chair. She was having a thoroughly lovely time, and when another glass of wine was placed in front of her, she settled back in her seat.

As she did so, Nathan's foot brushed against hers and she automatically moved hers away, only for it to happen again.

And a third time.

Oh, goodness, was he playing footsie?

A surge of desire swept over her, and she inhaled sharply at the unfamiliar feeling. Gosh, the wine was going to her head.

She caught his eye and smiled hesitantly, relieved when he grinned back at her. His foot found hers again and this time, instead of moving her own away, she slipped it out of her shoe and ran her toes along what she hoped was the top of his foot.

His expression didn't change, but hers did as she realised that unless Nathan possessed incredibly hairy feet it wasn't Nathan's foot she was stroking…

Stricken, she bent down and looked under the table.

Patch stared lovingly back at her.

Megan straightened up, her cheeks flooding with colour. 'I'm just going to step outside for a moment,' she said to no one in particular, then fanned her face with her hands to indicate she was hot.

Hurriedly, she got up from the table and fled out of the bar, feeling certain that flames of mortification must be trailing along in her wake. She hadn't been telling fibs – she honestly did feel hot. And silly.

As soon as she stepped outside, the freezing air hit her and she took a deep lungful of it. At least the sleet had stopped so she wouldn't have to go back in looking like a drowned rat. Maybe she could wait here until someone went in, and she could ask them to fetch her coat for her, to save her having to go back inside.

Feeling like an idiot, she slumped against the wall, her breath misting around her head and waited.

No one went in.

But someone did come out, and it was the very person she was hoping not to see.

'Nathan,' she said, in resignation. It would have to be him, wouldn't it?

'Are you okay? I saw you leave in a hurry.'

'I'm fine, just a bit hot.'

'I noticed Patch was cosying up to you. He's like a hot water bottle.' He joined her in leaning against the wall.

'Yes, that must have been it,' she said, feeling the chill of the bricks on her back.

'Thank you for coming.'

'You're welcome. I didn't know it was a surprise, though. You didn't seem too pleased.'

'I don't do parties, especially when I'm the guest of honour.'

'Sorry.'

'What for?'

'I wouldn't have made you a cake if I'd known you wouldn't like your party.'

'I like my cake. It's a wonderful cake and it looks just like Patch.' Nathan pushed himself up off the wall and turned to face her. 'Thank you. You knew exactly what I'd like.'

Megan smiled.

Nathan smiled back.

Before she could register what was happening, either she moved towards him or he took a step closer to her, but whatever it was she was suddenly in his arms and his mouth was on hers, and she was kissing him.

He tasted of real ale and icing, and the stubble on his chin rasped against her skin.

It was intoxicating and terrifying, and her breath caught in her throat as she breathed in the tantalising scent of him. Her legs shaking, he deepened the kiss until he was crushing her to him, and the low moan he made in the back of his throat sent her dizzy with desire.

Then the bang of the pub door dragged her abruptly back to her senses, and with a gasp she pulled away, horrified at what she'd done.

Tears gathering in her eyes, Megan took a step back, then another, ignoring the imploring hand Nathan held out to her and the beseeching look in his eyes.

She couldn't do this. She wasn't ready.

She didn't know if she ever would be.

And with that, she fled, back to her heartache and away from the promise of a love-filled future.

CHAPTER EIGHT

'I told you it was going to snow,' Nathan said to Petra, 'and Amos agreed with me. He said he could smell it in the air.'

Large fat flakes were drifting lazily to the ground, but Nathan knew this was only the start of it. Very soon they would be turning to flurries, and they would fall thick and fast, but he had a feeling it wouldn't last long.

'It might be a good idea for you to ring Megan,' he said to his boss. They were both in the office, Petra scowling at the laptop, and Nathan rubbing one of the jobs off the whiteboard.

'Why can't you do it?' she asked.

'I think it would be better coming from you. She said she'd be able to get time off work at a moment's notice, but I bet you she doesn't even realise it's snowing up here. It's probably just drizzling lower down.'

'I still can't see why you don't ring her.'

Nathan scowled. The last thing he wanted to do was to ring Megan. Tell a lie, he *did* want to speak to Megan, he wanted to hear her voice, he wanted to see her smile, her pretty face, the way she wrinkled her nose when she was thinking… He wanted to kiss her again (and again, and again) but she'd made it very clear how she felt about him.

He understood, guessing it was too much, too soon, and she wasn't ready.

Maybe she never would be. He hoped that wasn't the case: she was too beautiful, too young and too lovely to never love again. But she'd made herself clear when she'd left the Black Horse on Saturday evening.

He'd not hurt this bad in a long time, but he'd get over it. He just had to be patient, and avoid any contact with her again, for his own peace of mind as well as for hers.

It didn't prevent him from constantly thinking about her though, and since Saturday she'd taken up permanent residence in his mind. And in his heart.

'*You* should phone her,' he insisted. 'I've got to take some silage down to the fields.'

The horses and ponies were out as usual, all of them wearing nice thick winter rugs so they wouldn't feel the cold, but if the snow began to stick they'd appreciate some extra fodder. There wasn't much nourishment in the grass at this time of year, and all the animals benefited from some supplementary feed.

'Does that mean you're not going to be able to take her out on the ride?' Petra asked.

'Doubt it. I probably won't have time.'

'Why? What else do you have to do today?'

They both looked at the whiteboard; most of the jobs had been there for a while, because they were difficult to do in the winter. They could sit there until spring, it was of no consequence, but Nathan decided now was as good time as any to have a go at fixing the baler.

He had an idea what was wrong with it and he knew it wouldn't take too long to mend, but he'd been putting it off, because while the weather had been relatively dry although cold, there was always something else that needed doing outside.

Not today though. Cold and snowing didn't entice him to work outdoors, so he might as well tackle the baler.

Petra narrowed her eyes at him. 'Okay, I'll take her out,' she agreed, and he lingered for a moment as she picked up the phone and dialled Megan's number.

'Hi Megan, it's Petra up at the stables on Muddypuddle Lane. I just thought I'd let you know it's snowing quite heavily up here so if you want to go for a ride you'd best make your way up smartish. Half an hour?' Petra looked at Nathan. 'That's fine.' There was a pause, then Petra said, 'I'll be taking you today, out if that's okay? Good, see you in a bit. All done,' Petra said to him after she ended the call. 'Can you do me a favour and bring Hercules and Sherbet in for me after you've taken the silage down?'

Nathan nodded, feeling dejected. He would have loved nothing better than to have gone riding with Megan, but he had no intention of being around when she showed up. He was doing what was right, for the right reasons. He didn't need to open himself to heartache, and he didn't need to subject her to his puppy dog eyes. She had no clue he was starting to have feelings for her, and he wanted it to stay that way.

Starting? Ha, that was a joke. It had crept up on him unannounced and ambushed him. He wasn't *starting* at all: he already had them.

It didn't take him long to load up the trailer and take it down to the fields, then he went back for the two horses and took them into the barn ready to be tacked up. After that he went in search of Petra to tell her the horses were ready for her.

He found her just coming out of the house, but she wasn't dressed for riding. She was wearing a pair of jeans, smart leather boots, and her best waxed cotton jacket.

'Where are you going?' he asked her.

'Sorry, Nathan, I've just had a phone call from the bank, and I need to pop out for a while. It can't wait, so you will have to go riding with Megan. That's okay, isn't it?'

Nathan was savvy enough to know that she wasn't asking him, she was telling him, and he had a feeling she'd planned this all along. She was up to something, but he just had to concentrate on getting through the next few hours, and by this evening Megan Barnes would be out of his life for good and he could go back to his usual insular existence.

The problem was, he had a worrying feeling he didn't *want* to go back to it!

When Petra phoned, Megan had been seriously tempted to say she couldn't get out of work, but she decided she might as well get this business over and done with. She knew she wouldn't feel right until she'd done what Jeremy wanted, which was to go horseback riding in the snow. It was his final gift to her, and she had to see it through.

After today there would be no reason for her to set foot anywhere near the stables on Muddypuddle Lane, and therefore she wouldn't see Nathan again.

Hopefully she wouldn't see him today, either. She missed him though, his dry quiet ways, his steadiness, his solidity, but that was ridiculous considering she'd only known him a few weeks. The fact that she was still thinking about him was proof she needed to distance herself from him. She'd soon get over her silly infatuation and return to the way she was before.

Actually, that was quite a worrying thought. Did she honestly want to return to the miserable lacklustre person she'd been since Jeremy died?

No, she didn't.

She'd never forget her husband, of course she wouldn't – he'd always be there in her heart and her soul – but it was time to start living again.

Thankfully, Petra would be accompanying her today, so Megan should be able to stay out of Nathan's way. Her heart squeezed a little and her stomach churned, but she ignored it. She should never have kissed him, and she only had herself to blame if she was feeling rotten, but her vague guilt was more to do with how happy she'd felt in Nathan's arms and the nagging feeling that she didn't have any right to be happy. Any and all brief moments of contentment since Jeremy was gone made her feel like that, but it was lessening. She just didn't think she had been prepared for her intense reaction to Nathan's kiss, and it had taken her totally by surprise. She just hoped her erratic behaviour hadn't ruined his birthday.

Informing work she was taking the rest of the day off, she hurried home to change into her riding gear, grabbed a couple of slices of cake and made her way to the stables.

Although only two miles out of Picklewick, it was

two uphill miles, and with each hundred or so foot of elevation the drizzle in the lower lying areas turned to sleet, then to soggy snowflakes which dissolved immediately upon impact, and eventually, as she pulled into the stables on Muddypuddle Lane, the snow was falling in fat thick flakes which stuck to everything they came into contact with.

It wasn't ideal weather to go riding in, and Megan hoped Petra knew what she was doing. Maybe they wouldn't go as far as the disused farmhouse. It was probably best if they didn't. The last thing Megan wanted to do was to get lost, or stuck in a snowdrift.

When she'd gone riding in the snow as a teenager, it had been purely accidental. There had already been snow on the ground and it had lain there for a while, and as she and her friends had set off, the sky had been clear. It was a very cold, very crisp winter morning, but by the time they got halfway around the looped circuit of the mountain and were starting to head back towards the riding stables, clouds had billowed in and snow had started to fall. It had been magical, but possibly only in hindsight. When she thought back on it, Megan had remembered feeling very cold and slightly alarmed. The horses, though, knew where they were going, and just plodded, heads down, towards their nice warm stables.

Had she told Jeremy that part, the fact that she'd got soaked through and freezing, and she'd been scared about being lost?

She didn't think she had. She'd just told him how she'd turned her face up to the sky and the snowflakes had melted on her eyelashes and on her tongue, and that the world had been silent and still, and so very pretty.

Now that she was older, she thought about what could have gone wrong.

But surely Petra wouldn't have agreed to allow her to ride in the snow, if it was at all dangerous? Maybe they should wait for it to stop?

She was here now though, so she might as well carry on with it, but suggest they do a couple of laps of a field instead, rather than risk going up onto the hillside. It wouldn't be much fun anyway if she couldn't see more than a hand in front of her face.

Megan carefully parked the car, got out and slipped on her waterproof jacket. Then she went into the office and picked up her helmet. It wasn't *her* helmet of course, but she was beginning to think of it in those terms, and she stroked it before she put it on her head, thinking this would be the last time she'd borrow it.

This afternoon was going to be full of last times.

'Hello?' The steadily falling snow muffled her voice as she went back outside, but the visibility wasn't too poor: the other side of the valley was still discernible, more or less, and she hoped this was as bad as it would get, although the snow was already starting to stick and she could see her footprints across the yard, which led her to worry how she was going to get home if it got any worse.

She heard a voice call from the direction of one of the barns, and as she realised who it was, her heart somersaulted and her breath caught in her throat.

'I didn't expect to see you,' she said, as she walked in out of the snow to find Nathan saddling the horses.

'Sorry,' he said. 'I know Petra was supposed to be taking you, but she's had to go out.'

Somehow Megan wasn't as surprised as she should have been. It seemed inevitable Nathan would be the one to go riding with her today. Fitting, almost. A kind of final goodbye.

Gosh, she was starting to get a bit morbid, so to shake the feeling she stepped forward with a smile and patted the satchel which she had slung diagonally over her shoulder and across her chest.

'I've got cake,' she said.

'And I've got a flask of hot chocolate.' He pointed to a small rucksack on top of a bale of hay. 'Don't worry,' he added, as he glanced out through the wide-open doors. 'The snow will stop in a minute.'

'It will? Are you some kind of weather guru?'

'Not exactly. Look at the sky.'

Megan glanced up, and sure enough, the occasional hint of blue could be seen between the clouds, and even as she watched the falling snowflakes became lighter.

'Quick,' Nathan said. 'Let's get out into it so that at least you can say you've ridden in the snow.'

'I don't quite think snow actually falling was what I meant.'

'I thought that was the whole point of these rides?'

'Yes, it was, but I think Jeremy got slightly the wrong end of the stick. He meant me to go riding when it was snowing, but I meant riding in the snow. There is a difference.'

'There is. Are you still happy to go out? It's only a couple of inches deep, maybe a little more on the hillside.'

'Let's go.' The decision was made, and there was no point in backing out of it now. She was here, the horses were ready, there was snow on the ground and still some falling. She didn't think she could go through this a second time, seeing Nathan's ruggedly handsome face and having to say goodbye to him all over again.

The horses didn't seem to mind being out in the weather one little bit. Their ears were pricked and Sherbet pranced slightly as if she was excited. Megan patted her neck and shushed her, and once again the mare fell into step behind Hercules, who arched his neck and lifted his tail, showing off slightly.

They made their way along the path above the fields, and when Megan looked back everything was blanketed in a thin layer of white; the scene was monochrome, in shades of grey, with her bright red car in the stables' car park being the only splash of colour for miles around.

Megan was soon lost in thought as she gazed at Nathan's back, gently swaying to the rhythm of the horse. Today was bittersweet; bitter because she was coming to the end of Jeremy's gifts and also because she wouldn't visit the stables again. But sweet because she was experiencing the last thing that Jeremy had organised for her, and also because she was on horseback and she was with a man she would dearly have loved to have gotten to know much, much better, if only she dared.

'Shit!' Nathan exclaimed. He pulled his horse to a sudden stop, and Sherbet almost walked into the back of Hercules.

The mare jerked, and Megan was jolted out of her reverie.

'What is it?' she asked.

'Look over there.' He pointed, and at first Megan couldn't see anything, and when she did, she wasn't quite sure of its significance.

'The fence has been cut,' Nathan explained.

'How can you tell?'

'Because I was in that field a couple of hours ago, and it was intact then. Not only that, but I also can't see any sign of Storm or Midnight.'

'Don't they belong to Charity and Luca?'

'That's right; they were in here with Mabel, that horse over there, and the two Shetlands. They are still here, but there's no sign of the others. Do you mind if we take a closer look?'

Megan could tell he was worried, even though he was trying to hide it. 'Of course not.'

'There's a gate further along. We don't use it often, but we should be able to get through it. If not, would you mind waiting here with the horses while I go on foot?'

'I don't mind at all,' she replied, but when they got to the gate, thankfully Nathan was able to open it with a bit of a struggle and a lot more cursing, and when he held it open for her, she led the two horses through before getting back on again. Nathan jumped into the saddle and took the lead once more.

The field was a large one, stretching from the path they were just on, right down to the road. It had fences along three sides and a dry stone wall running alongside the road which Megan knew carried on for a fair few miles. When they got closer to the fence even Megan could tell that it hadn't just collapsed – it had been cut. The wire had been peeled back to allow enough room for a horse to walk through, and there were hoofprints leading through it and across the neighbouring field.

But what was more worrying were the boot prints

which accompanied the two sets of hooves.

'Rustlers,' Nathan muttered.

'Do you really think the horses have been stolen?' Megan asked incredulously.

'Pretty sure of it. Why else would you cut a fence and lead two horses out?' He turned to her and she could see the anger in his eyes and the hardness of his jaw. 'If you hadn't wanted to go for a ride in the snow, we wouldn't have noticed they were missing until this evening. Thank you.'

She was about to argue he had nothing to thank her for and it had been pure luck, when he swivelled in his saddle, his eyes scanning the road, and cried, 'There! See it?'

Megan saw a boxy dark blue vehicle parked on the road by the side of the wall. It was some distance away, and she had to squint to see it. 'Do you think it's the thieves?'

'It might be. Let's assume it is.' Nathan undid a couple of zips and thrust his hand into a pocket deep inside his jacket. Pulling out a mobile phone, he stabbed at it, put it to his ear, listened for a second, then swore. 'No signal.' Shaking his head, he put his phone away. 'I'm going to see what's what,' he said, 'but I'd like you to do me a favour, if you can. I can't get any signal to phone Petra or the police, so could you go back to the stables and ring them from there? Tell them we've had two horses stolen.'

'Do you think it's wise to go down there?' She narrowed her eyes at the barely visible horsebox on the road.

'I'm going to have to,' Nathan said. His face was grim.

'It might be dangerous,' she pointed out. If she

thought pleading might work, she'd beg him not to go – she'd had enough worry over the years with Jeremy and his job, although she suspected she hadn't known the half of it, thank goodness. The last thing she wanted was to worry about Nathan.

Nathan nodded in acknowledgement. 'It might be, but I can't do nothing. Please go back to the stables, as fast as you can, but don't put yourself at any risk. I'll be back soon.'

There was nothing else for it. Megan knew that time was critical and she had to get in touch with the police as soon as possible, but she wasn't happy about leaving him on his own.

'Please take care,' she whispered. 'I'd hate it if anything happened to you.'

Nathan shot her a surprised look, and for one second she thought she'd gone too far and said something inappropriate. But then a smile lit up his face, and it was that which kept her warm as she turned her horse and headed back up the field.

Nathan watched her go, a frown creasing his forehead. Although it was only about half a mile back to the stables, he didn't like her going alone. But on the other hand, he couldn't simply sit on his horse and do nothing when there was a chance he might be able to stop the thieves. And he certainly couldn't allow her to go with him. What if that horsebox really did belong to the rustlers? He'd never forgive himself if he put her in harm's way.

Pushing his concern for Megan to the back of his mind, Nathan concentrated on what was happening down the road, and anger coursed through him.

How dare anyone come onto Petra's property and steal what wasn't theirs! If he caught them, he would...

He sighed. The chances of catching them were slim; it had been snowing for nearly two hours on and off, and although the tracks looked relatively fresh, he suspected the horses were long gone, and the vehicle in the layby down on the road was probably someone making a quick phone call.

Nevertheless, he followed the tracks straight across the field as the ground angled steadily downwards towards the layby and a gate set into the wall. It would probably only have taken the thieves minutes to park up, use bolt cutters on the gate, walk up the field and snip the fence, before catching the two horses and returning the way they'd come. It would have taken them half an hour, if that. God knows where those animals were now. They could be twenty miles away in any direction.

Gritting his teeth, his jaw aching from tension, Nathan drew closer, but as he did so he spied a horse's dark head above the top of the wall. The vehicle was definitely a horsebox: its back end was open and a ramp was down. Nathan could see two men at the front end of the horse trying to encourage it up the ramp, but the animal was having none of it. Midnight hated horseboxes and he would do anything in his power not to get into one. Luca's horse could be a bit of a handful at the best of times, but he could be an absolute nightmare to load, as the two men were finding out.

Nathan sat a little straighter in the saddle and craned his neck to peer into the back of the box. He could see a horse's rump in its gloomy depths. That must be Storm. They wouldn't have had any trouble with her at all and it was only because Midnight was refusing to get in it, that the thieves hadn't already driven off.

There was no time to lose. At any moment Midnight might give in and allow himself to be led onto the van and then they'd be away, and Nathan wouldn't have a hope in hell of catching them.

There *was* one thing he could do though – he could get the registration. The horsebox would probably be stolen, but it was better than nothing. It meant he'd have to get quite a bit closer though, so he led Hercules to a low-growing bush and slipped off his back, tying the reins firmly to the bare branches. The horse immediately pawed at the snow to reach the poor grazing underneath, lowered his head and began to nibble on the grass.

Nathan left him to it, and hunched over, scurrying down the field until he came to the wall. Using it as a shield, he crept along it, trying to get as close to the horsebox as he dared.

He could hear the two men cursing, and the gelding's annoyed squeals and snorts. The horse's hooves clattered on the tarmac, and the noise would hopefully cover any sound Nathan might make.

He was just about to stick his head over the wall and try to read the number plate, when a thought struck him…and his hand went to his pocket as a plan began to form.

With her heart in her mouth and fear for Nathan making her pulse soar, Megan headed back to the stables, all the while glancing over her shoulder to check on Nathan's progress. He was going to get hurt, she simply knew it, and the thought made her blood run cold.

She'd only trotted Sherbet for a few paces, when she tried phoning the stables. No signal.

A few more paces and still nothing.

'Come on,' she muttered, and Sherbet flicked her ears back. 'Not you, you're a good girl,' she told the horse, not wanting the mare to pick up on her nerves.

When Megan glanced back again, the field with its mutilated fence was out of sight, and so was Nathan, and her worry escalated to slightly short of panic.

Thank god, she finally had a signal.

She didn't bother with 999, though. Instead, she called a familiar number and prayed the man on the other end was available and close by.

'Fonzo, it's Megan. I need your help.'

'Whatever you need, you've got it.'

'Where are you?'

'Where do you want me to be?'

'On the road going east out of Picklewick, there's a blue van – I think it's a horsebox – pulled into a layby about three to four miles out of the village. I believe the occupants are attempting to steal two horses. A friend of mine has gone to try to stop them.'

'On my way. ETA five to seven minutes. Megan, are you okay? You're not in any danger?'

'I'm safe. I'm on the track above the road.'

'Good. Stay there. Jeremy would come back to

haunt me if I let anything happen to you. Leave it to the police – I'll radio it in.'

'Thanks, Fonzo.' She heard him activate his car's siren and guessed it wouldn't be too long before Nathan heard it, too. 'And Fonz? Please make sure Nathan isn't hurt.'

'Nathan?'

'My friend.'

'Describe him.'

Megan did the best she could.

'Got it. You take care. I'll speak to you later.'

Fonzo ended the call, and Megan blew out her cheeks. She could rely on him utterly, the same way she could rely on any of Jeremy's former colleagues. Fonzo had partnered with Jeremy for several years before Jeremy had become ill, and she knew her husband's death had hit Fonzo hard. She'd never forget the tears running down his cheeks, or the words he'd said at Jeremy's funeral. The service had been memorable and moving, the police presence giving it added poignancy. Even now, almost two years on, all Megan needed to do was pick up the phone and someone would be there for her. And boy, was she glad of that now. If she'd gone through the emergency services' switchboard it would have taken longer for them to send a vehicle, and she had a feeling time wasn't on Nathan's side.

There was one more call Megan had to make before she turned Sherbet around and headed back to Nathan, and she got through to the stables on the first try.

To her surprise, Petra answered.

'I thought you were out,' Megan began, before swiftly adding, 'Never mind. I've got some bad news.'

She told Petra exactly what she'd told the police, with the added information that they were on their way. 'One of them is, at least – he was my husband's partner, but he's called for backup. If that van is trying to steal your horses, there's a fair chance they'll be stopped before they get too far.'

Petra had been remarkably quiet as Megan relayed what had happened, but as soon as she stopped, Petra swore loudly.

'Where did you last see Nathan?' Petra demanded.

'Halfway down the field heading towards the layby.'

'I know it. I'm on my way. Where are you?'

'I'm on the track above the fields.'

'Okay, I'll tell Amos to expect you. He'll see to Sherbet. And Megan? *Thank you.*'

Petra ended the call abruptly and Megan guessed she was probably leaping into the Land Rover this very second. Although she'd heard the concern and fear in Petra's voice, she'd also heard a core of steel and determination underlying it, and she knew that in a crisis such as this, the woman wouldn't fall apart.

And neither would Megan, who had already turned around and was trotting back along the path, dread coursing through her. If anything should happen to Nathan, she'd never be able to forgive herself.

There were certain things Nathan always carried with him, his mobile phone being one of them, although that was next to useless at this very moment. Another thing was his multipurpose knife. It was rare he didn't find a use for it when he was out and about on the farm. He never took it to the village with him, but he was never without it when he was at work. And as he reached for it, he knew exactly what use he'd put it to today.

Stealthily he crept further along the wall until he was level with the cab. Risking a quick peep, he saw the men had their backs to him, trying to control Midnight who was practically sitting on his haunches and refusing to budge.

Taking a chance, in one fluid movement Nathan scaled the wall and dropped down silently onto the other side, the grassy verge and the snow cushioning any noise his boots might otherwise have made.

Crouching, he moved around to the front of the vehicle, out of sight of the men, then pulled his knife out of his pocket and opened it. It wasn't a very big knife and the blade wasn't very long, but it should hopefully serve the purpose.

Without hesitation, Nathan drew his arm back and plunged it with all his might into the driver's side wheel, the blade sinking up to its hilt in the rubber.

Crumbs, that had been easier than he'd anticipated, Nathan thought, before jerking the blade free, but as he did it made a loud popping hiss that could be heard even above the noise of the horse and the cursing of the two men.

Nathan flinched and stuck his head around the bumper, fearing the worst.

It was as he thought, the thieves had heard it, and they had both turned around.

He quickly snatched his head back, but he knew he'd been seen. One of them shouted, 'Oi!' and Nathan swallowed nervously. He could stick up for himself, but he was no superhero and he didn't fancy his chances against two of them. And neither did he want to risk a confrontation when he had a knife in his hand.

Leaping to his feet, he drew his arm back and threw the knife as far as he could into the field. Then he debated whether to run or fight. But as he dithered he heard a scraping noise. Damn it! One of them was holding a tyre iron in his hand and dragging it menacingly across the tarmac.

That decided it – he'd have to run. The pair of them might have twenty years on him, but he was fit and he knew the terrain like the back of his hand, and he hoped they wouldn't be bothered to chase him, but would be more interested in getting Midnight into the van and making their escape.

He dreaded to think what they'd do though, when they found out they couldn't. They might well decide to take their anger out on him, and as much as he loved the horses, he wasn't going to risk his life for them.

Nathan propelled himself forward and dived towards the wall, scrambling up and over it. But as he landed on the other side, his foot slipped from underneath him and he fell backwards. His head hit the stone wall with a sickening thud, and for a second lights exploded in his eyes and his vision blurred.

He lay there, winded and dazed, unable to focus.

Thanking god he was still wearing his hard hat, he vaguely wondered how much protection it would provide if the men decided to give him a good kicking and, feeling sick, he heard the clang of metal on stone and the scrabble of boots as one, or both of them attempted to scale the wall.

Bracing himself, all he could do was to lie there and await his fate, and hope it wouldn't be too bad.

'Rozzers!' one of the men shouted.

Nathan took a second to understand what had been said, and as he did so he heard sirens in the distance, and he closed his eyes and let out a breath.

'Thank you,' he whispered, his lips numb. Megan had probably got a signal a short distance along the track and he thanked god for her.

Trying to gather his wits, he heard the thud of boots on the road, the rattle of the ramp being lifted and the sound of a horse's hooves. He guessed they'd let Midnight go and were now trying to get away with Storm. The engine started and revved, and the horsebox lurched into motion.

They wouldn't get far, not with a punctured tyre.

Terrified Midnight would panic at the sound of the approaching sirens, Nathan dragged himself to his feet and slumped against the wall. He felt dizzy and his head ached, but at least he could now focus properly. And what he saw turned his heart to ice.

Midnight was careering down the road, his head high, his tail out like a streamer, and from his stiff movements Nathan could tell the horse was petrified.

There was only one thing for it.

Hauling himself up onto the wall, Nathan balanced precariously on its top.

Flashing blue lights in the distance signified the imminent arrival of the police, and he knew Midnight would whirl around and head back in his direction. The horse was wearing a halter and he also had a lead rope attached to it. Nathan's only chance of stopping the creature's headlong flight would be to throw himself at the lead rope and hope he caught hold of it. The horse might drag him, but his weight should slow the animal down enough to get him into the field.

As a plan, it stank, but Nathan couldn't see any other option.

He more or less fell off the wall as he tried to get down, and while he waited anxiously for Midnight to gallop back up the road, he prayed no one came past him going in the other direction, because they'd meet the horse head on and—

A crunch from behind made him cry out, and he lurched around.

The horsebox had come to a halt further up the road and was listing on the punctured side, the damaged wheel in a ditch. The two men tumbled out of the cab, staggered, then ran, as a horse's squealing neigh rang out.

Nathan felt sick – Storm was trapped in the box, possibly injured and certainly terrified, and he hesitated, torn between wanting to help her and needing to catch Midnight.

Hooves galloping up the road had him spinning back to face Midnight's direction again. Steeling himself for what was about to happen, his head pounded and his pulse raced, and he swallowed convulsively.

The animal came into view—

And Nathan sagged with relief. Petra was astride Midnight, hunched low over the horse's back as the beast raced down the centre of the road; but it was a controlled gallop and not the frantic headlong flight

Nathan had been expecting.

Instinctively he dashed to the gate, swung it open and stood back. With a yell, Petra leant to the side, guiding the panicked creature towards it, and the pair of them plunged through the opening and charged up the slope. Nathan caught a glimpse of wide nostrils and flattened ears, and saw Petra's triumphant expression.

One down, one to go, he thought wildly, as he pulled the gate shut and stumbled up the road towards the horsebox.

Storm was still neighing, her calls sending shivers of fear through him, and when he reached the back of the horsebox and fumbled with the fastenings with numb, unresponsive fingers, he dreaded what he might find.

'It's okay, my sweet, it's okay, I'm here, we'll soon get you out,' he crooned, forcing himself to remain calm, knowing she would sense his fear if he didn't. Taking a deep, steadying breath, he undid the back and opened the door, then dropped the ramp down slowly.

Sirens were loud behind him, blue flashing lights illuminating the interior of the box, and he didn't want to look, but he knew he had to…

Storm was balancing awkwardly, trying to compensate for the tilt of the floor under her hooves as the vehicle canted over, but apart from the fear in her eyes and the flaring of her nostrils, she seemed unharmed, and he let his breath out in a whoosh.

Startled, Storm jerked her head, and Nathan hastily resumed speaking to her in a soothing, calm tone until she relaxed enough for him to approach without the risk of him getting hurt.

'There's a good girl,' he murmured. 'Who's a good girl. We'll soon get you out of this nasty horsebox.'

Slowly and gently, careful not to alarm her any more than she was already, he inched forward until he was able to untie the rope, then he backed her up until she felt the slope of the ramp under her hooves, and he guided her down it.

As Nathan tied her to the outside of the box, relief and spent adrenalin made him feel sick and giddy, and he leant against the side of the vehicle, his heart labouring and his head spinning, before he leisurely slipped to the ground.

The last thing he saw was Megan's tear-stained face, and the last thing he heard was her crying, 'Don't die, Nathan. I love you. Please don't die.'

CHAPTER NINE

'You're a bloody idiot, that's what you are,' Amos said. 'Tell him, Petra, tell him what an idiot he is.'

'I don't need to – I think you've told him enough times,' Petra replied.

She gave Nathan one of her looks, but he didn't take offence. He knew they were right, he had been an idiot; but, damn it, people shouldn't be allowed to get away with taking things that didn't belong to them. Especially animals. They had feelings and people who loved them. It wasn't like nicking a quad bike (although that was bad enough), or stealing a telly.

'I give up,' Amos said, throwing his hands in the air. 'Perhaps you can make him see sense.' This last was aimed at Megan.

Nathan winced as he turned his head. Megan was sitting on the sofa in Petra's living room. She was worrying at her lips with her teeth, and they looked red and very kissable. He couldn't take his eyes off her mouth.

'You might have died,' she repeated. She'd mentioned this at least twenty times over the course of the past five hours. An ambulance had shown up at some point whilst he was lying in the lane and had taken him to the hospital to be checked out, and Megan had refused to leave his side.

'But I didn't,' he replied for the twentieth time. 'I'm still here.' His tone was gentle – he understood what this was costing her. That she'd come back for him meant the world to him. It had also worried him senseless when he'd realised she hadn't obeyed his instruction to return to the stables. His own safety meant nothing compared to hers.

He vaguely remembered some copper giving her short shrift too, but it was only when he was waiting to be seen by a doctor that he'd discovered Jeremy had been a policeman, and the main reason the "rozzers" had shown up so fast was because Megan had phoned one of them directly, and hadn't dialled 999.

'They should have kept you in for observation,' Amos grumbled. 'In my day, they would have.'

'It's still your day,' Harry said.

Everyone was gathered in the living room of the stables, along with the two dogs, the cat, and Fred, the cockerel, who had managed to sneak in amidst all the fuss. So much for being advised to get some rest, Nathan thought, although rest was the last thing on his mind. He was exhausted and his head hurt something rotten, but he was also high on adrenalin. Not from the attempted theft, but from what Megan had said to him as he lay on the tarmac, feeling less than splendid.

He'd tried to speak to her about it when they were waiting at the hospital for him to be checked over, but she'd refused to discuss it, and for a while he'd wondered if he'd imagined it. But surely not, because the first thing he'd said when he'd come round was 'I love you, too,' and she'd smiled so widely it was as though the sun had come out.

A huge yawn escaped him and he briefly closed his eyes.

Maybe he was tired, after all.

'Come on, everyone out,' Petra ordered. She was looking knackered, too. It had been a rough day all round. But at least the thieves had been arrested, the horses were in their stalls, neither of them the worse for their ordeal, and the only injury was his mild concussion. His helmet had saved him from what could have been a fractured skull if he hadn't been wearing it, and since he'd returned to the stables he'd been fussed over and coddled, and treated like a hero, much to his chagrin and embarrassment.

'Someone should stay with him,' Amos advised, looking pointedly at Megan.

'It's late, I should be getting home,' she said.

'Stay here for the night,' Petra suggested. 'It's dark and icy, and driving in those conditions should be avoided. We've got a couple of spare rooms.'

'I'd also better be going.' Nathan struggled to sit up, but Megan, who was nearest to him, having not moved further from him than a hair's breadth, pushed him back down.

'Not on your nelly. Petra, tell him. He can't go home like this.'

'Megan is right. You should both stay the night.'

Amos beamed. 'I've got a nice pot of hearty stew on the stove and some fresh bread to go with it. We'll have a bite to eat later, but it won't be ready for an hour, so let's leave Nathan in peace for a bit.'

'Megan, will you stay with him?' Petra asked, and Nathan narrowed his eyes at her. The sly cat was up to something and he had a pretty good idea what it was.

'Only if Nathan wants me to,' Megan said, darting a glance at him.

'I want you to,' he confirmed. They needed to have a chat about what they'd said to each other. Words such as those couldn't be unspoken, but he wanted to check it wasn't the heat of the moment that had been responsible for them.

He hoped to god that wasn't the case. Because, to his immense surprise, he found he meant what he'd said when he'd told her he loved her. Nathan couldn't believe he felt this way when he'd only known her for such a short time. Was that possible, or was his head injury more severe than the doctor had thought?

The room cleared, leaving him and Megan alone except for Patch, who had curled up at his master's feet and refused to move. Bemused, Nathan waited for the door to snick shut, then he turned his gaze on her. 'You said you love me. Is that true?'

'Do you honestly want to do this right now?'

He nodded, then wished he hadn't.

'Is the headache really bad?' she asked, seeing his pained face. 'I can get you some—' She made to rise, but he grabbed hold of her hand and pulled her back down. He felt as weak as a kitten, so he was grateful she sank into her chair without a fight.

'I'm fine,' he said. 'It's nothing I can't handle. Will you answer my question?'

She looked like a rabbit faced with a fox, all wide-eyed frozen terror. 'Do I have to?'

'I love you.'

'So you said.'

'I mean it.'

'We've only known each other for a couple of months.'

'We've known each other forever.'

'Jeremy…' She shrugged helplessly. 'I still love him.'

'Of course you do. I wouldn't expect anything else.'

'You don't mind?'

'Why would I?' Nathan shuffled in his seat, the cushions sucking him down. 'He's part of you.'

'But—'

'There is no but, not unless you want there to be.' He had to convince her. She was right in that they'd not known each other long, and they both had their issues – her husband, his reluctance to share his life with anyone – but the thought of not seeing her again made his very soul ache. She'd changed him, without meaning to, and without him realising, but there was no going back to the way he'd been before he'd met her. He didn't think she could go back, either. When he'd first set eyes on her she'd been in a dark place, but now light was shining out of her, and she was beginning to come to life again. He so desperately wanted it to be with him.

'Okay, I admit it. It's true – I do love you.' She said it defiantly.

'Good, I'm glad.'

'Where do we go from here?' More defiance, as though she was daring him to come up with a plan that she could pick apart.

'I've no idea. Shall we take it one day at a time?'

She shrugged. Her head was lowered so he couldn't see her face. 'I suppose.' Then she peeped at him from underneath her lashes.

It was such a flirtatious and provocative thing for her to do that his breath hitched.

'How's the head?' she asked again.

'What head?'

'The one on your shoulders, that nearly got knocked off.'

'Can't feel a thing,' he replied, cheerfully. It was true, he felt no pain, only a burgeoning elation and a quiet joy.

'In that case, kiss me,' she commanded.

For once in his life, Nathan was happy to do as he was told.

And when his lips met hers, he knew he would be happy to kiss her for the rest of his life.

'Are you sure you're okay?' Megan shot Nathan a worried look. It was far too soon for him to be on the back of a horse, but he'd insisted on riding today. Apparently, he "owed" her a ride to compensate for the one that ended so abruptly and so dramatically less than a week ago.

'I'm fine, stop fussing.'

'I like fussing. And you secretly like to be fussed over,' she replied, inching Sherbet closer to Hercules so she could nudge Nathan with her knee.

'Do not,' he retorted, but his broad grin gave him away.

They'd seen each other every day since the horse-rustling incident, and Megan couldn't get enough of him.

She still felt disloyal to Jeremy and she had an inkling the feeling might never entirely go away, but she also felt she had her husband's blessing, and she wondered if her falling in love again had been the sole purpose behind all those gifts. Although, to be fair, she still couldn't see how planting a wildflower garden at the back of their house was going to move that forward. It had been a solitary experience, except for her frequent visits to the garden centre and her chats with the middle-aged couple who ran it.

Nevertheless, she embraced her newfound happiness and was determined never to make Nathan feel second best. Because he wasn't. Nathan was lovely, kind, thoughtful, and sexy, and she vowed to try to make him happy every single day; he deserved nothing less. They both deserved a second chance at love, and although theirs was new and fresh, it didn't mean there was no depth to it.

And who'd have guessed that the surly, reticent man she'd met in December would turn out to be such a romantic? As this ride across the hills on a blimmin' freezing but very bright day in January testified.

Snow lay thickly on the ground, drifting to a couple of feet deep in places, and the horses' breath steamed around their heads as they plodded gamely up the blanketed path. The air was calm and incredibly still, and Megan could see for miles. The only sound was the crunch of snow underfoot, the jingle of the tack, and the occasional bleat of a sheep from the fields far below.

When they came to the ruined farmhouse, Nathan tied the horses to a scrubby tree growing through the middle of it, and he brushed the snow off the remains of one of the walls and spread a blanket over it for her to sit on.

With a cup of hot chocolate in one hand and a slice of her latest creation in the other (red velvet cake with a Valentine heart decoration on the top), Megan's soul was filled with peace and her heart brimmed with happiness. And when they'd finished their drinks and Nathan gathered her in his arms, she was warmed from the inside out by his love.

He was her future, and she felt so incredibly excited to embrace all that life had to offer.

Magical, that's what their love was…*magical.*

THE END

About Etti

Etti Summers is the author of wonderfully romantic fiction with happy ever afters guaranteed.
She is also a wife, a mum, a pink gin enthusiast, a veggie grower and a keen reader.

Acknowledgements

My family deserves a great deal of thanks, mainly for putting up with my incessant daydreaming. Love you to the moon and back xxx

Thanks to my lovely editor and friend, Catherine Mills, for her support and advice.

My friends also get a huge hug for all the love and encouragement, even if they don't understand all the wittering on about story arcs!

Finally, I can't go without sharing my heartfelt gratitude to you, my readers.
You make the writing worthwhile xxx

Printed in Great Britain
by Amazon